W9-DCG-168

TEMPTING TROUBLE

SHADOWY ASSASSINS (S.A.S.S.) SERIES
BOOK THREE

GENNITA LOW

DEDICATION

To Mother and Father,

my troublesome Stash, and Mike, my Ranger Buddy

SIMPLE TIMELINE

```
BIG BAD WOLF
     |
    INTO
   DANGER    →FACING FEAR    →    TEMPTING TROUBLE
                   |                        /
(simultaneous)
           PROTECTOR                 /
              |          →    VIRTUALLY HIS
           HUNTER                |
              |          →    VIRTUALLY HERS
           SLEEPER
              |
           PIRATE
```

TEMPTING TROUBLE

aka

"GRACE HAPPENS"

CHAPTER ONE

It was safari hot and the sky a blinding blue. Her eyes were closed, but she knew exactly where she was. It always started this way, with the heat, the heavy languorous heat. Yet she never felt uncomfortable, never sweated in this steamy warmth that was like a fiery whip. If she opened her eyes, slowly, she would see that beautiful blue that seemed to fill her whole being, and she knew she would lie there admiring the blinding brightness until she wasn't sure whether she was staring at or drowning in it. And always, always, that magical moment, when she heard the growl, she would feel her own heat, inside, begin to grow.

It was a dream she was familiar with, for she'd read the pages repeatedly as a rite of passage into secret adult fantasies. Little girls dreamed of princes and fairy kingdoms; growing girls salivated over Hollywood stars and the cutest boys in class. But not Grace. One day, young Grace had read of the long courting ritual of the lioness and her mate, and sometimes, deep in secretive sleep, it would invade her dreams, and she would be her, that lioness. She had made this her escape world, as her father had taught her during their lessons. Some operatives, he told her, chose memories, some focused on repeated text. Whatever it took, he advised, to drown out the present. Grace was only sixteen when her father started training her, and at that age, she much preferred fantasy…

She always knew when he came, silent and sure-footed. He stood in the same place, his mane shining against the blue of the sky, his magnificent body rippling with sinewy muscles as he pawed the grass demandingly. Impatiently. As always, he looked straight at her, and as always, she would purr in excitement at that look he gave her.

Yes, he was here, and he was hungry. He pawed again, a deep rumble starting in his chest. She stretched, working from her shoulders, then pushing up with her hind legs, letting him see her behind. The rumbling increased in volume as she slowly walked back and forth within his line of vision, mewing back love call for love call. She knew he was hungry for her, but she wanted to play. It was part of their dance. At each pass, she moved closer to her mate, sauntering back and forth, glancing at him, now and then turning around to let him see her rump, angled with feline invitation. The rumbling was like distant thunder by now.

He was the lone male waiting for her, her king, her lord and master, but he knew this moment was hers. She could feel his need reaching out as he caught the scent of her heat. He tossed and shook his head in male frustration, his golden mane catching sunlight. He began growling in between the deep rumbling of his chest, the fire in his eyes calling to her to come closer, daring her to disobey him.

She reveled in the power that she held over him. His restlessness spurred her to tease him even more. She wanted him to see how beautiful and strong she was. She wanted to push him to the limit, and circling closer, swayed her hips in front of his face. She thrilled for that moment every time, always, when his patience snapped. His head reared back, revealing his strong muscular throat, and he let out the roar of ownership. The female in her shivered at his blatant sexuality, that roar that told her that the game was over, that she was in his territory, in his power. As some distant call of nature released his bondage, he sprang on her back, his huge paws clamping on her shoulders, forcing her to the ground. He roared again, in triumph, and the whole world reverberated with his claim of ownership. As he marked her with his teeth, she threw back her head to stare up adoringly at her lover, her mate, and his warrior eyes, staring back into hers, were the same hypnotic blue as the sky.

SUMMER, WASHINGTON D.C.

The nagging ringing of the phone finally got through her dreams. In the darkened room, Grace lifted herself on one elbow, eyes still shut, and groped for the nightstand, muttering at the insistent sound. She stretched out lazily, and reluctantly picked up the receiver.

"Hello?"

"Grace? It's me, Tim."

Grace groaned inwardly. Not again. "Not now, Tim. I've an appointment with my boss. Besides, we've already been through this."

With a sigh, Grace peered at the alarm clock next to the radio. She had about an hour and the half to make her appointment with Edgar Maddux, department head. Wanting to look both relaxed and confident, she didn't think she could stand another drawn-out argument.

"Geez, Grace, it's Saturday!" Tim protested, his voice sulky. "Do you get overtime, or something?"

"Nope. It's just a meeting, Tim, some sort of review of my first month on the job. I'm an intern, you know, everybody's slave." Grace sat up. "I told you I'd be too busy learning the ropes."

"Too busy for me, you mean. I don't understand why you took this job without consulting me."

"Don't start again," Grace warned. "I've told you, I don't need to consult you about anything. You want me with you all the time, Tim. I can't twiddle my thumbs all summer. We talked about this last spring, and all last night, and I'm tired of it."

She really was. Tim just wouldn't accept their being apart. It was really time to rethink this relationship thing.

"Well, I'm not going to twiddle my thumbs waiting for you while you work in

D.C. I might not be available when you get back," Tim, in turn, warned her. He paused, waiting for her to placate him.

Grace's lips curved into an exasperated smile. Emotional blackmail never worked with her, and truthfully, after last night, she didn't even feel guilty about being so mean to him. So she coolly said, "Got to go. I can't be late."

She could just see the shock on his face. She grimaced. How could she make him see she felt suffocated by his need to spend every moment with her?

"Wait! Grace, please let me come and see you. I promise I won't yell at you again."

She should refuse, but if they discussed it any longer, she knew she would really be late. Maybe a last talk would smooth everything out, and they could part as friends. She had nothing against Tim, except maybe his attitude about women in general.

"OK," she relented. "We'll talk again later, all right? 'Bye."

A hot shower helped restore some of her usual good humor, and as she dried her hair, she contemplated her relationship with Tim. Their talk would have to wait. Right now, her job was number one. She stuck her tongue out at her reflection. Trying to prove she could do the job in spite of her youth was her main problem. Why, oh why, did she have to look so fresh and innocent?

Grace had known ever since she was twelve her face and her nature were two different creatures, that people judged her from her face, and that her true nature, when she sprang it on them, would either cause consternation or amusement. That was the problem. Tim wanted a sweet and mild-mannered girlfriend, and had come to realize she was far from it.

But she *was* sweet and mild-mannered, Grace insisted silently, as she dabbed on blush and applied lipstick. To a point. When she wanted to be. She preened mockingly.

One reason why she took this internship as a translator in D.C., away from her home in Ohio, was she wanted distance between Tim and her, needing the few months before college commenced again to sort out her feelings. There was so much she couldn't reveal to Tim, or anyone, knowing just too well there weren't many she could trust. After all, she was a lot more than she seemed.

Never assume anything. She should know that better than anybody. Her father's unique education had seen to that.

***

Assumptions could kill.

The thought ran through Lance Mercy's mind as he glanced around the room, before he beckoned to his friend to join him. They needed only to exchange a look before both their gazes settled on the woman lying against the generous pillows of the sofa, legs tucked in to the side comfortably, an arm hugging a big pillow against her body. She looked serene, her eyes riveted still on the flickering images on the television. The dim lights cast mysterious shadows in the room. A drink sat on the coffee table with a piece of half-eaten pizza next to it and magazines lay at the foot of the sofa as if they'd been paged through while the woman watched television. One could see the woman had assumed life was as ordinary today as the day before, except that, right now, she was very dead, in a very unordinary manner.

Lance walked to stand in front of the sofa. In a cozy little room, his lanky frame should move awkwardly, but he maneuvered his body with the grace of one familiar with tight situations.

His companion joined him and they studied the dead woman dispassionately. In their kind of business, there were basically two kinds of cancellations. One was messy and slow, leaving a trail of clues. Lance Mercy, COS's top undercover operative, preferred the second kind—quick, clean and bloodless, a relatively painless process. Of course, the latter way was an art form, the first sure sign of a professional job, and some cancellations needed the anonymity of a common criminal. Thus, the first kind was usually the first option.

"He wanted us to know this wasn't an accident," he said to the older man, at the same time taking in all the details of the scene, vaguely noting it was quite apt an episode of the Twilight Zone was on at the moment. If not for the odd angle of the woman's neck, everything was in order, not a hair out of place. Her soulless eyes stared flatly ahead; her lips had a slight astonished twist to them.

The other man, Dan Kershaw, nodded, the etched lines on his forehead and the furrows around his mouth deepening, as he contemplated his own conclusions. "It was done quickly," he commented. "He watched her for some time."

Lance looked up and saw Dan's and his own reflection staring back. "The closet," he murmured, indicating the mirrored sliding door a few feet behind the sofa. He walked around it and slid the door to one side, squatting down in one fluid motion to examine the floor. "He stood here, kept watch, decided the moment, and cancelled her." Satisfied that no clues could be found, he added, "Charlie will be upset when he finds out. From what you told me, I think he's fond of her."

"Charlie's very good at what he does. Even Command isn't sure whether he's really fond of her, or not," Dan told him, looking at Lance's image in the mirror, noting the changes of his former underling from eager student to the now suave and watchful man. The old recklessness was still in those blue eyes. Part of his charm. He pulled out his cell phone. "Yes, it's me. Cancellation confirmed. The note wasn't a fake. No, Charlie isn't here. I don't think he knows. Right, we will." He hung up. "Let's get out of here. You're admiring the guy's work too much, as it is. This isn't one of your jungle ruins."

Lance smiled at the older man. "The guy's an artist. I appreciate good art, in and out of the jungle," he responded, deliberately leaning a shoulder against the kitchen doorframe, knowing it would annoy his old mentor. Privately, he was suspicious about the whole staged scene here. It was too perfect, too clean. A person who took time to create, he reasoned, deserved a measure of his respect, and certainly wouldn't be easily dismissed. The murderer was deliberately sending a message. *Track me. I am one of you.*

"Uh huh, there's just a matter of taste," Dan said, frowning slightly at Lance. "Surely you know better than to touch anything, even after five years on and off in the Far East. We'd better move before your 'artist' gets to the real target."

That, in turn, wiped away the smirk on Lance's face. He straightened from the doorway, his plan to keep teasing Dan forgotten. "I thought we had the guy secured."

"Wrong. We don't have the guy. At the moment he's hiding out in Chinatown."

Lance glanced again at the dead woman. "That wasn't what she told Charlie.

Was she lying?"

Dan shrugged. Information was information. It changed and varied from mouth to mouth. He walked to the front door. Lance followed, closing the door with a decisive click. The summer sunshine was bright after the dim setting inside the penthouse. Birds chirped overhead in the heavily blooming trees.

"What next?" Lance asked, as they headed toward their car, two conservatively dressed Washington businessmen.

"Command said they'll bring our boy in a crowd. We're going to a rally on Monday."

"A rally, huh? What kind?" Lance tugged on his tie, loosening it.

"Anti-abortion." Dan grinned at the upraised brows of the younger man. "Pretty appropriate, don't you think, since abortion is considered murder by the activists?"

"Why this rally?" Lance asked, as he expertly pulled out and maneuvered between two speeding vehicles.

"The clinic's owned by a Chinese doctor, so there should Asians around. Our boy can move without too much attention." Dan lit a cigarette. "There's information counteragents are likely to be there."

"Command's got moles working for us?"

"No, they've got a great source."

As usual, Dan's answer was vague. Lance had known him for eight years, long enough to know when the older man was holding back information. That was the nature of their business: reveal only what was necessary, and keep what was necessary to a minimum. As he'd been doing for the past five years, he kept his own opinions to himself as he drove. The assignment was unraveling, a carefully planned six-month project careening toward an explosive ending, something Command was trying to avoid.

Weaving in and out of traffic, he sifted through the facts. Someone had panicked about three months ago, making the crucial mistake of speeding things up. Mistakes were made. Information was leaked. He suspected the leak came from the senator's office, which irritated him, since he was in charge of that part of the operation. Dan, who was responsible for enemy information and target movement, hadn't received any warning from his sources. If the timetable had run smoothly, in six months, they would have what they needed—the names of the arms dealers; the list of US senators and council members in Chinese pockets; the name of the mole who was leaking their information. But all the current news of moles and arms had spooked the target.

"Agnes Lin was our bridge, getting that student visa for the informant," Lance said. "Whoever killed her is getting too close." Outside of Dan and himself, the informant/scholar was the only one who knew they were after the list of arms dealers. The lower level operatives had been told the present assignment was a local one, of little value to the international arena, only important to COS Command for future use. Except for a select few, no one on the team even knew Lance was one of them, since they'd only heard of him under his code name. The nature of his expertise called for undercover work, mostly done alone and overseas. He had only reluctantly agreed to do this one assignment because Dan called and requested his help. A mole needed to be smoked out and they needed an unidentifiable tracker. So here he was, stuck in the plodding world of organized surveillance, the kind he'd always hated, and counting down the days back to his freedom.

There was a good side to this. His mother was very happy to have him around for so long.

"We're to move quickly now," Dan admitted with a frown. "We have to make some adjustments to the timetable."

Lance slowed down for a passing car. Timetables were the foundation of wrong assumptions, and accidents happened on wrong assumptions. Agnes Lin already became the first. They needed more information. Who was going to help them find it?

***

Information had been Ed Maddux's world for over a quarter of a century. He breathed it; he chewed and swallowed it daily. It was no wonder he was a detail man. Everything he did had an exacting touch, from the way he folded his shirts to the number of times he chewed before swallowing his food. He believed everything added up to a whole, and the more details there were, the more complex the big picture was. He was one of the consortium's success stories; he'd stayed within its structures, learning from the bottom up, taking each step unhurriedly, knowing the insides and outsides of each phase before moving on. Edgar Maddux, GNE director, was born the day he took his first translating job. There wasn't any past since that moment, and he had only known one future.

Now he was in charge of the future. Retired from the field, he was reassigned to administration to reorganize and train, to observe and update the details, and under his watch, GNE hoped to make him the point man of the new and improved picture.

That wasn't the only reason he requested administrative work, of course. He silently returned the gaze of the woman sitting across from him. Everything about her called to him, from the wary alertness in her gray-green eyes to the soft scent that clung to her. Just as he remembered.

He'd known her for almost twenty-five years. Funny how time brought people together after a long absence and they could communicate like they had never been apart for years. She hadn't changed much, except for that professional conservative façade she now assumed. There was a time when Sandra Smythe and he worked regularly as partners, and she was another person then, not this controlled and guarded creature. Time hadn't marred that classical beauty. She was still his 'English rose,' with the wide generous mouth and dimples. He realized with a start she was studying him as well, and he mentally retreated.

"She fits the profile," Ed said, as if the file in front of him had been on his mind the last five minutes.

"Yes," Sandra agreed, taking a sip of her coffee and savoring it slowly. "She is very observant and speaks the two languages we need, Chinese and Malay. Her translations have been excellent."

"Is she suitable for Level Two work?"

"Definitely. She's a natural. However, she seems to think only of the three month-long internship as a plus for her resume, so I don't know whether she'll stay."

"Were we that young once?" he asked, giving her a rueful smile. "Twenty-two years old. Sometimes I forget how young they are when they first start."

Sandra caught her breath. She had forgotten how potent that smile could be. Blinking, she gave a quick answering smile, "It's like culture shock, isn't it, coming back to administration again? It's certainly a drastic change, from Level Five work to my boring domain. No regrets? Giving up all that adventure?"

Ed took a sip from his cup. "No," he told her, his eyes never leaving her face, "traveling is hard on a forty-five year old body. It's good to wake up in the morning and not have to figure

which language I'm supposed to be speaking today. I suppose that's the reason you retired from field work, what, three years ago?"

"Yes." She decided to change the subject. Reminiscing wasn't her favorite thing to do. "Shall I send her in?" Ed felt her retreating too. So they were both back to square one. He let it go. "All right," he said, flipping through the papers in the file before him.

Sandra stood up, not understanding the sense of loss that hung between them. Briskly, she gathered her notes and put them into her folder. "She isn't a typical twenty two year-old. You'll see a marked improvement in her already," she told him. She walked to the door, hesitated, then turned around. "I…I didn't get a chance to really welcome you back, Ed. I know you'll do fine, but if you have any questions…"

"I know I can count on you if I've trouble adjusting, Sandy," Ed quietly assured her. "Thanks."

After the door closed behind her, Ed fought the urge to light a cigarette. He wanted to let his thoughts wander over memories and choices. He wanted to think about Sandra Smythe. However, right now, the top priority was recruiting, and of the new crop of translators and analysts, Grace O'Connor had shown she was recorder material.

Five minutes later, his new intern sat before him. Deliberately, he studied her for a few silent moments, letting her reaction tell him about her. Instead of being nervous or looking around his large office, she too sat in silence and returned his contemplation easily. If she felt uncomfortable, she didn't show it. She sat like one used to being looked over. He wondered at her ease as he deliberately drew the silence out even longer. The artless smile, the youthful cocky attitude in the way she sat, the air of patience—he was intrigued.

This wasn't the first time he had noticed these traits about her. There was something very practiced in the way Grace O'Connor behaved that wasn't very obvious, but Ed had a couple of decades of observation skills behind him and everything about this young woman had a touch of secrecy. Maybe it was the little bold light in her slightly slanted eyes which contrasted so starkly with the wide-eyed innocence of youth, or the quick way she took in little details of the people around her, unlike the self-absorbed fashion of her age group. Despite proof of her age in his file, she didn't act like an untrained, inexperienced intern. He decided to push her further.

"How do you find your new job so far, Miss O'Connor? Any questions? Any comments?" Ed asked, picking up his pen.

Grace looked at his hands as he moved the file closer to him. Always look at the hands, her father had said. They gave good clues. Big, capable hands. Definitely the hands of someone used to taking charge.

"It's been educational so far," she answered. "I've never read so many U.N. treaties and speeches in my life. Translation is a lot different with all those big political words."

"It takes getting used to," Ed agreed. "It's good practice, though, for the future."

He watched her eyebrows lift speculatively. He liked the way she reined in her questions, as she weighed her options. An easily read face, he made a mental note. Not suitable for certain kinds of field work, unless more training was given. Trainable?

Grace thought she heard more than a friendly comment. One of the few things she'd discovered at GNE was that everybody seemed to be saying two things at the same time. She kept having the feeling of being a test mouse in a maze being trained to memorize every turn and corner. A few times in the past month, with her usual droll sense of humor, she'd been tempted to surprise her superiors by demanding to know where the cheese was. Instinct told her there was more to GNE, more to her internship. His silence seemed calculated, as if he was gauging her reaction. But the man didn't know she had had years of dealing with that kind of silence.

Looking around the room, taking in the bookcases and the surprising presence of a basket of roses, she casually asked, "I was just wondering how my evaluation was going, sir? Did I mess up and cause World War Three?" She wanted to see him smile and was pleased to catch a slight lift at the corners of his mouth.

"Nothing that a few more peace accords won't straighten out. Your work is good, Miss O'Connor. We are pleased with it, very few mistakes." Ed tapped his pen on the file, deciding to spring one on her. "We're ready to put you out in the field."

"Put me out in the field," Grace echoed. "Is that a GNEism?" She was thinking of a piece of cheese in a mousetrap.

Ed liked the way she fenced with words while stalling for time to evaluate. GNEism—he had to remember that one for Sandy. "Field work," he explained, "is the traveling part of your internship. We want to start close, attend a rally in D.C." He had wanted to wait until close to the end of her internship to test her, but for a rare impulsive moment, he had surprised himself by this decision. He wanted this young woman's reactions without the usual detail training. It would be interesting to see how she would handle fieldwork, what she would do on her own. If she was good material... "Tell me, Miss O'Connor—"

"Grace. Call me Grace."

"Grace, then. What do you think the scope of GNE covers?"

"You mean what kind of business GNE does?" Grace could all but smell the cheese around the corner somewhere. "Translation for foreign corporations, political bodies like the U.N., even entertainment subjects like books and movies. To put it formally, GNE provides a valuable service for the international market, which is getting more integrated as the world economy becomes more tied together by trade treaties and currency dependability." She cocked her head, a wry smile on her lips. "Am I using the correct U.N. lingo?"

Ed smiled back, amused. The girl had a smart mouth, quite a surprise to him. "Nice summary," he commented, as he jotted in his file again. "GNE's main business is, as you said, to provide the link between two foreign bodies. Our clients need quick translation service with non-sensitive documents so their staff can handle the more important translations, and we are perfect for the job. Our translators are well-trained and most of them go on to actually work for these foreign corporations later on." At least, on the surface, he silently added.

Grace wished that she was standing behind Ed Maddux, so she could read over his shoulder. All the future possibilities jumped out at her, and she eagerly leaned forward. "So, for those interested in translation, this is good practice, and those who want a poli-sci future can hone it on the dry treatise language, right?"

"Yes."

"You said, main business," Grace pointed out. Damn it, she was going for the cheese. "What are the other services we provide?"

"Let's hear your analysis. What kinds of other work do you think GNE is in?"

Grace clasped her hands together. "The traveling must be part of it," she ventured. This lab test was proving most stimulating. "A personal translator for visiting executives? An overseas intermediary? Speechwriting for political people? Analysis of foreign reports? You mentioned rally—what kind? I would guess my attendance wouldn't be for me to support the cause, so you're sending me to—what—learn something for GNE's foreign links?"

Ed inhaled, taken by surprise. He could all but hear each click of her logic, like clockwork while she rolled off her analysis as if she'd been thinking about his question for a while, instead of a few seconds. Every conclusion she made was closer to the truth than he had expected. He clicked his ballpoint pen as he looked at her thoughtfully.

We do provide a certain amount of those kinds of services," he acknowledged. He paused, trying to decide whether to give her the standard GNE line, or to go a little further, so he could see her mind at work again. He went for the latter choice. "GNE deals with information, Grace. We collect data, record and report them. We function as an objective observer for any events of importance or interest. Our field agents travel to experience first-hand, report in detail all they see and hear, the whole event as an uninvolved party." Level Two, that is, he added silently.

Cheese! Cheese! Grace quelled down her excitement with difficulty. "Report to whom?"

Ed put down his pen, and put his palms together, tapping the fingers against each other as he considered the answer. "We really don't have a specific group to whom we report, although we know, from experience, what kinds of reports interest whom. We just record the information and sell it to whoever asks for it."

"Too vague," Grace demanded, forgetting she was the employee in her impatience to get all the specific details. She knew it. She knew GNE was more than just a simple translation service. "Observe. Report. Sell. What do you mean?"

Ed liked the way she deconstructed chunks of information into short sentences. "Why don't we put it to a test?" he suggested, leaning back into his chair. "Attend the rally, come back and report to me."

"But what am I supposed to do there?"

"Exactly what I told you—observe and report. Participate, but only objectively." At her slow nod, he continued, "The rally is outside an abortion clinic this Monday."

Grace sat back, blinking. "A what?" She hadn't expected that. What did that have to do with translation?

"An abortion clinic," Ed repeated gently. "You're there to record the event, not form an opinion or be an activist. One thing to keep in mind. The Global Network Exchange Consortium is not a news service." Ed closed his file, clicking his ballpoint pen. "We'll drive you there. Miss Smythe will take care of everything. Dress casual, of course, to blend in."

The meeting with the department director was over. Grace walked back to her car, full of questions. Nothing seemed to fit. She had assumed that they would test her, maybe set up a meeting with some foreign executives to test her social skills, but an abortion rally?

Global Network Exchange is not a news service. Well, yeah. Like she didn't know that one. All that information was worth a great deal.

She eased out into traffic. Dad was right. Never assume. Ever. The cheese was dangling right under her nose, but she hadn't gotten to it yet. She liked getting to the bottom of things, and this translation business might prove to be more fun than a way to polish her language resume. Except that in her book, fun usually meant trouble.

She grinned impishly. She could hear her dad's voice already, calling out her nickname in that low warning tone, "What have you done now, Trouble?"

All her life, trouble always found her—that was, if she didn't find it first. She couldn't help it if she was tempted by shiny mysterious puzzles. She was a superspy's daughter, after all. Collecting information and dissecting it to fit a pattern were in her genes. She winked at the bemused man in the car next to her at the red light. She had already forgotten about Tim.

CHAPTER TWO

Monday morning.

It was hot, and tempers were rising with the heat. Grace moved among the confusion of big-lettered placards flashing in the bright sunlight as groups of voices chanted in the crowd, "It's a baby, not a fetus! It's a baby, not a fetus!" in between spurts of arguments. She had been to rallies before. They were nothing new to college life, but it was more intense here. People with signs, screaming, chanting. Police officers. TV cameramen. Reporters with microphones. A group of Chinese nuns hovered nearby in prayer. Another group of younger people milled around, maliciously trying to interrupt. She dutifully noted all these, telling herself that she was a human camera.

The escalating tension was apparently in danger of erupting into a full scale mini-war, but she refused to be nervous, knowing Sandra Smythe was out there somewhere studying her mouse scurrying around looking for that cheese. She knew this was a pivotal point in her internship; if she passed this test, GNE was going to reveal something new, and far more interesting.

Meanwhile, walking the perimeter of the throng of humanity, Lance Mercy was wishing it were the real thing instead of the human jungle he was in. He blended with the crowd, moving in the same ease in his jeans as he did in his tailored clothes.

He checked every Asian face, looking for a sign, but each one looked right through him. Impatiently, he raked his fingers through his thick hair. Where the hell was the guy?

Nearby, Grace lifted her dark hair from the nape of her neck, deftly tying it in a loose ponytail. The heat was stifling. She wondered how these people had the energy to shout and march. Drifting closer to the group of nuns in prayer, she watched for a few moments, feeling sorry for them as she noted the sweat glistening on their foreheads. Those habits must be a torture. She leaned against a nearby tree, taking respite under its shade.

Lance kept walking. A lone woman under a tree about forty feet away caught his attention. She didn't look exactly Asian, but she wasn't Caucasian either. Something about the way she stood reminded him of a distant memory, and suddenly, his senses came to full alert, sensing she wasn't there as a participant. Was she a messenger? He studied closely, noting the way she herself was studying those around her. He decided to move nearer.

As she stood there, Grace kept her eye out for anything unusual. This was all fine and dandy, but why the hell was she there? She circled the tree, trying to decide her next move, reluctant to leave the shade. At first, there were just people passing by, moving in and out of her vision, and then, without warning, there he was, striding toward her with measured, graceful steps that reminded her of a lion she saw on some National Geographic program. *Hello, gorgeous guy ahead.*

Tousled dark blond hair. Strong jaw. She couldn't help but notice him; he had the most seductive walk. He walked like the earth belonged to him, all sinewy purpose—smooth, sleek, powerful—drawing her attention like a predator would any wary, wise little animal.

Grace's eyes widened slightly. Mr. Smooth, it seemed, was heading straight for her, and his eyes pinned her to her spot. It was impossible to make them out, but she was absolutely certain they were blue, that they were intently on her. Out of nowhere, a shiver ran up her spine despite the heat, and without stopping to question why, she slid sideways from the tree into the crowd nearby, obscuring herself from the advancing man.

Her move surprised him enough to slow him down, and he started scanning the moving heads around. Huh. He *was* looking at her. Was he connected to GNE? Peeking between two standing bodies, she studied the man as he scanned the crowd.

N..iice, she mouthed a silent drawl. He was tall; from where she stood, he was easily the tallest of those around him. And he was very muscular, something her bodybuilding self noticed immediately. Her eyes were drawn to the well-defined muscles of a tight tee-shirt revealing a broad chest that tapered gently down to jeans molding a definite male frame of lean hips and muscular legs. *Wow*, she mouthed. At that same moment, he turned his head and their eyes met.

Grace inhaled, startled by the directness of the man's gaze, and even with twenty some feet separating them, she felt the heat of his perusal. There was something unnerving about the way he kept his eyes on her and whatever the reason he had for coming to her. Grace was sure it wasn't because he wanted to be friends. There was nothing at all friendly about that intent look. She took in the impossibly handsome features, from the masculine flare of his straight nose to those lips that any hot-blooded female would kill to have a taste of, and desire flared unexpectedly.

Right in the middle of an abortion rally, Grace wanted that man's baby. She bit back the quick laughter forming as he continued advancing. Never shy, she stared boldly back, arching a brow. The tall, handsome stranger paused and glared back at her. Why the man was angry? She couldn't decide whether she wanted to meet him or disappear into the crowd.

Any decision was interrupted by a voice coming from a loudspeaker. "Your attention please. This is the police. Do not panic. Please move away from the clinic now. There has been a bomb threat called in. Please move away from the area immediately. Do not panic."

Immediately, confusion took over. Grace stepped back in the melee and stomped on someone's foot. She turned to apologize.

"Sorry, are you okay?" she asked, holding on to the nun she almost knocked over.

The woman mumbled something as she tried to keep her balance. Grace hung on, taken aback by how much weight was pulling on her arm, and looking down, she gasped with the realization they were a man's hands. She looked up quickly, her mouth open in surprise. A man's face peered out at her from the nun's wimple. He was about to say something to her when one of the other nuns grabbed his arm and said urgently in Chinese, "Run!"

All the nuns looked up at something behind Grace, and fear formed on their faces before the disguised nun turned and fled in the opposite direction. She turned to see the cause of their reaction. Three Chinese men were running toward them, too well-attired to be there for a rally, and they seemed to be aware that their nun was…not a nun. Grace looked at them, turned back, looked at the retreating nuns, then turned sideways, and caught Mr. Smooth's gaze again. The commotion took less than a minute, but she had the odd feeling everything was in slow motion.

From where he was, Lance swore when he saw the young woman grab hold of one of the two nuns. So that was where the damned man was hiding. The two of them exchanged some hurried words and she pushed the nun away, who high-tailed it. He swore again, trying to push through the crowd in front of him. The mystery woman looked in one direction and back at the running nun; then, she turned back to meet his eyes questioningly. Big brown eyes. He could see her clearly now. Something was happening. He glanced to her left and saw the three Chinese operatives pushing their way through.

Shit, someone had spilled on them. Lance cursed again, shoving harder. Damn it, what the hell was happening? Who was this woman? The loudspeaker continued its urgent demands and the crowd became a sea of panic, slowing him, and most importantly, slowing the three others.

Grace had a split second to decide. The Men In Black or Mr. Smooth? Neither, she concluded, suddenly disliking her role as a mouse. Sometimes, being short was a good thing. She hunched down behind two burly men and moved quickly with the herd, letting her training take over.

"Thanks, Dad," she muttered, as she always did whenever her father's tutelage proved useful.

"Move! Move!" Policemen were cordoning off the area, and sirens filled the air as ATF bomb squads started to arrive.

How did she do that? Lance stared at the empty spot where the woman was last seen standing. That was twice. Nobody had done that to him in a long time. And he still had to get to that nun before one of those Asian goons. Looking farther ahead, he cursed aloud again as he saw all the black habits scattering in different directions. It was too late. It would seem they had an escape plan after all. The other three pursuers appeared to think so too, as they stopped, consulted each other, and headed back to their car. Lance's eyes narrowed. It had a diplomatic license plate.

From the safety of a shrub, Grace saw her "nun" being dragged off in the opposite direction, by a third party of two men into another car. Her "nun" sure was popular with the boys. Details, she had them. Hmm. How was her information important to Ed Maddux? As far as she could tell, what she'd just witnessed had nothing to do with the abortion rally.

***

"Fake bomb scare disrupts anti-abortion rally. Details at eleven."

Lance sat cleaning and oiling his 9mm Bersa, not even glancing up at the television. Inserting a cotton-tipped cleaning rod into the barrel, he gently rolled back and forth with his forefinger and thumb, then pulled it out to examine for dirt. He shined a small pin light down into the barrel, checking for smears.

A specific set of knocks on his door interrupted him. He cocked his head, heard the pattern repeated, and resumed what he was doing without glancing up. Dan Kershaw let himself into the spacious penthouse, impeccably dressed as usual. He put a box of pizza on the table where Lance was cleaning his weapons.

"Knowing you," he commented, "you've probably not eaten yet."

"Thanks," Lance said, wiped his hands on his jeans and opened the box to grab a slice. "Has Command called you yet?"

"Yes." Dan went to the stove and poured himself a cup of coffee. "They still want your personal report about what happened this morning. They want the rat, Lance. Whoever it is, it's someone real close to us. He's gotten every one of our moves so far, taking us down step by step. We can't afford to have one in our midst."

Lance nodded grimly. He took a swig of beer to wash down the food, staring at the ceiling thoughtfully. "Got to work fast," he said. "This whole operation is in jeopardy, if what you saw was really our guy being escorted off. Did you have a good look?"

"No," Dan answered, shaking his head. "I was on the other side of the crowd. The cops were everywhere and I couldn't get any

19

closer. Damn good trick, that bomb threat." He stared at the television for a few seconds, then added, "Nothing on that girl you saw either. Are you sure she's with the Chinese scholar?"

"She talked to him. I saw him grab her arm and she said something, warned him enough to get him running from the three goons," Lance told him, frowning as he recalled the morning's events. "She's definitely not with the Chinese government. That makes her one of the other group, the one that caught our guy."

"But you said our guy talked to her," Dan pointed out. "If she was working for someone who would harm him, surely he wouldn't have revealed himself to her."

"Maybe he thought she was one of us."

"Possible." Dan watched the younger man wolf down the piece of pizza in several bites.

"What?" Lance asked, an eyebrow cocked as he caught the older man's smile. "What's so amusing? Command is screaming for results and you're smiling? We haven't any answers so far. No knowledge of our scholar's whereabouts. No knowledge of who our new enemy is. Zilch about that mystery woman who evaded me."

"She must be an operative, obviously trained with specific evasive techniques, if she were able to get rid of you, Mercy," Dan said softly. "You know how tough it is to lose a tracker, especially one with your know-how. She must've known about you."

Lance scowled. He hated working like this, depending on invisible faces to pull strings while he jumped from situation to situation without his own personal decisions as a safety net. These last five years alone had honed his skills unsuited for team projects. Give him one-man missions—tracking missing combat soldiers and POWs in tropical jungles; or finding war criminals for COS Command; or zeroing in on cocaine gangs in South American jungles; even doing stints tracking CIA agents on the lam. Working alone had a good benefit—his own rules, his own time. This particular assignment was like swimming in mud for him. In fact, he would prefer to do just that than go through these last three or four months of inactive covertness. He was a natural hunter, a man used to prowling on the loose, sniffing on the heels of his prey. Without that freedom, the head games of poli-warfare bored him to tears.

"What did she look like?" Dan interrupted Lance's reverie. "I'll send a few fingers out to other agencies to trace any likenesses."

Lance chewed slowly. "Small built, maybe five three? I was quite a ways from her," he said, in between bites, remembering the cocky stance, the pert expression, and not mentioning it, "but as I got closer, she appeared taller. Petite, though. Dark eyes, brownish hair, mixed heritage with possibly some Asian blood. Young, and very quick, needless to say. Twice she moved faster than I'd anticipated, and you're right. She knows me. I recall quite clearly how she looked right at me to let me know she knew who I was."

"How? You said you didn't talk to her then," Dan wondered. "Any special features you remember? She doesn't sound remarkably noticeable, the way you described her. But of course, that's perfect for an evasion expert."

Lance devoured yet another slice of pizza, staring challengingly at Dan's pointed gaze at the almost empty cardboard box. "I just know," he told the older man. He couldn't just say that all the girl had done was arched her eyebrow at him. How could he explain that those big brown eyes had spoken volumes? The first time was like a punch in his gut, so strong was the jolt of their eyes meeting. The second time, with just a look, she conveyed to him the oncoming danger. Hadn't she deliberately let him know about the three agents coming in her direction? Then she had mocked him, and them, by showing exactly who she was and what she could do. By disappearing so quickly, she'd let them know in her own way she wasn't there by mistake.

"Hey, Mercy, quit taking off every time I mention that woman, will you?" Dan's voice was filled with quiet amusement. "You can't simply tell Command 'I just know'! What else did she do to betray herself?"

Lance shrugged. He picked up some loose bullets, arranging them in random patterns on the table. "Nothing. She's well trained, tell Command that. And young, a lot younger than an experienced agent should be. Maybe that's what caught me off guard."

"OK. I'll put out the word." Dan finished his coffee and stood up.

"What's the next step?" Lance asked, picking up his beer and gulping it down.

"We'll have to buy information."

"Off the street? Information like that would be hard to get. This isn't the usual black market underworld info that can be bought." Lance crushed the aluminum can noisily, then wiped his hands on his dirty jeans.

"Our information source isn't the usual off the street mouthpiece, Mercy," Dan told him, as he put the used cup into the basin. "You've always worked in your controlled little niche, always stayed away from the ones with lots of red tape, so you don't know how much one can get from our other source."

"They are that good?"

Dan nodded. "And that popular. Everyone in the game goes to them eventually."

Lance frowned. "Then everyone has the same information?" he asked.

"Most of it. They're non-aligned. Recorders. We call them ghosts among ourselves and they're essential to all of us doing covert investigation, black or white agencies. They record everything. It's up to us to ask the right question and they'll supply the information. Like the rally today—they'll answer any call for information, from what political groups were present, to which groups fund which senators, to the specific minute replay of the rally itself. The question has to be specific, maybe like 'Did anyone see a group of nuns and what happened to them at the rally?' and most of the time, some recorder has that information. It's his or her job to notice anything unusual. Anyway, this source tries to grant every wish, like the genie in the bottle." He grinned, pleased with the analogy.

"Ghosts," Lance repeated the word that caught his attention.

"Untouchables," Dan further explained. "We can't touch them. It's an unspoken alliance among all of us. Recorders, being non-aligned, cannot be cancelled."

"Honesty among thieves," Lance mocked, his tone unbelieving. "You mean to tell me, in all your years, you'd never seen one of these recorders cancelled by our operatives because the person knew too much or got too close?" When Dan just shrugged, he continued probing, "How could this source of information have so much power? Unless they know something we don't?"

"You just answered yourself," Dan said, turning towards the door. "Information —knowledge—is power. And they're tough on those who hurt their own; they've been known to withhold information rather than cultivate any client who makes the mistake of biting the hand that feeds them. Just like us, Lance. Command has a long memory too." He opened the apartment door, and added, "I'll let you know when I get something about the rally."

Lance nodded, walking over and holding the door open as Dan slipped out. "There usually isn't any loyalty among thieves either," he jibed, wanting to know more. This was the first time he had gotten so much from his old mentor and he was reluctant to let him go.

"Ghosts aren't thieves, Lance," Dan retorted. "In fact, they have been friends more times to agents than anything else. Their eyes and ears are valuable."

"You won't find ghosts in my jungles." Lance's grin was smug as he jammed his hands into his pockets.

"You'd be surprised, Mercy." Dan jabbed at the elevator button, then looked back at him. "There's a saying among us older operatives."

He paused, obviously waiting for a response, and Lance obliged, lips quirking. "Oh?"

The elevator door slid open and Dan turned and said, "Yes. It's common knowledge among all old hands that every good covert agent should have a ghost as his sidekick."

"That's a saying?" Lance crossed his arms now, openly amused. "All of you are walking around with an imaginary friend, then."

"No, only the good ones, Mercy," Dan said, smiling back at his former student. "All the others work without the advantage of knowledge, which could be the upper hand one needs to survive in key situations. A good ghost is a wonderful sidekick." He disappeared into the elevator.

"And how do you catch a good ghost?" Lance loudly addressed the empty hallway.

"A good operative finds that out himself." Dan's reply was muffled as the elevator doors closed.

"Sounds just like some crap kung fu movie," Lance muttered as he closed and locked his door. "A good agent must follow his heart to find ghost. Ah, so. Then good agent will get ancient secrets."

He shook his head and resumed his cleaning activity at the table. It was a soothing exercise for him, staying prepared, getting mentally focused, as if he were still living on the edge. From the TV, some newswoman was giving a short editorial piece.

"The abortion rally was declared a success by both sides, each claiming they had achieved what they had set out to do. The public, however, had a difficult time deciding the issue, since the rally was constantly more a battle of emotional words than a dissemination of objective information. The bomb threat further incited an already mob-like attitude. As our own camera recorded the scene this morning, one can feel the big picture playing out like a morality play. As one man said, 'So that no one can dispute the historical significance of this issue of the last several decades, we need every bit of this recorded.'"

Lance looked up, his forehead creasing thoughtfully. His long strong fingers caressed his Bersa slowly as he reflected on those final words.

***

At the GNE offices, Ed slowly flipped through the folder, now and then pausing and glancing up meaningfully at Sandra. His cigarette smoldered, forgotten in the ashtray, as he read each page. When he reached the end, he closed the file, steepled his hands and rested his chin on them, his gray eyes thoughtful.

Sandra, having sat through the whole reading in silence, acknowledged quiet agreement with a smile. She knew him so well, remembered still every one of his expressions. "Impressive, isn't she?" She was very pleased with their new find.

Ed nodded, tapping his chin on his steepled fingers. "Very. The only thing wrong was that she interfered. She actually got in the way."

"She didn't even know what was happening, Ed. This was a blind assignment. We were there just to test her observation skills, how she'd handle herself in a crowded situation. Everything that happened was a bonus revelation of her skills."

Ed looked at Sandra, his eyes glinting. He watched her usually bland ones widened slightly as she realized the assignment wasn't that "blind." "And from your debriefing," he said, his voice smooth and unrevealing, his eyes still holding Sandra's, "I can tell she was quite good in a crowd."

"It was very interesting, watching her at work," Sandra told him, her mind still busy deciphering the look Ed gave her. "When she realized that she was seeing something unusual, she didn't panic. She actually, by reflex, looked for cause and motive, targeting the three Asian operatives and the other man in seconds. Then, she had the sense to move away from the action, Ed. There wasn't any confused pause or even any sign of fear, just a moment when she considered her options."

"And you said you saw her escape four people," Ed remarked. That was what caught his

interest. It wasn't an easy feat, evading four trained operatives, and there wasn't any doubt they were that, from Sandy's observations. Sandra's enthusiasm elicited a slow smile from him. The Sandra Smythe of today seldom showed any emotions other than calm professionalism. He hadn't seen this kind of impulsive reaction from her since he came back.

"That was a beautiful thing to see. Quick and catlike. She's going to be a pleasure to train. She already has the natural basics."

"And she still has no idea what it was she saw?" Ed asked. He had his own speculations about the incident but their job was just to tell the surface story. Recorders didn't interpret events.

"She hasn't asked any questions."

"Another strange quality about our young lady," he observed. "She's unusually composed and observant. I checked her background to see what her parents' occupations were but her mother is deceased and her father's whereabouts, according to her, is unknown, so there aren't any influences from that direction. She has no contact with any law enforcement officer or ever had a relationship with any military personnel. So where do you think she learned her skills?"

Sandra shrugged. "I prefer to think they came naturally for her and she worked with them unconsciously as a means of protection, being an only child, orphaned and taken care of by her single grandparent. She was probably a loner and a lonely child, and that accounts for her maturity and attention to detail," she offered as a theory. "I like her. I can see potential in her and we need someone like her—she speaks the languages we're weak at, and is far more advanced than the rest of our trainees. We'll use her as long as we can."

Ed agreed. Although Grace O'Connor would be by far the youngest they'd ever put out into fieldwork, she appeared to be capable of rising to the challenge. Perhaps they ought to move her slowly in, acquainting her with the easier aspects of being a recorder. On the other hand, she was already in the middle of something, just by being herself, without any prior training. "So are you thinking what I'm thinking about Grace and what she saw at the rally?"

Sandra smiled knowingly again. "I want to see more," she told him, eyes alight with an excitement that brought back certain memories to Ed Maddux. "Let's assign her to the Chinese ambassador's ball this Friday. I bet she'll pick up from where she left off."

***

Friday night.

Grace walked with her group, right behind the senator and his wife, showing her

ID tag and invitation Sandra had earlier put in her assignment envelope. The man checked his own sheet and waved her in. She'd followed the instructions on her appearance—plain jacket-top, conservative skirt, low heels—while humming the tune to Mission Impossible.

Look sedate, Sandra had advised. She was to try to be unnoticed, a part of the scene. Rarely did a recorder stand out. Grace had chosen one of her least favorite jackets, the one Tim bought for her birthday.

Sandra had been reassuring. "Don't worry," she'd said. "You're not crashing the event. Your pass is legit. You're there as an interpreter for the senator and his aides, so if you're asked, tell them the truth. Interpreters are quite normal at these affairs. The secret to blending in, Grace, is to answer all questions as truthfully as you can, without jeopardizing yourself and us. Do you think you can handle this?"

Grace suppressed a grin. *Oh yes, ma'am I can handle blending and pretending.* "Yes. I'll learn to be a good recorder, or whatever it is you said this position is." She suspected there was more to this information selling business than simply attending rallies and functions.

"Remember our first rule—do not ask questions or bring attention to yourself. If you cause a scene, that can influence events."

"But what if I get caught in the middle, like the first time?"

"But you got out of it, remember?" Sandra reminded her. "You'll do all right, Grace.

Listen, watch, remember. That's all. It might be just a nice party, and in that case, you'll have a good time. That's the usual Level Two experience, anyway. Don't think it's always adventure."

So Grace found herself standing quietly near the aides, sipping water. They were mostly young men and women, mingling among themselves as the party began to warm up. The ball was given in honor of the new trade agreement between China and the U.S., and every senator attending was eager to talk trade with the ambassador, wanting to offer business opportunities from their own respective states. Grace listened attentively to the trade discussions mixed with gossip and ordinary conversations, keeping an eye on the Chinese ambassador and his aides. She moved easily through the groups, giving some translation help between a Chinese aide and American one. One senator sent her to bring over some files for him and she had to hunt down the right aide for the task, who then pulled her along in case he needed an interpreter.

An hour later she went in search of food at the buffet table. She was slightly hoarse. It was like flexing a new muscle, this interpreting business, but it was surprisingly enjoyable and educational. Eyeing the sumptuous feast before her, she decided all business should be discussed around good food.

The Chinese buffet spread out on a long table, tray upon tray of exotic looking dishes. Asian food was one of her weaknesses, having been brought up with her grandmother's home cooking. She stood there, knowing with regret that her eyes were bigger than her stomach. She wanted to try everything, and with gusto, she started heaping generous amounts of butterfly shrimp fried rice and five-spiced roasted pork on her plate. Looking around, she found an empty corner table and sat down. She took a moment to admire the pretty colors of the food before attacking. The spicy aroma almost made her moan. Oh, yeah. This was a good side benefit to her new job.

Lance excused himself from the bright chatter of the ambassador's secretaries. The last hour had gone by quickly, and he still hadn't seen Senator Richards make any move toward the ambassador. He gave a polite smile to a pretty female interpreter who stopped to inquire whether he needed her help and shook his head, although he eyed her appreciatively. Another time. Right now, according to the report Dan received from Command, their source gave some information of a nun being seen taken away in a vehicle. Even the license plate was given, and it hadn't taken long to trace it to a vehicle registered under one of the senator's men.

He had his doubts about the report. Of course, they knew that the senator was knee deep in the Chinese's pockets when it came to trade votes on the floor, but why the need to kidnap the Chinese informer? If these recorders were so accurate, then how come they couldn't just tell Command the reason? And did they ask about the woman he—

He almost dropped his glass of wine when he saw her sitting by herself. She was deeply engrossed in her meal, not even looking up during the minute or two he stood studying her. Like him, she was no longer in casual clothes; she looked like any of the young people working for the senators. Her hair was secured from her face, a light trace of lipstick was all she had on as makeup, and she was dressed in an absolutely boring jacket and skirt ensemble that covered what he recalled very well was a lithe shapely body. He frowned, wondering how she'd managed to slip in and marveling at her audacity to sit and eat like she was doing at the moment. Her enthusiasm at her present chore betrayed her professional cover.

Grace was licking her sticky fingers when someone pulled out a chair and sat next to her, trapping her to the wall. Surprised, she looked up and her eyes widened at her unexpected companion. Mr. Smooth—all groomed—was looking at her, his blue, blue eyes raking her appearance. He looked slightly amused, as if comparing what he remembered of her from that Monday morning to her fashion statement at the moment. Suited up, he looked as delicious as the food she'd just consumed. He was even better close-up, she decided, unconsciously licking her lips, drawing his unforgettable eyes down to settle there.

"It seems that we finally get close enough to speak," he said. He had a nice deep drawl, hypnotically low.

Grace continued to stare at him, wondering whether it was lust or fear that had her heart pounding so. Her trained instincts sensed the alertness behind his easy repose, the toughness inside those deceptively civilized clothes. Everything about the man hummed of danger.

"Who are you?" he demanded impatiently, as he grew tired of her silence. "How did you get in here?"

"I'm working," she replied, feeling her temper rising at the tone of his voice. She curbed it. "Are you in need of my services?" She instantly regretted saying that, as unwanted images of a different sort of service came unbidden. What was wrong with her? She had never been so quickly attracted, especially to older men, and Mr. Smooth was—what—ten years older, she surmised. At least. He was very, very old. *Yeah, keep telling yourself that.*

"Depends," Lance taunted, waiting a beat, "on what services you offer."

"I'm an interpreter," she explained, in as mild a voice as she could, "and as you can see, I'm taking a break."

"May I see your invitation and ID tag?"

"Are you with security?"

"No."

"Do you have any authority to ask to see my tag?" Grace wiped her fingers on a napkin.

"I'm with Senator Richards' detail," Lance curtly informed her. A small lie. "I want to know who you are and why you were at the rally on Monday. I also want to know who you work for and what you're after."

It was a command, implacable and snotty. He spoke like a man used to people snapping to attention. Sorry, Mr. Smooth. The only snapping this woman did was at the heels of rude snotty men. Tell the truth, she recalled Sandy's words.

"In that case," Grace gave him one of her patented plastic smiles, "may I know by whom I'm being interrogated? I'm Grace O'Connor, since you're just dying to know."

"Your ID tag," Lance requested again, ignoring her sarcasm.

Grace shook her head. "Your name, sir." She knew that she was not to cause a scene but there was no way she would allow this man to treat her like that. Not when she'd actually contemplated having his baby last Monday.

Lance looked down at her. She seemed too young to be an operative, looking more like eighteen. "Lance Mercy," he told her.

"Lance Mercy," she repeated, managing to prevent a smirk. Poor man. With that name, no wonder he had an attitude problem. "You know I can't marry you now. Grace Mercy sounds absolutely scary."

He didn't rise to her bait at all. A slight quirk to those gorgeous lips but he just kept looking at her. She gave an exaggerated sigh before handing him her plastic tag, which had her name and position boldly printed on it.

"I was hired by Senator Richards' office as interpreter for this. Here's my tag and invitation. My name ought to be in the list of guests as well. I'm sure you'll have no trouble finding my name there; it's under the letter O."

Lance looked at it and found it seemingly authentic enough. "What were you doing at the rally?" he asked, deliberately making her madder by being rude. Not that it flustered her at all. She'd tried distracting him, joking about their names together…hinting about future intimacies, perhaps? But something about her made him mad and he refused to flirt.

Maybe it was the two times she'd managed to slip away from him, but he'd never had an ego problem before. She might be too young but he doubted those liquid brown eyes missed much. They were too bright with intelligence, with some mysterious shadows lurking behind the boldness. And the little hellion wasn't too shy to eat him with those cat eyes either. No, she couldn't possibly be eighteen.

"Well?" he persisted.

"It's a free country, Mr. Mercy," Grace pointed out smoothly. "It was a rally open to anyone."

"But you weren't there for the rally." He leant a little closer, his knee bumping slightly with hers.

Grace crossed her legs, adjusting her position a little away. "Nor were you," she retorted, her voice icier than before. She didn't like threats. "I don't know why you're so curious, but I'm not going to answer any more of your questions. I've done nothing wrong."

"You don't fool me, Grace," Lance said, deliberately bumping her knee again with his. It was going to take more than words to rattle her. She wanted to flirt? She was going to get more than that. "You'll tell me what you were doing there and where the nun disappeared to after you talked to her." He leaned forward and tipped her chin with his forefinger, noting her startled gaze. "You're too young for this game, babe. You're way out of your league against me."

God, but he smelled good, Grace thought, even though her mind was rebelling against the obvious attempt at intimidation. She hadn't any idea what the man wanted, but she was sure he wouldn't believe her if she told him so. She stared into his compelling eyes, her own round with innocence. "What game?" she drolly questioned.

"One more time. Where is that nun?" He enunciated the words carefully, threateningly.

Grace grasped his forefinger, which seemed to be burning a hole under her chin, and pushed it away. The trick to a game of intimidation, she knew, was not to show a disadvantage. Deliberately, she held on to his finger, settling his hand down on his knee. She was surprised he didn't resist.

"I don't know," she answered coldly, wondering whether honesty actually helped her situation. "I wasn't there to find out where nuns go in their free time." She tightened her hold on his finger, wanting to push him as he'd tried to push her. "And I'm not babe. It's Miss O'Connor to you."

Her hand felt warm around his finger, and she didn't seem to be aware that her thumb was caressing his palm. It was a tantalizing motion, round and round. He looked at her closely, seeing the faint pulse at the nape of her neck. Miss O'Connor may look outwardly calm but her heart rate was telling him a different story. "So tell me," he invited, his voice going an octave lower, "Why were you there?"

An impish gleam of mischief entered those fascinating cat eyes of hers, both surprising and intriguing him. Her lips curved back to reveal little white teeth. "If you must know, Mr. Mercy," she chuckled, "I was out there looking for cheese."

With that, she burst out in peals of delighted laughter at what Lance assumed was her own private joke. She had a pretty laugh, bubbly and husky, and it came out easily, typical of someone who laughed a lot. Many of the guests glanced in their direction; she had the kind of laugh that drew people to her.

"Do I need an interpreter to understand that statement?" Lance interrupted her merriment. He was growing more fascinated by the second. He didn't like the feeling one bit. A stray lock of hair had fallen across her cheekbone and he felt a sudden urge to reach out to tuck it behind her ear.

"Believe me, you wouldn't find it interesting," Grace answered, still smiling, her tension wonderfully gone. "I'm sorry I can't help you, but I really don't know where that nun went or anything else. I was just there at the wrong time, that's all. What did you think I was, a spy or something?" She tilted her head inquiringly, and added, "What's so important about that nun anyway?"

Was she telling the truth? She was an accomplished actress, if she weren't. "How old are you?" Lance abruptly changed the subject.

"Twenty-two," Grace's reply was soft and mocking. "Way out of *your* league, babe."

Lance held her gaze for a moment. "Aren't you, Grace?" He let his eyes slide down from her face to the front of her jacket in a slow perusal.

Grace could feel his heat, his taunts a challenge to her quicksilver nature. Her body responded at the sound of her name on his lips, at his intimate look. Thank goodness there wasn't much to see, she thought with relief, with that chunky jacket with its severe buttoned front.

"Depends," she came back, feeling reckless, knowing that baiting him was possibly dangerous her health. To her heart anyway. He was having the strangest effect on it, erratically speeding up whenever he gave her that lazy knowing look.

"Are you going to hold onto my finger all night?"

Looking down, Grace was embarrassed to find out she was indeed doing just that, her thumb absently moving round and round, dandling the callused flesh under his forefinger in a soft exploration. She hastily released his finger, feeling a flush spreading up her neck.

"I…think I've answered enough questions for one night. May I go back to work now, Mr. Mercy?" She sounded disgustingly breathy. She couldn't stand up from her chair since she was trapped in the corner.

"Of course, but this isn't over. You haven't told me everything." He stood up and allowed her to make her escape.

Grace shook her head. "If you keep asking me questions, you'll make me more curious about what's going on. And you don't want that, do you?"

"And you're not curious now?" Lance walked with her a little way as she headed toward a group of aides beckoning to her.

Grace couldn't help herself. She wanted to rattle that damned arrogance. Before turning away, she deliberately looked him over from head to toe, then said, "Frankly, I'm curious why a man like you would make it a habit of chasing after men dressed as nuns."

Lance's eyes narrowed thoughtfully as she strutted off before he could make a reply. He smiled reluctantly at her play with "habit" and "nun." She did have a way with words, whoever she was, first joking about not marrying him because of their names together. He allowed a reluctant smile. That *was* funny. His mother would find it funny. But then his mother also named him, so he'd better not even mentioned this joke to her ever or she would start getting ideas.

That brought on a frown. Damn if that woman hadn't distracted him yet again. He'd better check her out. If she were indeed working for Senator Richards, she would find out soon enough that she wouldn't be getting rid of him so easily.

CHAPTER THREE

Curiouser and curiouser. Grace felt like Nancy Drew without the clues. She should call it The Mystery of the Transvestite Nun. On cue, she smoothly repeated in Chinese the advantages of having American-made farm machinery parts to the solemn-looking Chinese man standing next to her. The senator for whom she was interpreting was animatedly charting out China's output of farm produce in five-year increments. The Chinese aide looked totally disinterested. But maybe it was just a cultural thing. Her grandmother had the same look when she used to try to convince her she needed more allowance money. She quickly hid her own amusement, taking a sip from her glass of water.

Much later, as she stopped to refill her glass, a middle-aged Chinese man approached her. He was quite short, even shorter than she was, and his face was fanned with lines caused by constant smoking.

"You have Asian blood," he said, matter-of-factly, in Chinese, without any introduction.

"Some Chinese," agreed Grace. "My grandmother's from Mainland China. She married an American."

"You speak Chinese as a mother tongue." Again, it was a statement.

Grace nodded. "Yes, I speak both Cantonese and Mandarin. I was taught by my grandmother and mother."

"Good. We want a native speaker to translate for us, so that nothing is misunderstood. Come with me, please."

Grace followed him, moving behind an eight-paneled Chinese screen depicting swans in repose on a lake, with mother-of-pearl inlay. There was a smaller group of men there, sitting on the Chinese designed sofa and stiff-backed chairs. She could immediately tell these men were of more considerable influence than the ones talking with the other senators. They were older and had an air of quiet authority. Traditional Chinese cups sat on the coffee tables next to them. Senator Richards, whom she recognized, was also present with his aide. The Chinese man who had taken her there gestured for her to sit between the two groups.

"Be sure you repeat to the senator in English word for word what we say. His aide understands Chinese also, but we do not trust his phrasing," the man said to Grace. She nodded obediently. Asking for the names of the various gentlemen around her, she then turned to smile at her employer. Of course, the man didn't know she was really his part-time contract employee for that week; most of the senators were too busy to know every underling.

"Good evening, Senator," she greeted pleasantly. He seemed distracted, nodding back slightly. The aide judiciously took out his notepad, as if to catch her mistakes. "I'll repeat exactly what the Chinese ambassador and Mr. Wang and Mr. Lee say. They were just unsure of several things being discussed."

The senator nodded again.

The one named Mr. Lee calmly said, "We are sorry we missed our sick little brother. He's a long way from home."

Grace repeated, translating his words, very carefully emphasizing on the "little," since the Chinese language used different words for elder and younger siblings.

Senator Richards smiled and replied, "I'm sure you'll be glad to see him." He had a wonderful speaking voice, the kind hired to tell a good story on the radio, and it flowed out of him like soft silk. "I'll see what I can do about his health."

"We are grateful that you have taken care of him for us and we are indebted to you for your kindness," the same Chinese man continued.

Grace noted he spoke in polite rather than personal terms when mentioning this brother. Regretfully, she couldn't convey this in English, except perhaps to use stilted formal English.

"It was the least we could do, Mr. Lee. I know you'd have helped me too if I were ever in need of your aid," the senator said, sipping his champagne, his eyes intently on Mr. Lee. "I've heard he is still unwell and needs your attention."

"Of course. We always take care of our own. 'The wind blows and the grass moves'. Your generosity is most appreciated. You will definitely hear good news on Monday regarding our trade contract."

Grace frowned. Mr. Lee used an old Chinese proverb. Depending on the situation, it could mean several things. It was up to her to get it right. She considered for a second, then chose the most likely pertaining to the conversation. Knowing Mr. Lee was closely listening, she translated his words, replacing the proverb with, "It's just a small problem." She looked at him questioningly when she came to that particular line and, after a moment, he nodded.

"How wonderful," enthused Senator Richards, his face alight with pleasure. "I'm so glad that my state's doing business with your country. My constituents will be happy with the news."

"And they will remember come voting day," one of the other gentlemen commented, a slight smile tugging the corners of his lips. Grace translated; the senator had no comment.

"When that is done, we will be free to take care of our responsibilities," Mr. Lee stated.

"Oh, of course. Our Charity Invitation on Tuesday night, if you like, is the perfect time. You know how important charity is to me, so I cannot be with you then, but it'll all be ready in Room 103."

"It is not wise to do business in the evening, Senator," the third Chinese gentleman observed.

Grace studied the very distinguished looking man, with his neatly trimmed beard and haughty eyes. The others seemed to defer to him.

"It's always good if it's for charity, Mr. Ambassador. Besides, the Chinese government will look good with a big donation. The media will be at the function." Senator Richard's voice was persuasive.

"I see. And this donation is, of course, to the usual foundation?"

There was slight amusement among the men after Grace translated that question.

"That would be wonderful," the senator answered, smiling and composed. "And you can leave from the private entrance after our business in Room 103 to avoid any unnecessary delays with the media."

"Thank you, we don't want any delays at all," replied Mr. Lee. "We are confident that our agreement will be carried out successfully."

***

Lance caught glimpses of Grace throughout the evening. She appeared hard at work; constantly the mouthpiece for some senator or key aide who had been instructed to discuss with certain Chinese aides.

In those clothes, she looked the part, earnest and perfectly conservative, but Lance remembered the curves underneath. She checked out on the guest list, so she was who she'd said she was. However, the coincidence of her being here was still suspicious.

At least, that was what Lance told himself, as he followed her movements whenever she was in the vicinity. There was something about her that drew him to her—that surprising tart sense of humor, the liquid brown eyes that could light up with anger or laughter, the fluid grace. He wanted to know who this young woman was, and he was determined to see her without her current disguise. He quirked his lips. She couldn't keep running away every time, not when he intended to catch her by surprise.

It was long past her bedtime when Grace unlocked the door to her apartment, humming her favorite group's latest hit. Whew. Home. Translation was more work than she'd anticipated. Throwing her satchel on the armchair, she strolled into her dark bedroom, impatiently unbuttoning her jacket blouse and shrugging it off. She sat down on the vanity stool and unstrapped her heels, giving a moan of pleasure after discarding the tortuous things. Ugh, how did anyone wear these things for more than three hours? Closing her eyes, she grumbled softly as she rubbed her arches, savoring the feel of her thumbs. Oh, what she wouldn't give to have Tim there to give her a foot rub.

She arched her back like a cat, yawned and blinked sleepily as she went over the events of the night. Lazily, she unhooked the back of her bra. So much to think about—what with debriefing and then trying to understand that mysterious—

Grace froze. Slowly, she turned her head toward the direction of her bed. Her heart started thudding hard when she confirmed the slight movement she'd caught in the darkness. Someone was in her bed. Someone big, lying there with his hands clasped behind his head. She could pick out his outline from the stream of light coming from her living room.

"Pity. I'd hoped to see more of you before you caught me."

Lance had been lying there for at least half an hour, after walking around her apartment and picking things up here and there to clue himself in about the woman's personality. He'd enjoyed being in her bed, taking in her slightly fruity scent, imagining her curling up where he was. He refused to picture her there with that boy in the photo on one of the dressers, the one with his arm casually across her shoulders.

Lance hadn't expected her to drop her top so quickly, and the whole spectacle of her sitting there in the half-darkness with only her bra and skirt, rubbing her feet, her eyes closed, making throaty moans, had kept him silent. Here was Grace O'Connor without her disguise, all sensuous and sexy, with the shadows and light adding an intimacy to her movements. His quick arousal—fierce and sudden—took him by surprise. He'd watched more intimate revelations in his line of business and very little elicited this kind of reaction any more.

But she appeared to have breached that part of him too. He'd silently willed her to take her bra off and when she'd reached back to comply, he was all but ready to stride off the bed and drag her back into it with him. It was both a relief and a disappointment when she finally realized she wasn't alone.

Grace heard the voice of the very devil she'd been thinking about, and half-naked as she was, she pivoted to make a mad dash out of her bedroom. Her intruder was faster than she'd thought. One moment, he was lounging there on her sheets, all heavy with indolence, and the next he leapt like a big hunting cat and pounced.

She gasped as he gave her a linebacker's tackle, and as his weight came down, she shrieked in furious protest, pulling herself back enough to try to land a punch into his solar plexus. She didn't miss her target by much and it was a solid enough punch that produced a grunt from her assailant. Fear and panic gave her the strength to push him off enough so she could roll over to get up. His hand grasped her right ankle as she got to her knees, pulling her off balance. She landed on her front, sprawled every which way. Desperately, she reached down with one hand and pried his third finger out, pulling it back cruelly. He yelped, cursing loud and strong, and let her ankle go.

Breathlessly gasping for air now, Grace made another attempt to stand up, her tight skirt restricting her movements. The door was just a scant few yards away, and if she could just get to it… Lance rolled over like a log against the back of her feet, flipping her backwards as she made her frantic flight. She landed on her posterior, legs flailing as his limbs and hers tangled together in a ball of flesh and clothing.

The next few minutes were a furious rugby-like grapple. In the darkness, Grace wasn't even sure which part of him she was punching and biting, and she didn't particularly care. A part of her registered her attacker wasn't trying to kill her, just subdue her, and her fear turned into anger as she felt him hold her down limb by limb until she lay panting and perspiring under his male heat.

To her humiliation, she realized that they were upside down to each other: his knees held down her arms, his body lay between her legs, his hands were bands of steel around her calves, while his arms gripped her thighs. She was trapped in a classic wrestling pin down, unable to move. She didn't want to know where his head was.

Her skirt had ridden up during their struggle and she could feel his rasped breathing against the inside of her naked thighs. Oh…shit.

"You little hellcat," Lance muttered, soft and grim, after he caught his breath. "You just betrayed your training with those moves." She'd stunned him with her agility. Although he knew she fought him out of panic, part of him refused to allay her fears. She'd almost got him where it hurt. If it hadn't been for his superb reflexes, he'd be lying flat on his back right now. "So, little Miss Intern, care to tell me what agency you work for?"

Grace tried unsuccessfully to pry loose. She dared not buck under him. She had an uncomfortable feeling about the location of his face. Dripping sweat ran down her neck as she tried to calm down. Agency. He thought she was an operative, which made him one too, since he recognized her evasive tactics.

"I don't know what you're talking about," she said. After a few more minutes of trying to break his hold, she demanded, "Let me go! How did you know where I live, anyway?"

"I made it my business to know as much as possible about you since last Monday. And let's stop this nonsense about your innocence, OK? I know you're somehow involved. Your every move shouts covert training, Grace. And, being that," there was a pause, then he softly challenged, "you ought to have an idea what I am."

Grace felt the deliberate scrape of Lance's day-old stubble against the inside of her thigh. Shock reverberated through her system. Wild hysteria bubbled up. Of all the luck. Damn, damn, damn. She should have known, should have recognized his specialty.

Why, oh why didn't she think of her father's lessons about spy classifications and operative specialties? Loner type, an expert in search and destroy, mode of operation focused on seduction of mind and senses. Lance Mercy was a trained tracker. She could have kicked herself. She'd felt the pull of his powerful personality from the very beginning. Why hadn't she realized it sooner?

As if to punish her silence, Lance scraped his chin along her skin again, and it took all her will power not to propel her hip upward in response. "Stop it." Her voice was hushed, as realization of her predicament dried her throat up.

"I want an answer." His tone was deceptively quiet.

"I'm thinking," she muttered back.

She needed time to prepare herself, time she didn't have. A tracker—a good one—came from the school of interrogation. They were taught to be ruthless in order to get answers. A tracker on seduction mode knew all the points of pain and pleasure to manipulate the human body, knew where to touch to stimulate and elicit a response from the victim, whether through fear, pain, or pleasure. A tracker hunted, retrieved, destroyed. Her father had warned her of the nature of this kind of trained field operative. She knew she had to hold him off while she worked to control her own surging emotions.

"Don't!" This time Grace shouted, as she felt his teeth nibble on her flesh. She was hot. Feverish.

"Are you going to keep pretending you know nothing?"

"But it's the truth!" She bit out between clenched teeth. "I don't know what's happening."

"So tell me what you know."

If he was working for an outfit that planned to kill that disguised nun, Grace sure wasn't going to give him any helpful information. She tried desperately to remember her instructions. Sexual intimidation was to be countered with either indifference or retaliation. She didn't think she was up to try the latter, not with his heady musky scent slowly enveloping her senses in the heavy darkness. She gave another strangled cry as the nibbling started again. Soft, then hard. Again.

"What do you think you're doing?" She curbed the urge to thrash her legs.

"You know exactly what I'm doing," Lance told her, in between bites. She was too still. Her body was rigid from trying not to move under him. He listened to her heightened breathing. She might be afraid but her fear wasn't the kind a woman showed when being attacked by a stranger. No, she was still very much in control. It was that odd mix of fear and anticipation again, as if she liked being on the edge. And it excited him.

Lance understood desire; he was trained to control and enjoy it. The emotion had never blinded or overcome him like it was threatening to now. His need to take her was almost supplanting the tracker initiative of first mastering the intended victim. Somehow, he couldn't see Grace O'Connor as a victim. He wanted a response from her and he would have one tonight. Easing his weight off her a little, he waited with cunning for her first deep intake of air. And attacked. He laid his chin gently against her crotch and at the same time slid his hands from her calves down to her firm little buttocks. He smiled in the dark at the loud whoosh of air that escaped her lips at this assault. But she still didn't move a damned muscle. He frowned.

Grace squeezed her eyes tightly shut, concentrating on her muscles rather than the intimate sensations roiling through her. She knew she mustn't give in to that need to respond physically to Lance Mercy's sexual onslaught. Indifference. *You told me what to expect, Dad, but you didn't tell me I might like it!* That was what made it so difficult to be indifferent. She wanted his touch, had wanted him since setting eyes on his masculine form at the rally. Now she didn't know how long she could resist his expertise.

Lance wanted to have her so badly he realized that he would have to stop soon. He couldn't achieve his end if he satisfied his own need. That wouldn't serve any purpose except his own. He was suddenly even unsure whether there was ever any other purpose except his own when he'd decided to break into her apartment. She pulled at him without even trying, even when she obviously intensely disliked him.

Grace's eyes flew open as soon as he released her. She lay there staring up into the darkness as she felt him nearby where he'd rolled away from her body, his breathing heavy, as if he was having trouble controlling himself. He was granting her a reprieve. Why?

Sitting up carefully, she scooted back a little ways, still looking at Lance's inert body. Sheer relief sent shivers up and down her spine. Another minute and she didn't think she could have resisted him any longer. She wondered whether he knew how close to victory he was. She pulled her skirt back down, covering her thighs. She resnapped her bra.

"A little late for that, sweetheart," he drawled, amused.

Grace glared back. "I'm going to call the police if you don't leave my apartment now," she warned him, at the same time considering her sanity for possibly jeopardizing her life.

Lance sat up, raking his hair with one careless hand. "No, you won't. I let you go because I wanted to, Grace. Don't make me change my mind."

She swallowed. No, next time he might succeed. "Then leave," she said, as calmly as she could. "I told you the truth tonight. I know nothing about what's going on. And, I'm not an...agent."

He snorted in disbelief. "Yeah, and you didn't know what I was doing either, I bet."

Grace was silent about that. She knew what he'd started to do but to admit that meant having to explain her own knowledge, about how she knew how to evade trackers and their methods. At least, she corrected herself wryly, thanks to Dad, in theory.

"You were trying to seduce me," she finally conceded, knowing if she weren't honest, he would know. "It's an easy enough conclusion, Mr. Mercy. You were...using your mouth in a very explicit manner." She refused to recall the feel of those white teeth of his against her thighs.

Lance smiled at her words. The woman knew how to play with fire, he would grant her that. "Mr. Mercy sounds a little stilted after we've enjoyed such close rapport, don't you think?" he taunted, standing up and walking toward her.

His movements once again reminded Grace of a lion stalking his prey. She scooted back even more, until her back hit the side of her bed. Light flooded the room when he turned on her bedside lamp. She blinked several times, focusing her attention on his body as he loomed over her. He was clothed all in black, looking dangerous and sexy. Shadows caused by his light stubble added contours to his face. His blue eyes glittered with a suppressed emotion she couldn't quite describe. His hair was enticingly mussed up. A scratch lined one side of his face from cheek to jawbone. Obviously, she'd given him a mark to remember for a few days, she noted with satisfaction. Funny how a few hours could change a man's face. All clean-cut one hour and downright macho and remote another. She tried to imagine how he would look in the morning, just awakened. It was a disturbing little fantasy.

She gave a start when he held out his hand, and after a moment's hesitation, she let him help her up. He gave her a slight push so that she sat down on her bed. She looked at him warily as he sat down beside her. His smile was slow and taunting.

"Ah, the little intern is nervous. Poor Grace." She flinched when he followed temptation and pushed her untidy curls away from her flushed face. In fact, he couldn't seem to keep his hands off the woman. Still half out of her clothes, she didn't seem to be aware of how delectable she looked on her bed.

No, Grace O'Connor wasn't a shy woman. Not by a long shot. Her slender build hid her strength; her body, soft as it looked, was well-toned and, as he'd found out half an hour ago, incredibly nimble. Her lower lip was dangerously close to a pout, her brown eyes dark and stormy between anger and fear. All that hidden strength and passion in one sexy package. How far would she let him push her?

As if reading his mind, Grace said in a bored tone, "This is all I know. You seem to be…an agent. There seems to be a male nun on the loose. You seem to think I know where he is. You seem to think I am an agent too. That's it. Now you can go and leave me alone."

She looked about her, then picked up a shirt from the floor.

"Not enough," he said.

"Well, I've nothing else you want!"

43

Her lack of inhibition and nerves continued to intrigue him. Maybe he *should* push her, no matter how young she looked. Looks were deceptive in his business."Oh, I wouldn't say that," Lance said, reaching out and twining his finger around one of her loose curls.

She shook her head, her lips pursed. "OK, Mercy, you can quit that kind of game. I'm not going to let you play with my mind."

"Yes, I noticed how strong you are," Lance commented softly, ignoring her attempts to stop his playing with her hair. He took great pleasure at taunting a response from her. "In fact—"

The shrill ringing of the phone startled them out of the growing tension. Grace stared at it, dreading to pick it up, knowing who the caller was.

"Answer it," Lance ordered. Her expression gave her away. Handler?

"No," she said. No freaking way. This wasn't the time for a long drawn out conversation with her caller.

"Then I will."

"No!" Grace dove across the bed in a panic to get to the phone before him and snatching it up from the bedside table, she barely had time to catch her breath "Hello? Uh, hi, swee…Tim."

Lance's smile turned particularly nasty. He would wager all the money in his wallet "Tim" was the young fellow in the photo on her dresser, the one that he'd somehow taken a great dislike. Deliberately, he leaned closer to the sprawled woman. She was too busy listening to her boyfriend to notice what he was doing until he delicately pulled one of her bra straps off her shoulder. He felt her shudder as he touched her.

"Yes, I've…been to a dinner party. I…I just came in."

Lance knew that she wouldn't be able to fight him when her concentration was elsewhere.

The moment was perfect for attack. She didn't seem to want her boyfriend knowing there was a man in her apartment at this hour of the night, which was odd, if she were afraid for her life. How many chances was he going to give her?

He moved over her, effectively trapping her between the bed and his body, and pulled her head backward to reveal her throat. He placed his lips on her pulse.

Grace gasped aloud at the first touch of his lips on the sensitive spot. "Nothing! I…I stubbed my toe, that's…all." White spots blinded her vision as she stared over a muscular forearm, her eyes focusing on her pillow. Her mind skittered with sensations beyond her control. She couldn't think, much less answer Tim's questions. She dimly registered the impatience and irritation in his voice, although she couldn't actually hear any of the words. Desperately, she tried to control herself. "OK, OK, sure, Tuesday."

When he started nibbling, Grace swallowed another gasp. What was wrong with her? Her limbs had grown helpless and heavy. She was sinking fast. Inching her free hand with difficulty, she reached for, and groped under, her pillow. Her eyes fluttered closed as his teeth traveled down her neck, reaching lower and... Without another word, she cocked the barrel of her .38 silver Walther PPK against his dark blond head. He went still.

"I miss you too, babe," Grace mumbled, not really concentrating, replying to Tim's questions without really paying attention, as she watched Lance's head rise up slowly. She eyed him with what she hoped was a cold stare. "Me too, I wish you were here now."

Lance sneered down at her and she nudged the cold nose of the gun against him, to let him know what she thought of that. His eyes were a glittering blue as he stilled his movements.

"Bye now." She pushed the dial button and lay the receiver on the bed, her other hand still steadily holding her gun. "Get off me. I mean it. I do know how to use this."

He slowly sat up, his eyes never leaving hers. There was no fear in them.

"Your hands," Grace ordered briskly. "Keep them in sight. Now, get off my bed and back out of my room."

She kept her gun aimed at him as he obeyed. She followed, arms stretched out, holding on to her weapon, as he moved backwards into the living area of her apartment.

"Now, go to the door," she continued, "open it and let yourself out, Mr. Mercy. I've enough of your bullying tonight. I'm not going to keep telling you the same thing over and over. If you want proof, think about this. If I knew where this runaway man is, why would I show up at the ball?"

"Bargain power. Profit. Blackmail." Lance listed all the possibilities.

Grace shook her head. "Not out in the open where everyone could trace me. Even you found me quite easily, didn't you?" She nodded at his slow scowl. "Now go home and think on it. Good bye."

She waved her gun in the direction of her doorway. Lance opened the door, stepped outside, his dark clothes seeming to merge with the shadows.

"Good night then," he greeted in his now familiar sardonic voice. He started to close the door, cocked his head, and added, "By the way, you don't think I'd leave a loaded gun under your pillow for you, do you?"

With that damn charming quirk of his lips, he swung the door shut, and he was gone. She stared at the closed door for a long moment, then lunged forward to lock it. Laying her head against the wood paneling, she allowed her body to finally succumb to all the charged emotions within her. Trembling, she released the cartridge to her gun and found it empty. The bastard had been playing with her.

She trudged back into her bedroom, walked tiredly into the bathroom, setting the gun on the dresser on her way by. She stared at the sight of herself in the mirror. Her hair was a mass of tangles, her lips were redder than usual, her eyes had a feverish look about them. Worse, her skirt was a destroyed wrinkled mess. Yup. She looked quite ravaged. Every part of her body tingled still from his touch. Her neck felt sensitive against her disheveled hair. Dropping her skirt, she patted the inside of her thighs. Her face flamed at the memory of what he did. Damn it. She acted like a dumbass instead of her father's daughter. Where was her usual control?

Determinedly, she went about getting ready for bed, forcing herself into her normal routine to deal with the shocky aftereffects, knowing familiarity would help to settle her pumping adrenaline. As she climbed into bed, she realized she couldn't sleep on it without thinking about Lance Mercy. She bit her lip.

Problem number one: she simply had to get rid of these lusty thoughts about the man. So odd. He was hardly her type and it was irritating he could make her act like some *squee*ing teenager around him.

Problem number two: she had to decide what to do with her suspicions. Problem number three: she must find out which side Lance Mercy worked for, whether he was planning to help or kill off the Chinese man. She turned restlessly in the dark. Sleep first.

Tomorrow she would buy the biggest deadbolt lock she could find in D.C. before a tracker named Lance Mercy decided to visit again.

"A tracker," she mumbled, eyelids drooping, mind wandering between slumber and alertness. Why had he stopped, when he could have taken her?

***

When Lance slipped into his apartment in the early hours of the morning, Dan was already there, writing in his notepad while waiting for his report about tonight's function. He didn't bother to make excuses for his tardiness, of what sidetracked him. Dan looked up, then smiled in amusement.

"Been on the prowl? Oh. Seems like you're the one attacked this time. Looks like the lady gave you as good as she got."

Lance touched the side of his face. "So that's why it's been burning. That hellcat's got to be declawed," he remarked. He rubbed the scratch absently. "She's one hell of a fighter."

Dan's brows lifted. "Does that mean what I think it meant? Our mystery girl has evaded you again? What happened? Did she lose you?"

"Not exactly," Lance answered ruefully, reluctant to discuss it. It was just as well his identity was kept from Charlie and the few others. Lance liked to work alone and hadn't taken to this sharing plans stuff. He preferred improvising. Just as he did tonight.

"Did you try to imprint her?" Dan asked.

Lance shrugged. "It didn't start out that way," he said, and told Dan the gist of it.

The older man was silent as he considered the information given. "She *could* be telling the truth. However, that doesn't explain her incredible ability to escape you, Lance. Those times at the rally may have been sheer luck, but tonight," he shook his head in certainty, "she resisted you. Succeeded too, if you're admitting as much. Or did you let her go?"

Lance frowned. "Are you interrogating me?"

"No. You're a tracker. You do your job and I'll do mine. I trained you in my field, Lance, so you know I'm just assimilating the given facts to reach some sort of conclusion. What you told me points to an operative, and I might add, an agent trained in evasive tactics, in information assimilation, like me, and in manipulating surroundings. The only thing against this conclusion is her youth. She's too young to be this good, to be able to match you. Notice I didn't say outmatch." Dan's tone of voice was wry.

"Oh, I noticed," Lance, likewise, retorted. He threw himself on his sofa, stretching out the length of it. "Yes, Grace O'Connor is an enigma, all right."

"She's got you intrigued," Dan observed. No one had ever outfoxed the Big Cat, as Lance was often called in the Asian jungles and underground networks, as long as he'd known him, and enemy or not, that young woman was matching his former student wit for wit. He grinned. Maybe he would call her Little Cat. She did look like one, from the photo on file, with those slightly slanted almond-shaped eyes and the bold, yet child-like, gaze.

"Dan, that grin of yours means you've gotten a good joke on me again," Lance said lazily, cradling the back of his head with his hands. "One of these days, you'll have to share with me these jokes you make at my expense. It's only fair."

"One day," Dan agreed. "Let me think over what you just told me about Grace O'Connor for the night. I'll let you know my conclusions sometime in the next few days."

Lance nodded. He wondered whether Dan could read between the lines how out of control his own desire for the girl was. He'd stopped because of that and nothing else. Okay, maybe her youth made him hesitate. He quickly discarded the notion. He'd fended off younger, deadlier enemies out in the field. Maybe DC had made him soft in the head.

No. He'd stopped because she'd pulled a gun on him. Loaded or not, her quick thinking had forced an acknowledgement. He admired her self-preserving tactic enough to let her go, to give her the victory this time, even though he'd unloaded the weapon when he first found it. He was on tracker mode and a weapon wouldn't have stopped him anyhow, although he admitted that when he tasted her soft skin as she lay there trying to converse sensibly with that boyfriend of hers, his mind wasn't on tracker mode at all. In fact, he was just determined to show Grace how little that boy of hers actually meant to her when she was lying in his arms.

In a rare moment of stunned embarrassment, he realized he'd been jealous and had allowed that jealousy to turn off his training. When he was seducing Grace that second time, he was doing it as a man who wanted to make her forget about that chump on the phone. With a start, he realized that he didn't care for a man in Grace O'Connor's life.

"Are you ready to tell me about tonight's event?" Dan asked. He knew the younger man was prone to silence due to his loner nature and needed prodding when it came to information. A tracker hated to share. His own training required extreme patience and understanding of human nature, and Lance Mercy, he knew, wasn't an easy man with whom to team up. He was the best in his field and best-suited out of civilization, and it'd taken their former teacher-trainee relationship to get him to come home for this assignment.

"Something is brewing. I saw K.K. Wang there. We both know he seldom shows up in the States—he hates the U.S.," Lance told him, picking up the TV remote control. "Richards is pushing hard for the trade deal with China and he and the ambassador had several very public discussions on possible trade agreements."

"I can get that from CNN. They're analyzing everything on TV these days," Dan said, gesturing at the box. Lance kept clicking the channels. "Of course, there wasn't any mention of Wang."

"Follow him and we eventually get our Chinese guy," Lance advised, pausing long enough to look at some writhing bodies on a music channel.

"Are you going to?"

"Nope." Lance clicked the button again.

"Why?"

"It'd be too late by then. K.K. Wang is the Beijing Butcher, Dan."

"Ah. Our scholar won't be alive for long if he ends up in Wang's hands," Dan concluded. "Damn. So, we've got to get to him before the Chinese do."

"Uh-huh," Lance agreed noncommittally. "Do you know they have hundreds of channels on TV these days and there isn't anything worth watching? Did I help track and destroy rival satellite projects so we could monopolize the airwaves with this junk?"

"That's right, Lance," Dan replied, amused again. "You're the reason Western civilization is in rapid decline."

"Ha, fucking funny," Lance retorted. "This dispersion of information isn't helping to give any semblance of reality, is it? It's disjointed and entertaining, but there's something missing."

"It's news for the masses. Surely you know that's how it's done. Our information differs from the daily dosage of commercialized truths. Or, it could be all about you."

Lance ignored the dig. Dan was always trying to point out the world didn't revolve around what he wanted. "So how does Command deal with the information age, as the press seems so fond of calling it?"

"Every agency grows with the times. We may be in one of the deepest recesses in the system, but we're the fastest to adapt. You should go back to Command one of these days before losing yourself again in those jungles of yours. You'd be surprised to see the new changes—the new equipment, the speed with which we can transmit information."

Just more red tape for you to bombard me with," shrugged Lance cynically. "Besides, certain commandos in there still hold a grudge against me. I gather you want more info so you can go ask that genie bottle of yours for more wish questions?"

"That's a good analogy, isn't it? Yes, that would please Command, thank you," Dan grinned, standing up to stretch his cramped muscles. "It's late. Hurry up, so I can leave you to sulk alone." He politely muffled a yawn.

Surprised, Lance asked, "Sulk?"

All that blather about information and the dispersion of it, as you've been philosophizing," Dan mocked. "You want to know what she knows. You want information about her."

"And that makes me sulk?" Lance arched an eyebrow. "I thought I was just doing my job, covering all angles."

"But of course," Dan agreed. "You want to have your cake and eat it too."

Lance gave a smile the older man recognized too well. When he was training under him, he would give that exact same look and smile whenever he saw a way to solve a particularly tough assignment. It was a smirk much like what a warrior about to lay siege on some unfortunate castle would give.

"Indeed." Lance's comeback was both an answer and a question.

"So, is there something else you want to tell me before I report to Command?"

"Yeah," Lance picked up the remote again. "Ask your genie where and when the next meeting between Wang and the good senator will be. Wang doesn't like to wait long, so I'm assuming the action will take place within the next few days. Do you think your genie will have an answer?"

"Are you sure that there's going to be a next meeting? How do you know that the scholar hasn't been handed over yet?"

"Richards wants more votes. The only way he gets that is to be popular—the senator that brings jobs and prosperity sounds like a good slogan. I know China hasn't signed anything with the state yet, but tonight's main rumor was Richards getting the ultimate assurance from the ambassador," Lance told him. "There's no reason to give China what they're seeking until the dotted line is signed."

"Hmm. So the next meeting is the only time they could come together without generating suspicions." Dan rubbed his chin. "OK, I'll contact Command tonight. Talk to you 0700 hours."

"Yeah."

"Don't watch too much TV, Lance. It's bad for you, all that dispersed information."

"Uh-huh," Lance grunted, settling more comfortably into his couch. "Lock the door behind you."

He couldn't sleep. She was haunting him. Her scent clung to his clothes and his skin, the taste of her was like some drug, the pleasure of it playing havoc at the edge of alertness. With his eyes closed, he saw her again, half-naked under him on that bed, her soft breasts almost spilling out of her bra. His body responded to the memory and he cursed softly. He supposed he could take a shower and wash her scent off but he continued to lie where he was, letting the hard ache of his desire torture in a slow burn. He kept changing the channels, his mind not really registering any of the flickering images as he tried to focus on the facts of his mission.

Over and over, Grace popped up at the end of each thought. She was the key, somehow, although nothing about her made sense. There wasn't any other agency that would want the Chinese scholar's information; this wasn't of international significance. It couldn't be a news agency like these TV cable syndications, could it? Was Grace an investigative reporter?

For the umpteenth time, he told himself she was too young to be what she seemed to be, and even if one so young was given this kind of assignment, there would usually be an older agent close by to advise and instruct. Yet, she seemed to work quite independently. Plus, her background appeared normal enough for a college student—straight A's, boyfriend, internship, bank and savings account.

He scowled again at the thought of the boyfriend. The guy was going to be a problem if he were to have her. *No, when he did have her.* For an instant, he analyzed his adamancy. She was, after all, not really his type. He liked his women more mature, in age and experience, and her youth pointed to a certain naiveté about life and relationships. No, she wouldn't be any good for him. He should let her be. But she had resisted, a sly voice whispered in his head, interrupting the voice of reason. She didn't give in.

That decided it. Lance Mercy could never resist a challenge.

CHAPTER FOUR

Grace was in a foul mood. Her sleep hadn't been restful, filled with vague dream images that had awakened her in strange heated limbo. Her body tingled with an unfamiliar ache she couldn't describe, settling low in the pit of her stomach. To make matters worse, as she took a shower in the morning, she discovered three purplish discolorations on her thighs. Then, when she looked in the mirror, her worst fears were confirmed. There was the beginning of a magnificent bruise right in the hollow of her throat. Groaning, she had cursed a certain man all the tortures of hell. A hickey. She had a hickey the size of a small tomato that promised to become an impressive blend of rich colors by tomorrow.

It was summer. There wasn't any way she wouldn't attract attention if she showed up at debriefing with a turtleneck top! Ed Maddux would easily be able to deduce the reason. Finally, she tied on a short neckerchief, knotting it jauntily over the telltale bruise. There was nothing more she could do.

At least it was Saturday, so she could look a little more casual than usual. D.C. wasn't quite her type of town. Everyone was always too dressed up in case they were seen. Politicians were like movie stars these days, dressed and coached by experts so the media wouldn't catch them in an awkward moment. The absurd thought of them maybe hiding a hickey from the public eye made her laugh out loud, and she felt less upset. She never stayed angry for long, anyway. Life had too many funny moments.

"You look tired, Grace. Long night?" Ed Maddux asked. "Are you sure you want to continue doing Level Two work? We don't need to move so fast with your training. There's plenty to learn where you were before."

Grace firmly shook her head. "I told you at the last debriefing I don't intend to work past summer. This internship is very interesting but I want to finish my education and get my degree. Level Two is just fine."

Ed studied her for a moment longer. "All right, I'll let you continue for now. Are you ready for debriefing?"

"Not yet, sir. I have a few questions," Grace said. She hesitated for a second, wanting to word them just right. "Can a recorder be unobjective once in a while?"

Ed leaned back in his chair. The girl learned quickly, already asking questions most trainees never considered until their second, or even third, year with GNE. "Most of us can never be totally unobjective," he answered smoothly, "but our observations—the ones we report to our clients—must be as unadorned as possible by our biases. GNE is called a non-aligned entity. That's why we've such a huge client base and also the reason we don't get in trouble with anyone. We give the same information without prejudice."

"So we just sell them the same report I type out and each of these…agencies…have the same footing? What would be the advantage?" Grace was puzzled. If everyone knew about the same thing, then why would there be a need to spy on each other? They could all just read up every field agent's report, go home and party.

"It doesn't quite exactly work that way. Each client, Grace, has a different problem, or a different agenda. They don't just ask for a report of, let's say, the function last night. They can get that from the media or their own operative and aides." Ed clicked his ballpoint pen, punctuating the air as he explained. He decided to see that wonderful clockwork-like mind of hers clicking for him. "Can you deduce, from what I've told you, how each agency can buy the same information and yet act differently according to their agenda?"

He watched the furrow between her brows appear and disappear.

"Same info, different agenda," Grace summarized Ed's explanation, frowning, her teeth worrying her lower lip. Her eyes brightened as they met his. "Different agenda, different motives. Different motives, different questions."

She paused dramatically. Ed wasn't even surprised any more by her ability to dissect things into simple truths. This was extraordinary. He had to find a way to keep this girl with GNE somehow.

"Very impressive," he praised.

"So you're saying, we sell our information based on the questions they ask. We don't give them the same report over and over."

"Essentially and simplistically, yes. That is the basics of GNE marketing mission. It's supply and demand, very profitable to both sides. Now, why the objectivity problem, Grace?"

He understood the phase very well. Every field operative went through it, still had problems with it now and then. It wasn't an easy job, to just stand and observe, to not interfere, and to be coldly objective while the world could be falling apart around oneself. He'd his own moments when his own control failed him and he had to become involved, and it took a lot of training to keep one's perspectives in focus. Grace's eyes, he realized, looked troubled, as if she had been making some difficult decisions.

"It's not because of what you saw at the rally, is it?" he questioned, a little sharply.

Grace nodded. "I can see it's all tied together somehow, that incident, the chase, the ball last night. I can feel it and I'm not sure I want to be responsible for information that might lead to the death of anyone." Unconsciously, she fingered the knot on her neckerchief.

"It's a recorder's moral dilemma," Ed agreed. He sighed. He hadn't expected this problem with her this soon. "On the other hand, your information may help save someone's life."

"That's it," she admitted. "I'm all torn up inside. It could or it might, or whatever, just doesn't cut it with me. Part of me wants to tip the scale in the good guy's favor."

"That's not our job and won't solve your problem." He told himself to be patient with her. She had so much to learn about the world. "You're assuming you know who the good guy, as you call it, is."

"I can't compartmentalize my emotions and maybe that's a problem with this job," Grace said quietly, but her eyes met his challengingly. "Ms. Smythe said from the beginning GNE likes their operatives to think and make decisions, not just follow orders. I'm not trying to break any rules. I just want you to know I'm having a problem with my conscience."

"Ms. Smythe and I are here to help all our trainees," Ed gently reminded her. "We know how difficult this job can be. That's why I advised earlier that you might not want to work at Level Two yet. You have the choice to work in research and translation until you're better trained."

"Maybe so," She considered for a moment, and added, "but I think I can handle it. I never assume, Mr. Maddux. I always try to find out the truth first before jumping to conclusions. Don't worry, I know the first rule during observation out in the field is to stay out of the way. My question is does this rule apply when the operative isn't on assignment?"

Ed smiled in amusement. He, too, paused to consider the question. The girl didn't need further training. She already had everything she needed to be a field operative, including the ability to get information in between diverted conversation. Once again, he chose not to give the standard answer.

"Only a Level Three operative can work independently while not on assignment," he said softly, watching Grace's face closely. Her bold brown eyes gazed back thoughtfully. "It's dangerous to do Level Three work without any prior training. And you aren't trained in any kind of covert activities, are you, Grace?" There it was, an open invitation for her to confide.

Grace cocked her head and clicked and unclicked her ballpoint pen, unconsciously imitating Ed. She had to tread carefully here. Ed Maddux, from what she'd heard, had been one of the very best of GNE operatives, and no doubt saw more than she wished.

"I don't think there was such a course offered in college, although I'm sure that it'd be a popular one." She shifted position, changing the subject at the same time. "Now that I know what Level Three work is, I'm ready for the debriefing."

A good fisherman stayed patient and reeled in his fish slowly and steadily. Ed opened his file and leaning forward, he turned on the device on the table.

"Very well." He stated the day's date and time, "Report #B83442. Ambassador Ball, Washington D.C., dated…"

Grace gave her report on the event, answering Ed's questions about the people she recognized, the conversations she overheard, down to the mundane description of Chinese etiquette at official meetings. She sensed Ed's immense interest in the translation job she did for the Chinese ambassador and the senator, as he jotted down quick notes in his folder. He gave her a long look when she brought up the use of the Chinese proverb and its different meanings.

"Basically, the 'no trouble' interpretation was the most diplomatic, but that saying came from an ancient war time story about an escaping man whose family had been beheaded by a ruling warlord. It could be used as a threat, but I didn't think it flowed with the conversation."

"Interesting. How did you know about the proverb's story?"

"My grandmother loved ancient Chinese war stories."

When they were finished, Ed turned off the device and stood up.

"That took longer than usual. You should take a break," he suggested. He was still amazed at her ability to give details without once looking at any notes. Most of the trainees needed to refer to their own notes to make sure they remembered correctly. There had been no hesitation in her answers; she gave exacting descriptions, down to Wang's panda bear tiepin. An incongruous image for the Butcher of Beijing indeed. And the proverb and her different interpretation of that line in connection with the whole conversation further emphasized her talent in this field of work.

Grace glanced at her cell phone. It was almost lunchtime. "It's okay," she said, leaning back in her chair, stretching out her legs. "I can do that when I get something to eat."

"Why don't you do that now and come back later to type the report?"

"Fine," she readily agreed. "May I suggest another thing?"

"Go ahead."

"I can do the report from home if you give me the security clearance for password usage. That way the report will be filed for immediate use."

Ed liked the idea very much. The good thing about new blood was they were always willing to improvise. Older ones tended to stick to the old methods.

"Do that," he said, "but don't print it."

Grace cocked her head, her eyes narrowing. "Of course not," she said, amusing Ed with the slightly chiding tone of her voice. "There are other ways to store and transfer data. Tyler and I have been working on a program on our own to enhance the reports."

Ed had to smile at her enthusiasm. They all adjusted so easily to all these gadgets. No confusion, no fear, only wonder. It made him feel old for the first time, seeing how the world could be through her eyes. "Is that so?" he asked, as he walked with her out of his office. "A hacker-safe program?"

"Nothing is that, but it's our own program and we have put some failsafe codes and devices into our maze. It'd be like a fingerprint so we could trace who handled or accessed the files. High tech recorders. Neat, huh?"

"High tech recorders," he repeated, shaking his head as he stored away yet another Grace GNEism for Sandy later. "Quite...neat..."

He watched her leave. They would have to give her another assignment. This one had gotten more complicated and his instincts told him danger was imminent. No need to put her in unnecessary danger. Besides, she needed to learn to let go; she was getting too attached to this assignment. Recalling the sly way she inveigled information she wanted, even from an old pro like him, he wondered whether he wasn't just trying to tempt her to outwit him.

By three p.m., when she pulled into her parking space at her apartment complex, Grace was contemplating a good hour in the tub to soak away a day of frustration. Her boss was right. She was too close to her assignment, but her mind had rebelled at having been ordered to stop. It was like a kid being asked to put down her favorite candy after just one bite. She wanted to continue her assignment. She liked to finish what she started, and she said as much as part of her protest but Ed had firmly stood his ground.

"This has been a beginner's course for you," he told her in that calm way of his.

"You have really done very well."

"So why end my assignment now?"

"Because you need to learn to disassociate yourself from your task, Grace. You're excited because you think you know everything, and there's danger in such a presumption. Also—" He waved away another interruption. "The charity event doesn't need an interpreter and everyone working for the senator knows you as one. The Chinese Ambassador's donation is to be a media surprise. Your being there will be questioned."

Ed's second reason made sense, but she had the odd notion if her superiors really wanted her at the charity event, they'd find a way. Grace knew a smoke screen when she saw it, having played one most of her life. She knew she was taken off because Ed feared she might end up endangering herself. She understood, but that didn't mean she would comply.

She'd muttered some vague comment and left Ed's office for her smaller one she shared with two other trainees. She seldom saw them these days, now that she was immersed in Level Two work, but they still left notes on the board for each other.

Hey you, snotty Level Two! Call me!—Tyler.

G. Need help with program. Call me too!—Lisa.

She'd replied to the messages and then gathered her pile of work into her satchel, having decided to do her report back home. She didn't feel like being cooped up in there. It was Saturday and she wasn't involved with the stupid assignment any more, so what's a few more hours on a report? Let them eat cheese, she snorted childishly, kicking a crunched piece of paper out of her way. This mouse was going home to play.

So the sight of Lance Mercy leaning against her apartment door made her feel like snarling and spitting. Her face must have said as much, because he straightened from his indolent pose, amusement softening his handsome face as he watched her march wrathfully down the hallway toward him.

"You!" Grace put her hands on her hips, glaring. "Don't you ever quit? If I didn't know any better, I'd think that you're some stupid ghost haunting my miserable life! Why don't you leave me alone?"

Lance grinned down at her. She had a wildness about her when she let loose all that passion she kept controlled. She looked like an entirely different person—a lot older and unmistakably sexual.

"Well?" She jabbed her forefinger into his chest. "You don't scare me, Mr. Agent Smart. Why don't you pick—Hey!" She squealed when he unceremoniously lifted her into his arms, putting her at eye level with him. Those laser blue eyes shut her up.

"...you up?" He finished for her, still amused. "I've been waiting for you for about an hour. Notice I didn't let myself in."

Grace snorted rudely, her hands on his shoulders. "Another day and you won't be able to do that," she retorted, thinking of the nice deadbolt lock in her satchel bag. "And I meant pick someone your own size to bully. Let me down, you don't have to manhandle me all the time!"

A neighbor walked by, her eyes lighting up with curiosity at the sight of Grace in Lance's arms. "Hi Grace," she greeted, stopping by them.

Lance didn't let her down, and Grace was forced to look over her shoulder to see her visitor. She groaned silently. It had to be Mary Tucker, of course, the resident gossip. It was that kind of a day.

"Good evening, Mary." Grace managed a nonchalant smile.

She rudely chose not to introduce Lance, even though she knew it wouldn't deter Mary Tucker. She was the kind of woman who liked to collect dirt on people, which she then churned into gossipy articles for Beaucoup, the glossy pseudo political magazine that followed the lifestyles and doings of the influential and notorious.

"I haven't seen you lately. You must be working late all the time," Mary chatted on, looking at Lance. "Oh, you're not Tim! I thought—oh, never mind, well, how are you? I'm Mary Tucker, Grace's neighbor down the hall. You look familiar."

Lance merely nodded, but didn't offer his name. "Nice to meet you. Sorry, can't shake your hand, mine are rather full at the moment, I'm afraid."

Grace glared at him, then gave Mary an awkward smile. "I've been busy. Umm…and I'm late again." She pulled her apartment key from the side pocket of her shoulder bag and dangled it in front of Lance. "Please, won't you open the door? We're *so* late!" She wanted to pull his hair and slap his face silly, but instead had to get away from Mary's unabashed nosiness. That meant letting the man into her apartment.

Lance, still holding her easily against his body with just one arm around her waist, took the keys with the free hand and turned to unlock her door. Mary still stood there, ignoring the blatant hint.

"Well, you must come over for dinner some time," she cooed, as Lance strode into the apartment. "You have to bring your friend here along, too. Or Tim, of course."

Grace stared over Lance's shoulder, knowing the woman was going to keep bringing Tim's name up until the door slammed in her face. "Sure. 'Bye. Can you close the door?" She muttered to Lance, a tight little smile on her face. Oh, he was deliberately making this difficult, the pig.

Lance's smile was charming as he turned to face Mary Tucker. Grace gritted her teeth and dug her nails into his shoulders as she found herself looking at her apartment from the abnormal height of six foot plus. This was getting ridiculous.

"Goodbye, Ms. Tucker," Lance said pleasantly.

"Don't be a stranger!" Mary kept on hounding, her voice cloyingly sweet. "It's so hard to get hold of her, you know!"

Grace groaned inwardly. She could all but see Mary winking.

"Oh yes, I'm forever trying to catch hold of her," Lance agreed, his tone mockingly conspiratorial. "I won't let go so easily now that I caught the busy lady."

He heard her sigh when he finally closed the door. She rested her chin on his left shoulder as he shifted his weight, bracing for her verbal and physical attack. Oh, he'd done that to make her madder. There was something arousing about watching her in a rage. To his astonishment, she started to shake in silent laughter until she could no longer contain her mirth, soft laughter bubbling out into peals of pure amusement.

Lance changed his mind.

Her laughter was even more arousing, with the husky throaty beginning that seemed to go an octave lower, caressing the depths of her throat, and coming out delightfully rich and melodious.

"Omygod," Grace gasped out, her laughter trailing off, "what did you think you were doing? A ballroom waltz with a floppy air doll? You couldn't just let me down so I could have a normal conversation? All that turning and facing and turning was a little too much, don't you think?"

Lance joined in the laughter. "It was a tango, actually," he told her. "We'd the right facial expressions too, with the head turns."

She started to chuckle again at the mental picture of their impromptu "tango." He sat down on the nearby sofa with her on top of him, and the both of them laughed a good long minute.

"Did you have to bait her about catching me when I'm busy?" Grace choked out, her head against his chest. "You're so going to get me in trouble when she tells this to my other neighbors. She's the resident gossip, you know."

He glanced down and frowned. Then he reached out for the loosened neckerchief. He did it so quickly she didn't even know it was off until she saw him tossing it over the back of the sofa. Immediately, awareness of her position returned, and she tried to get off him, but his hand held her chin as he examined the dark bruise on her neck. Her color rose.

"If you so much as smirk, I'll put a matching scratch on the other side of your pretty face," she warned, her eyes narrowing.

"Seems like we've branded each other."

He ran a finger over the bruise lightly. She jerked her chin away. He was a tracker, she reminded herself. Don't be fooled. It was so damn strange to feel so comfortable with this stranger, with someone who had insulted her every time they met. She patted down her blouse and pants self-consciously.

"You have a bad habit of wrinkling up my work clothes," she told him.

"They seem to always get in the way," he agreed, still smiling.

Grace didn't want to flirt with him, didn't want to feel the pull of attraction whenever she looked at his lips. "Yeah. You seem to always be in my way too," she muttered. "Why are you here again, Mercy? I thought I told you last night I didn't know where your runaway nun was."

Lance watched as the layers of self-control fell back and rearranged themselves. The urge to strip her bare, physically as well as mentally, for himself, was becoming a temptation he couldn't resist.

"What must I do to convince you?" Grace further demanded.

"Come with me to Chinatown tonight."

"What?"

"Come with me to Chinatown to talk to the nuns who were at the rally," he repeated. "Prove to me that you don't know them."

"How did you find them?" she asked, then shrugged. "Of course, you're an operative. It's your job." She stood up and went to the kitchen, opening the refrigerator. "So what do you want me to say to these nuns?"

"Why don't you just come with me and find out?" he challenged. "Or, are you afraid they'll betray you?"

She poured orange juice into a glass. She gestured the container at him and poured him a glass when he nodded. "Are they expecting me?"

"They're expecting me," he answered, moving to stand behind her. "I've some questions for them. You can play interpreter."

"I don't play, I am an interpreter. If you still don't believe me, I don't see why I need to prove anything to you."

"This is your chance. Make me believe you." He gulped down the glass of juice and handed it back to her.

Grace studied him warily. She didn't have to do it, but maybe it would get the irritating man off her back. He was too smart to play games with and would certainly see through her, the more time he spent with her. The idea of meeting those nuns was tempting, though. It would clear certain doubts about Lance Mercy. Part of her wanted to tell him about her suspicions, but she was bound by her job. Anyway, if he were really an operative, his bureau would get the information soon enough. As soon as she submitted it, she wryly added.

"So if I go along, you'll believe that I'm not an agent?" she asked, as she rinsed out the glasses.

"No. It would prove you don't know who the man was and where he is now, that's all. Surely you don't expect me to fall for the student intern act." He put a hand on either side of the sink, effectively trapping her. "I don't know exactly for whom you work, but I'll find out, Grace. I'm very good at going after...what I want."

In that position, Grace was forced to look up at him. She wished she were six feet tall, just so he couldn't play this intimidation game with her. *Be indifferent or retaliate.* To hell with indifference. Bracing her weight with her hands, she pushed up and sat on the side of the sink, so that her face was level with his once again. His eyes narrowed as she put one of her hands on each side of his face.

"Why, Lance," she drawled his name out for the first time, exaggeratingly batting her lashes, "that promise is fraught with possibilities!"

She leaned closer and softly planted a light kiss on his sensual lips, rubbing hers against them like she'd wanted to from the very beginning. She felt his facial muscles tense in response. Oh, she liked this way much better. Heat slowly unfurled all the way down to her toes. Desire. There was something dark and tempting about him, something lacking in her life these days. Without further self-examination, she slipped a tentative tongue between those masculine lips. She needed to taste him. The fierceness of her need hit with such force she pushed herself against his body, wanting more, disregarding the danger of wanting someone like him.

Lance put his hands at her waist, gripping her as she invaded his mouth. He was taken by surprise at her bold initiative. Either the girl didn't know the danger she was in or she was crazy enough to think she could handle him. The reason didn't matter the moment she touched her tongue to his. A palpable pleasure vibrated where they touched, rushing down to the gathering pressure in his groin.

He put his hand behind her neck, pulling her closer, deepening the kiss, and she moved her hands from his jaw to link them behind his neck. She tasted of orange and mint, that sweet fruity combination that had been haunting him all last night and all that day. He wanted more. Nudging her legs apart, he stepped between them, moving his hand from her waist to her lower back, pressing her closer. She made an incoherent sound and immediately wrapped her legs around his hips, fiercely gathering him in with her strong thigh muscles.

Her fingers played restlessly with his hair, tugging on it for a brief moment when his hands pulled her blouse loose from the confinement of her pants, and slipped beneath to touch her warm flesh. He swallowed her cry when he pushed away the confining bra and cupped her breast.

Grace responded with mindless pleasure. He was an exquisite kisser. His tongue, his lips, his teeth skillfully excited and conquered, taking and giving pleasure with mere flicks and strokes. She blinked in surprise when he finally lifted his lips from hers, ending the intimate contact.

He looked at her, heat in his eyes. "Promising enough?" His voice was husky, his breathing uneven.

She tried to gather her wits about her. What on earth made her kiss him? She'd almost given herself away…but he tasted so delicious, a part of her decided the danger was worth it. "Fraught with possibilities," she repeated again, her voice low and warm.

Reluctantly, she unwrapped her legs from around him. She must really stop this bad habit of either having him haul her around or attaching herself to his definitely muscular body.

"I gather you don't want to try out the other possibilities." His smile was crooked as he let her go just as reluctantly.

Actually, Grace wouldn't mind kissing him all over again, but she quickly dampened the urge. "No thanks," she kept her voice light. "Too dangerous."

"Coward."

"Like you told me before, I'm way out of your league," Grace reminded him, with a slight taunting smile. She gave him a slight push. "Come on, let me off the counter. We'll play it safe and go get your nuns instead."

Lance shook his head. Damn if the woman didn't have a twisted sense of humor, talking about getting nuns at a time like this. Stepping out from between her thighs, he helped her jump off the sink counter. He felt vaguely irritated, not liking the feeling of being dismissed. He was aware of her pretense, and part of him wanted to make her admit she wanted him.

"You're a cool little thing, aren't you?" he remarked instead, as he watched her retie the neckerchief, following her as she headed to the door. "Are you sure you're really as young as you look?"

Grace turned to face him at the entrance, her eyes serious. "Why? Because I don't act coy? Because I know what I want? You think just because you're so much older you can talk down to me. Well, that's where you're wrong."

Lance chucked her chin and retorted with impatient amusement, "Yes, I do have this grandfatherly reaction to you, don't you know."

She grinned back, satisfied that her little dig hit the mark. She wanted to remove herself from the raw sexuality that seemed to grip her whenever he got too close. She wasn't comfortable with this new sensation. It was too intimate. Too demanding.

"Well, you know how it is with dirty old men," she said, as they stepped out of the apartment. Cautiously, she looked left and right. "Thank God. I was afraid she would still be here with her ear to the door."

CHAPTER FIVE

Lance was still muttering about the last jibe about dirty old men when Grace caught sight of his car in the parking lot. She gave a low whistle of appreciation and walked around the gleaming silver BMW.

She arched a delicate brow at him. "Yours or your agency's?" she asked, running a finger slowly along the fender, then peeking through the window.

"One thing about being elderly," Lance said, as he opened the passenger door for her, "we have all those nest eggs with which to enjoy life."

"I'll keep you in mind if I need a sugar daddy," she told him.

Lance got into the car. Smart mouth. A bundle of sass, that was what she was. He wondered briefly whether he was going to have a perpetual hard on whenever they were together, which couldn't be too good for an old man like him.

Grace covertly studied him. That quirk of his lips was too cute. Glad to know she could keep him amused. She noticed the casual confidence in his right hand as he changed gears, the strength in the way he glided the car through traffic. She already knew they could be seductive as well as unyielding in their strength, understood how those deceptively gentle and long elegant fingers could turn deft and powerful. Geez, she was getting turned on thinking about those hands on her again. She looked away, trying to think of something else.

"Do you really need me to translate for you when we see the nuns?"

"A few of them speak English and the rest choose not to."

"Are they really the same nuns who were at the rally?" she asked, recalling how a few of them had moved suspiciously fast for nuns. Not that she knew how fast nuns ran in general. She grinned at the image that brought.

"You don't seem to think so." Lance glanced briefly at her, as he made a turn. What was amusing her now? "Would you remember them?"

"Oh, now you think I'm no longer acquainted with our nuns?" she teased. "I see. You're just trying to trip me up." At his frown, she added, laughter gathering in her voice, "Oh, now we're back at playing serious spies out on a caper, are we?"

"It's not fun and games, Grace," he warned, turning into the Chinese part of town.

Grace looked around. "That's the problem with old folks. Don't know how to have perspective," she commented, noting that he was going towards a particularly bad section of town. "Uh, I hope you're going to park closer to the main Chinatown area if you intend to drive this wonderful vehicle again."

Lance looked at her again. "You're familiar with Chinatown," he observed.

"Hey, I do have a drop or two of Chinese blood in me, you know," she told him, giving a shrug, then grinned impishly at him. "The genes need real nourishment now and then. I come here often enough."

Lance parked the car by a restaurant that Grace recognized as one favored by the locals. She got out and followed him as he headed down a narrow alley that led to the side entrance. Chinese music blared from the back kitchen window. Lance banged on it and an irritated face popped into view. The man's face cleared when he saw his visitor.

"Wah*, if it's not my favorite big cat come to look for some scraps," he exclaimed, smiling broadly. The head disappeared and moments later, the man appeared at the kitchen door. He looked like an Oriental Pillsbury Doughboy, short and plumpish, but with Popeye sized shoulders and forearms. Splattered food stained his apron and a lopsided cook's hat sat on his head. He studied Lance up and down, then offered his arm, a big crooked smile on his face.

"You're looking fat from all that Western junk, man. Look at you, just shameful. You've gone downhill."

Lance laughed easily, shaking the little man's hand. "We can't all eat good food all the time, Fat Joe," he said. Turning to Grace, he added, "Grace, this is Fat Joe, a good friend. This is Grace."

She noticed that *she* wasn't a good friend. "Nice to meet you," she greeted in Cantonese.

"Hey, your gal's speaking my kinda talk," he exclaimed again, in English. "Aiyah*, you look like you're little bit Chinese, yes?" He changed to the dialect she was using. "One of your parents is Chinese, right?"

"Actually, my grandmother. She's from Canton," Grace explained.

Fat Joe gestured them toward the door. "Come on in back into my office. It's a little too, ah, open out here." He winked at Grace. "You have to stay for dinner. OK? I'll cook you any dish you want."

Grace smiled back, liking the man, "Thanks, Fat Joe."

"It's actually Fatt Choy," he confided, then gave Lance a mocking glare. "Those white folks, they can't pronounce worth a damn, so it's Fat Joe this and Fat Joe that." He broke into hearty laughter and Grace joined him.

Lance registered the quick camaraderie with interest. Funny how Fat Joe had never told him that joke about his name before. And he knew his pronunciation would have been right if Fat Joe had wanted him to use his real name. Quizzically, he studied Grace as she followed the little man through a corridor past the steamy kitchen. The two of them were chatting like they were old friends. She had a way of getting to people. Must be those mischievous brown eyes.

Fat Joe's office was actually a store room. It was stuffed full of food cans and sacks of flour and exotic-sounding Chinese food. Boxes and boxes of canned Chinese spices stacked one whole side of the wall. Grace squeezed into a little space between jars of "thousand year-old eggs" and a big bin of rice. Fat Joe and Lance took up the rest of the space, with Lance towering over shelves of soy sauce.

---

* Chinese exclamation, meaning "Hey!" or "Wow!"

"Nice office," Lance dryly commented, looking around.

Fat Joe snickered. "Hey, better than that hellhole you always make me meet you at in Hong Kong," he shot back. Pointing to a couple of upside down crates, he said, "Have a nice office seat."

Grace shook her head; Lance gingerly sat his long-legged form on the one closest to Grace. She found herself admiring thick blond-streaked hair and finger-tempting muscular shoulders. Not fair. The man must have an ugly something that would repulse her.

"I wondered how long before you get hold of me once I heard you were in town," Fat Joe continued, untying his apron. "'Sbeen a long time since I seen the Big Cat on the prowl."

Grace tilted her head. That was the second time he'd used that term. Big Cat. Well, she supposed everyone had a nickname. Didn't she call him Mr. Smooth? It was an apt name, Big Cat. More like a big lion cat, with that hair and golden tan. She could smell his clean male smell from where she was, mixed with shampoo and aftershave. Funny how she had never considered herself a cat person, she thought morosely as she fought the urge to wrap her arms around his shoulders and burrow her face in his neck.

"It's good to see you doing well away from your old trade," Lance said lazily. "I did wonder whether you would die of boredom."

"Oh, you can't be bored for long with a name like mine," Fat Joe grinned back, cheekily winking at Grace, "eh, Grace?"

"Nope, can't be bored when you're busy being prosperous," Grace agreed. She explained, for Lance's benefit, "Fatt Choy means Very Prosperous."

Lance didn't correct her assumption he didn't speak Chinese. After all, he'd told her he needed a translator. He ignored Fat Joe's knowing chuckle. "Well, so now we know why he's always been able to make money out of nothing," he jibed.

"Nothing!" Fat Joe looked indignant. "I worked my ass off before you came and destroyed my operations..."

"Schemes," interjected Lance mildly, "but we can quibble about this another time, old friend. I need the information."

"They aren't willing to see you, Big Cat." Fat Joe opened a roll of paper towels and tore some out of it to wipe his hands and face. "They don't trust you and your friends any more. They claimed last time was a set up and only someone from your group could have leaked the information out to the ones who captured David Cheng."

Lance's expression was unrevealing. "True. Do they know it wasn't the Chinese government who has him now?"

"Yeah, they figured that out, since their other sources are still alive. If they had him, the Beijing Butcher would have their necks by now too. No, your mole works for the other group, whoever they are," Fat Joe said. "Be careful, Big Cat, there's a rat in your midst."

Grace listened, fascinated. This was the world she could only have imagined a few months ago. These men, easy as their conversation appeared, were dangerous men. They had the keen air of alertness about them, something she'd always noticed about her father, a vibrant current brought about from living at the edge all the time. She had a taste of it only once when she was sixteen and she'd never forgotten that precious, wild and wonderful year she'd spent alone with her father. It was the only year with which she'd any kind of connected relationship with her only parent.

"So, are they abandoning this man now that he's close to freedom?" Lance was asking, as she listened on. "They shouldn't give up so easily."

"The Sisters are always willing to help those in need, Big Cat. They just cannot afford the exposure. It'll harm too many who depend on the...ah...tender mercies of the Christian God." Fat Joe took down a few cans from a nearby shelf. "Tell you what. I'll pass along whatever messages you have for them and see whether they'll trust me with the answer."

"Can't do that, Fat Joe," Lance shook his head.

"Don't trust me, my man?"

"I wouldn't want to put you in the position to run away again," Lance explained, his gaze steady.

Fat Joe paused for the first time in the little room. "That high a price, huh? Must be some chili-pepper hot info we're dealing with here. And I thought it was just a couple of high position political names."

Grace's ears pricked up. So, here was more cheese in her new little maze.

"You just pass along this message." Lance stood up, making the room even smaller. He nudged the crate aside with his foot, then took Grace's hand in his. "Tell them there is only one way to win their little war and that's through me. They don't have to deal with any other names any more. Just me. And you can vouch for me, eh?"

Fat Joe grinned, then turned and opened the door. "Yeah, count on it," he answered, as they stepped back outside. He placed a hand behind Grace's elbow. "Now, what do you want to eat, Grace? All that talk makes me hungry for something spicy."

Grace looked up at Lance, unsure about his plans. She was there, after all, to meet with these nuns who were now refusing to see him. In answer, he let go of her hand and placed an arm across her shoulders, smiling almost boyishly. For the first time since they met, she felt him relaxed.

"We'll insult Fat Joe if we leave without dinner," he told her. "Nothing like his spicy dishes, trust me."

Lance discovered Grace always ate like the way he saw her that first time—she attacked and consumed food with the fierce concentration of a child with a favorite toy. In between bites, she cajoled Fat Joe, or Fatt Choy as she now correctly called him, to tell her bits and pieces of his past along with bawdy Chinese jokes at which she laughed with genuine amusement. She seemed so sweet but he knew better. Her mind was busy thinking about the nuns and the missing man.

As he always did with a potential opponent, he had sat back and studied her for hours the night before, going over what he'd seen and heard and comparing it with what she'd said and shown through her actions. He'd been trained to key in on strengths and weaknesses; a tracker needed to know when and where to strike. He made several conclusions last night. One of them was to keep her around him for a while, to see what she would do. Another was more personal and it didn't have anything to do with the mission. The third was the more serious decision of whether she was indeed a dangerous mole planted to find out about him.

Already, watching her with Fat Joe, he could tell when something was important to her. Grace O'Connor never hid her enthusiasm and her delight was refreshingly straightforward. When captivated with a story, she gave it her undivided attention, charming both the teller and even himself, with her sparkling brown eyes. He wondered whether they would have the same look when he was inside her, if she would stare straight into his eyes when she climaxed. Damn it. He couldn't seem to stop making love to her in his mind. Surreptitiously, he adjusted his jeans.

Later, on their way back to her apartment, Grace was very quiet. The sports car easily moved through D.C.'s many one-way streets, its purring engine the only sound heard as Lance pulled away from the busy Saturday night traffic into the quieter streets.

"I guess it was a wasted evening for you," she finally said. "You didn't get to meet the nuns."

"Yeah, but it wasn't entirely a waste." He glanced at her, his lips quirking. "I got to watch you devour that mountain of food. That was a memorable feat."

"I wasn't the only one with a remarkable appetite," Grace grinned back unabashedly. "You almost beat me to that last helping of spicy orange chicken."

"I was just being a gentleman. I didn't want you to cause a scene and embarrass Fat Joe."

"Hah! Like you could eat another bite after that ton of crispy pork you piled on your rice!" Grace retorted, then laughed aloud. "Do you think Fat Joe will ever let us eat there again?"

"He's seen me eat before," Lance assured her, then smiled wickedly, "but I don't know about you. He was either very fascinated or shocked out of his shoes at the empty plates you left behind."

"He was extremely pleased!" Grace pouted in jest, knowing she was being teased. "And it's polite and flattering according to Chinese custom when a guest finishes all the food."

Lance pulled into the parking lot at her complex and turned off the car. It was a pleasant evening, with a slight breeze fluttering in from the outside darkness.

"He was more than flattered," he remarked, turning towards her. "Tell me Grace, how do you do it? How do you get every man to try to solve your mystery?"

Grace stiffened, glad that the evening shadows hid her surprise. She hadn't known she was that easy to read. "I don't know what you're talking about," she said quietly.

His hand reached out for hers and she watched, mesmerized, as he spread it open, holding it with one hand while drawing imaginary lines in her palm with the forefinger of the other.

"It's your eyes, sweetheart. They hold a man in endless fascination."

Grace smiled. If anyone's eyes fascinated, it would be his own electric blue ones, the color that matched the deepening twilight outside. "Oh yes," she said, injecting humor into the growing sexual awareness, "they've been known to drive men crazy. Why, just last Monday I had a bunch of them falling all over me."

Lance couldn't help but smile at her reference to the rally. She was the wittiest as hell and dead-pan funny. He enjoyed women. They were warm and giving or sexy and manipulative, and he hadn't missed many other combinations in between, but very few had ever made him laugh or enjoy a match of wits. They had all had secrets, including this one, but none had intrigued like she did. Some had the misfortune enough to try to kill him but none had ever been able to double-cross him with their seductive talk. He'd enjoyed them because he was a sensual man, and he'd taken care of business without any emotional entanglements. But Grace O'Connor defied any categories. She was and wasn't what she seemed. Most of all, she was saying no when her body language was projecting the opposite, immediately affecting the male instinct in him to go on the chase.

He lifted her unresisting hand to his lips, kissing her palm. "So what now?" He murmured.

Grace nearly moaned aloud when his tongue flicked out where his lips had been. The man was definitely still hungry. She sought to bring him back to earth. "Are you convinced now I don't know where this Chinese man is?" He paused in between kisses. *Good, maybe*

he'll let me go now.

Actually, Lance had already made up his mind earlier she wasn't working for whoever kidnapped David Cheng. He just wasn't sure exactly where she stood within the whole matrix. It annoyed him, not being able to figure her out. Even more so, it maddened him she kept slipping in and out of his grasp so effortlessly. This evening, he'd revealed more to her than to any woman he'd known, yet he didn't feel she would be a danger to him. He couldn't understand how he knew that either and he was trying to prove himself wrong at every opportunity, which further irritated him because he was a man who lived by and trusted his instincts.

He also instinctively understood she was trying to slip out of reach again. Not. So. Fast. He punctuated each silent word by kissing the tip of her fingers, pleased to hear the little quickened breaths she was trying to hide.

"When are you going to let me make love to you?" he asked, his voice deep and sexy, the growing darkness giving it a caressing quality.

Her body's response to that question shocked Grace more than anything else. She hadn't expected a direct hit and her mind scrambled as her invisible defensive wall became a pile of dust at the invading army of erotic thoughts tumbling through her mind. Heat churned in her gut, urging her to touch that dark masculine form in the shadows and—Grace squeezed her eyes shut, then tried to free her hand from Lance's, but he wouldn't allow it.

"Let me go." She sounded like she had just run a few miles at top speed.

"You can't run forever," Lance told her, his voice still low and seductive, his breath hot against her palm. "When?"

"I have a boyfriend," she reminded him. Desperately reminded herself. Even if they didn't get along anymore, she added silently. She used Tim as a shield against this potent man because she knew, with the instinct of the hunted, she would fall prey to him, if she didn't step away with care.

"You're involved with a boy," he corrected her, confidence brimming in his voice. "You're with him because you can control him, Grace, admit it. Let me show you what it's like to make love with a man."

Grace gulped. She would have called him conceited if she weren't so turned on by his words. With a few kisses, he'd reduced her to a quivering pile of wanton flesh, all but discarding her schooled feminist notion of death to all dominating men. Here was one man who seemed able to dominate her at will, whenever he chose. And Grace was suddenly afraid.

"I have feelings for him," she protested weakly. She wanted to lie and say 'I love him,' but somehow she didn't think he would believe her. His next words proved that.

"Sweetheart, you didn't kiss me like you have any deep affection for your…boyfriend," Lance drawled, pulling her closer. He sensed her confusion and sought to use it to his advantage.

Grace looked at those tempting male lips and fought with herself. Being an only child who literally brought herself up, she never had to deny herself anything she wanted. However, she didn't need the kind of complication that Lance Mercy represented and she resented, most of all, a man who could come and go as he pleased. Just like her father.

"I kiss everyone that way," she told him coolly. He paused in the middle of drawing her closer. In the gathering darkness, she could feel the first hint of temper coming alive. So she added, for good measure, "It's not just the eyes, you see, that drive all my men wild."

"Is that a promise?"

Grace tugged at her hand again but still found it imprisoned. Short of another tussle, she was trapped in this car until he decided to let go. All she could do was to keep dousing out his ardor. Temper was definitely a good replacement for passion. At least, she hoped so.

"I never promise," she said, giving an indifferent shrug. "It was just a kiss, after all. Can't

you just let it go at that?"

"Just a kiss." His voice was soft, but it cut like sharp jagged glass through her demeanor. He leaned towards her, his face inches away, and currents of anticipation raced up and down her spine. "When I have you in bed with me—and I will—be sure to remember those words when I kiss you. There." He softly touched her lips with his. "There." With his free hand, he ran a light finger over her aching nipple. "And especially there," he whispered, as his hand moved lower. Much lower.

Grace stopped breathing, her lips parted in mid-gasp. His blue eyes looked into hers, fierce and determined, and she felt like a deer caught in oncoming headlights. "Lance..." she whispered hoarsely, no longer sure what she wanted.

Helplessly, she watched those lips descend inexorably onto hers. His musky male scent played havoc on her already tizzy senses, and all she wanted was for him to continue. He kissed her gently, like the soft breeze wafting in through the car window. He persuaded without force as he took and tasted with his tongue, possessing her mouth as surely as he possessed her mind at the moment. She responded blindly, for once unable to stop herself. There was something in the way his tongue touched hers that made her go limp inside. When he finally released her lips, she could only stare mutely at him. His hand remained where it was, not moving, and it was arousing to know, at any moment, he might.

Lance studied her, seeing the passion in her eyes. And fear. And why not? She was, after all, barely grown up. He had the unfair advantage of experience to seduce her. He should let her go, if he had any morals. Looking down, he noted the sensual lines of her face, the parted lips that kissed like a woman who knew how to pleasure, the half-closed eyes that beckoned with promises. It was good he had never been a man concerned with morals.

"Will you be home tomorrow?" he asked, his breath warm against her cheek.

"Yes." She wanted to see him. No, she didn't. "No."

"Say yes," he commanded, knowing an advantage when he saw one. Advantage with this

woman, he suspected, was probably a rare thing. Better take all that he could.

"Yes."

"I'll call you." He kissed her lightly again. "Aren't you lucky you left all that personal info in your file? Now you can run, little Miss Intern." He released her.

Aroused, vaguely disappointed, and not a little unsatisfied, Grace stepped out of the car, taking a deep breath—like a prisoner just tasting freedom. She didn't turn around to look at him as she walked into her apartment complex, but she knew that he was watching. He was just waiting for the right moment to pounce.

***

Across the state line in Reston, Virginia, in a quiet restaurant, Ed and Sandra were finishing their coffee and dessert. The evening had been pleasant, with warm conversation about the D.C. art culture, real estate property prices, and the best restaurant they'd ever eaten in. The last subject brought many memories to the surface—the cheapest, noisiest *trattoria* in Florence, Italy, so well hidden in the cobble-stoned alleys, only the locals knew how to find it, and so dark was the trail at night, only the brave ones dared to risk their lives for the food.

That little dark place had been their secret, and their younger selves had returned again and again until even the locals didn't look at them any more. He would order the *spaghetti vongole* and she always went for the *pollo cacciatore*. Rizo would come out from the kitchen and hug them, kissing them soundly on the cheeks, whenever they showed up. In his loud voice, he would insist the *Chianti* was on the house.

Florentine nights and Italian wine. Sandy could think of them without too much yearning now. She sipped her coffee, smiling at her companion across the table.

Florentine beauty and Italian passion. Ed never forgot. Through the years, he'd kept that memory of the restaurant visits close to his heart. His gaze settled on Sandy. He wondered how much his companion chose to remember.

They didn't discuss business. Recorders, even retired ones, seldom did. Sharing could contaminate information. Recorders who had relationships with each other kept their working lives separate, and seldom asked each other's opinion. The really good ones became partners as they advanced up the levels and some of these partnerships enjoyed the greatest success in work and love.

But Ed knew only too well the danger and downfall in certain relationships. Recorders were also control freaks by nature, little emotional time bombs waiting to explode. It didn't take a psychologist to understand a recorder always formed a relationship with someone who kept him or her on the edge. They needed the challenge, the giving and taking of power. He'd never found someone who held that kind of control over him, but he knew that Sandy did, soon after Florence.

That confrontation long ago when she'd admitted to having ghosted for someone still seemed like it happened yesterday. It was all she had said, but that was enough of an explanation. He'd known her well enough to know the implication. It took a very special agent to get a recorder to become his or her ghost. That kind of relationship was remarkable and rare because it took a great deal of trust and dependency between two individuals trained to be uncompromising, independent and secretive.

Ed had been jealous that day long ago. It had marred their relationship since. Then, three years later, he'd heard her abrupt retirement from the field, transferring to administration. He wondered about that still.

"You're quiet tonight," Sandra interrupted his reverie. "What are you thinking about?"

"Something that I shouldn't at dinner." Ed smiled.

Misunderstanding, she nodded, smiling back. "Yes, it's terribly difficult to enjoy a meal when you think about work."

He chose not to correct her. "It's the inactivity," he told her instead. "I sometimes find myself missing the running around, hands-on aspect of the assignment. Now it's all in my head, with a lot of what-if questions."

"It takes getting used to," Sandra agreed. She had enjoyed watching him while they conversed, studying the intelligent face with its high forehead and strong jaw line. He'd aged nicely. The lines around his gray eyes added a certain depth to his face.

"I catch myself being envious of the trainees. They're at the starting line, all set to take off, and have so much energy and excitement."

"I know. It's painful as well as a relief, isn't it?" She nodded to the waitress, who refilled her cup with coffee. "You want that air of adventure, yet it's kind of satisfying to know you've been through that before and don't need to do it again."

"Hmmm. I don't know. It's still too new for me," Ed said. "I still want to do it. I guess it's still in my blood. Take Grace's situation, for example. I find myself playing observer through her. At times, I wonder whether I'm pushing the kid too far."

"Is that why you pulled her off her assignment? It's unprecedented, you know, taking a recorder out of the game."

"Ah, but Grace sets the record for precedence," he pointed out. "She has been jumping all sorts of hurdles as it was, out recording without even a training session. She was attempting to sneak by me into Level Three, can you imagine that? Of course, she didn't really know what she was doing, since she was acting out of instinct."

Sandra rested her elbow on the table and laid her chin on her hand. "So that was the reason. She was doing so well, Ed. I wouldn't have pulled her off, dangerous or not."

That was always the difference between them, Ed realized. He'd always preferred to wait, whereas Sandy always wanted to be in the middle of the action. That was how he'd lost her too.

He picked up the bill set discreetly at the side of the table, put his credit card in the folder and handed it to the waiter. "Don't you get the feeling, Sandy, our new trainee seems to know more than she's telling? That she is more than just good at her job?"

"Yes, I do." Sandra acquiesced. She'd already noticed all that, but it didn't bother her to think that Grace O'Connor could have been trained outside of GNE. "It hasn't interfered with her job."

"And we both agree she's very good."

She nodded without hesitation. "I *know* she's very good. What's more, I like her."

"And we both also agree she's always one step ahead."

Sandra nodded again.

"So," he continued softly, "what makes you think that she won't find a way to be at this convention?"

Sandra's breath caught as she looked at Ed. Then she laughed softly. "You're testing her!" she exclaimed, looking amused and exasperated at the same time. "You're actually using the old kitty and toy test. Talk about old times."

It would be a perfect test for Grace. The toy was moved from place to place while the curious kitten, getting bolder as it became more and more challenged, followed it.

"You haven't forgotten," Ed said, a faint smile on his lips as they left the restaurant.

"Of course not. That's how they knew I could do Level Three."

CHAPTER SIX

The blue in his eyes was oddly familiar as her lord lion visibly stalked her, and with female cunning, she kept herself just barely out of his reach. With delicate insolence, she tossed her long tail right in his face and delighted in his obvious response. He was more impatient than usual, the low rumbling emitting from his chest purred louder as she padded ever closer. Then, just to make him mad, she sat on her haunches and began to lick her paws, using her tongue to tantalize him as she flicked it in and out. Cocking her golden brown head, she yawned, but she kept a jaunty eye on him.

He wasn't going to sit still and wait this time, and she thought she was going to die from excitement as he started moving toward her, his muscular flanks rippling with purpose, his eyes intent and possessive. Her own purring filled the air as she caught the musky scent that was uniquely his. Lazily, she blinked her large cat eyes at her handsome lover as he sauntered among the tall grasses toward her. Her cat heart swelled with desire. Ten feet. Eight feet. Not. So. Fast. With a long graceful leap, she pranced off, purring with glee. Glancing back as she took off, she saw the surefire blue of surprise in his beautiful eyes and then with a short roar, he kicked off with those powerful back legs and started to run full speed. At her. Her loving lord and master wasn't pleased at being tricked.

***

When Grace was upset or nervous, she exercised until she dropped in exhaustion. Two restless nights. Two dream-filled toss-and-turn nights. She had finished her report and morosely watched television late into the night, just to avoid that bed. When she'd finally crawled into it, tired enough to fall into a sleeping state, she found herself teased by phantom lips and fingers, waking up several times in heated disbelief. Vague, teasing dreams left her aroused and aching. And each time, she'd groped for somebody by her and came up empty.

She gritted her teeth as she jogged on the machine in the gym downstairs from her apartment. She missed Tim, that was all. She was looking for Tim. She kept repeating those words over and over as she panted the miles away on the machine. After another fifteen minutes, she slowed down to a walk, perspiration sticking her cutoff tee-shirt to her body. She put her hands on her hips, refusing to stop, even though her muscles were screaming in protest.

Exercise put more oxygen into brain cells, cleaning all those bad stinky thoughts away. Things would look a lot clearer after an hour or two of good old-fashioned sweating. At least, it had always worked that way before. A good hard run, and she could understand the frustration of a father who consistently missed the times he'd promised to show up. A good hard swim, and she could deal with a problem at school. A good hard session with the weights, and she could forget an argument. However, she had never exorcised lust and yearning before, and to her dismay, she found exercise wasn't the cure.

She hit the free weights next, determined to punish her body for betraying her. She went through her sets, working on arms, shoulders, then her back, and lastly, her legs. She was mid-way through her second set of sit-ups on the apparatus when she saw his reflection in the mirror. At first, she thought it was merely her imagination playing tricks, but he was solid and real as could be when she leaned back and dangled upside down from the equipment. She remained like that, looking at him from that angle.

"I thought you said that you would call," she said, feeling the weight of her hair streaming down onto the floor.

"I did," Lance said, walking toward her. "You didn't pick up the phone."

"Let me guess. You don't know how to take a hint, right?" She was flippant as she dangled her arms downward, her heart rate a trifle too fast to be comfortable in her upside-down position. "How did you find me anyway?"

Lance stood over the apparatus, studying her tempting pose. She hadn't realized yet that he could see down her tiny tee-shirt. Or maybe she did, and was teasing him. "My new buddy, Mary Tucker, told me she saw you heading down here when I happened to bump into her outside your apartment." He grinned at Grace's scowl. "She told me your workout schedule—Sunday, Wednesday, Friday—like clockwork."

Grace pulled herself up to a sitting position, unlocking her ankles from the rollers that kept her anchored in place while upside down. She stood up to face her nemesis. She felt like killing Mary Tucker. Then Lance Mercy. And anybody else who crossed her path at the moment. Ignoring Lance, she went for a sip of water at the water fountain.

Lance eyed her derriere appreciatively as she bent down for a drink. She had a well-toned body, a tempting ass and legs that made his mouth water. Why was he always thinking about eating when she was around?

Her temper was very evident, from her tense shoulders and petulant lips. He didn't blame her. He would be feeling a little unsettled too if he were being pestered by someone like himself. He'd spent last night deciding what to do with the girl. It wasn't a difficult choice once he'd decided the course of action. Either frighten her enough to make her reveal her secrets or seduce her to find out what she was. He didn't think she was a danger to him personally, but he wasn't going to underestimate her possible danger to the mission and perhaps, Command. She was definitely hiding something and he intended to get to the bottom of it. Since frightening her didn't sound as attractive, he logically chose seduction.

"You're a serious bodybuilder," he commented, admiring the slight ripple of her abs revealed by the cut-off tee-shirt. He wanted to run his hands across that flat belly and feel those ripples for himself.

Grace sat down on the bench press stool, wiping her mouth on her sleeve. Now she wished she were properly dressed instead of being in her scruffy cut-offs and shorts. Somehow, it made her feel naked without the security of her tailored clothing.

"It's my hobby," she told him, then added for good measure, "My boyfriend trains with me." She watched with satisfaction at the appearance of a sneer on his face.

Lance resented this new odd feeling of jealousy, that someone was touching what he was claiming for his own. For God's sake, he hadn't even met the pup. "I guess I just have to work out with you some time," he taunted back, deliberately looking her curves up and down.

Grace ignored the urge to cross her arms. That was too defensive. She put her hands on her hips instead. "I don't think that would work out," she tossed back, her eyes challenging.

Lance squatted down, startling her. "Tell me, sweetheart, are you as good with your tongue in bed as out of it?"

Oh, that was classic. Grace rolled her eyes dramatically. She'd swatted away dozens of pick-up lines in college bars better than that. The chance to squash Mr. Smooth here too was irresistible. Flicking back her untidy mane of hair in a tantalizing manner, she gave him her best 'come hither' smile, and drolly replied, "I've been known to destroy souls brave enough to try and find out. But tell me, Lance, do you spend all your time thinking about sex? Don't you have some stuff to do, like saving the world or something?"

Lance laughed easily. The woman endlessly antagonized and amused him, and it had only been three days. "I could do a little of both at the same time. Actually, I came by to ask you just that."

"What? To have sex and save the world?" Grace inquired lightly, pointing to a towel draped over the steel bar over the bench press.

Lance pulled it off and handed it to her. "That too," he said, undaunted by her sarcasm. "Are you free later this afternoon?"

"Are we going nun-chasing again?" she sneered, wiping her face. "This nun fetish is getting to be a habit."

"One day, you have got to try these lines of yours on a friend of mine," he told her, shaking his head. "He would enjoy those little puns and wordplays."

She grinned. Tim seldom got her jokes or found them funny. Then she frowned. Oh no, she was not going to start making comparisons.

"What is it?" he asked her softly, feeling the sudden shift in her mood.

She shook her head. "Nothing. Tell me why you're here instead."

"I need you to come with me to the senator's place at four this afternoon," Lance explained. "You were translating for some of his aides the other night, and I want you to point out to me if you saw any of them with him today."

Grace looked at him thoughtfully. "Why?"

"Did you translate for any one of his aides?" Lance countered her question with another.

"There were so many, who knows?" Grace shrugged. "It's all privileged information as far as I'm concerned."

Lance frowned. "What do you mean?"

"Surely you wouldn't want me to go around telling anyone who asks me about your discussion with somebody else, would you?"

"If I were stupid enough to openly discuss something private with a third party present, especially in this town, then I deserve to have the subject broadcasted," he said, and stood up. He pulled her on her feet too and Grace felt a tug of resentment at his bossy ways. "Why, did you hear something interesting?"

She looked up at him innocently as she walked out of the gym. "Why, Lance, you know everything being said that night was of interest to someone or other. Why can't you just look at that same file from which you checked my name and see all who were present?"

"I know all the names in there. I'm only interested in the few who had personal contact with the senator." One of them had to be leaking the information, he silently added. He had three names that were Command "plants," and he needed to narrow the list to one. Grace was the easiest way to achieve that without too many suspicious questions. They were getting too close to a confrontation for him to risk his identity being uncovered by a traitor.

Grace picked up the clues immediately. "One list with names of the senator's aides to be narrowed down to a second smaller list." She bit her lower lip, focusing inwards as they walked down the passageway toward the stairwell. "Smaller list contains names of aides who were with the senator that night." She nodded in comprehension, concluding, "You want the few in the senator's confidence."

Lance's glance was intense, his eyes guarded. "I don't suppose you could name them too, could you?"

"Oh, give me time," she replied airily. "What's in this for me?"

"You're an employee, so you'll do as you're told."

"No, I'm not," Grace said, stopping in front of her apartment. "My services were retained for only that particular function, none other."

"By the Council for Asian Trade, of which I am the deputy chief, so I say you're hired again," Lance told her.

The unexpected piece of revelation made her pause in the middle of turning the key. He could almost see the information being processed and stored in her quick little brain in that fraction of a second. The moment passed, the door swung open, and she stepped inside.

"Deputy chief, huh? And here I was misled somehow into thinking you were top security guy or something." She studied him thoughtfully as he walked across her living room to the kitchen, seemingly at ease with her small apartment. She sniffed crossly. Of course he would be; he'd been in here three consecutive days!

"It's only for a few times, today and Tuesday night."

That got her full attention. "Tuesday night?" She kept her voice casual.

"There's this charity convention. I heard it's one of the *in* places to be seen at this time of year. The Senator invited me and I would like you to go with me."

"There's no need for translators for that event," Grace informed him. "I know, because my firm already mentioned it to me."

Lance opened and closed all the counter drawers, looking at the contents. She frowned at this intrusion of her private space, but she didn't say anything, too busy thinking about this unexpected bonus that had fallen her way.

"Yes, let's just say that being the deputy chief, I know better. Senator Richards informed me in his call the Chinese trade group will be there to present a *surprise* donation, quote unquote," Lance said, finally turning around to look directly at her. "I want you there to study the aides. I want to know if any one of them approached the Chinese reps to help them translate. It's important, Grace." He omitted the fact he suspected no translation help was given, only messages.

To hide her excitement, Grace turned and casually flipped through the wall calendar. She fought to keep a triumphant smile off her face. "I see," she said nonchalantly. "Well, my calendar doesn't indicate any major appointment for that evening. What luck! I might be able to squeeze you in after all."

Actually, she wanted to jump up and down in glee. She had found a way to be there. What incredible luck indeed.

"You'll be going as my date, so I'd prefer you leave that ugly working outfit you wore at home." He came behind her and turned her around to face him, lightly caressing her shoulders. "Something soft and sexy would be nice. Something you squeeze into would be very nice." Sliding his hands down to her waist, he tickled her flat tummy with his thumbs, and huskily added, "I must say, though, this cut-off tee-shirt is pretty distracting."

Lance found it difficult to keep his hands off her whenever she stood this close to him. She looked awfully cute in her tight shorts. He wanted to spend the whole day exploring what she hid under those clothes.

"When..." Grace ignored the warm hands moving on her flesh. "When is this afternoon meeting?"

"Four o'clock, with the senator," he murmured into her hair. "Hmm, you smell good."

"Liar. I'm all sweaty and dirty," she murmured back into his chest, giving in to the urge to get close to his hard male body, "and I'm staining your nice shirt."

He didn't seem to mind her sweat and dirt, gathering her even closer. She was temptingly soft, just as he remembered. "I'll come pick you up around three."

"I've a few errands to run but I'll be back by then." Grace rummaged deeper into his shirt, breathing in his masculine scent. "Is this one supposed to be a date too? I mean, how am I supposed to act around you and the senator?"

"Friendly. It's a casual meeting. He called and told me about this big secret surprise and wanted me to know all his plans, so it's not too formal." Lance pinched her derriere gently to stop her squirming.

"Ow."

"Just checking to see whether you're paying any attention. You seemed preoccupied," he teased. "What were you trying to do, babe, get into my clothes with me?"

Grace rested her head against his chest, listening to the strong heartbeat. "I was being friendly, like you ordered." His rumble of laughter echoed under her ear.

"That's what I like, an obedient employee."

"I think this wouldn't be proper in the employer-employee rule book, don't you agree?" She looked up, amusement in her eyes. "I can't date my boss."

"We'll just have to reword your position," he solemnly told her. "You're now an independent contractor, subbing out your services to the Council for Asian Trade. You also happen to be a...friend of mine." He let her go reluctantly. "You'd better go get ready and do your errands. I'll see you at three." If he stayed any longer, he would take her right there in her kitchen.

Grace nodded, sliding her hands down his chest to the leather belt at his pants, hooking her thumbs into the front loops. "We'll have to discuss my salary. I expect to be paid well." The heat in his blue eyes, sending delicious tingles down her spine, prompted her to add, "And I meant to be paid with money, Mr. Mercy," and she stuck out her tongue, wrinkling her nose, because that came out wrong too.

Lance's answering smile was slow and lazy. "I'll make sure you won't have anything to complain about, Miss O'Connor. You really shouldn't hold your employer hostage by the pants, though, sweetheart. You might be surprised at the outcome."

She laughed and unhooked her thumbs. He was quite a funny guy, once you got pass that suspicious nature. When the door closed behind him, she finally let loose, jumping up and down, and bouncing on her sofa in youthful jubilation, whooping out "Yes! Yes! Yes!" while doing some silly Blues Brothers moves.

With the senator and those Chinese representatives meeting at the convention, she would at last have a chance to figure out how they would meet in this Room 103. She had her own suspicions they were talking about the missing scholar but nothing in their conversation betrayed anything, just an ambivalent discussion of a sick relative and of taking care of him. Except for that proverb. She frowned. Could the relative be David Cheng, and if so, how would the Chinese take care of him? If her translation was right, and he was just a "small problem," what would that mean?

A cold feeling sobered her excitement. Could the senator and his men be the ones who snatched the missing scholar? *Her* male nun? But why would he give the poor man back to the Chinese, after taking the trouble to "save" him from the same Chinese group at the rally? She frowned, recalling the conversation. An agreement in Room 103. A private donation for the media and some kind of fund. And she also recalled Fat Joe's comment about high-powered names being at stake. All the pieces were there but was her puzzle done right? David Cheng, a scholar, with some kind of information everyone seemed to want, or want to hide—the senator, the Chinese representatives, Lance Mercy. And Lance Mercy wasn't one of the senator's men, she was sure of that by now. She bit her lip, trying to decipher the puzzle. A deputy chief. What in the world was that? He was no political player; he'd more than revealed himself to her he was some kind of undercover operative, maybe CIA or one of the other agencies. Grace knew she was very close to reaching the end of her maze. She only needed to know that important information everyone was going after.

As she got ready, Grace went over her plans. One, she must find out where the Chinese scholar was. Two, she couldn't tell Lance her theory without revealing GNE, and besides, she might be wrong about everything anyway. Three, if she were to continue, she must be prepared for danger, and if what she suspected were, in fact, true, then this thing was big, and there was only one person she knew who could handle it, one person whom she trusted.

But first, she had to drop off her report at GNE. They would be there waiting for it, those working drones who always seemed to be present to process all the incoming bits and pieces of information into a network of files that would eventually end up in someone's questing hands. She wondered whether any of it would ever end up in Lance's. It was a strange feeling, like she could influence some event with a few well-chosen words. They ask the question, Ed had told her, and we sell them the answer. She'd deliberately written her report with Lance's questions in mind. Of course, he already had the information about the Chinese's fake surprise appearance, but would he be quick enough to ask about Room 103? She rubbed her nose, a little furrow appearing between her brows. How could she be sure he would know what question to ask? And most important, why should she care?

She was still musing about it when she checked in, and looking up, was surprised to find Sandra Smythe at GNE. Usually, there would just be the processors, or drones, as she'd privately called them, busy at their computers, with the supervisors seldom seen. She would sign in, drop off her translation to B.B., the head drone, answer a few questions, collect her receipt and that was it. Sundays were for the workaholics. Even GNE, the supermart of the information highway, would be quiet. Usually, she liked to stay a couple of hours, playing with the computers and learning the programs. Glancing at her watch, she saw she'd plenty of time to make it back to her place for her "date." Good. She needed to get hold of Tyler. There was a favor she needed to ask.

"Hello, Sandra," she greeted her supervisor in the hallway leading to her office.

Sandra Smythe was, as usual, impeccable, in a dark red jacket and skirt ensemble, with a silver broach pinned on her lapel. She looked cool and elegant, with her hair swept into a tidy French knot and flawless makeup on her enviable smooth skin. For the umpteenth time, Grace wondered how the woman could stay this perfect the whole day, every day. And on those heels too. The woman had her utmost respect. "It's unusual to see you here on a Sunday."

"Hello, Grace, handing in your report?"

"Yes. Everything is ready."

"Good. Ed told me you won't need to go to the charity event since the embassy didn't ask for an interpreter."

"Ed already explained he didn't want anyone wondering *why* I'm there, if I went," Grace said, emphasizing so she could justify her news. She hesitated, then added, "I guess I have to tell you because you're my supervisor. I'm going to the event after all."

Sandy lifted a questioning brow. "I see," she said.

"It's not what you think. I'm not gate crashing or anything. I was invited." Grace rushed through her explanation. "You see, he wanted me to go there as his date."

"He?"

"Oh. The deputy chief of the Council for Asian Trade. His name is Lance Mercy."

Sandra gestured to a nearby sofa and walked toward it. "Sit down, Grace. I have a few questions."

Oh-oh. She felt like a child caught in the middle of a scam. She sat down.

Sandra could feel the nervous energy emanating from her intern. In her light summer blouse and khaki pants, she looked like any fresh-faced college grad in D.C. surroundings. Sandra suspected, for reasons of her own, Grace counted on that assumption a lot. One thing she liked about the young woman was her ability to grasp facts and her direct way in saying what she was thinking.

"Lancelot Mercy," Sandra intoned thoughtfully, "deputy chief-slash-unofficial advisor of smoothing the trade negotiations between China and the States. He was highly recommended by the Secretary of Commerce because of his intimate knowledge of Asian politics and history, along with a healthy respect for his prowess in Asia."

"Prowess?" Grace repeated. *Lancelot?*

"My dear girl, Lance Mercy is no ordinary Washington bureaucrat. In fact, he's very seldom in the States. He's mostly a wealthy adventurer with a surprising number of political connections in foreign countries, mostly because of his philanthropic donations to social causes in Third World countries." Sandra smiled at Grace's stunned expression. "I see you don't know that about your new friend. He's from a very wealthy family around here."

"We just met," Grace admitted lightly. She wondered whether Sandy recognized Lance as the same person in the rally. "I didn't know he's such an important person."

"Important? No, he isn't important, per se, but he has influence, especially in business dealings with Third World and Asian countries." Sandra folded her hands on her lap. "Mr. Mercy is much sought after by international businesses that are looking for new markets in Asia. He talks their talk and knows what level to pull to get the right people to meet with the business corporations. At least, that's how American big business views him."

Grace cocked her head. "And how does the U.S. government view him?" She was beginning to see an entirely new Lance Mercy. *Lancelot!*

Sandra smiled. Quick at grasping facts and very direct in conversation. "Ah, Lancelot Mercy is somewhat of a mystery to those who keep an eye on these things. He is exceptionally young to make such an impression in international circles, yet he mostly keeps to himself, dealing behind the scenes. He is known among us recorders as the ultimate insider's insider. Most U. S. government branches only know him as a wealthy man who backs a number of social causes in Asia and a few other countries. He likes restoration of historic places and is particularly fond of South East Asian jungles. He is famous for his forays into the tropical jungles for months on end, purportedly to look at ancient ruins and temples. The locals over there give him a lot of free rein, since he pours in quite a bit of money to sponsor university chairs and other educational and humanitarian causes."

"Wow. He's Indiana Jones without the professor thing." Grace was more than stunned. She couldn't quite picture Lance Mercy as a do-gooder, but it was an excellent front for a tracker. And now she knew the source of his wealth. But...*Lancelot*?! That name was going to boggle her for the rest of the day.

"So, why do you think he asked you out to this convention?"

"Well, actually," Grace shrugged, resigned to tell a little bit of the truth, "he asked me to go as a favor. The senator had already informed him of the media surprise I told you about, and since he's the deputy whatever of that council, he wanted to attend. He's taking me along, in case he needed a translator." That was certainly part of the truth. She looked directly at Sandra. She was beginning to understand the rules around here, she thought with a touch of cynicism. *We'd talk but let's keep the real information minimal.* "It's like a part time gig, I guess, and I didn't think it would interfere with my job here. I won't let it, Sandra, if that's your worry."

"Confidentiality is important in our business, Grace," Sandra warned. There was an odd look on her face for a moment, then it was gone.

"I'd never undermine GNE's reputation," Grace assured her supervisor. "I haven't told anything to anyone."

"Yes, but if you get involved with someone like Lance Mercy..."

"I can handle it."

Sandra gave a small sigh. How was it she sometimes heard her own self when Grace spoke? She wanted Grace to succeed, but she didn't want her to learn the hard way. Yet she also knew she couldn't protect the young woman forever. If she were to learn to become a good recorder, she had to experiment on her own. She had to be left alone to figure things out.

"They call us ghosts, you know," Sandra said softly.

Grace frowned, puzzled. That strange expression was back on her supervisor's face. "Excuse me?"

"Our clients. You should know by now that some of them are different government branches. Others are underground figures and international organizations. They all have a name for people like us; they call us ghosts."

"Why?" This was getting beyond intriguing now.

'Because we're untouchable, which is their term for people they've universally agreed are their common ground, or property. That means they can't...harm us because we are neutral agents for their use." She smiled as she watched Grace's eyes widened at her words. "Do you understand me, Grace?

"I...yes, yes I do," Grace answered, her eyes alight with humor. "We're shareware, public domain."

Sandra's lips lifted slightly. Must be one of those GNEisms about which Ed had been telling her. The girl had a cocky little intellect, more was the pity she was so determined to return to school. "There is danger in this job," she explained, refusing to let the instructional mood evaporate. "They don't necessarily know they hurt a ghost, since we don't reveal ourselves. However, if you keep interfering instead of performing your role as mere observer, they might hurt you on purpose."

Grace studied Sandra closely. The older woman was trying to scare her enough to be afraid, and she suddenly felt a warm appreciation for her concern. But she had never let fear get in the way of adventure. Her father had taken the usual fears she once had and helped her to mold them into challenges instead.

"I'll never interfere when I'm working as an observer, Sandra," she hedged her answer, smiling at the obvious insinuation she would break the rules, or at least, bend them, when she wasn't on the job. Her father had also taught her to talk between the lines—frog's hair-splitting, he called it. Her smile widened at the recollection.

"If you agree to observe for someone other than this agency, Grace, you're essentially ghosting for that person, and that is my main point." Sandra wanted her to understand that her actions had consequences. "There is no protection when you're not working as our observer."

"That's an interesting concept, ghosting." She was quite amazed at all the information with which Sandra Smythe was plying her. Why? A warning?

Sandra surprised them both by laughing out loud. Grace stared, astonished to see the usually composed Ms. Smythe in unrestrained mirth.

"I see the more I tell you, the more attractive the whole business of ghosting is," she chuckled. "Quite the opposite of my intended result. Okay, have it your way. You want to go independent with this project, fine. Just be careful. When you're someone's ghost, you belong to that person in a very private way, girl. I don't think you're aware of what you're doing."

"I don't intend to be anyone's ghost," Grace sniffed, "and I certainly won't ever allow myself to be recognized as a belonging."

Sandra stood up, signaling an end to their conversation, and surprised her again by laying a hand on her shoulder. "You belong to that person," she said, in a hushed tone, her eyes oddly far away, "because you have to trust each other's information to be correct and have to act on it by instinct. That kind of trust runs really deep, and is a rare commodity in the kind of business your Lance Mercy is in, Grace, let alone between operatives from different agencies. It's an intimate bonding, and very difficult to adjust to."

Grace felt a shiver down her spine. What a strange concept. She shook her head firmly. "That isn't for me, so have no fear that I might end up ghosting or bonding, or whatever. I'm just learning the ropes to be a good recorder, in case I want to return after my education is finished. You see, I don't want to belong to any operative or person."

Sandra nodded, a small smile still on her lips. That odd expression had disappeared and she looked like her usual supervisor self again, slightly remote. "Go ahead and step into the water," she said enigmatically. "I'm here when and if you have further questions."

What a weird business to be in. Grace shook her head and wandered into her little office, pleased to find the person she was looking for.

"Tyler, sweetheart," she called out, walking to the young man at work at his terminal.

Tyler glanced up, hair unkempt, leftover crumbs from some previous meal at the corner of his lips, and smiled broadly. "Well, well, if it isn't snotty Miss Level Two deigning to visit us mere paper pushers," he sneered, his hand shooting out to pull her hair.

Grace laughed. She liked Tyler. They were the same age and had gotten along well from day one since their internship started. He was intelligent and had a talent with computers. Grace enjoyed bantering with him.

"Missed me, huh?" she teased.

"No way. I like the office without all your junk," he countered, sweeping the room with one hand. "What brings you to our domain on a Sunday, anyway?"

"Oh, like I can't ask the same of you," she retorted, eyebrows raised.

"Work," Tyler dolefully explained, gesturing to the pile next to the computer. "Some stupid Chinese speeches about trade for some newspaper article. Not as important as actually translating for the Chinese ambassador, you know." He pulled her hair again.

"Quit that, you monkey."

"Tell me, was it fun? What was the best part—meeting them big wigs or actually pretending that you know what they were saying?" Tyler rocked his chair back and forth. He was a nervous young man, always jiggling things around.

"Actually, the best thing was the food," Grace confided, grinning. "Everything else was…the same thing as you're doing now, except I have to smile while doing it."

"Yeah, yeah, rub in the part about the food," Tyler turned his lips down in mock sorrow. "We unenlightened ones have to get our own."

"Well, do me a favor, and I'll buy you a meal next time," she said, sitting down beside him.

"Okay, deal. What can I do for you, sweetness?"

Grace lowered her voice slightly. "How good are you at hacking our dear GNE mainframe? Not too deeply, just a couple of levels from our usual domain."

Tyler's smile broadened even more. "Ai, ai, I smell trouble," he said in sing-song. When she pinched him, he ran a hand through his untidy dark hair. "All right, all right! It's an easy task, sweetness, nothing to it. They don't have a strong enough firewall to keep out the likes of *moi*."

"I need information, the kind that you need passwords to get access to, know what I mean?"

"Yeah? You aren't going to sell out on our agency, are you?" Tyler popped a stick of chewing gum into his mouth. He eyed her appreciatively, wiggling his brows in exaggeration.

"Don't be silly. And stop ogling. I just want to find out about a client or whether such a person exists in our files, and if so, what we have on him."

"Done. For lunch, I'm cheap. Name?"

"Code name 'Big Cat.' That's all I want."

"You want the 'Big Cat,'" Tyler chewed thoughtfully. "Nice spy name. Sounds like a perfect job for me—digging up info about spies."

"Will you keep it between us?" Grace punched him again. "Your voice carries, you know."

"Easy, woman, I bruise easy! How am I going to explain to my girlfriend tonight?" Tyler complained, then dropped to a mock sotto-voce, "Give me tonight. Maybe part of tomorrow. You want the 'Big Cat,' I give you the 'Big Cat.'" He grinned, cracked his fingers, and added, "You look like a cat yourself at the moment, Grace, all smug and licking her chops."

Grace plucked an imaginary feather from her lips, smiling back. "Meow," she said in sultry repose. So far, life had been improving since last night, she concurred.

CHAPTER SEVEN

It was a casual meeting indeed, right by a huge swimming pool. Senator Richards sat on a lounge chair in his swimming trunks, a drink on the table next to him, and some rumpled papers in his hand. People were swimming in the pool while others milled around in small groups. Security stood discreetly close by. It looked like any typical Sunday afternoon in which family and friends relaxed and enjoyed life away from work.

Grace looked around. Sculpture dotted the patio, and inside and through the patio doors she could see gleaming marble floors and expensive furniture in a living room bigger than her grandmother's home. These people certainly didn't shop where she did.

"Ah, there you are, Lance," Senator Richards called to them above playful yells around the pool. "Come on over."

The senator stood up from his chair, beckoning them. He was a slightly built man, with the well-toned body of a regular swimmer. It was easy to see why he'd been so popular in the past two elections. He was spry and pleasant looking, exuding the confidence of a man who knew what he wanted and where he was going. His voice was rich and resonant, perfect for speech delivery.

"James," Lance nodded briefly.

"How nice—you brought a guest," Senator Richards eyed Grace speculatively.

"This is Grace," Lance introduced, his hand light and sure on the small of her back. "We have a dinner to go to later, so I thought I'd bring her along for our meeting."

The senator flashed his made-for-TV smile at Grace. "Of course. Have a seat, both of you. This shouldn't take long. I believe we've met before, haven't we?"

"Yes, Senator Richards," Grace replied. "I was one of the interpreters at the function last week."

"Oh yes, I remember now," Senator Richards said, his smile dimming a little. "Did you have a good time?"

"I was there to work." Grace smiled artlessly, then confided, "It was quite exciting actually, as it was my first time interpreting for such distinguished people."

"A novice, how delightful," he murmured. "Everything must seem like an adventure to you right now."

"Oh yes, very much so. I met so many people, I'm having a difficult time remembering who is who." She gestured helplessly. "And the food was superb! My mouth still waters whenever I think about the feast!"

Lance wanted to laugh. What the hell was she up to now? This was the first time he had seen her pull a dumb act on anyone. He wondered whether she did it often.

"But I remember you spoke Chinese so well," the senator commented, taking a sip from his glass.

Lance eyed Grace quizzically. She didn't mention to him she did any translation for the senator that night. Right now she was beaming at the older man, leaning back on the lounge chair. She crossed her legs. Provocatively.

"Thank you, Senator, that really gives me confidence. I didn't want to mess up my first time on assignment. I was so nervous, I could barely remember what went on."

A maid appeared. Lance asked for a cold beer and Grace, a glass of orange juice.

"Nothing stronger, Grace?" the senator asked.

"Oh no, I don't drink," Grace declined, then turned to look around. "What beautiful sculpture."

"Why don't you go look at them while the Senator and I have a talk, sweetheart." Lance chipped in, an enigmatic expression on his face.

Her face was beginning to hurt from all the smiling. "Could I?"

"Go ahead, make yourself at home," Richards told her. "All our talk will just bore you."

Right. You male chauvinist pig. Grace obediently stood up, gave a bright smile, then walked off to dutifully look at the statues. And the aides. She gave her best imitation of Marilyn Monroe's sashay, wishing she had on a blond wig.

Lance already knew from the telltale gleam in her eyes that she was having fun. There was simply very little fear in her once she decided to act upon something. She attacked everything with a passionate gusto—food, challenges, any obstacles—and laughed through it all.

"She's very effusive about everything," Richards commented, studying Grace as she chatted with the maid who was serving her a drink.

"Yes, she is," Lance agreed lazily, settling back in the lounge chair.

"Did you just meet her?"

"She caught my eye at the party last Friday," Lance said truthfully.

The senator laughed. "I should've known a pretty thing like her couldn't possibly walk by without catching your attention." He stared thoughtfully at Grace again. "How's her work?"

"How would I know?" Lance shrugged. "She told me she only works part time as an independent."

"Yes, yes, I'd imagine that you're not taking her out to dinner to discuss work."

Lance shrugged again, smiling nonchalantly. "So, what is it that's so urgent?"

"Well, you know how unexpected this marvelous contribution from the Chinese is," Richards began, "and I want to milk it for what it's worth, publicity-wise. It would be great for generating support for the trade negotiations."

"And for future votes," Lance added wryly.

"Ah, well, it's always good to have the future in mind." The senator looked pleased with himself. "Look, Lance, the board was set up by the Committee for Foreign Trade to oversee and advise the business side of the negotiations. Your name came highly recommended by very powerful people up the ladder, and I feel I need you to understand my side of the issue here."

Lance drank down his beer. The guy was slick. All these months, he'd walked in and out of the senator's office, working closely with his staff, and the man had shown nothing short of amazing savvy in his dealings with the Chinese representatives. One couldn't tell from their public talks the senator had any other dealings with them than the most appropriate of political discussions. He made it no secret he had voted in favor of any trade deals with the country, and certainly that wasn't a crime, if he'd voted with his conscience.

However, Command intel had known since last year certain senators, including James Richards, had been on the take from the Chinese government. So far, that had meant votes in terms of trade exchange. Command hadn't any interest in interfering with that particular problem, and had handed over the relevant information to the other agencies within the CIA and FBI. What they wanted were the names on the other list, the ones containing the arms deals China was secretly making, and Senator James Richards currently had the man who had the information. Lance was very sure of this last fact, although there wasn't any proof. His tracker instincts pointed to the smooth politician before him. Something big was going to happen this Tuesday night. He could taste the senator's excitement.

James Richards kept on outlining the importance of business and trade with China. It was obviously a rehearsal of a future speech. Lance impatiently waved it away. "I know the potential of trade between our country and China, James. My curiosity lies in the reason you want me at this convention at all. You said they wanted to make a public donation, and that sounds wonderful for your popularity points, but why do I need to stand around shaking their hands, thanking their generosity for your cause? In other words, what's in it for me?"

"Come on, Lance, credit me with a higher business IQ," said James, not offended at having been cut off. "Your presence here would catch the attention of the business community—those who are still on the fence about the new trade agreement. Everyone knows about your ability to open doors. Once they know you're in, they too will drop their hats into the ring."

"I'm flattered." Lance crossed his legs at the ankles, lazily glancing at the people prancing in the pool, "Nice to think everyone has such great confidence in my power to persuade."

"Well, your last project in Malaysia really opened some eyes, I heard," James said. "Tell me, why did you accept this advisory position from our dear Commerce Secretary? You're a busy man, seldom in D.C., and here you are, out of your favorite part-time vocation of chasing forgotten ruins."

Suspicion simmered to the surface. Lance smiled, totally relaxed. This was when he functioned at his best, while standing at the edge of being uncovered.

"My family is here and I haven't been home in a while. Also, China has many relics," he pointed out.

"Ah, you're trying to open doors for yourself." James Richards understood that kind of ambition. Maybe he did have something in common with the enigmatic Lance Mercy, who had been forced on him four months ago by the irritating Department of Commerce. He'd resented and resisted the forming of the watchdog board, but knew the Commerce Secretary wasn't going to let him take all the credit for the whole trade deal; everyone wanted a finger in the pie, if it were a success. As a politician, Richards understood this political ploy all too well.

"I am, primarily, interested in business opportunities," Lance responded.

"So then you *will* come on Tuesday night?" Richards urged. "It'd be an ideal situation to solidify your new friendships." And ideal for him to know exactly where everyone was while his own plans took place, he added silently. He needed to exercise extreme caution to carry off this private deal with the Chinese. Everything must look proper. Every media source must have a record of the event. He wanted photos and publicity shots of himself, the Chinese representatives, Lance Mercy, and the Commerce board cohorts together.

Lance appeared to consider for a second, then nodded. "All right, but it's a favor for your benefit, not mine. You owe me one for the future, Senator."

"Thank you. I'll send over notes and details to your office tomorrow." Richards sat back, relaxing. "Now, where is that charming girl you brought?"

Lance glanced in the direction of muted laughter and saw Grace standing by a copy of Michelangelo's David among the rose bushes, chatting merrily with someone. He heard male laughter.

"There she is," Richards nodded in the same direction. "I see she's made another conquest, Lance. Better go get her."

***

Grace had been pretending to study the replica of David when a young man a few years older than her approached and introduced himself as Charlie Bines.

"Grace O'Connor. Nice to meet you." Grace shook his hand, checking him out. Boyish face, easy to read. Friendly eyes.

"Oh, yes, you were the one taking notes last Friday," Grace recalled. Actually, she'd already recognized him earlier when he'd walked past the pool area. "Sorry, there were so many people there—I tend to get confused as to where I've met anyone."

"That's understandable. I heard you're relatively new at your job, so it's bound to be a little overwhelming right now. So…umm…I see that you came with Mr. Mercy." He nodded at the two men in the distance.

Grace glanced over at the two men conversing. "He told me this would be quick," she said, pursing her lips in mock impatience. "I hope so. I don't like to work during weekends. I don't know how you do it."

"Oh well, you need to give up something if you want to climb the ladder in this city," Charlie said. His smile was crooked and infectiously charming. She couldn't help smiling back.

"Not too much, I hope," she joked, "or you'll end up a bore yakking on about charitable contributions." She jutted her chin meaningfully towards the senator and Lance.

Charlie laughed. "Don't let them know you find them boring when they talk about contributions. They'll never let you work for them again."

"Oh no, I'm good when I'm working, Mr. Bines." Grace flirted. "I'm a professional."

They laughed together. "You were excellent that night when you worked with the senator and the ambassador. You looked…different," Charlie said.

"Like I said, I'm a professional when I work, but I don't work all the time. I want to learn about everything in D.C. There is so much to do around here."

"If you want to," Charlie said, somewhat shyly, "well, don't take me wrong, but if you like, we could do lunch some time and I can show you around the senator's offices."

"Really?" Grace beamed. Here was a way to look for more clues. "You've got a deal. Here's my card. Call and leave a message. Usually I'm running around town."

Charlie looked at it and put it in his pocket. "I'm looking forward to it."

It was nice getting to know someone around her age. Maybe it'd be fun to get to know him. *If I weren't already with Lan*—her mind screeched to a halt. Tim. She did say Tim, didn't she?

"What's the matter?" Charlie asked.

Her shock must be showing on her face. She swallowed, for once without a quick answer. "Oh, nothing." She gave a nervous laugh, running her fingers lightly through her hair. She did say 'with Tim,' didn't she?

"Are you sure? You looked like I suddenly grew horns or something." Charlie patted his head. "Whew."

Grace laughed, regaining her composure. "I certainly wouldn't notice," she teased him, laying a gentle hand against David's marble thigh. "Not with this perfect specimen of manhood around."

"Ouch."

They laughed together.

"Enjoying the art, Grace?" Lance's low voice cut into their merriment, effectively separating them as if he were physically standing in between their bodies.

She turned. Funny how she could stand near one man and feel absolutely nothing, and how another could just say her name, and her mind would start uttering sentences in three different languages. She was beginning to feel uneasy with Lance's effect on her.

"Lovely art work," she said. "Mr. Bines and I were discussing art and men who suddenly grow horns. Weren't we, Charlie?"

The aide coughed in answer, swallowing either in amusement or nervousness, she couldn't tell. "Yes," he mumbled.

Lance refused to dwell on the unexpected urge to stake his claim to the aide standing beside Grace. He knew what Charlie Bines was and wanted to remove Grace from being used. The aide was a Command plant and his assignment in this mission was to garner information from the female staff around Senator Richards and the Chinese representatives. From observing the younger man these last few months, he knew Bines was good at what he did. His last imprint, Agnes Lin, gave him access to almost everything they had needed before she was murdered.

He noted Bines didn't seem to be suffering overmuch at her death, although he had earlier assumed that the man had grown fond of the woman. That must be part of his success, to be able to immerse himself in his role so much that even an old hand like him was convinced otherwise.

Having familiarized himself with Bines' file, as well as others in the mission, Lance could only marvel at the younger man's skill. Behind the middle-of-the-road-looks and unassuming demeanor, Charlie Bines was a master manipulator. Command apparently used his unthreatening manners to seduce a woman's trust.

Lance wanted Grace out of the young operative's vicinity. Bines may be doing his job, insinuating himself into a woman's confidence, but he wasn't going to be given a chance to seduce Grace in any way, shape or form. Not if Lance had anything to say about it.

A short silence grated uncomfortably between them. Grace returned her attention to the replica of David. "I would like to see the real thing some day," she said.

"A naked man or a man with horns?" Lance placed a hand under her elbow and guided her back toward the poolside, obviously dismissing the young aide, who had respectfully receded into the background.

"Don't be obtuse." Grace wrinkled her nose. Then, turning to wave apologetically at Charlie, she added, "Or rude."

"You were supposed to find out the aides who were around the senator, not check them out," he told her, sarcasm creeping into his voice.

"I've been looking around," Grace retorted. "So what's wrong with a little conversation? You didn't tell me I wasn't allowed to talk with anyone." She was mad enough not to tell him about Charlie being one of the aides present the other night.

Since they were back by the pool, Lance didn't give her an answer, but the glint in his eyes spoke volumes. Men were such strange creatures. They thought putting an arm across one's shoulders, or around one's waist, or holding one's hand, made one their property. Or, at least, that was how they signaled to each other. She mentally shrugged. Idiots. Grace O'Connor wasn't that easy to handcuff.

It was all fluff and light conversation now that she sat with the two men. She bet they weren't so casual when she was practically ordered to walk around the place. She was probably seen by the senator as just some young bimbo at Lance's beck and call, and she resented that.

"Well, it was nice meeting you, Grace." The politician remained unfailingly charming as they said goodbye. "I'm sure we'll meet again at some future function."

"I'm sure we will," she said politely.

"Actually, you'll be seeing us in a few days, James, at the convention."

Lance put his arm around Grace's waist and drew her closer. It took all her willpower not to roll her eyes heavenward at his possessive gesture. Instead, she worked on looking suitably pleased at being told she was going out with her sugar daddy.

"Wonderful. You'll enjoy the affair, Grace. It's one of the few big events of the year. Everyone wants an invitation."

"Sounds exciting. I know I'll enjoy myself! Goodbye."

Lance held her hand as they walked out to the driveway toward his car, nodding to a few people who obviously worked under him. They all looked speculatively at Grace.

"Do you mind?" she asked in irritation, keeping her voice down.

"Mind what?" He slowed his gait to let her keep up with him.

"Not overdoing the 'this is my current plaything' act?" she demanded. "It's too obvious."

"I want it obvious. I want to let everyone know we might have frequent pillow talks." Lance lifted her hand to his lips. "Besides, I do want you as my plaything."

Grace ignored the last comment. Reaching his car, she stared up at him. "You're using me as bait?" She couldn't believe the man's arrogance.

Lance paused at the passenger door, key in hand. His eyes were direct and challenging, making her knees wobbly as they swept the length of her. "Afraid?" he challenged. "Don't want to save your nun?"

"Afraid?" She tossed her head back with indignation. "Do I look afraid? I just wanted to make sure you understand being used as bait jacks up my fee quite a bit." She watched his brows rise. "Hazard pay, you know."

He laughed. "Okay, bill me. I want everything listed, item by item." The passenger door swung open.

"Of course," Grace said, getting into the vehicle. "You could use me as your tax deduction, or do you people pay any—" She stopped, a frown on her face, one foot in the vehicle.

"What is it?" Lance looked in the direction of her gaze. Two limousines had driven up the driveway past them and were now parking in front of the mansion. The drivers got out and went into the residence. "What is it, Grace?"

"Hmm?" Dozens of thoughts processed in her mind.

Lance looked at the vehicles again. They were alike, standard transportation for diplomats and other VIPs. He got into his car and started the engine.

As they drove out of the grounds, he ordered, "Tell me."

"I think one of the drivers was at the rally," Grace told him, "but I'm not sure. He looked familiar."

Lance nodded. "I'll check the two of them out tomorrow, bring you some photos so you can point him out to me." He made a turn. "We know the senator's got David Cheng. I even know why, but I now want to know where and when they're going to return him to the Chinese government."

Grace swallowed, trying to hide her excitement. "How are you going to find out?"

"I don't have much time," Lance said, his fingers tapping on the steering wheel. It had to be during this charity media circus. But how? How would the exchange be made? He could only hope Dan got some answers from his source.

"Much time for what?" Grace pressed. Getting no answer, she looked out of the car window. "I can't help you if you don't tell me anything."

"Sweetheart, I know you haven't been long at this game," his glance was brief but the mockery was there in his eyes and his voice, "but surely even you know we don't simply share information with everyone."

He still thought her an operative. She asked softly, "Even someone you're trying to seduce?"

"Especially someone I'm trying to seduce," he replied, his voice equally soft.

"I see." Grace calmly smoothed her pants with the palms of her hands. "Don't you think that sometimes two heads are better than one? That if you don't let me in a little, I'll only give you just exactly what you ask and no more?"

"Exactly. I need you to do exactly what I ask and no more," he told her curtly.

"So, just to be specific, I'm to keep my eyes on the aides anywhere near Senator Richards and no more," Grace said, her eyes solemn as she looked at him.

Lance frowned, glancing briefly at her, before concentrating on the traffic. "That's right," he agreed. "That's all I'll need from you."

You're so wrong, Lance Mercy. Grace calmly looked ahead. *I have the answers to your questions and now you're going to just have to pay for it.*

There was much to plan tonight, and not much time, like Lance said, if what she'd discovered was really part of the senator's plan. She studied his profile from under her lashes. He was deep in thought. She could tell from the set of those sensual lips. His fingers continued tapping to the tune of his thoughts on the steering wheel. She could sing his query to each tap—How would they do it…How would they do it…?

She smiled secretively. It wasn't the aides who got out of those limousines that had caught her by surprise. It was the license plate of one of the cars. Part of it distinctly read 103.

CHAPTER EIGHT

There was nothing more intoxicating than the heavy perfume of blooming roses in the heat of late summer. August seemed to invite the sweet fragrance to hang heavy and linger with the languor of a satisfied lover.

Sandra walked up the garden path, her nose lifting instinctively to breathe in the different scents wafting around her. Riots of roses nodded off the hedge that followed the picket fence. Long canes climbed and twined around an arch over the little gate, heavy with dangling white blooms. She walked through the arch, following the path that led around the little house. Rose bushes, big and small, pregnant with buds and flowers, crowded each other along the pathway, seeming to beg for attention, until finally, she gave in to the urge, and plucked one single white rose off a bush.

Soft classical music came from further back in the garden, and she kept going until she spotted the owner. She stood there in silence, watching him at work.

Ed viewed roses as the ultimate paradox to his philosophy. A methodical man, he believed everything had a season, and this, he concluded, was what made sense of things, of life. It only stood to reason, then, that there was a pattern to do things—first things went first, and second belonged to second—and throughout his adult life, he'd lived by these rules.

However, the art of rose gardening was his venture into chaos. He had adhered to all the seasonal rules to growing these plants—how to feed them, when to prune them, where to plant them. With the dedication of a worshipper, each month meant a different step in the process. Except for one little odd thing.

Ed's roses didn't follow seasonal rules. They grew with little regard to a normal schedule, blooming off-season, sometimes twice a season, sometimes year-round. The only time they stopped was in winter, when they finally slept, but the rest of the year was one long season of growth, much to the bewilderment of their gardener. His roses seemed to be able to take care of themselves, and their ignorance of their natural laws was a puzzle for a methodical man like Ed. But he was secretly pleased with his rogue roses; he fancied them a reflection of his soul. In this chaotic world, he could lose himself, tending to each rose bush like a long lost lover or beloved child, shearing and pruning, caressing the little flowers and big bright ones, and absorbing each scent like they belonged to a different woman.

His years of training brought the intruder's presence to his attention. Looking up from the arm-like canes of a climbing rose, he saw Sandra framed by his bevy of flower children, a bloom in her hand. She was in her current persona of crisp and tailored clothes, but Ed remembered a softer version of Sandra Smythe, one who used to favor billowing skirts and sleeveless blouses, one who wore her hair loosely framed around her dainty face. His English rose, he used to call her. Pivoting toward the work table, he turned the radio down.

"Hello, Ed, I hope I'm not interrupting," his English rose spoke, moving closer.

"Sandy?" Ed wasn't sure who he was greeting, the Sandy of his memory, or the collected creature standing before him. "What a...surprise."

She took in the disheveled hair, the grimy hands, the smears on his clothes. He looked like the Ed she used to know. He'd always liked the outside better.

"It's too hot to stay in the house. I was restless," she explained. "I thought I'd catch you puttering among your children." She waved her hand, indicating the plants.

"It's perfect weather to be outside," Ed agreed, heading to a nearby cooler. "Would you like something to drink?"

"Sure."

"Soda? Beer?"

"Soda. Pepsi, if you have any."

He washed his hands in the sink, then opened the cooler, picking out a can and handing it to her. "You look like you're dressed to go out."

Sandra sat on the garden chair and opened the can. "I just got back from the office, actually. I'd a few things to discuss with B.B. that couldn't wait."

"Anything I have to know?"

"Nothing that I can't take care of myself. It has to do with the oil observation. Some misunderstanding of instructions."

Ed frowned. "From translation?"

Sandy nodded, giving a sigh. "One word and the whole thing was red-flagged."

Ed moved several pots of plants around. "You mean our high-tech recorders are fallible?"

"You're talking about Grace, aren't you?" She lazily twirled the rose she picked earlier between her thumb and forefinger. "Sounds like one of her terms."

"Of course, who else? I should call her Miss GNEism." He laughed.

"As a matter of fact, I saw her today at the institute. She submitted her report," Sandy said, giving him a contemplative look. "She told me she was going to the event on Tuesday night."

Ed paused in the act of sweeping dirt off his work table. He returned Sandra's gaze, amusement mixed with surprise in his eyes. "So soon? What's she planning to do, work as a waitress there? The tickets to that event must be the hottest in town right now."

He watched the slow curve of her smile in fascination. He wanted to trace it with his finger; he wanted to ask her why she never let her hair down any more. But he just dusted the dirt off his hands.

"Grace O'Connor got herself a date," she said, her smile widening.

"And who did she manage to get ahold of who happened to have an invitation or a ticket?"

"Lancelot Mercy."

Ed's response was a low whistle. "Now how did she manage that?" he wondered out loud. "*The* Lance Mercy?" At Sandra's nod, he pressed on, slightly incredulous, "The Lance Mercy who was supposedly vacationing on the Malaysian east coast a year ago, but our observer instead saw him among prisoners in a Cambodian campsite? He negotiated an exchange, I recall."

"The one and only."

"Dangerous," Ed commented quietly.

"Yes," agreed Sandy. "He saved that other operative. I recall a sensational report from our operative, how Lance Mercy gambled with his own life for another agent's, but that's Command. They never leave their men behind. And he has always been known to enjoy living dangerously."

"I meant dangerous...couple," Ed told her. "He and Grace are two similar creatures, in mind and spirit. I wonder whether she's ghosting for him."

"She's on the verge of doing just that." Sandra filled him in on Grace's few details about how and why Lance had hired her for that event. "I did explain to her about ghosting, but she kept denying she was doing it."

"That doesn't surprise me. Her psychological profile from the test strongly suggests a need to control and dominate, and ghosting is partly a surrender of those two elements."

"I prefer to describe it as an exercise in patience and compromise," Sandra corrected him, a strained note entering her voice.

He looked down, hiding his gaze. Of course she knew it first hand, tasting the bitter-sweetness of past jealousy kindling again in his throat. Instead, he said, "She's barely old enough to understand the meaning of those words. Level Three is dangerous work and with a man like Lance Mercy around her, there's bound to be trouble. I don't want Grace to get hurt."

"You know, Ed, I think she can take care of herself." Sandra reiterated her confidence in the girl. "There's a lot more than mere intelligence behind those observant eyes of hers. I've a feeling she's well-trained in handling dangerous situations."

"What makes you think that?"

She stood up and walked to a rose bush tied to a trellis. Purplish-fuchsia blooms waved merrily in little clusters. "Look at this beautiful plant."

"A floribunda," Ed told her, coming near her and absently fingering the petals.

Her attention was arrested by the soft loving touch of his fingers on his flowers. She ignored a little flash of pain. Blinking away memories she'd thought were forgotten, she bent to take a whiff from a cluster of the blossoms. "It's beautiful, perfectly shaped, and its scent is heavenly. It draws everyone closer, invites people to enjoy its fragrance and abundance, yet," she delicately fingered the green stems, "it's the thorniest thing I've ever seen in my life. One miscalculated brush, and you have a scar."

Ed smiled. "You've got to protect yourself when you're that tempting," he acknowledged. And with sudden insight, he understood Sandra's own protective armor. "So, what are you saying, our Grace is a thorny creature?"

"I think she has a lot more up her sleeve than you and I suspect. You can mold her like you shape this beautiful plant to the trellis, and she is resilient enough to grow the way you want her, but in her own time, and by her own rules. You should know roses, Ed, they are your specialty."

"Only because I don't seem to have any control over them," he ruefully admitted, wondering whether she was aware of her new layer of thorns that she, in fact, had grown without his care these past years.

"But you nurture them and they love you for it," Sandra said, smiling up at him. "Just as our little Miss GNEism will, if we handle her right."

He laughed softly. "Actually, I prefer her a little wild, like she is now. Keeps me on my toes. I'd hate to prune that away."

Unexpectedly, he lifted an escaped tendril from Sandra's knot and tucked it behind her ear. Her eyes shot up to meet his, wariness enlarging her pupils. Ed murmured, "Your thorns are showing."

"We weren't talking about me," she firmly said. She wanted to turn away, but didn't.

"A rose by any other name…"

"You're mixing your metaphors…."

"…would smell just as sweet," he finished, ignoring her prim protest. "I've always known my roses by their scents, Sandy. Each one is different, unique; each one has its own taste."

Sandra couldn't tear her eyes away from his gray ones, now cloudy with an emotion she recognized. Time stood still.

"And what does your favorite rose taste like?" she mouthed breathlessly. She should turn away now, turn away and step back, do something to break the moment.

She didn't. She couldn't.

"I'm about to find out," Ed calmly told her, and bent his head toward her upturned face as the heady perfume of roses invaded their senses.

The fragrant silence lazily waited as roses, big and small, peered over each other for a better look.

***

"A deadbolt. What a good idea," remarked Lance from behind Grace. "This should deter some intruders." He went to the kitchen and put the two bottles of wine in the freezer.

"Yes, I've been having problems with unwanted visitors. Order a pizza, will you, while I get into something comfy?" Grace went into her bedroom. Her head popped out of the doorway, and she added, "And don't come in. I've reloaded my .38."

Lance looked properly shocked. "Go in your bedroom? Never crossed my mind."

"Yeah, keep it that way," she warned, and disappeared back into her room. Then she yelled out, "I want pepperoni on my half."

Lance looked toward the bedroom as he pulled out his cell. There were three ways a tracker worked to trap his prey. The first was a silent hunt in which the intended victim was stalked until the appropriate moment. Usually, the main motive was to frighten the target enough so he or she would make a mistake, revealing vital clues. The second way was less subtle. The target ran and the tracker hunted, and cancellation would usually be sudden and quick. The third way was the cat and mouse game of mind control. To seduce with body and mind, the target's physical and mental states would be stalked, hunted, and taken prisoner.

After placing the order, he made himself comfortable on Grace's sofa, surveying the cozy little living room. He wanted the woman who lived in this apartment. He'd been stalking and hunting her like a tracker on a mission, putting himself in her world physically and mentally. It amused him to see her fight him. It'd been a surprise to discover her strength—she was mentally very strong, and had fended him off with astonishing ease. She was a puzzle—a deliberate thinker sometimes, with the training to piece odd information together into a coherent pattern, and a total innocent at other times, walking heedlessly into dangerous situations with nary a thought. He'd concluded, besides sheer luck, that quick tongue of hers was what saved her little hide most of the times.

It was her soft chocolate eyes that convinced him she was more than she seemed. They were bold and challenging, and invaded by a velvety passion whenever she was aroused. He could drown in those eyes when she looked at him that way. Those weren't the eyes of an innocent.

Lance was familiar with want and desire. They were natural to him, controllable and often channeled into completing a mission. But this feeling building in him was beyond desire. He realized he not only wanted Grace, but there was a growing need to be with her. This growing hunger for the young woman was disconcerting for a man like him. He had always been in control of a situation, especially one that included a seduction.

The thought of her taking off her clothes in the bedroom teased his already sensitive predicament. Raking his hair with impatient fingers, he adjusted his pants. Not yet. He needed to first lull this fiercely independent and sensual woman into surrendering her mind. That was his ultimate goal, and it wasn't going to be easy.

Lance's smile was slow and sensual as he looked at the closed door. He didn't want it to be easy. Let her have her little victories, but she would be his sooner or later.

CHAPTER NINE

Grace stretched out lazily on her favorite chair, a huge chaise lounge that belonged to her grandmother. It always reminded her of the elegant furniture Hollywood movie stars used to own in the Fifties, opulent and inviting, large enough for two, set low to the ground to make the reclining individual feel like a rajah lying under the ministrations of his slaves. She had it refurbished in a more modern color, splurging her savings on velvet over the cheaper material. It was a decision she never regretted; the chaise was the most comfortable thing in her life. Her cocoon, her nest.

Her eyes were alert on Lance as he ate a slice of pizza. He, too, appeared relaxed, his lean form sexily inviting as he lay on her couch. She should just jump his bones and satisfy her curiosity about that body. She forced herself to look away. Dammit, she simply had to stop these thoughts! The man wasn't a college peer with whom she could have a mild flirtation; this was a man of experience who would take everything she was willing to offer and ten times more. A tracker, Grace, for heaven's sake. *He would use you and if he didn't kill you afterwards, he'd swat you away like a bothersome fly.* All trackers, her father had warned, sought to control through the power of seduction, physically and mentally. She couldn't help wondering which part of her Lance wanted to seduce first—her body or her mind.

Submit or retaliate. She didn't know which choice to make. She couldn't be indifferent, that was for sure. Every time she kissed him, every part of her was far from indifferent. Submit or retaliate.

She wanted to do both and recognized the irrational humor in her predicament.

"Tell me what your plans are at the charity," she said, forcing herself to think about safer topics.

Lance chewed slowly, then sat up. "You're to stay by me for a while when we make our social rounds. I want you to be seen as my companion by both the guests and the senator's staff, so they won't question why you're there. If you lose me, mingle around. I'll find you. Meanwhile, my men will work to cover the exits and will be on the alert."

"On the alert for what?" Grace asked, although she already knew the answer.

"I've a feeling that the Chinese reps have more than a donation to give while they are there. I suspect they'll be retrieving our missing nun."

Grace was careful not to show any reaction. Mr. Smooth was actually quite good at his job. Even without her information, he'd gotten very close to the truth. Another point to remind her that this man was an excellent tracker.

"So you intend to get him from them? How are you going to accomplish that?"

Lance gave her a meaningful look. "Sorry, that information would best be just between my men and me."

Grace shrugged. "Suit yourself. I just wanted to help out as much as possible."

"You'll help tremendously if you could identify those aides," Lance assured her. "I need to know who followed the senator's order to nab David Cheng."

"Why don't you be more forthright, and just admit the truth to me?" Grace demanded.

"Why don't you tell me what you mean?" he countered. He leaned back, his head tilted, studying her with hooded eyes.

"You're after the aides in the senator's confidence," Grace replied, the corner of her mouth lifting in a sarcastic smirk. "Obviously, there could only be a handful who know the good senator's motives. The question is, which one of them is helping him with information about where our scholar was meeting you and your people? Fat Joe also mentioned about a rat in your midst. Tada…! Two and two makes one of them an agent of yours, who therefore must be a traitor. You obviously have more than one man working undercover with the senator, or you would've known exactly who the bad guy selling you out is. How am I doing so far?"

Lance crossed his arms, his blue eyes piercing sharp. "Very impressive," he said softly.

Grace bowed her head in mocking reply. "So, anyway," she continued, "after we've done the social thing, I'm supposed to mill around while keeping an eye on the senator, am I right?"

"Yes."

"Okay, no problem. Anything else?"

"Yes. If I have to take off, you're not to follow. I don't know what's going to happen, and if you tag along, it'd be another surprise element to handle. Stay away. I'll return to pick you up later. This bash should go on for a while. Clear?"

Grace tucked her legs up against her body, wrapping her arms around them and resting her chin on her knees. It was the only way she could stop herself from jumping up and down in glee. Not follow him, eh? A plan was starting to form.

"All right," she meekly acquiesced.

Her lack of protests made him frown. "You look suspiciously mischievous," he said, standing up and walking over to the chaise. "Don't follow me. Don't expect to tag along. You'd only be in the way. I want your word on this, Grace. Let me handle this my way."

"Oh, you have my word not to follow you," she assured him with a mildness that deepened his frown. "I'm going to let you handle it your way." As she would handle it hers, way out of his way.

He stared down at her, sitting there so wide-eyed. She was up to something; there wasn't a doubt about that. Too agreeable. Damn it. "I trust you to keep your word," he pressed on, this time more forcefully.

"Oh, stop repeating the same thing," she pouted. "I give you my word. Agent Smart's honor." She placed a hand over her heart.

"Good, let's drink that wine in the fridge to seal the deal."

"I don't drink," Grace said.

"Not at all?"

"Zilch. Nada. I don't drink," she repeated.

"Why?"

"I don't like it," she confessed. "Tastes terrible."

Lance laughed. An operative not trained to drink alcohol? Another puzzling part of her make-up. Well, being her age might allow some sort of adjustment in her training, he supposed.

"Have a glass of wine with me," he persuaded. "Come on, you'll like this. It's quite mild."

It was Grace's turn to be suspicious. "One glass?" she asked. "You're not trying to get me drunk, right?"

"I won't let you get totally drunk. Agent Smart's honor," Lance returned her mocking salute, then held out a hand to help her off the chaise.

A few minutes later, in the kitchen, Grace took several tentative sips, and was surprised to find the wine pleasantly smooth. It wasn't too sweet, just right, with a tangy aftertaste.

"Well?" He cocked a brow.

"It's good," she admitted, taking another sip. "Usually alcohol tastes like medicine to me. I don't know a thing about wine or liquor."

"You're at the right age to start learning," he told her, filling her glass again, then bringing the bottle with him back to the living room. This time he took her previous place on the chaise lounge. "Hmm, this is a great chair to curl up in."

Grace liked the sight of him in her favorite chair. Too much. Another place he'd managed to invade. She took another sip of her wine, this time swishing the liquid over her tongue to prolong the flavor.

"Come sit over here by me," Lance invited from where he was, patting the space next to him.

Tempting. She shook her head.

"Come on," he cajoled, his gaze roving lazily over her. His voice had lowered to a husky growl. "I promise I won't attack you. I won't make any moves."

She took another sip, then sat down at the end of the chaise, by his feet. "It's safer when I can see what you're doing," she told him.

He leaned back against the huge sofa pillow, amusement lighting his handsome features. "A toast then," he said, bringing up his glass.

Leaning forward, she clinked her glass to his. "To what?"

"To sweet shy maidens," he mocked, and laughed when she choked on her wine.

"To wolves in sheep clothing," she retaliated. Feeling reckless and excited, she tossed off the rest of her wine.

"Don't drink it down so fast, sweetheart," Lance warned. "You'll get tipsy and then I'll have to take advantage of you."

In fact, he could tell she was already having a relaxed buzz. Hmm. She hadn't lied about not drinking. Her cheeks were tantalizingly rosy and her sparkling brown eyes were daring him to touch her. She was damned inviting. Filling her glass again, he gave it to her, his eyes quietly bland. After a moment's hesitation, she took it.

"I'm going to nurse this one," she declared, then turned sideways to kick off her shoes. "It's getting warm."

"That's what happens when you drink wine down quickly. Give me your feet."

"What?"

"Turn towards me, lift your legs up and give me your feet."

Grace complied, curiosity prompting her to obey. "Why?"

"I remember a certain sight of you massaging your feet with obvious enjoyment," Lance said, smiling at the flush that appeared. He set down his glass and held one foot in his hands. She stared at her foot in fascination as he began massaging slowly. "I want to see that look on your face again."

It was so warm, and she was turning into jello. Grace had sensitive feet that were partial to slow caressing foot rubs, and the feel of his fingers pressing and rubbing her soles sent erotic trills through her system. She forgot about nursing her wine, swallowing down another big gulp.

"Did you know there is a spot at the bottom of your foot, a nerve ending, that corresponds to each part of your body?" Low and seductive, his voice melted all resistance. "This, for example," he continued, pinching just below her big toe, "corresponds to your neck. If you rub it right, your neck-aches go away."

"Hmm…" Grace was aching all over.

"And this," he continued, as he slowly rubbed another spot that made her moan in pleasure, "is your heart. I could massage it till it's practically mine."

She stared into those mocking sea blue eyes, very aware he was playing with her. His fingers continued to knead, pressing all the right places. The man's talents were definitely wasted as an operative.

"And this," his voice was soft, hypnotic, "is the most important nerve." He smiled wickedly when she looked back at him questioningly, his eyes sliding suggestively down her body to show her where he meant. "I could rub this several ways."

Grace could hear the drumming of her heartbeat echoing in her head. Closing her eyes, she felt his strong finger suggestively tracing that spot over and over. He wasn't touching any other part of her body, but it felt like he was intimately touching her all over. She slumped back, weak as a newborn. So. Good.

"I think I've found your Achilles' heel," she heard that dark velvet voice continue. He took her other foot and kneaded it the same way. With her head against his bent knee, she opened her eyes to look at him again, watching the slow movements of his long fingers. His touch was magic.

She heard that hypnotic voice ask, "What do you want, Grace?"

Desire bloomed like a flower in the pit of her belly, seductively urged by the effect of the wine she'd drunk. So, this was tipsy, she hazily analyzed. But she wasn't drunk, and she wasn't without her common sense. Submit or retaliate.

Retaliate.

She licked her lower lip and his eyes followed the motion. "I want," she whispered, slowly straightening from her slouch against his knee, "I want…"

His amazing blue eyes reminded her of midnight in the plains of Ohio, far from the city lights. Suddenly, she wanted to see him under those millions of stars that appeared over her house back home; she wished she could lie with him in the woods in the hills and watch the countless fireflies twinkle like the Milky Way in the darkness. She blinked, confused at the image. She'd never before wanted to share her private moments with anyone.

"What do you want?" he persisted. He had the air of a man assured of a conquest.

"…to play a game," Grace finished, and nearly laughed at the look on his face. For a moment, she'd diverted that animal magnetism enough to escape and she made good use of it. "It's an interesting one too."

"You want to play a game." His voice was slightly incredulous.

"Don't stop that heavenly massage, though," she urged him, giving him a naughty grin. She didn't want him to stop that, just wanted to control the situation. "We can play it while you finish…stimulating me."

Except for the slight flare of his nostrils, Lance didn't betray any emotion. Instead, he leaned over, set aside the glass in her hand, and pulled her unresisting body until she ended up half lying on top of him in the oversized chaise. His hand traveled up and down her small back as they looked at each other face to face.

"So, what's this game you have in mind?"

The feel of his body under hers was arousing. One of her legs rested intimately over part of his thighs, and she deliberately rubbed against it, sliding closer between his legs. His eyes never left her face, even as he kept his earlier promise, not making any move at all.

"It's like this. You get to ask me three questions and I get to do the same to you. There are three rules. One, you cannot give a yes or no answer. Two, you cannot ask a question concerning work. Lastly, you must answer as truthfully as you can."

Lance gave a hoot of laughter, shaking his head. He had done versions of this game years ago. It was the standard way to begin training in evasive tactics. A carefully constructed truth from a trained operative could escape lie detectors, and the advanced operative with a higher level of training learned to answer "correctly" even under the influence of drugs and truth serum. All of them started out with the usual game of answering three questions; it was used to train the mind to recognize nuances in the telling of facts. As a tracker, he had the skills to interrogate over these evasive tactics. Did the woman think she could divert him so easily? Didn't she know he would recognize what she was doing with such a silly exercise?

"Well?" She arched a delicately shaped brow at him. "Afraid of my questions?"

"Not at all," he answered, "but I get to make one more rule."

"What is that?"

"That each question must be preceded by a swallow of wine."

Grace gazed with disbelief at his proposal. "Do you think I'm stupid enough to fall for that? You're trying to take advantage of my low tolerance of alcohol."

He shrugged. "Hey, all's unfair in espionage and spy games. We're playing the covert game of your choice, after all."

"It's not a spy game," Grace insisted. That is, her father never told her it was one. Just a mental exercise, he'd said, a way to learn how to think. "I called them wish questions, you know, since you get to ask whatever you wish. Just pretend I'm a genie and I can grant you three answers."

"If you were a genie," Lance mocked, "I wouldn't be asking you dumb questions. I'd make you grant me real wishes, like having you naked in my arms right now, moaning my name." He fingered the collar of her oversized tee-shirt suggestively. "We can still do that. Or you can accept my rule and we'll play your game."

"But I don't want to get drunk!" she protested.

"I don't want you drunk either, babe." He gave her that smile she couldn't resist. "Just loosen you up a little."

"Well, at least you're honest about your intentions," she grumbled, twirling a loose tendril of his hair around her finger.

"I won't do anything you don't want me to," promised Lance solemnly, but that cajoling quirk was back. "Trust me."

Grace fell against Lance's shoulder and gurgled with amusement. She trusted him like she would a hungry lion. She knew the man long enough to understand why they called him Big Cat. Big Hungry Cat, she amended, still laughing.

The warmth in her belly was powerfully seductive. She couldn't decide whether it came from the wine or his body, but it made her feel powerful and reckless. God, the man was a challenge. Well, time to see how good Dad's lessons were.

"You ask first," she declared. "Give me that glass of wine."

Lance took a drink from his glass, then handed it to her. "First question. Where did you cultivate your many talents?"

She adjusted to a half-sitting position, propping an elbow on one of the chaise's arms. "Define talent," she said. "Remember the second rule."

"Are you saying that your talents have to do with your work? Then you're admitting you're an operative," Lance argued. "By talent, I mean, your skills in evasive tactics."

Grace considered for a moment. It was a smart question, trapping her either way. If she said it did break Rule Two, then of course he was right, she might as well admit she was an operative, which she wasn't. If she answered the question, then of course she was still admitting she was at least trained as one. Blasted tracker know-how.

"Okay, you win," she finally gave in. "I'm not admitting anything, mind you. I started when I was sixteen, training extensively for one year."

His brows shot up. His tone was disbelieving. "Sixteen? That's really young to be recruited by any agency."

"I didn't say I was recruited, did I?"

"You must be very good if they picked you to be trained that young," he persisted, trying to make her own up to it.

"I was taught by the best." Grace made her answer vague, and using her best evasive weapon, she teased the buttons of his shirt with her fingers. She succeeded to divert those eyes for a few seconds. "My turn to ask."

"Drink."

She tentatively took a sip.

"That's a wussy sip. More."

She made a face at him and obliged. She giggled. "My face is getting numb. Is that normal?"

"Only for beginners," he drawled, his eyes dark blue slits.

She handed the glass back to him. "My first question is," she swayed a little closer, her dark hair dangling over his chest, "what do you do in the jungle besides look at ruins?"

Lance smiled. She'd obviously prepared for this game. He wondered how she would handle reality. "I look for the truth. The jungle hides and reveals much."

"Pfft! Don't use fortune cookie language with me!" Grace poked a finger in his chest. "Say you were hunting if you daren't tell me the truth!" Her face may feel numb, but her brain certainly wasn't.

"Okay, I hunt," Lance agreed, amused. "It's how I live—I hunt and I get to make up my own rules."

"The law of the jungle," she finished for him. "You suffer from kingdom-envy."

"Pardon?"

"Kingdom-envy," she repeated, grinning. "You fancy yourself king of the jungle, wild and free."

Lance laughed. "So you think that I want to be Tarzan?"

Grace shook her head, her fingers still tracing the buttons on his shirt. She wiggled her brows. "No, I think you're a big cat." She undid the top two buttons. "And you fancy the jungle as your domain."

"Fascinating," murmured Lance, finishing the wine off from the glass they shared. "Second question, then. Who is Grace O'Connor?"

The most delicious smile appeared on her lips, and he felt the blood leaving his brain and rushing to a currently more needful area of his body. The woman was a witch.

"Who is Grace O'Connor..." she repeated softly and slowly, drawing circles on the small exposed area of his chest revealed by the unbuttoned shirt. Dude certainly knew how to ask the right questions. "She is a normal, ambitious intern from Ohio trying to fatten up her resume."

"Bull," he scoffed.

"She is an airhead in D.C. out to date the political insiders on Capitol Hill?"

"Likely story."

Grace tilted her head a little. "She is...an operative disguised as an intern trying to steal every other agency's thunder?"

His laughter was rich with mockery. "Closer to the truth than the other two versions," said Lance, watching her fingers curiously.

"Okay, last offering. Grace O'Connor is a smart woman trying not to be seduced." She undid two more buttons.

He couldn't take his eyes off her moving hands sliding over his chest. They felt very warm. He nonchalantly topped off the now empty glass and handed it back to her.

"Your turn," he said.

"This could be addictive," she remarked, as she drank from the glass, then handed it back. "Question number two. Which is more important to you—the chase or the goal?"

He stared intently at her. She was leading to something with these questions. Yet she didn't look like she was trying to pump information. Right now, actually, with her flushed face bending toward his, her eyes slightly feverish, and her lips impossibly tempting, she looked like she had other things on her mind.

"They're both equally important," he answered, "but the chase is always more exciting since there are so many possibilities. The goal, on the other hand, has only one conclusion."

Her hands traveled lower, pulling his shirt out of his pants. He sucked in his stomach as she slowly undid the rest of the buttons, the back of her fingers brushing the flat of his belly.

"You're telling me you never fail in getting what you want," Grace said, cocking her head in mockery, "and that foregone conclusion makes the goal less exciting than the chase."

"Maybe less exciting is the wrong word," Lance amended, his eyes following one tiptoeing finger with concentrated effort. He still didn't make a move. "Let me make this more positive. What I really meant to say is the goal is a lot more satisfying than the chase. Better?"

He inhaled sharply when she laid her cheek against his chest, nuzzling against him like a contented kitten. A certain part of him hardened even more. It dawned on him she'd reversed the role of tracker and prey with the ease of a pro. He took in a deep breath.

Taking a deep swallow of wine, he said, "Last question."

"Hmm, don't waste it," she murmured into his chest. A pink tongue flicked out.

His voice lowered to a low demanding growl. "When are you going to give me what I want?"

Grace lifted her head and touched her cheeks with her hands. God, she felt incredibly warm. "That's a loaded question," she said, her voice sounding as husky as his. "Define what it is you want."

"I want everything," Lance told her. Her body. Her mind. Her secrets. She was fast becoming an obsession.

Grace lay her head back onto his chest, running her fingers in the soft mat of his hair. Did he mean he wanted the information he was always thinking she had? Or did he mean something else? It would be so easy to give in to her feelings, but he would eat her alive and spit her out. That, she knew, would be the foregone conclusion.

Lance's hand began to slowly pull up the back of her tee-shirt. "I'll keep myself occupied while you think of the answer," he said. He almost groaned aloud. Damn woman was braless. He smoothed his hands quickly to the sides of her slim body, only to be stopped from moving to her front when she grabbed his wrists. He obediently stilled his movements.

Grace kissed his chest, then moved up sinuously against his hard body until their faces were inches apart. Every part of her body was on fire, and her heart was clamoring in the quiet of the apartment. He didn't attempt to move his hands from where she'd stopped them, seemingly content to let her make the calls. Except for that seductive glimmer in those blue eyes.

She felt reckless, like a gambler on the last the roll of the dice. "You can't have everything you want all the time," she whispered, her breath mingling with his.

"Is that your answer?" he whispered back.

"Yes."

"You're wrong, you know," he told her, moving his hands again.

She impeded his progress by squashing her front against his chest. He smiled at her then, a dangerous raffish smile that tempted her to give him a thorough kissing. For a moment, she thought he was going pull her shirt off.

Instead, he put his hands to the back of her head, and added, "I always get what I want."

She stared into those eyes. She was playing with fire. There would come a time, she was sure, when this man's control would reach an end, and then—she shivered slightly at the dark fantasies that intruded her wine-filled mind. His smile widened. Grace narrowed her eyes.

"I still have one question," she reminded him.

Having her so near, it was a challenge not to ravish her right there and then. "Fire away," he drawled slowly, "but only after you finish the wine."

Grace turned to look at the glass on the table nearby. "But it's almost half full!"

"So?"

"I've a feeling you have lecherous plans for me when I'm totally incapapated, I mean, incapacicated. No, I mean…" She started giggling hard. "See, it's happening."

Then it's already too late," Lance pointed out logically. "Finish it, sweetheart. I promise I'll take care of you."

"That's what I'm afraid of," she said. "Oh, hell, why not?" She sat up astride his chest, leaned over to pick the glass off the table, and drank the wine down slowly. "Satisfied?"

"Uh-huh. Now, what's your question, O Drunken One?"

"Don't mock me," Grace warned, glaring down at him, then bursting into giggles. "You have two heads."

Nothing like seeing a controlled intelligent female tipsy, Lance thought in amusement, as he watched the woman astride him push her hair out of her eyes. He wondered whether she understood how vulnerable she was at the moment, even though he'd allowed her to be in charge. That was just reverse psychology on his part, of course. The more she thought herself still in control, the more he could lead her where he wanted to take her.

"The better to outthink you with," he drolly said, enjoying the sudden alertness dawning in her brown eyes. She did have an amazing ability to still think logically even when under the influence. He frowned. Extensive training.

Grace wondered at what he was thinking. A part of her knew what he was attempting to do, but she didn't panic; she was confident she was good enough to submerge her secrets if she were in danger. But the attraction pulling her to him was out of her scope of experience, and all she wanted was to give in to the urge to make passionate love with the handsome devil, lying there with that Mephistopheles smile, seducing her with his sexy eyes.

"When you find out that you can't have what you want," she started, licking her lower lip, "what will you do?"

Lance blinked. As a man used to getting his own way, the thought of failure had seldom crossed his mind. He met resistance with the weapons available to him—with his easy charm, or his determination, or with force. As a tracker, giving up was never an option, not even when he was assigned the toughest missions, like that challenging one that took him almost a year.

"I have several options," Lance told Grace truthfully, tracing her lips with his forefinger. "I could release you. Or, I could take you anyway, or," he lowered his voice, "I could destroy you."

He carefully studied her reaction. She surprised him by laughing.

"I'd be scared, if you didn't have four eyes," she blubbered in between peals of laughter. She bent her head and kissed him hard on the lips. "There, I accept your challenge."

"Kiss me again," he demanded.

She did so, touching his lips with first her tongue, then teasing them with her own soft lips, giving him a kiss soft as the flutter of butterfly wings. Lance growled at the taste of her, wine and desire mixed with her uniqueness, and without warning, he put a hand to the back of her neck and applied enough pressure to deepen the kiss.

She was dangerous, he thought, as his cock painfully protested its restriction within his pants. She turned the tables on him, becoming the seducer, without seeming to even try. What was

Grace O'Connor? Whom did she work for? Why did he want her so much? These thoughts scattered when she responded to him as demandingly as he did her.

Grace finally came up for air, panting. The warmth was making her eyes heavy. With a sigh, she buried her face in his neck and yawned indelicately.

"I'm falling asleep," she declared sleepily.

"Then go to sleep, babe," he told her.

His voice was like warm honey. Everything was heating her up—his hands, his skin, even his voice. "No, you'd just take advantage of my poor body," she said, but she obediently closed her eyes. Wine was not for her, she belatedly concluded.

"But of course," her seducer admitted. "Wasn't that the point of the whole game? You're going to stay in my arms all night. There, now you can rest easy, knowing I'm staying with you."

"I've never been carried to bed inde…" she struggled with that elusive word again, "indecapidated…" Pouting at the failed attempt, she added, "I don't like wine!"

Grace felt his smile rather than saw it.

"Try love words, babe," he teased. "Wine and love words flow together. Say something sexy." He bent his head and kissed the corner of her mouth. "Say 'Make love to me, Lance.' Go on."

He wanted to hear her talk sexy to him, like she meant it. Her expressive almond-shaped eyes deepened to almost black when she lifted her head to look at him. Slowly, she licked her lower lip.

Lance's jaw dropped at the string of sexy sentences that flowed dark and suggestive out of her mouth. All in Malay.

"Malay," he voiced unnecessarily.

"For a Malaysian Big Cat," she saucily pointed out.

"I didn't know that you could speak Malay."

"Never assume anything, Lance," she said, smothering another big yawn, "especially about me."

"I won't," he said, promising to get into her head and learn her secrets, one by one. *It would be easier if you first gained her trust.*

"Lance?" she sleepily interrupted his reverie.

"Hmm?"

"One freebie question for me?"

"Okay."

Grace yawned again, trying to focus. "Why me?" she asked.

There was a short silence and she bit him in the neck, trying to hurry him. She was getting very sleepy.

"I don't know," he finally replied softly, his sigh gentle against her forehead. "Shhh…"

Grace fell asleep in his arms. He stroked her hair back and adjusted her so she was lying beside him, with one arm protectively around her. He studied her for a long while, desiring her with an urgency that brought up all kinds of questions to his mind.

"I don't know," he repeated, his eyes roaming possessively over the sleeping girl. "You're a puzzle. I just know that I have to have you. All of you."

CHAPTER TEN

"Goddammit, you have him for almost a week, and still can't get a stupid piece of information from him?" Senator James Richards barked at the speakerphone on his desk. His usually smooth composed face was lined in irritation, and his voice was higher than normal. "I thought you were trained to do stuff like this! We don't have much time left!"

"He's been preprogrammed to stand the kind of pain you wanted me to use on him." The voice over the speakerphone was blurred by static. "You specifically disallowed any scarring or blood, Senator. He has a strong mind."

"Sleep deprivation can break minds of any strength!" Richards said curtly, crumbling a piece of paper in disgust. "Has he said nothing at all besides the fact he was supposed to meet with…what the hell is that name—"

"Big Cat."

"Yes, that ridiculous name. What good is that information for me? I want the list of names! I want to know who else is in their pockets, do you hear me?" The senator's frustration was very evident as he shoved his notes in front of him, almost knocking over his glass of wine.

"Big Cat may not mean anything to you, Senator, but it's of significance to me." The speaker crackled for a second. "If they sent the Big Cat to search for our prisoner, we have to get him out of our hands as soon as possible."

"Afraid of him? That's a first. I never thought your kind would be afraid."

"I'm not afraid, Senator," the voice came back calm and confident, "but I'm wary. Big Cat is synonymous with the tracker business, and that tells me that this scholar is very important to certain people. He may have more information than we thought."

"Spare me the details. Who is this Big Cat?" Richard demanded. "Can't you get rid of him if he gets too close? Can't you go behind his back, like you've been doing all along?"

"Senator, even my agency keeps secrets from its own." The man said sardonically. "As for getting rid of him, I just told you, he's a tracker. It'd be difficult to get rid of a tracker, much less one of his caliber. However, finding out his identity might be worth quite a bit to me."

"Don't you dare get sidetracked from your job!" Richards yelled into the speaker, pounding his hand on the cherry wood desk. "If we return the man on Tuesday night without the information, I stand to lose supporting votes when we meet for the trade deals when Congress reconvenes. I need the names to hold over the Committee, damn it!"

"There is one bloodless way left, but it could be dangerous to the health of our scholar."

"What is it?" At this stage, Richards was willing to give anything a try. That list was worth it.

"It's a new experimental drug similar to truth serum. If administered in the right dosage, we ought to be able to get him to recall certain events. On the other hand—"

"Well, do it!" Richards ordered. "Just don't get him killed or our Chinese friends won't be too happy. I gather they want him to reveal his associates, which is none of my business. I only want those other names, do you hear me?"

"Loud and clear, Senator, but the drug is experimental, like I said. A wrong move and our guy may go into a coma or suffer from brain damage."

"Then it's up to you to make sure you give him the right dosage, isn't it?" What was the matter with these people? They were supposed to be professionals. They should know how to handle these things without even consulting him. The senator wished he could be there in person to question the Chinese man, but it was too risky to be anywhere close.

***

Despite urgent demands from his body, duty called. Lance thought about the scholar and picked up his cell phone.

"Dan, Lance here."

"Where is here?"

"I'm at Grace's apartment," Lance replied, the phone cradled under his chin as he shrugged off his shirt. He dropped it over the back of the sofa.

"Uh, huh. I see," came the dry reply. "Did you meet with the senator?"

"Yes, everything is set. I want extra bodies for Tuesday night. I want more firepower and cowboys."

"No problem. I've contacted Homeland Security so they know what's going on. They'll probably alert the Agency."

"Damn it, why do you have to let them know this soon?" Calling Homeland Security was standard operating procedure and Lance didn't have to like it, but getting the CIA involved was another matter. Sure, they couldn't do much, this being a federal case, but with international entities like the Beijing Butcher involved, they'd make sure to send someone. He'd spent enough time in tough positions when the guns at the CIA, wanting the loot for themselves, had sent their boys out to play their own games.

"Don't worry. I was very specific this time about interference. They know about the missile smugglers list. I told them if they get any of our men killed, they'll answer to the NSA themselves."

"Oh, I bet they liked that," Lance noted as he unbuttoned his pants.

Holding itself as an independent agency, the CIA hated conferring with the National Security Agency. However, that second list with the names of arms dealers selling illegal weapons to China was an NSA matter. The CIA spied, gathered information about governments; the NSA handled the security of the country. As such they were inevitably tied, yet both stressed their independence. The CIA went for groundwork; the NSA went for satellite systems, missile warfare. And Command was their little bastard, unacknowledged, but always useful.

"The department head had the look of a man with a toothache when he realized he wasn't going to let his cowboys in this time," Dan said.

Lance heard the amusement at the other end. The rivalry between sibling agencies was often a joke among them. Information was information. A mission was a mission, whether one or the other accomplished it. COS operatives like themselves never needed the credit sought by the CIA or the NSA, preferring to live in the shadows. Safer. They also seldom dealt with betrayal because of the layers of anonymous government red tape camouflaging their existence.

Until now. He paused, narrowing his eyes in realization. Their mole was a double-agent after the same information they wanted and the Chinese tried to conceal. The senator was involved, but he was interested only in the list of his partners in crime, so to speak. But what if Agnes Lin's murderer, a.k.a Senator Richard's man, also knew about the second list and was after that too? It would mean that the hired killer was not just a goon, but also an operative. For whom? He glanced down at Grace, sleeping like a child, a hand under her cheek. His frown deepened. Too many damned agencies involved in this.

"Hello? Lance?" Dan cut in.

"I'm here. I just thought of something. I'll let you know once I've worked it out. Meet me at 0900 hours and we'll discuss the plans," Lance said, pulling down his pants. "We'll walk around the convention building to gauge exit routes.

"Will do. I also received a source report. Seems like a meeting is scheduled for Room 103."

"Good, we'll check that out tomorrow too, maybe even position a man close by." Lance stepped out of his pants. "Not a word to anyone in our unit, Dan. We've got to seal this from the mole. He'll be suspicious as it is with the extra men, but I'm hoping he'll miscalculate it as precaution on our part. I want to get him next, after I've retrieved our scholar."

"0900 hours then," Dan agreed. "I assume I'm to reach you at Miss O'Connor's quarters if I need you?"

"Yes." He ignored the tinge of amusement returning in his friend's voice.

"You don't have a matching scratch on your face yet, I suppose?"

"Not yet," Lance wryly replied. "'Night, Dan."

"Uh, huh."

He draped his pants over his shirt, then turned and walked back to the chaise lounge where Grace was fast asleep. He watched her for a long moment, then scooped her up into his arms, her head high on his shoulder. She was very light, even in deep sleep, and her sweet feminine scent tantalized him as she shifted in his arms, instinctively burrowing deeper. Having already memorized her bedroom from the previous visit, he didn't bother to turn on the main light. Sure-footed, used to walking in the dark, he headed for the bed.

She whimpered softly when he lay her down, then stretched like a feline in her favorite spot, a hand automatically going under her pillow. He smiled wryly. Turning the bedside light on, he climbed in on the opposite side and picked up the pillow. As expected, her hand was lying casually close to her .38. He picked up the weapon and discharged the cartridge. It was loaded, as she'd earlier warned. Snapping it back in place, he clicked the safety notch, then put the weapon under the bed, on his side. Better keep this away from her. He smiled to himself, then shook his head. Never a dull moment with this woman, even in sleep—that was for sure.

Her bed was comfortably large, something for which he was grateful. He frowned, realizing that meant her young pup was a big man too. Jumping out of bed, he went to the dresser and turned the bothersome photographs to face the wall. Better. When he resumed his place, Grace curled up against him with natural ease, one leg inserting itself between his thighs, a hand on his chest.

Lance didn't sleep much, making do with three or four hours of rest. He liked pushing himself, reveled in it. All his senses functioned at their peak when he overworked his physical state. His mind analyzed better; his sense of awareness seemed heightened. He studied the sleeping woman snuggling against him.

Grace the enigma. In many ways, she was his complete opposite. Unlike him, her physical state was an armor to her inner abilities. There was a deliberation in her physical movements, and she appeared to revel in melee. The more action surrounding her, he'd noticed, the more her mental awareness sharpened. She seemed to be able to dissect mass information into digestible chunks without trouble. He didn't know her, yet it seemed like he'd known her forever. Something about her was vaguely familiar, but he couldn't put a finger on it. A man used to internalization, he accepted this strange combination of contradictions in this new relationship.

Shifting to his side, he ran a finger lightly over her jaw line. Her eyes fluttered open.

"It's not time yet, is it?" she asked, drowsiness slurring her voice sexily.

"For?"

"For you to seduce me," she said, rubbing his chest absently.

"But I am seducing you," Lance gently informed her, getting even more curious about the way she thought. She never seemed to be afraid and always went on the attack first, no matter what the situation.

She yawned, then smugly said, "See? You do like the chase better." She closed her eyes and immediately fell back asleep.

He laughed softly. God, she drew him like a magnet. If he ever clamped down on her, he would never let go. He grimaced. Of course he would let go. He had to. His life wasn't here in this city of talking heads. His was a whirlwind of danger and death. There wasn't any place in his life for a young woman like Grace O'Connor, who appeared very at home in D.C.

He reached back and turned off the light. He lay there thinking in the darkness, his mind clicking along in tracker mode, removing obstacles and creating possibilities. Tomorrow would be all preparation, and the day after would be his kind of day—action on the agenda. His hand caressed Grace possessively as his mind wandered, returning sometimes to savor the feel of her body. She was silky smooth all over, and so soft he wanted to nibble everywhere. He sighed. She may be soft, but he was hard as a rock. It was interesting, how she could arouse him without trying, and how she could drive him crazy with those clever fingers, then fall asleep at a drop of a hat. Granted she was slightly drunk, but her mind was still needle-sharp. And, let's not forget she spoke in Malay too, he noted, before finally closing his eyes. Lazily enjoying the feel of her body heat against his, he wondered briefly whether she would survive in his world if he did carry her off.

***

They would have to let him go, the man thought, as he smoked. They had no choice. They couldn't push him too far. A dead man wouldn't please the Beijing Butcher. Too bad. He was just beginning to enjoy himself. He liked this new drug. It certainly was a powerful weapon of persuasion.

The man finished his cigarette, ground it out, and called the senator. He came to the phone immediately, his voice hurried and hoarse from lack of sleep.

"It's done," he informed the politician, not even waiting for the question. "The man obviously knows very little or nothing. I had him relate events leading to our capture of him, and all he'd been able to tell was the arranged meeting with the Big Cat, of whom he couldn't even give a description. All he kept mumbling was Big Cat and Shia Yi."

"Sa what?" the senator asked. "What in hell does that mean? Is that a code?"

"I think that we've got the wrong man, senator. Shia Yi, in Chinese, means shark. I suspect that's the person with information that you and I want."

"Well, press him on the whereabouts of this Shark." James muttered several expletives over the phone.

"No good, Senator," the man spoke calmly over the string of curses. "I'd doubled the dosage. Another one and his brain will be fried. Your Chinese buddies won't be too happy about that."

"Then how are you going to find out who this other person is? We both know how important that information is to me. Don't forget that your neck is stuck out just like mine, boy."

"I'll try other avenues. Before he passed out, he did mention about bumping into a woman just before he was to meet the Big Cat. Maybe she is the Shark. I got a description of her—young, small frame, brown hair, brown eyes…"

"That could be anybody, for God's sake!" James's sarcasm blasted over the line.

The man sighed. If not for the importance of his assignment, he would have been tempted to leave the senator to find someone else to do his dirty work. He abhorred impatient people, especially stupid, impatient self-important people. "We work with what we're given, which is, surprisingly, a lot. I've got a code name, a description, and a few other things. How many female operatives have that code name? No, she'll be easy to trace. I'll make a few calls to my friends to check out that name for me."

"Fine. Take care of it and make sure everything goes as planned tomorrow night. I don't want to fuck this up, so if you want to get paid, you'd better get the return done right. That Mr. Wang strikes me as someone who wants things done as expected. For the kind of cash they're donating, it'd better be exactly per their instructions."

No, you wouldn't want to mess with the Beijing Butcher. Of course, what would the stupid senator know about the Beijing Butcher? He was only interested in lining his off-shore coffers. "I'll take care of it," he assured the worried man. "Either way, at least the poor bastard would be back in Chinese hands, out of our way."

"Yes, but it'd make me feel much better if he'd given the list of names. Those names could have bought me quite a bit of influence, know what I mean? Damn. One wasted week."

The man lit another cigarette after getting off the phone. He didn't care what the senator wanted; his assignment was entirely something else—a second list of names the scholar had supposedly smuggled out. The senator could go to hell, for all he cared. He was nothing—a conduit for the real assignment—the man had no idea how unimportant he was in the scheme of things.

That piece of information was his ticket to the big leagues, and he couldn't help but laugh out loud at Command. They didn't even know there was another, more important, list, and obviously, they were also after the wrong man too, since it was a woman who was the handler. The man pieced together what had happened at the rally. Agnes must have held back one piece of information from him. Damn it. He should have made sure he'd gotten everything from her first.

Obviously, the real person with the list was this Shark, a female operative, and David Cheng here was some sort of a go-between for her and the Big Cat. That made sense. The Chinese underground movement was almost as secretive as Command, and it wasn't likely to reveal any of the key people working against their country. So, David Cheng was just mere decoration.

Damn, he had to admire the plan. If only he hadn't cancelled Agnes. But he'd thought it best to be rid of her. She would have known something was wrong when the scholar disappeared in the rally and might have contacted someone higher up from him. Then he would be caught.

Shit. One fucking mistake. He should have been more patient, gambled a little. But it was too late now. He would just have to work a little harder to get that list.

He wondered who this Shark could be; he'd never heard of her. Perhaps the others had. He glanced at the Chinese man, slumped over unconscious on the chair where he was securely tied. Poor bastard. The Beijing Butcher was going to make mince meat of him. Maybe it would be an act of mercy if he did overdose Cheng by mistake after all. These Chinese scum were fucking well-programmed. This one didn't scream through all the hours under his care, and he knew he was good at extracting information. Too bad he couldn't hurt him a little more, but the senator was scared to death about returning damaged goods. When he finally did break, it was just the Big Cat's name he kept muttering, then later, the Shark, over and over, shaking his head at every question. Who the hell is this Sa Yi? He called out Big Cat in English, and the Shark in Chinese, so he was quite positive that the latter was Asian.

That was his other regret. He wished they had waited a little longer before capturing the man. If he'd seen what the Big Cat looked like, that kind of information could be worth a bundle. Nabbing the Big Cat's identity would give his resume a major boost indeed. Not that he was complaining about the reward once he accomplished this mission.

He smiled. He felt powerful, privy to all the things going on, since he was playing both sides of the table. Everyone else knew only part of the truth, was only after one agenda. He knew differently, because he knew each group's agenda. The senator had hired him for his own motive; his agency wanted to get the same list to see who had been bought out by another government; as for himself and his group, they were making sure they remained undiscovered. That Chinese scholar held all the information each of them sought; at least, he admitted, that was what they had all assumed.

He shrugged. He would find this Shark and then he would have everything everyone wanted. He had a feeling about the female he glimpsed from the car, the one who was talking to Cheng before he recognized the Chinese guards Wang had personally trained. She'd had her back to him and they were too far away for him to see her anyway, and it had happened so quickly at that time, he hadn't suspected her of being part of the game. Another mistake. He should have paid better attention. He vowed to be more vigilant about details. He would have to be, if he were to prove to the others he could handle the more rewarding operations. Once he had all these different lists, he would make use of them to rise up to play with the big boys.

Money and power. Those were two things that turned the world.

CHAPTER ELEVEN

Grace was having her favorite dream again. This particular one was remarkably vivid, so real she felt the heat roasting her cheek as she lay on her side. She stretched and got on her feet, peering curiously over the tall grass behind which she was resting. There her lion mate was, so close this time, that every purr from his chest seemed to unfurl animal heat in her direction, inviting her to draw closer. He was standing still, as always, and his watchful eyes were a dazzling blue, like the sky behind him. A memory nagged at her subconscious as she prowled around his tautly muscled body. Those eyes disturbed her more than usual.

A golden aura bathed the two of them as she stepped closer. His male heat was overpowering, tantalizing her to nudge against him. She wanted to tease him and sensed his excitement as his purrs turned into rumbles. Soon, she thought, soon he would turn and pounce—

The dull buzz of the alarm clock melted away the curtain of dreams. Grace moaned in disgust, trying to hang on to the last vestiges of her erotic images as they dissolved into forgetfulness. Someone turned off the culprit.

She slowly stretched, rubbing against the rocklike muscles she was using as her pillow. She felt them ripple under her right cheek and side of her body as, eyes still closed, she uncurled and moved lazily.

All that heat could drive a woman crazy. She ran her hand possessively over a taut stomach and a broad muscular chest. She explored it with teasing fingers, rubbing over the little nipples, then skimming through the downy chest hair—her eyes flew open, a small gasp escaping her lips. *Tim didn't have chest hair.*

The previous night's activities filled her mind as she slowly tilted her head back. A pair of blue eyes, not Tim's green, regarded her with sleepy interest.

"Don't even say his name," his husky morning voice told her, soft and mocking, "or I'll have to really show you I'm not him."

His eyes told her that he knew exactly the moment when she realized she wasn't caressing Tim; after all, her fingers were still tangled in that mat of hair that betrayed his identity. A flush crept up her neck and over her face, a delicate hue that added a doll-like quality to her, with her untamed hair spread across his arm and shoulder.

Grace cautiously checked under the sheets and, to her relief, discovered she was still in her oversized tee-shirt. She tried to sit up, but he turned and trapped her body under his. Her eyes widened. He certainly wasn't wearing anything.

"Cat got your tongue?" he asked, his lips quirking. His morning stubble made him look even more dangerous than usual.

The morning ritual of slowly awakened awareness was replaced by wired tension. There was no slow awareness where Lance Mercy was concerned. Grace's body, as always, reacted without any control whenever he was anywhere near her. Every part of her screamed for his touch; every molecule in her brain was knocking itself silly between her ears. She was sure if she rattled her head from side-to-side, every cell that governed common sense and intelligence would roll out in defeat.

"I think I'm still drunk," she managed to say, her voice throaty from sleep and lust.

"Do I still have four eyes and two heads?"

"What?"

"That's what you said I had last night." His lips quirked down at her. He ignored her attempts to move from under him, adding, with a grin, "You're cute when you're tipsy."

Grace frowned. "You did that on purpose," she accused. "Why?"

"For fun," Lance mocked. "It was fun, don't you remember?"

"I…" Damn it, she couldn't remember beyond the third question she asked.

"You unbuttoned my shirt, teased the hell out of me, put your face on my chest. You snuggled like a kitten, told me to carry you to bed," he told her.

Grace closed her eyes at the litany of crimes she committed the night before, as he continued, "Then, this morning, you accuse *me* of taking advantage of you? I feel cheap and abused."

There definitely was laughter in his voice. She opened one eye. "We didn't do anything," she cautiously stated. "We just slept together, right?"

"Sweetheart, if you don't remember it, then we didn't do it," Lance assured her, his eyes gleaming with mirth. "Believe me, I always make sure the ladies find our nights memorable."

He did want her. So, why didn't he seduce her? Puzzled, she asked, without embarrassment, "Why? Why did you stop?"

He leaned so close she wanted to pull him down for a morning kiss. "Because if I started, I wouldn't stop for a long time," he told her, his condition very evident against her thigh. He nudged against her shamelessly, grinning as she squirmed against him. "I wouldn't be satisfied for quite a while." He kissed the corner of her lips. "And today would be a necessary interruption. When we make love, sweetheart, I'll take my time, and I want you wide awake and wanting me, the way I want you. I won't let anything interrupt us, short of a world war."

Grace stared, mesmerized by his words. "Oh," she squeaked weakly. He could seduce her with mere words. This was getting bad.

"What, no protests? No outrage?" He nuzzled her neck. "I'm just now getting used to your usual prim little answers to deny me."

Deny him? How could she when he was lying naked on her, his need hot and obvious against her thigh? She was having difficulty not reaching down to see how it would feel like…God, she had to stop this madness.

"I need…" she began, licking suddenly dry lips.

"Yes?" he whispered.

"…the bathroom," she finished.

Lance put his forehead against hers, fighting the urge to push her legs apart. The need to take her was getting uncontrollable. He wondered when he finally did, whether the feeling would go and he would be normal again. "So do I. Want to go together?"

"Nope," she said, shaking her head. "You go first. Then I've to get ready for work."

He gave her a kiss that banished that notion from her thoughts. She responded with a fervent frenzy, as his hands raked through her mussed-up hair to slant her head to meet his more intimately. His tongue lazily thrust into her mouth in imitation to the slight movement of his lower body and Grace moaned softly at the double assault.

"Think about that while I'm in the bathroom," he huskily ordered, when he released her mouth. Rolling away abruptly, he threw back the sheets and strolled across the room into the bathroom, totally comfortable with his nudity.

From the bed, Grace stared at the nice view. His broad back was a tanned broad expanse of muscle. Her eyes traveled down the dip of his backbone, moving to that narrow waist, and heavens, but the man did have a sexy ass. Besides the obvious. Groaning aloud, she pulled the sheets over her head, wondering at her predicament. What was going on with her usual cool and collected self?

As she got out of bed, she turned to look at the twin indentations on the pillows. She couldn't believe they'd actually spent the night in bed and not done anything. Everything the man did, everything he said, indicated his intentions. The sexual pull she felt for him was palpably exciting, almost like a drug. The more she saw of him, the more she wanted him. Ugh, he probably had the same effect on every one of his women.

The thought cooled her off considerably. She certainly wasn't going to be in line with Princess von Whatever for Mr. Mercy, thank you. They all could have him. She straightened the bed and picked up clothes and linens from the floor. She scowled. If she saw him with one of those glammed-up society types, she would puke. All over the both of them.

Pulling out her working clothes from the closet, she muttered to herself about hurting various strategic body parts. She stuck out her tongue at her untidy reflection in the closet mirror. Things were getting out of hand. She had a man she'd known barely a week in her bathroom while she trampled around half-naked in her own apartment being jealous of his imagined girlfriends. Meanwhile, her estranged boyfriend waited for her return to Ohio.

What a mess. Nothing like guilt to dampen one's passion, she grimaced in disgust. The problem was it wasn't guilt of what she wanted to do, but guilt over having to hurt Tim's feelings. She'd never kidded herself she was in love with him. All these nine months they had been together, she'd never shared her secret self with him, and had never wanted to. It was a comfortable relationship, like an old shoe. She knew they would break up soon, more from boredom than anything else.

Before this internship came up, Tim never baited, never fought, seldom even argued with her, unlike—she frowned. There, she was doing it again, making comparisons. She didn't want to do that; she wasn't making a choice between Tim and *him*. She glared at the closed bathroom door. There wasn't any comparison, none whatsoever. Tim was wonderful and considerate, a great person. She chose to ignore his unreasonable demands of late. Lance, on the other hand, was dominating, rude and...and...a great kisser. And insufferably, abominably sexy.

Grace's shoulders slumped in defeat. So what if she kept listing Tim's virtues if, at the thought of Lance's kisses, her body lit up like Christmas lights? She was attracted to him, she might as well admit it. And she knew she would have to break up with Tim soon, and hurt him. She couldn't go out with one man when her mind was hankering after another, even one with whom she couldn't allow herself to get involved.

She rapped sharply. "Hey, if you use up all my hot water, I'm going to shoot you," she yelled, then realized she hadn't seen her .38 when she was making up her bed. She rapped again. "Where did you hide it?"

The door opened. Her jaw dropped. He stood there in wet nakedness, except for a towel draped low on his hip. Never had her towel looked so good.

"Where did I hide what?" he asked.

"The...gun," Grace replied, her eyes following the rivulets down his hairy chest, down to his belly button, down to the towel. Oh my.

She quickly looked up and met his amused gaze. Flushing, she turned her back to him. "Don't say it," she snapped.

"I was just going to tell you where the gun is." His voice held barely suppressed laughter. "Want me to show you?"

She made a sound of exasperated laughter and gathered clothes into her arms. Turning around, she deliberately walked past him, averting her gaze. "I've to get ready," she said. "You can leave any time you like." Closing the door behind her, she turned the lock.

Lance grinned at the sound. He didn't mind making her mad at him; it was fast becoming a hobby to watch her get angry or aroused. He returned her .38 under her pillow, went out to the living room and picked up his clothes.

Tomorrow night. After securing their missing scholar. Tomorrow would be Grace O'Connor's last day as a free woman. In twenty-four hours, he'd make sure those wings of hers got clipped. Shoving his hands into his pants, he whistled as he sauntered into the kitchen.

***

Sandra hesitated a fraction outside Ed's office, then gave a crisp knock and entered.

Ed looked up from across the room and smiled gently. "Good morning," he said, standing up.

She walked slowly toward his desk, her eyes steady. "Do you have a few minutes?" she asked, her voice polite.

"Of course," Ed said, hungrily taking in the cool whiteness of her loose fitting jacket and matching knee-length skirt. She wore demure pearl studs in her ears, as well as a pearl choker. All that frosty white, he reflected, to hide the heat of last night. She was perfectly groomed again, and his fingers itched to run through her silky hair, to loosen it from the confining pins and leave it tangled and wild.

He hadn't been able to sleep after she left. There were too many things to remember. He'd thought they had crossed a small bridge together in their present relationship, but in the cold light of this morning, he could just make out the canyon that yawned between them. He carefully sat down as she settled into the seat opposite him.

"I think one of us ought to go to the Charity Invitational," Sandy said, her voice business-like, her face expressionless. "There are certain things I want to record."

Ed studied her, his own eyes guarded. It never failed to amaze him how she could hold two conversations with a person at the same time. Aloud, she was discussing business, and yet, he heard her silent words as if they were being announced through a loudspeaker. Yesterday was an aberration, she was saying.

"Do you want to go, or do you want me to go?" He asked, then added, "Or would you prefer we go together? Like old times?"

Sandra blinked, then composed herself. "Ed," she began, "I don't want to talk about last night."

"Nothing happened last night, Sandy," he told her, clicking his pen. "We shared a few kisses, and you ran away."

Sandra knew, from practiced control, that Ed wouldn't be able to tell the turmoil underneath her calm façade. She'd barely slept last night, too disturbed by her responses to his kisses. She felt bitter and angry with herself. She'd thought she was beyond feeling that way for anyone again, after three years of tight discipline. But the sight of him among the roses, the fragrance of the flowers mingled with his warm masculine scent, had evoked the fiercest kind of pleasure-pain in her, the same feeling that had burned her and nearly consumed her so long ago. She'd hoped three long years would douse that fire.

She was wrong.

"Nothing's going to happen beyond that," she firmly informed him, noticing for the first time the tension in his hands, even though his expression remained the same. "I cannot let emotions get mixed up with business again, Ed."

"You're letting your fear come between us," Ed said quietly. He leaned back, forcing the wave of bitterness to recede. "Why didn't you ever call me these last three years—when you've obviously finished with him?"

The silence was heavy. He regretted bringing the subject up, but it was one question that hung between them. That man she wouldn't mention was forever the shadow between him and Sandy. She was his ghost, his lover, and the bitterness crept up his throat again. She'd chosen him, and now, when it was over, it seemed her old lover had become the ghost, haunting her.

Sandra gripped the seat of her chair, forcing herself to breathe normally. She didn't want to remember, and certainly didn't want to be reminded. "Let's leave him out of this," she said, angry that she couldn't keep the hoarseness out of her voice.

He shook his head. "He had you for two years. Something happened. I want to know, Sandy, even though you won't tell me who he was. I want to understand why you've hidden yourself in administration for three years instead of calling me."

"Why, so you could tell me 'I told you so'?" She asked bitterly. "I do have my pride, Ed."

"The hell with your pride!" He walked around his desk in three quick strides, and pulled her out of her chair. "Are you saying you let your pride stop you from calling me all these years? That you've been hiding here because of your damned pride?"

Sandra jerked her chin up defensively. Ed never yelled, but when he was furious, the steel in his carefully enunciated sentences was just as effective.

"I was not hiding," she retorted, and pushed against his chest. "I'm perfectly fine where I am, where I choose to be."

"Yes, that's why you put on this front, this mask. You're fine!" Ed shook her, anger coursing through him like a forest fire. "This isn't you. I knew you, Sandy. Is this what you choose to be—this cold and controlled person, carefully put together to face the world? You're fine. Do you think you can deceive me?"

"Stop it!" Sandra held on to his suit, trying to keep from stumbling. "Ed, stop it!"

He released her and turned his back to her, walking to the sideboard to get something to drink. She drew in a shaky breath.

"Do you think I wasn't tempted to get hold of you?" She stared at his stiff back. "We didn't exactly part with the kindest of words, Ed. I've known you for twenty some years. I know exactly how much pride you have, how hurt you were. Don't you think I didn't know why you chose to go to the farthest places possible with the most dangerous situations? You were nursing your own pride. Contacting you would just reopen your wounds, and I didn't want to do that."

Ed crushed the napkin in his hand, then forced himself to drink down his cup of coffee. He wished he stocked something stronger in the cabinet. Pride. The coffee tasted like bile with the realization of what they'd both allowed to come between them. They both chose pride over need, and accepted the pain that came with that choice. He sighed. It was difficult to catch up with five years of emotions in one morning.

He looked down into his cup, trying to find an answer to the future. "Sandy," he said, "I've never forgotten."

"Or forgiven," she finished for him, soft but sure.

Ed swung to face her. "I was hurt and angry for a long time," he admitted, "but I forgave you a long time ago."

"Then you're a more generous person than I. I'm sorry I hurt you, but I'm not sorry for what I did."

The unexpected pain from a realized truth slammed into him. "You still love him, don't you?" His accusation was resigned, tinged with anger. "You're still his."

Sandra fought hard for a measure of control. She would not break down, not now. "I'm no longer the Sandy you loved, nor the one who loved him," she woodenly said. Slowly, she sat down again, deliberately taking time to arrange her skirt. "Therefore, your conclusions are moot."

Ed stared at her. She was trying very hard to objectify, as if she were a recorder on the job again. There was, after all, three years' coat of the new Sandy under which to hide. He hitched a hip on the corner of his desk, looking down at her.

"Some day," he said, "I hope you'll tell me who the son of a bitch was, so I can wring his neck for hurting you. And some day, I hope you'll forget him and crawl from under that shell to meet me half way. It's not over for us, Sandy."

"Don't jump to conclusions over someone you've never met." Sandra's calmness had returned. "It didn't end the way you think. There were extraneous circumstances, and I made the choice, not him." Her voice gentled. "I can't become who I was, even for you. She's dead. To you, as well as him."

"No," his voice was firm, and just as gentle, "she's alive. I tasted her and she was vibrantly alive." He watched the slow flush bloom in her cheeks, and added, "You can deny all you want, but that Sandy is still in there. I never asked anything of you, and I won't begin today. Just consider this. It's been five years and I still miss you. I still want you, and I still—"

"Don't," she cut in, afraid of what he would say next. She wasn't ready for it. Not now. Not yet. "Don't. I need to think. I need time."

He had never been able to make himself hurt her or cause her pain, no matter how many times in his loneliness he'd imagined doing exactly that. He wanted things to fall back into place, in an orderly fashion. It didn't make sense to force the issue. He would give her what she wanted, like every other time.

"You've always had that from me," he said, resignation etching his face. He withdrew behind the desk and sat back down. "Now, the Charity Invitational. Should we both go?"

"I can arrange that," Sandy replied, relief speeding through her. She needed time to be strong again, and he'd given it to her. She felt his anger and frustration, and that feeling of pleasure-pain emerged again. Ignoring it, she continued, "Our contacts will get us invitations. One more thing, I think I've found a way to keep Grace with us after the internship is over."

Ed reached for his pen. It was so easy to ignore chaos, to pretend the world was in order. "Let's hear it," he said, his eyes cool and flat as he too reassumed his façade.

CHAPTER TWELVE

He even cooked. Grace shook her head as she drove to work. She had come out of her bedroom, only to smell breakfast from her kitchen. The only complaint he had was the missing key ingredient—coffee.

"I'm going to have to dub you OJ queen," he'd quipped. "What do you do, survive on the stuff in place of a good meal?"

Grace had shrugged. She never ate breakfast, anyway, although now and then she indulged in some sausage and eggs, which was what he found in her fridge.

She recalled how he acted so familiar, like he belonged in her kitchen—in her life—and she wasn't comfortable with it. Of course, the whole of Sunday and last night leading to the breakfast was bizarre, to say the least. On the way out, he'd kissed her possessively in the parking lot, told her he would call, then waved nonchalantly at a staring Mary Tucker before purring off in his BMW. She had made her escape in her own vehicle before Mary had a chance to cross the parking lot.

So much to do, and one thing on her mind. Him. She had to focus on David Cheng, the missing scholar. His life was in danger.

Tyler didn't even look up from his desk when she entered the tiny office they shared. He looked exactly like he did yesterday, only messier. "Did you sleep here?" she asked dryly, walking over to his desk and sitting on the corner. "You need a change of clothes, buddy."

"I'm stuck in here all day, anyway," he mumbled, his fingers flying over the keyboard, "unlike some busy people I know who attend all kinds of functions."

"Ouch!" She grinned.

"Get me something to eat?"

"Later, lunch," she said, affectionately patting him on his stubbly chin.

"Yummy."

"Did you work on what I wanted?"

"Yeah, I got it," he told her, finally looking at her. He smiled, pushed his glasses on top of his head and rubbed his eyes. "Took me all night, but I cracked it, babe."

"You're sure you didn't get caught?" Grace asked, keeping an eye on the office door.

Tyler coughed indignantly. "Insults will cost you, my dear," he warned.

"I apologize, babe," she said, getting to her feet. "I just don't want you to get in trouble."

He swiveled around on his chair, watching her as she made her way to her own desk, his hands laced behind his neck. "It wasn't too difficult," he drawled cockily. "So easy, you could have done it yourself."

Grace moved several files around. "No," she shook her head, "I don't have the patience. That's why I asked for your help. If I could do it myself, I wouldn't have involved you."

Tyler rubbed his whiskered chin. "Yeah, you're right. I'm the Hackerator," he declared. "So, do you want it now?" When she nodded, he handed over a thin file, adding, "There isn't much."

She eagerly snatched it from him, took a deep breath, and opened the manila folder. As he'd said, there wasn't much, barely two pages. No identity was given. No description, no photos, no contacts. The information was skeletal, at best, and not what she'd expected. She'd thought there would be something more in-depth. If she were a client, wouldn't that be the expectation? Why then would the information be this scarce? There must be a logical explanation for this, but right now, her mind was on one crucial bit of information.

"Well, well, well," she breathed.

"Found something?" Tim asked, reaching for an opened box of cornflakes and pouring some stale-looking crumbs into his hand.

"You might say that."

"Actually, I was surprised at how little the damned file revealed. You'd think, with the trouble they went through encrypting it, there would be some deadly secrets, at least an identity of the guy," he said, voicing Grace's thoughts aloud. "Do you know who he is?"

"Hmm," she said, continuing to read. She had no desire to tell anyone what she knew, unless necessary.

"Mind explaining some of the stuff in there to me?"

Grace looked up. "Maybe. What do you want to know?"

Tyler was good at asking questions, a talent he seldom used, since he preferred to do his research through electronic means. However, when the fancy struck him, he was a pretty good investigator. "What is this agency that the Big C works for?" He wiped his mouth with his sleeve. " C.O.S. Unit. What do those letters stand for, do you know?"

She stretched out her legs, closing the file. Studying her shoes for a moment, she then softly said, "Covert Subversion Commando unit, also known as COS Command Center, or Triple C, among the surveillance world. It's a special forces intelligence battalion consisting of elite operatives culled from all the government branches—CIA, FBI, NSA, SEAL, you name it. COS Commandos are the grunts in the covert wars, the kind our government doesn't want the world to know we meddle in. Covert subversion is the gray area of gray areas, so to speak, and those in the unit operate in shadow, independent of the other branches. I'm not sure exactly which is under whom in the order of command, but COS is a combination of all that the others do."

Tyler gave a low whistle. "Wow, you learn something everyday," he remarked. "How would a sweet young thing like you know this, by the way? Not from Wiki, I'm sure."

Grace smiled. "Level Two, my dear," she lied without blinking, "gives you access to all kinds of information."

"So did what I found out help?"

She nodded slowly. "Yeah." Not enough, but it yielded that one important missing piece of information. The Big Cat a.k.a Lance Mercy was COS, far more dangerous than a mere insider millionaire with a penchant for rescuing scholars. And now it was obvious the information held by the Chinese man was of more importance than a list of greedy senators, as he'd told her yesterday.

She briefly wondered how much the information would cost, if he had to buy it from GNE. That is, she amended, if she got to the kidnapped victim first. She ignored the part of her that instinctively wanted to help Lance. Lie to her, would he? She was going to beat a tracker commando at his own game. He could track as well as he could, but she vowed to be at the finishing line before him.

"Must be something really big," Tyler commented, watching her and munching cornflakes at the same time. "Look at them big thought clouds over your head."

She laughed and went over to give him a quick peck on his cheek. "Thanks. Why don't you clean up so I won't be ashamed to be seen in public with you when we go for lunch?"

"Aw, you sure know how to flatter a guy…"

Laughing still, she walked over to the shredder and, within moments, the file was history. Tyler groaned. "Half a night's work," he moaned. "Babe, you killed me! I thought you needed the info!"

It's all up here, kiddo," she told him, tapping her head. "Photographic memory." She pulled out another file and headed for the door. "See you later."

"Ta."

Practically skipping to the front office, she was elated to know who Lance Mercy was, and a little apprehensive. She wondered how he would react if he knew the whole truth about her, whether he would still want to be so friendly. Not that she would ever volunteer to tell him.

"Grace!" Sandra called from her office when she walked by. When Grace retraced her steps and stuck her head through the office door, she picked up her briefcase, and instructed quietly, "Follow me."

They walked past the front office where the assignments and reports were gathered and distributed, passed Ed Maddux's office and the conference rooms. Grace's curiosity got the better of her. "Where are we going?"

She got the usual Sandra Smythe non-committal, "You'll see." They stepped into the elevator. Inserting a key, Sandy punched a code into the panel. The elevator door closed and they ascended past the third floor, which was the highest destination for those without the key.

Grace looked on with interest. She hadn't expected this move by her superiors. She followed Sandra down the corridors, which were secretive and silent, unlike the frenetic energy of ground floor, where she worked. Turning the corner, they stopped outside the closest door; there was a similar panel to the side. Sandra inserted the key here as well, punched in a code, and she heard a lock released.

It was a mini-library, with files upon files on one wall. Books lined another, and on the far end, a whole row of computers sat side by side. No one was in the room. She cocked her head, waiting for an explanation.

"We're giving you a key to use one of our libraries," Sandra waved at the room. "Here, you will find access to all Level Three operative privileges. You've shown a proficiency with computers, so I don't think you'll have any problems learning your way around our database."

"How much access?" Grace asked, not even bothering to conceal her surprise.

"More than you would need for your current little adventure," Sandra replied, smiling. "You can access the U.N. files, all Congress dialogues here and overseas, all current observations up to Level Three, most of the reports being requested by our clients, and most of all, check the background of any of your acquaintances."

Grace gave her supervisor a measured look. The last piece of information was thrown in as advice. "Why would I need to do that?"

Sandra walked to one of the computers. Opening her briefcase, she took out a magazine, thumbed to a bookmarked page and handed it to over. She watched while the younger girl looked curiously at the page, observing the flare of surprise that accompanied a hint of annoyance.

Grace immediately recognized the glossy Beaucoup. It was a gossip article about the Washington scene, and featured prominently on the page was a picture of Lance Mercy, international power broker, according to the writer, who went on to inform the reader of his new love interest, a Grace O'Connor. "Sources told us," the article smugly ended, "that the two would be going to the bash of the summer, the Charity Invitational, together." She wavered between exasperation and amusement. Yikes, Mary Tucker was better at this than she'd thought.

She glanced up at the watching Sandy and shrugged. "Gossip," she said. "I don't see what that's got to do with my need to check anyone's background, unless you're suggesting I check up on Lance?"

"Grace, I won't press for details on how much you know about your new friend, but don't underestimate my knowledge about what's going on," Sandra said, her expression turning cool. "This is Level Three work, and I'm the one granting you limited access because of your talents. Level Three, in brief explanation, is contract work. You're paid for good information, the kind that would bring GNE profits. Our field agents specialize, then pick and choose the different areas in which they wish to work. Some choose overseas observation; others remain here."

Sandra paused to let the significance of her words sink in. Her young prodigy didn't say anything, nor did she show any surprise. Maybe she wasn't as readable as she appeared. The probability of Grace's ability to project herself in various guises was getting higher by the week.

"At Level Three," she continued, "you make most of your own calls, but you must learn to understand the danger of your situation as well as your responsibilities. You add your own reports into the database, selling the information to us, so to speak. You'd be given your own code and your own choices of assignments."

How do I get paid?" Grace asked. Scenarios sieved through her mind, showing her all the possibilities available in this particular future. More than interesting. Very tempting.

"We set up an offshore account and your funds are transferred there. Level Three isn't for the squeamish, Grace, and certainly a lot more dangerous than you think. Many have quit."

"Even under the umbrella of non-alignment? I thought ghosts were untouchable?" Grace closed the magazine but didn't return it, feeling pleased she remembered all the strange terms Sandra had tossed at her in their last conversation.

Sandra would have given her subordinate a Grade A for insight. Nothing got by the girl, and she was privately pleased. This gamble on her part might actually pay off big dividends in the long run. Already, her psych and evaluation file on Grace O'Connor was getting thicker.

"You'll find out there are risks, especially with someone as cocky as you are," she told her, "but this is all in the future. We feel you can go far with our kind of work and that's why we're giving you this opportunity. We want you to have a taste of what your future with us might be like. Hopefully, you'll like it enough to stay with us."

"A test run, then," Grace murmured, tactfully not pointing out she was the one being tested.

Sandra nodded. "There's more but I'll leave that till the end of your current contract with us. Now, regarding background checks. You're associating with people who are or will be checking up on you, so you might as well return the favor. Our business is information, and you'll learn we're the best because our information is put to good use by our operatives. Knowledge is foresight, and foresight is power."

"Is there anything particular I should check up on about Lance?" Grace casually inquired. "Income bracket? Bank account?"

Sandra snapped her briefcase shut. "Level Three—your own little game. We have one more rule, and this clause is binding. We don't, not ever, sell our clients' personal information to anyone, so when you're ghosting for Lance Mercy," she waved away Grace's initial denial, "please keep everything confidential. You'll find all our files don't cross-reference any clients or their agents. Everything is kept separate."

Grace already knew that, having read one particular file that morning. "I understand perfectly," she said. She'd just solved the puzzle several seconds ago. "Bad for business. We can't have our clients eliminating each other, can we? We'd just lose our base."

Sandra laughed, then moved toward the door. "You've a good head for this, Grace. Consider the offer. Here are the keys and an envelope with all the security codes for this floor. Please memorize and then destroy."

"So I'm allowed to use this room for now without a contract? Or promotion?" She knew there would a price, and waited.

"Your little adventure, your own decisions," Sandy reiterated softly. "You decide what information you want to sell to us, and if it brings us big profits, I assure you, your next paycheck will be a lot fatter. Okay?"

Grace nodded, and changed the subject. She'd suddenly found a whole new way to play Save-A-Nun. "Sandra, is there any way to access maps of important buildings and parking lots in our databases?"

Sandra considered for a moment. "Yes," she replied, speculation in her voice. "We do have floor plans and blueprints of the parking lot and surrounding area of the convention center."

A silent communication passed between the two women, and they smiled at each other.

"Thank you," Grace quietly said.

The older woman nodded and said, "Be careful," before closing the door behind her.

Grace hugged the copy of Beaucoup to her chest, surveying her new playroom. Making money through information. Her father would be amused at her accomplishments, then frowned when she thought about her plans for tomorrow night. No, he would probably be quite angry with her. She sighed. So would Lance. Her lips twisted derisively. He could always be her client, but somehow, she knew deep down she would end up paying the price. He'd gotten under her skin. She actually felt foolishly guilty she was doing things behind his back. She rubbed her chin on the top of the magazine as she wondered how a ghost would give out information when recorders were gagged by confidentiality and sworn to secrecy about their work.

Hmm. Didn't ghosts leave clues? Chains clanging, mysterious footsteps, doors opening and closing without aid. A GNE ghost would find a way to let her favorite agent get the info. A snicker escaped her. She could always moan.

CHAPTER THIRTEEN

Tuesday night

Grace took in a deep breath. Time to put her game face on. She fingered a few loose tendrils, took a step back from the mirror, and twirled around. She felt prepared. She'd chosen this particular outfit because it would be easy to tuck into the workout stretch-pants she'd managed to squeeze into her purse, a black beaded sack with a surprising depth, yet looked sophisticated and fashionable. Lying within were her little pants, a pair of plastic gloves, a two-headed screwdriver, a small mirror, and the four magnetic strips she'd taken off her refrigerator.

Not exactly a lady's toilette, she grinned at her reflection. It was a risky plan she'd decided to undertake, but she knew she could do it. She had studied the blueprints and plans, cased out the convention center when she drove by that morning. After work, she'd parked her car close by and took a cab home. Everything she needed was in place. Now, everything else had to play out accordingly.

She stared at herself in the mirror, her face solemn as she critically examined her features. She looked…pretty damn good. Like a woman out with a hot date. Like a woman planning to make that hot date all hot too. Nope, not a thought about locating imprisoned male nuns was going through this young lady's head.

She peered closer, looking critically to make sure none of her apprehension showed outwardly. Fear, her father had said, was normal. Concentrating within, she crushed the nugget of fear, telling herself she could do this. It'd been five years since she felt this pumping, heart-churning feeling. She had missed it—the fear, the anticipation, the power of adrenaline. A moment later, she looked outward again, and was satisfied at the confidence in her eyes.

The doorbell rang. He was here. Her heart rate increased again, remembering his hard body against hers. She had missed him and couldn't squelch the irritation that came with it. It wasn't possible to miss someone whom she'd just met, damn it. But then, she'd never met someone with whom she felt so familiar so soon, like she'd known him for a long time. Something about his eyes stirred a dark yearning in her. Something about his possessive behavior shook her insides even when her intellect rebelled against it. He was a disturbing man, with disturbingly exciting intentions.

Her breath caught at the sight of Lance in evening attire. Tall and impossibly handsome, he exuded enough sexual magnetism to make her break into a sweat. He was nothing like anyone she'd ever dated, and therein, she told herself, laid the challenge. His blue eyes swept appreciatively over her slender curves revealed by the figure-hugging dress and traveled down the length of her legs.

"How did you get into that outfit?" he asked, stepping into the apartment. Christ. Another long, hard evening ahead. If it weren't for the operation, he would abandon the idea of a night out and just lock the door behind him, tear off that flimsy thing she called a dress, drag her into the bedroom, wrap those legs around his waist, and have her squirming under him. For the rest of the night. Hell, the next day too. Did she know what she was doing to him, looking like that? The dark maroon number stretched like a glove over her well-toned body. The simple plunging neckline and long sleeves gave him visions of tangling fingers drawing his head closer to explore the rounded curves of her cleavage. Her legs were perfect, tempting in tinted dark hose. He wanted to stroke her all over.

"I wrapped a wet swath of nylon and satin around my oiled body and hand-stitched it on. Then I had to blow dry the material slowly to get the wrinkles out," Grace told him solemnly.

Lance grinned. "Well, in that case, I'd better enjoy this privately for a few minutes." He sat down with an expectant expression, like a man inspecting goods. Giving a leer, he demanded, "Let's see the back."

She positioned her arms like a model and did a catwalk jiggle, slowly pirouetting in front of him, twitching her bottom teasingly when she turned to show him her back, which was also revealingly low.

His cock rose to the occasion, and he muttered a soft curse. "What do you have underneath?"

She turned back to face him, her hands on her hips. "A few drops of my favorite perfume. Like it?" She daringly stepped closer. "It's called Man-eater." She bit the inside of her cheek to keep from laughing.

She was her usual playful self, but he fancied a tension about her, a certain springy excitement. Behind her dark brown eyes lurked secrets that irked him because she wouldn't share them with him. Whatever it was, she exuded a cagey sexiness, the kind of signal that challenged any male within scenting distance. It was going to be a hell of a long night.

"I want to kiss you," he told her, lust making his voice a growling rumble, "but I don't want to mess up your makeup and hairdo. Give me a kiss."

"I thought you'd never ask."

Grace sat down on his lap, wrapped her arms around his neck and planted her lips on his. She kissed him softly, gently nibbling his lower lip and sliding her tongue in to meet his, dizzy with delight to touch him again. He sat there patiently as she explored his mouth, neither passive nor taking charge, just very controlled, subtly changing the kiss when he captured her tongue and sucked on it. Then it was his turn to invade her mouth.

Minutes could have been hours for all Grace cared. There was only texture and taste, his and hers mingled, a tender sharing of mindlessness. He seemed to draw her very soul out of her mouth, stripping away everything, until she was nothing but a quivering mass of need. Panting slightly, she laid her forehead against his. She couldn't deny it any longer. Every part of her wanted him, no matter how hard she fought the yearning.

Later," he promised, his voice a little unsteady and husky with passion. "Go put on your lipstick while I put these in the fridge."

She hadn't noticed the bottles he had brought in. "More wine? You're going to ply me with more wine?"

Lance shook his head. "Champagne," he said, "to celebrate after we get our lost nun."

She stood up, turning away slightly so he couldn't read her face. "You must be confident about getting the poor man back."

"We have the groups involved meeting tonight. We have the possible venue of exchange and a source even has the room number," he told her, his eyes watchful. She was certainly hiding something tonight. That nervous energy he felt was caused by something other than sexual excitement.

"You sound very sure," she said, taking out her lipstick.

He went to put away the champagne. "Something's going to happen tonight," he assured her. "You'll act as we agreed, Grace. Don't get in the way."

Grace always tried to be honest. "Of course," she agreed. "You won't even see me anywhere near you when you're face to face with the bad guys." She considered informing him of her suspicions, but what if she were wrong? No, she would do this her way. He had, after all, told her in no uncertain terms that he didn't need her help. Let him buy the information from GNE, and it would serve him right if she made a little money off his agency. Maybe she would give him a hint. Later.

"Check out the aides with the senator," Lance repeated his instructions. "See which one was also at the other function."

"Yes." She nodded and picked up her evening bag, hooking it over her shoulder, almost grinning with satisfaction at the weight from her little cache inside. "I'll do that and maybe a little more. You never know, I might even find out where your scholar is without any need of you dashing around the convention center." *There, that's hint number one, darling. Let's see whether you will ask politely.*

She looked so serious that for a moment, he almost believed her, but her eyes had a devilish glint. She must be teasing him. "Let's go." He put a hand on the small of her back. "For God's sake, Grace, show some fear, hmm? It might make you more cautious."

She locked the door. "Don't worry," she smiled mysteriously, "I can take care of myself."

"I told you this isn't cops and robbers—"

"Look, make up your mind," she interrupted, her voice like a patient teacher, "either I'm what you think I am, therefore I should know exactly what the dangers are, or, I'm a naïve innocent bystander, therefore I've no idea what you're talking about half the time. You can't treat me one way when it suits you, and another at other times."

Lance unlocked his car, helping her in. After he got in and secured his seatbelt, he said, "You told me the other night not to assume anything about you."

"That's right," she said, looking out of the window. She shouldn't have warned him, shouldn't have alerted that quick mind of his.

"You don't care to elaborate." He chose to be rhetorical, knowing she would be evasive again.

Grace turned and gave him an accusing stare. "You don't trust me, Lance, so why should I trust you?"

His face turned brooding, hers defiant. He understood she had scored a point; she knew her point would always be a matter of contention between them. He still wanted her in spite of her secretiveness; she mulled over her weakness, wondering if she could stop before it was too late. A heavy silence hung between them all the way to the Center, each reviewing their own evening's timetable.

By the time they arrived, there was already a crowd at the function. The Washington elite had shown up in full regalia for the Charity Invitational. The conventional guests were ushered by doormen to the public parking lot; the political guests were given security clearance stickers once their invitations were confirmed, and they drove to the rear secured parking lot. Grace had already memorized the locations from the maps she printed from the computer. No problem with getting around. Her only obstacle was to figure out how to slip in and out of the parking lot without her own security clearance card.

Excitement coursed through her as she surveyed the fashionably late crowd, recognizing many famous faces. She tensed when Lance gripped her lightly below the elbow.

"Why are you so nervous?" he murmured. She stood out among the guests, with her exotic mix of pretty almond-shaped eyes and soft, shapely lips emphasized by the small stubborn dimple beneath her lower lip. The figure-hugging dress was catching interested glances from the opposite sex, but she seemed self-absorbed tonight, her gaze darting around. She reminded him of a wary kitten left outside for the first time, sniffing at the different smells in the air.

"I'm not nervous. I'm just excited. I've never seen so many important people in one place. What do we do before..." she consulted the schedule in her invitation, "before the senator's speech?"

Grace was guessing everything would be normal until probably after the "surprise" guests' arrival and exit. The media should go a little crazier than usual with the sudden appearance of the Chinese ambassador and his contingent bearing gifts for good causes. While they were making their speeches and unveiling their donations, she would make her move for the secured parking. She looked at Lance from under her long lashes. Let's hope he wouldn't get too angry when she eluded him again.

"Mingle," he replied. "Separate, then come back together. I want to know where you are at all times."

"Even if I've to go to the bathroom?" she mocked.

"Yes," he said, gazing intently at her. "It's for your safety, so you won't be in harm's way."

She made an unlady-like sound. The man didn't want her sneaking off. She gave an artless shrug. "You're the boss."

Lance frowned. How come every time she gave a vague response, he had this odd feeling she was trying one of her evasive tactics? Did she have something up her sleeve? She had better follow every instruction he gave her. He had ordered a man stationed at every exit, and an extra one outside Room 103. Even the doorman was his own, instructed to put a tracking device on the good senator and the two aides Grace had recognized. He'd told Dan to instruct Charlie and the few others who worked undercover to keep an eye on those two. Lastly, the usher who opened the car doors was his only secret from everyone else. Some information must always be kept apart, he knew from experience, in case of further leaks. Every vehicle that came with the Chinese retinue would be tracked by a micro-device hooked to monitors in a van up the street, to pinpoint exactly where they were taking their scholar, once they had him.

Homeland Security had cooperated fully by supplying manpower and gadgets in exchange for the information of senator names involved with the Chinese vote-buying scheme. Lance had smiled cynically when he heard about their little payoff here. The agency wanted its own little glory in the adventure, too. Since that list was secondary to what Command was really after, he'd told Dan to inform them it was theirs, if the operation proved successful.

The window of opportunity to get the scholar alive was becoming smaller. If they didn't retrieve him tonight, Lance would have to track him alone and wrest him out of the hands of the Beijing Butcher. That shouldn't be too difficult a task, but he doubted the poor man's condition would be worth much once in the Butcher's hands. For his sake, the rescue better be before that.

He watched with interest as Grace moved around the growing crowd, stopping to talk to a few people he recognized were at the function where he'd first seen her. How long ago that seemed. Except for yesterday, they'd been together almost every day since. Yesterday, without her smart aleck comments, was strangely lacking something. A loner, he wasn't prepared by the need to see her, to touch her. It was definitely unnerving and unhealthy to his mind and frustrated libido. He let out a breath of frustration. That was all he needed, a loaded weapon in his pants while tracking after the Butcher with a loaded weapon in his hand. He looked at that glorious little body of hers again. He'd had to have her soon, to regain his concentration as well as peace of mind. Turning abruptly, he headed toward Senator Richards to play his role of supporter.

Grace checked out some of the exits, catching sight of the few men hovering at each point. This wasn't going to be easy. They were surreptitious, hardly noticeable, but her trained eyes noticed little things. Not all were operatives, though. Some looked a tad too uncomfortable in their new suits and ties. Must be their new shiny shoes hurting their toes. The thought made her grin as she watched one of them shift his weight from foot to foot. If not agents— cops? No, COS Command would never involve hometown cops. Well, she would choose the exit with the non-COS guards; they wouldn't even notice her. Absent-mindedly, she patted her beaded shoulder bag.

"Miss O'Connor!"

Turning, she found Charlie Bines walking to meet her. "Hey!" she greeted, smiling, genuinely pleased to see him. "I was starting to feel quite lost among the elite. How are you?"

"Better, now that I found you," he gallantly replied, looking her up and down with male admiration. "You look sensational."

"Thank you."

"Mr. Mercy is a lucky guy," Charlie went on. "I hope you're still going to let me show you around Capitol Hill soon."

"Of course!" Grace said. "I would like you to."

"You mean it?" His pleasure lit up his quiet face. There was something boyishly appealing about him, a certain shyness. "You aren't just being polite, are you?"

"Don't be silly, of course I meant it!" Grace linked her hand into the crook of his arm as he guided her through the crowd. "It would be wonderful to see D.C. and Capitol Hill. Everybody else treats me like a doll. They forget I'm here to learn, too." *Hey, Lance was paying her to gush, so gush she would.*

"Let's do something then," Charlie said, looking pleased. "May I call you in a couple of days? I'll take you away from the touristy routes and show you some behind-the-scenes stuff."

"Great!" That was exactly what she wanted. "Too crowded in the summer for touristy stuff, anyway."

"You're right, and too many rallies."

"Don't even talk about rallies. The last one I went to had a bomb scare. People are acting so crazy these days." She stopped a passing waiter to pick up a glass of what she hoped was punch. "It was even on TV last week. Did you see it?"

"Oh, that one." He frowned. "I hope that you weren't trampled or hurt. I read there was a record crowd that day. You should be careful about these things, Grace. D.C. can be dangerous place. Next time you want to attend a rally, take me with you."

Grace had to smile at the offer. The man was really rather sweet. "I'll call you whenever I get the urge," she teased, and they both laughed.

"The urge to do what, sweetheart?" Lance appeared out of nowhere, drawing her to his side. He nodded briefly at Charlie. "We've met before. Bines, right?"

"Yes, sir," Charlie said, offering a handshake. "It's been great helping out with your trade committee. The senator is very dedicated to his work."

The man was very convincing, Lance observed. He could go far at Command. "Glad to see everything is doing well," he agreed. "The sooner the details are ironed out, the better."

Grace took a step, deliberately moving away from Lance. This was the second time he'd done that to her, interrupting her conversation with Charlie. She had a feeling he didn't like her with the younger man. Well, too bad. She liked talking to him. "Excuse me, I need to look for the ladies' room. I'll see you later, Charlie." She slipped away, ignoring the narrowed gaze of her date.

Lance believed in choices. Some, he opined, were made for one already. When he held Grace captive under him that night he'd surprised her, he'd had several choices—force, kill, or seduce her. He had chosen seduction. Tonight, watching her with another man, he'd picked another option, to make Grace his, and his alone. Imprinting through seduction wasn't playing fair, but he was tired of sharing her, this woman who attracted men like flies to a ripened succulent fruit. He wasn't much into sharing.

She looked ravishing, even while running away from him. The way her too observant eyes sneaked peeks around the banquet room aroused him. The way light reflected off her rich dark mop of hair excited him. Hell, the way she moved, with that odd little bounce in her step, turned him on.

He had wanted to seduce her before, and had been doing it step-by-step, but watching her tonight, he knew that it wouldn't be enough. Something about her made him feel possessive, like a hunter after a prized animal. He wanted her marked, so that others would know she'd been taken. No, seduction wouldn't do at all.

Grace didn't know it, but she just had a choice made for her. She would be his.

She had almost made it across the room before he caught up with her. Still ignoring him, she headed for the restroom.

"What were you talking about?" he asked, keeping in step with her.

She glanced sideways and shrugged. "Nothing important."

"Tell me," he insisted.

"It was nothing important," she repeated, looking guarded. "It had nothing to do with work."

Lance didn't like that answer at all. There were many ways to gain the trust of someone like Grace, one of which was through insidious friendliness, something Charlie Bines appeared to amply project. He understood the younger man was just doing his job, collecting information from anyone who was close to the Chinese deal, and since Grace appeared to be dating the deputy advisor of the Council for Asian Trade, it was only logical to target her. But the fact that he was actually succeeding angered Lance. He didn't want her to like the undercover operative, didn't want her getting interested in anyone else except him.

"Did I tell you that you look beautiful tonight?" He changed the subject, lowering his voice. He banked down the fiery need that kicked in every time he was near her.

Grace paused in mid-stride, then swirled to face him. "No," she said softly, her eyes a melting chocolate brown. "Do you think so?"

"Radiantly so," he told her, taking her hand and raising it to his lips, a gesture both sensual and possessive. "Where are you running to this time?"

"I'm flattered I caught your attention." Her smile was shy, but her eyes were bold. "Why do you keep restricting me?"

He turned her hand over and placed a light kiss on her wrist, the tip of his tongue touching her pulse, enjoying the betraying jerk. "You're going to get my full attention later," he promised, feeling her quickening pulse, then moved in for the kill. "What do you know about Room 103?"

It was just a flick of his tongue, but Grace felt the fire of his promise down to her toes. He was on the attack again, she warned herself, even as she shivered with delight when his thumb stroked the inside of her wrist.

"I might be too busy later," she said, a little breathlessly. After all, she had a man to rescue. Recklessly, she added, "trying to find Room 103."

His brows came together, then smoothed back. "A beautiful woman like you," he said, ever so softly, "shouldn't look for trouble. Besides, how are you going to do that when you promised to stay out of the way?"

She smiled and withdrew her hand. He let her go, studying her carefully. "Haven't you heard?" she insouciantly asked. "Grace happens whenever there is trouble. Don't worry darling, we're looking for two entirely different things. You do what you have to do. You won't see me, I promise. Now, I really need to use the ladies' room."

She nodded to him as if she was a queen imperiously dismissing her knight, then turned and headed toward the restroom. Thoughtfully, Lance eyed her bare back, suspicion suddenly flashing bright red. He wished he could read her mind as well as he could read her emotions. He stalked off, instincts on alert mode.

CHAPTER FOURTEEN

In the dark, Grace knew her maroon top would blend in. She tucked the skirt into her capris, impatiently pulling off her heels and hiding them nearby. She quietly moved among the shrubs and walls. She passed her obstacles like a shadow, her stocking feet noiseless, moving into the cordoned-off area.

Voices approached. She crawled on her belly under her target car.

"Everything's taken care of, keys in, everything," one voice spoke quietly.

"Good. I don't want anyone to see you escorting them to the car. Too suspicious. Let their driver see it, then walk away, like the vehicle is part of their group. You don't have to say anything. They know which car to take, since they have used it before," another voice said.

"No one will notice. I've parked them less than ten feet away from theirs."

"Good," came the other voice again. "I just don't want to be anywhere near these vehicles when they take off. They've sent the Big Cat to sniff me out, and you'd better make a disappearing act at the end of the speeches too, know what I mean?"

Grace stiffened at the mention of 'Big Cat.' The man speaking must be the double agent. The rat, as Fat Joe called him. If only she could peek out from under the car.

"Who is the Big Cat?" the first voice asked.

"If I know, do you think I would be trying to conceal myself instead of canceling him?" demanded the second man, the one who seemed in charge. His voice, although low, was clipped and cold, giving Grace the shivers. "For all I know, he already knows about me and who I am."

"But you're sure he's around?"

"Believe me, that guy in there wouldn't be mumbling Big Cat's name over and over if he wasn't meeting him that afternoon. One day, I'll find out who he is, then I'll give the info to the other agencies. I know there are several who would be glad to have him as their personal guest."

Grace clenched her hands as she stared intently at the pair of shoes planted a few feet away from her face. She wished she could see who these two men were.

"Yeah, but let's not stand here too long. The speech ought to be done in five minutes or so and we'll give them an extra five for handshakes and photos. Then you lead the driver here, and he'll pick up General Wang to make it look like it's part of the entourage. I'll go make sure the guard lets them out with no questions."

"Right."

As their footsteps disappeared, Grace cautiously crawled out from under her hiding place. The two cars she'd seen parked outside Senator James' were side by side, with the back facing out to the driving lane. She double-checked the license plate, just to be sure. 103. She tapped lightly on the trunk, but no sound came from within. Knowing she didn't have much time to prove her theory, she moved to the front of the car, hiding in the protected shadows of the wall, and took out her screwdriver. The plates, to her relief, came off easily, and she crawled to the vehicle beside it and proceeded to do the same thing. Not wanting to risk being seen squatting in the driving lane, she slid underneath 103 again, pulling her beaded bag along with her. Taking out her mirror, she pushed upward on her back until she reached the rear of the car. She snaked her hand out, holding the mirror to check she had the right car.

Checking left and right to make sure no one was walking down the aisle, she then quickly plastered two magnetic strips onto the license plate. With a click, the stolen plate from the car next to it snapped into place. She used the mirror to adjust and straighten it.

Then she rolled out and went under the other vehicle and did the same thing. She could hear footsteps and people talking in the aisle. Hurriedly, she scooted out again, rolling and crawling as she made a quick escape. She smiled grimly. Part one of her plan was completed. The cars had been exchanged.

***

Inside the Convention center, it was getting quite obvious to Lance his date was not mingling or watching the new arrivals.

"Where is she?" he muttered, as Senator Richards introduced the surprise guests and revealed their significant donation that would help the worthy causes sponsored by the Charity Invitational.

The tiny electronic insert in his ear responded, "Can't see her in our cameras, sir."

"Check the exits. Did anyone see her?"

A few moments later, the voice answered, "North Exit, negative. West Exit, she passed him ten minutes ago. South Exit, thought he saw her."

"What do you mean, thought he saw her?"

Silence. The Chinese representative on stage beamed at the cameras, gesturing at the carved dragon to be auctioned off.

"South Exit reported he saw her standing near the restroom, but she must have gone in there because he didn't see her move from the spot."

Lance's face hardened. She'd done it again, and in front of three COS and CIA operatives. He should have stuck a tracking device on her. Dammit, if she got in the way—he didn't know what the hell he was going to do. But he couldn't worry about her right now.

"Are all tracking devices activated?" he asked softly, moving toward the banquet table, as if to get a drink. Most of the guests' attention was on the stage area.

"Affirmative. Ambassador vehicle number one, tagged green. Vehicle number two, tagged green."

He continued, his eyes on the ambassador and his men, "I've tagged all three human targets when I shook hands. Activate." He sipped his champagne.

"Affirmative. Human targets, tagged green."

Well, at least he knew where the main cast of characters was at any given moment, Lance thought sourly. "Room 103, any activity?"

Silence. Lance lifted his glass again, smiling at some comments a guest directed to him. He moved closer to the stage area.

"No one. No one going in or out," came the reply. "No security in sight, sir."

Something was wrong. If there were to be an exchange, it should be done now, while the ambassador was on stage. There should be activity in the scheduled place. Where did they have the scholar?

Damn. Where the hell was Grace? What did she know?

***

Time was her enemy. Grace watched as the car with the planted "103" license plate started, then moved slowly down toward the back entrance of the center. After counting to twenty, she crawled toward the real vehicle, opening the driver's door wide enough to jam a hand in there to pop the trunk. Thank God the cars were parked here by ushers who left the vehicles unlocked for quick exits. Closing the door, she moved quietly to the rear and pushed the hood up.

Anticipation made her hand shake. Her brown eyes widened in triumph. Inside was a man gagged and tied. She needed to get him out before the Chinese representatives finished their visit. Before their people came out. She briefly wondered what Lance was doing at that moment.

***

Lance half-listened as the ambassador's speech ended, moving out of the way as the media crowded in for photos and questions. The ambassador and his group stayed for another ten minutes then regretfully bade goodnight, not being able to stay for "the rest of the wonderful affair."

"No activity," the voice coming from his earpiece kept repeating. Room 103 was a dead end. Wrong information from your source, Dan. Lance hid his disgust as he calmly shook hands with the leaving diplomats, murmuring about looking forward to seeing them soon. Mr. Wang looked at him strangely, but Lance knew he couldn't recognize him from the last time they had met. That was four years ago, on a recon mission in Cambodia. He had long hair, sported a beard, and was covered in dirt then. Now, Lance took a perverse delight in tempting fate, meeting the Beijing Butcher's unreadable eyes with deliberate blandness.

***

Grace freed the man from the ropes and gag. He looked totally out of it. She could barely hold him up. The poor thing had obviously been tortured and drugged.

"It's me, recognize me?" She held his face as he tried to focus on her.

"Big Cat. Big Cat," he groaned in a hoarse whisper.

She hadn't the time to explain. "Yes, Big Cat," she said, reverting to Chinese. "You have got to come with me. Try to walk, David. Hurry."

God, he was heavy. She realized they weren't going to make it before someone came along to take the other VIP cars around them. She had to get the both of them out of the way for now. Her weightlifting was coming in handy.

***

Things were simply not going his way. Lance's gut feeling was to run out the back exit and wrench open the ambassador's limousine. Something was happening somewhere. And he knew, just knew, that Grace, his trouble in human form, was there in the midst of it all.

You won't even see me when you're after the guy. Didn't she hint to him about what she was intending to do? Her last few sentences kept coming back: *I'll find your nun for you while you're dashing around the convention center...*

He halted. She did try to tell him something else. What was it— they were looking for two different things. *Two different things.*

Her clue. He walked faster past Room 103 to another exit that also led to the rear parking lot. Dan stood waiting with a flak jacket, his gear and hood.

171

"Forget Room 103," Lance barked. He tore his jacket off, still talking to the hidden wire on him. "Check targets. Where are the human targets?"

"At stated exit. Check one, check two, check three, affirmative," the voice in his ear said in a calm monotone.

He unbuttoned his shirt, removed his pants, and donned the items handed to him. "Check vehicle targets." His mind was already picturing the parking area.

"All check green. Check one, check two, affirmative."

"What are they doing now?" The flak jacket cosseted his chest.

"Human targets getting in target vehicles."

Damn. "Where is the senator?"

"In banquet hall, all target aides in banquet hall."

His mind swerved back to the parking lot. Where was the damned exchange? "Go on."

"Human targets in vehicles. One human target in unmarked vehicle."

Lance broke into a run, pulling his hood on. "That's the one. Check outside. Confirm vehicle."

A few seconds later, "Unmarked vehicle unknown origin. No government plate. Leaving parking area with tagged one and tagged two."

"Car license plate?" Lance questioned calmly as he reached the waiting unmarked armored van at the end of the passage.

The door opened. He climbed in, hood secured. The four men inside saluted. Dan Kershaw followed. Lance glanced up at the screens in the vehicle and found it

"I'll be damned," he said, his voice soft and dangerous. The camera caught the leaving vehicle's license plate—103 was part of it. "She fucking knew."

She'd given him enough clues all along, and he hadn't paid attention.

"She?" queried Dan.

Lance gave an impatient wave. Turning to the man at the wheel, he ordered, "Move. I want that car."

"Yes, sir."

The chase was on. Lance barked more orders, instructing other armored vehicles in the vicinity, his eyes intent on the car shown on the screen. The Chinese contingent was one block ahead. He was going to get them.

Damn her, where the hell was she?

CHAPTER FIFTEEN

Grace waited until all the cars disappeared from sight, then counted the moving vehicles in obvious pursuit. She smiled. Bingo. Lance must have finally figured out her hint about Room 103. She'd begun to wonder about that thick head of his. Goodness, four truckloads. Were they trying to have a street war? She shook her head. Men loved to make a big noise. Something to do with pounding the chest. Or roaring ferociously. It's all about territory, this male thing.

Putting the car into gear, she drove back into the convention parking area, turning to the secured parking lot. The guard came out of the guardhouse, looked at the clearance tag she had stolen from Lance's BMW and waved her through. Smiling, she cautiously drove past the crowd at the back exit, hoping to be unnoticed. There were several people she recognized, including Charlie Bines. Obviously they had just escorted the Chinese representatives to their vehicles. She wondered who had gotten into the fake car.

She left the motor running and hurried to the semi-conscious man she'd left hidden, propped against a wall. She was worried about him; he was incoherent, and hardly able to stand up, repeatedly chanting 'Big Cat, Big Cat' like a prayer. She had to get some medical help fast.

***

174

Lance kept his eyes on the screen as they converged toward the cars they were following. "Call all units. I want them to B.O.L.O* for police vehicles. We don't need them between us yet," he ordered calmly. His mind was moving at a rapid rate as he planned his moves.

"Yes, sir."

The two armored vehicles sped behind the three cars ahead of them, then moved to overtake them when they reached a three-lane wide road, trapping the car with the 103 tag between the four of them, two on each side, one in front, and one at the back. The target car had no choice but to follow wherever the lead vehicle was going. The two vehicles in front immediately pulled over.

***

Stopping at a lit up street corner, Grace hurriedly checked on her passenger. "David! David!" She lightly slapped him, trying to wake him. His eyes opened, unfocused. She spoke to him in Chinese. "Wake up, David!"

His drugged state worried her. The bruises on his face hinted on hours of torture. She couldn't take him to a hospital, knowing he would end back in the hands of those who hurt him.

"Big Cat," he kept muttering.

"Yes, you're safe," she told him, trying to calm him down. "I know the Big Cat. You're going to be okay."

David Cheng struggled to understand. He heard someone telling him he was safe with the Big Cat. He fought against the wave of pain and nausea, pulling hard at the arms that held him. He had kept on repeating the name to suppress the pain and the drug, until he'd fainted from the effort. This person pulled him out of the car. He must tell them what he knew. Got to.

"Jeeah Lee," he whispered hoarsely, trying to form a sentence through his swollen lips. "Jeeah...jeeah lee..."

"What?" Grace ignored the pain shooting up her arm he was grabbing like a drowning man. "What did you say? What did they poison you with, David, do you know?"

---

* Be On Look Out, tactical term

Poison. David Cheng knew he was going to die. Can't. Not yet. Must tell.

He lifted his hand, stuffed his fingers into his mouth, groaning in pain.

"What are you doing?" Grace exclaimed. David looked like he was trying to gag himself. When she forcibly pulled his hand away from his face, she found blood dribbling at the corner of his lips.

"Jeeah lee!" His eyes suddenly cleared and focused on her. He gripped her arm again.

"Yes, yes, Jia li," she repeated, trying to placate him. Must be a code. "Big Cat will know about Jia li, Okay?"

David Cheng sighed, then opened the hand he'd pushed into his mouth. He had no choice. He was going to die. "Take this," he rasped out, saliva mixed with blood spilling out of his mouth. He unclenched the hand under Grace's face before darkness took over.

***

In the darkened parking lot of an abandoned building, the target sat in silence with headlights still on. The four armored vehicles surrounding it turned on their mega-wattage lights attached to their roofs. Lance opened the door and stepped out, his hood tight against his face. He gave the signal. Similarly hooded agents jumped out of the vehicles and surrounded the car, taking their positions.

Dan came forward with a loudspeaker. "Come out with your hands up. We don't wish any confrontation."

The car door slowly opened. "Diplomatic immunity," an accented voice yelled.

Lance took the loudspeaker from Dan. "You have it. Come on out. All of you." He hoped in his heart Grace wasn't in there with them. He didn't think so, but…

The doors swung open. Every operative trained his weapon at the car. Three figures emerged—all males—and Lance recognized one of them as the Beijing Butcher. Slowly, he advanced toward the surrounded men. They appeared unarmed, one of them holding some kind of beverage, as if they were celebrating in the vehicle. Out of the corner of his eye, he saw the other two Chinese diplomatic cars parked close by, watching the whole scene.

"I demand to know who is in charge," the Beijing Butcher, a.k.a. General Wang, said, his voice filled with cold fury.

"I am." Dan Kershaw stepped forward.

The general only gave him the barest of attention, then turned and glared at Lance. "And who are you people?" he demanded. "This is illegal. We are given diplomatic immunity and are not subjected to your tactics."

"You're free to leave," Lance told him, his voice muffled through the hood.

The older man hesitated, then said, "I still demand to know the reason behind this outrageous behavior. I will cite a complaint to your government for accosting me in my car."

"We apologize for the inconvenience, Mr. Wang," Dan calmly cut in. "For some reason, you're not in a diplomatic car registered to the Chinese government. Allow us to escort you to your waiting friends. I'm sure they're concerned about you."

Wang continued eyeing Lance. Then he shrugged, and nodded to his two men. They walked toward the two waiting vehicles, escorted by two of the masked agents. Giving one last look, the Butcher got into one of the cars. Lance watched them drive away, frowning.

Beside him, Dan ordered, "Open the car trunk."

Too easy, Lance thought.

"Yes, sir!" One of the men moved toward the abandoned vehicle.

Too willing. He didn't like the feeling creeping up on him. Too damned easy. Suspicion ricocheted through his tracker-trained mind the moment he noticed the bottle left on the trunk of the car.

"No!" Lance shouted and uncoiled into a leap, using his momentum to push the man to the ground and rolling with him away from the vehicle.

The car exploded into flames in astonishing silence. There was just a sound similar to opening a roaring oven, and the heat that ensued dropped everyone to the ground. Lance recognized it; he'd seen it before a year ago. A newly developed flame bomb, it was designed for small spaces and especially to be used not to cause damage to the surroundings. It was the new tool for arsonists to use to start a quick fire.

The place became a pandemonium of action. Lance sat up, watching his men extinguish the fire. Grimly, he walked toward the damaged car. It didn't look like his scholar survived after all.

***

"*Aiyah*, Grace, what a surprise!" Fat Joe opened the back entrance to the restaurant.

"I need you to come with me, Fatt Choy," Grace said, tugging at his dirty apron.

Sensing her urgency, he followed immediately and caught his breath when he saw the reclining man in her back seat. Checking his pulse, he asked, "Does the Big Cat know?"

She shook her head. "I only brought him here because of his condition. Can't take him to the hospital. I figure you can get hold of Lance for me."

"Why don't you hand him over yourself?" Fat Joe got into the car, adjusting the driver's seat to fit his wider body.

After a moment's hesitation, Grace got into the passenger's seat. "I'm not supposed to be interfering. I'm," she gestured helplessly, "ah, a ghost."

She hoped he understood. He cocked his head.

"I see." He nodded, driving down back alleys. "Non-aligns." He looked at her with new interest. "I did think you were somehow different. Guess I was right. Why did you come to me, little ghost?"

He smiled at her. Beyond a mere lift of a brow, he didn't register much surprise.

"You know the nuns," Grace pointed out, then impishly added, "and looked good with him that day too."

Fat Joe laughed. "Now I really know you're a ghost. You have the eyes of one."

"Fatt Choy? Don't mention how you got him."

"I understand. Anything else?"

"Yes. Tell him David's been chanting two things before he passed out. He kept saying 'Big Cat' and something that sounded like 'home' in Chinese."

"Home?"

"He kept saying 'jia li' or 'jeeah li,'" she explained. "It was rather garbled, but it sounded like 'home' in Chinese."

"I'll tell him. Jia li," Fat Joe repeated. He looked at the inert body of the scholar in the rearview mirror. "I wonder what that means."

"I assume that's code of some sort. Maybe Lance will know."

The car slowed. "You're too young for this kind of game, little ghost," Fat Joe told her as he stopped the car. "Lance will have my hide if he knows. You're going to get me in trouble."

Grace turned and grinned at him in the dimly lit alley. "Distract him. Cook him something good to eat."

Fat Joe grinned back.

***

"There's nobody in the trunk, sir!" the man stated the obvious.

"They tricked us!" Dan stared at the burned out shell.

"No." Lance got on his haunches, looking at the back of the car intently. He picked up some metallic remnant, turning it over in the light. The dangling license plate in front of him caught his attention. He made a sound of disgust, and added, "They were tricked."

Dan squatted down, grunting as his knees protested. Leaning closer, he examined the dangling plate and discovered what Lance saw. License plate with 103 was partially covering another plate. The flame bomb had loosened whatever held the fake plate in place.

"Obviously," Dan remarked, "the perp didn't have time to change the license plates properly, which," he glanced at Lance, his eyes watchful, "rules out the senator's men. They would have attached the fake plate more permanently."

Lance pulled at the plate and it came off easily. Turning it over, he removed the attached magnetic strip, which was identical to the one he'd just picked up. He scowled behind his hood, feeling the material stretching against his face.

"Damn," he uttered, and added several other stronger expletives. In the distance, police sirens sounded.

"You have to go before the cops get here," Dan said, getting up slowly. "I'll take care of the locals and Homeland. Do you have any idea who's behind this?"

Lance pocketed the strips. "I'll take care of it," he said, temper straining his voice. He'd opened a certain refrigerator enough times to recognize those magnetic strips.

CHAPTER SIXTEEN

Grace pulled up at her apartment around midnight. Nice job, she mentally patted herself on the back. She had saved the scholar from the stupid senator and the evil Chinese dudes, and he would be with Lance's people in a matter of hours. Hopefully, they would take care of him. She frowned. If they didn't, she had—she groped for and touched what the scholar gave her before he fainted—these. She'd carefully wrapped them in tissue paper. When she got back to her place, she'd better handle them with better care.

She stepped out of her car. Ugh, she must look a sight from all that crawling around. She knew her hair must be mussed up, her dress was partially torn where she'd snagged it somewhere, and there was dirt smeared all over her hose. Grinning, she imagined herself looking like she'd been rolling on the ground with her date.

She gave a small shriek of alarm when a dark shadow suddenly loomed before her and grabbed her by the shoulders. Under the soft building lights, she caught a glimpse of cold blue eyes and a mane of dark blond hair before her lips were bruisingly captured. Struggling from surprise, she tried to pull from the big hands on her shoulders, but he only gathered her against his chest with brutal power. Her gasp from the impact allowed him to plunder the inside of her mouth, and he attacked angrily, his tongue punishing, his hands trapping her, his body pushing her against her car. Her neck snapped backward at the onslaught of his kiss.

Heat. It engulfed her whole being, burning recklessly through her defenses. She tasted rage and desire, knew she was irrevocably being shown who was in charge. In spite of the initial protests, she fiercely gave in to the storm of need that blanketed them both. Frantically moving closer, responding wildly, she tore at his shirtfront, even though he still held on to her tightly.

He demanded and she willingly surrendered. Almost.

"What in the hell is going on?" A furious and familiar voice shot out into the semi-darkness. Grace heard it over the crescendo of emotions and struggled to free herself. Her captor released her lips, but not the commanding hold of her body. She turned toward the voice and blanched.

Shit. Shit, shit, shit.

"Hell," she muttered through passion-swollen lips, blinking rapidly.

"Grace?" The voice called her name, full of questions, mixed with incredulity and anger.

"Grace?" Her tormentor repeated above her turned head, still not releasing her.

She tried to step out of his arms, but they tightened like a predator around a prey. If he had sharp enough teeth, she distractedly mused, he would probably sink them in her right now to claim his killing. She slowed her breathing, telling herself to remain calm. Actually, she wanted to laugh. Hysterically.

"Who is he?"

Both men synchronized their accusations, one indignantly, the other in mocking reference. She closed her eyes briefly.

"Tim," she managed to choke out, "wha...what are you doing here?"

"I told you I'd be here Tuesday night when I called." Her estranged boyfriend stepped closer, anger and hurt in his face. "And you changed the locks to the apartment. How come?"

Oh God, she had forgotten. She'd been—she glared up at amused blue eyes—preoccupied. "I ..." She coughed and Lance pounded her back with a cheerfulness that earned him another baleful glare.

"You better let my girlfriend go now," Tim interrupted, snapping like a vicious puppy, obviously not in the mood to be polite to someone who was stealing his property.

"I don't see the lady complaining," Lance smoothly pointed out, then looked at Grace. "Darling, you really shouldn't play with fire. You might get burned."

She realized he was punishing her. Behind his eyes lurked the deep blue of a murderous temper. She could handle Tim's anger, but she didn't think she could control Lance's. *Be indifferent or retaliate*, her crazy mind yelled out a solution. As if she had a choice.

Retaliate.

She let her anger simmer over. "Let me go," she said in as steady a voice as she could.

"Not quite yet," he countered, his own dangerously soft. "There is the matter of something you have that I want." His hold tightened even more. He amended, "Actually, more than one thing you have that I want."

"Grace, I want an explanation for this," Tim demanded, stepping even closer. He wasn't as tall as Lance, but he was a muscular young man, with incredible strength, and he wasn't afraid to use it. He was gauging the man holding his girlfriend.

Grace easily read Tim's mind. Oh-oh. Talk about being caught between a rock and a hard place. Strangely, she didn't feel much beyond the initial shock of seeing Tim. No remorse. No guilt. Only she was very sorry she had hurt him.

"I know," she said. She owed him at least an explanation. She looked up at Lance, "Please, let me go."

"Where's David Cheng?" Lance demanded instead.

She blinked. "David?"

"Don't play with me, woman," he warned. "I know you have him somewhere."

"Don't be silly, I was at the Conven..." She stopped at the sight of the magnetic strips he was dangling in front of her face. "Oh."

"Yours, I believe," he sneered. "I think I warrant an explanation too."

Stupid, she berated herself, you stupid, careless—

"Grace!" Tim grabbed her arm, frustrated that she wasn't paying him attention. "Come with me, right now!"

"No." Sandwiched between two muscular bodies, Grace heard Lance answer for her. "She has to come with me."

"The hell she will!" Tim pulled furiously.

Grace's feet stumbled one way, while her upper body, held prisoner by her other tormentor, stayed in the same position. Maybe they could explain to each other, she thought sarcastically. Before she could tell them both what she thought of their manhandling talents, a voice sounded from the balcony.

"Is something wrong?"

This time, Grace groaned aloud.

"Oh, it's you, Lance! And Tim!" Mary Tucker's honey lilt floated down toward the tense trio under her balcony. "Where's Grace? Oh, there you are!"

Tim ignored the newcomer, still insistently pulling at Grace's arm. "You come with me right now, or we're through, Grace! Do you hear me?"

"Let go, Lance." Grace tried to twist out of his arms. She needed to take control of this situation before it got any further out of hand.

"Not until you answer a few questions," Lance told her, his voice hard and cold. "You can have her back once I'm finished with her, young man." His tone was deliberately insolent, insulting.

"You can't have her. She'll stay here," Tim insisted stubbornly.

That was it. Her indignation exploded into outrage. "Nobody," she emphasized, her eyes flashing from one man to the other. "Nobody is going to have me. I'm not some piece of property one of you own." She struggled violently now, tugging at her imprisoned arm from one man, and jerking her upper body from the other. "Come on, I'm sick of being squashed by all this macho hot air."

"How romantic!" Mary Tucker clapped her hands from above. All three ignored her.

"Let her go or I'll—"

"You two insufferable idiots can—"

"You're coming with me—"

All three spoke at once, much to the delight of their audience of one. A car drove into the parking area, halting right next to them. Ignoring it, they continued their overlapped conversation, until the window rolled down, and Dan cut in.

"Lance!" There was amusement and shock in his voice.

"Not now," Lance grounded out, hauling Grace with him toward his car.

She felt like a rag doll being tossed around by two pitbulls as her arm was unceremoniously pulled out from one captor's grasp to become prisoner to another's unyielding hold. Tim wasn't going to stand there and quietly watch his girlfriend being spirited away. He slapped a muscular arm on Lance's neck to pull him back for a punch. She ducked. Lance loosened his hold of her, neatly blocking the swing, then twisting his arm behind his back in one quick smooth move.

Freed, Grace sprang away. Ignoring Tim's howls of pain and string of curses, she skipped up the stairs two at a time. Behind her, she heard the man in the car say, "Lance, Fat Joe contacted me. He said he's got something you want."

Lance didn't even pause, automatically pinning Tim against the hood of a nearby car. "Really." He looked up and called out, "I'll be back later, Grace."

She turned in mid-flight. "Don't bother," she yelled back. "You won't be welcomed."

"Grace!" Tim yelled from his position. "Grace!"

"You're not welcome either." She leaned over the balcony, standing next to the avid Mary Tucker. "Yes, I did get a new bolt for the door and it'll stay locked tonight. Both of you can hug each other down there, maybe explain to each other that no, no, you don't actually own anyone by the name of Grace. You can even kiss and make up, then go home and play with your stupid toys." She wasn't really making sense, but who cared? She was angry and didn't appreciate Mary Tucker witnessing her being mauled by two stupid beasts. Men. And this wasn't even their domain, damn it! It was her apartment building, *her* place.

"You're going to be sorry for this!" Tim started ranting, something she had never thought him capable of. Sweet, easy-going Tim. "You lying, cheating, conniving…"

"Shut up," Lance ordered. "She hasn't done anything."

Grace raised her eyebrows in amazement. Defending her, was he?

"You expect me to believe that?" Tim bitterly asked, struggling to stand up. "Grace! I want you to explain this!"

She hesitated, then called down, "Not tonight. I'm not in the mood. Tomorrow. Good night."

Without a backward glance, she walked down the passage toward her apartment. She had a goodbye speech to practice. She sighed. Maybe two.

"Grace!" Both voices called out in unison after her, one in frustration, the other with quiet command. She ignored them both. Behind her, she heard Mary's delighted giggle.

"Grace," Lance repeated softly. There was a thread of violence this time, but she refused to turn around, even though the hair at the back of her neck stood up. She turned the key in the lock. A distant flash of lightning illuminated the passage for an instant before he continued, "Your play time is over."

Grace carefully closed the door behind her. Outside, she thought she heard a faint rumble of a coming storm. Strange how it made her think of a growling lion.

Downstairs, Lance got into Dan's car. "Let's go," he said shortly. "I'll pick up my car later."

Dan drove off. Checking his rearview mirror, he watched the sight of the forlorn young man staring up at the apartment building. "That was an interesting episode," he remarked.

Lance sighed. "I suppose you aren't going to be polite and drop the subject," he said.

"I may be past my prime in, ah, certain aspects, son," Dan couldn't help teasing, "but I still can recognize a love triangle when I see one."

"There is no love triangle," Lance said, exasperated. He ran impatient fingers through his hair. "Tell me what Fat Joe said."

"He just said, 'Tell the Big Cat I have the guy. Come get him, and bring the medics.'"

"Bring the medics?" Lance frowned.

"Yes. I've already taken care of that," Dan told him. He waited a beat. "So, do you think your Miss O'Connor has anything to do with this?"

"I know she did," Lance curtly replied, his hand automatically rubbing the magnetic strips in his pocket.

"Interesting woman, this Grace," Dan murmured, looking at Lance when there was a red light. "I ran a few diagnostics on a profile like her. She has remarkably high-level training, similar to someone with years of experience."

"And yet she acts like she hasn't any field training," Lance mused thoughtfully. He'd seen it in her, that very raw aspect of her character, mixing the expected with innocence. He'd found himself drawn to the same unsophisticated sexuality.

"Yes, which points to the fact she might have special one-on-one training, extensively, but no prior experience in missions."

"She did mention she spent one year training when she was sixteen," Lance told him. She also said she wasn't recruited, he remembered.

Dan's eyebrows lifted. He stepped on the gas as the traffic light turned green. "Sixteen? Impossible, but here she is, qualified to be on par with some of our own."

"Tell me about it." Lance's lips quirked. "She beat every one of our operatives at the exits tonight and got to David Cheng before we did. What I want to know is, how did she get her information faster than us?"

"She didn't tell you?"

"All she would say was, 'whenever there is trouble, Grace happens'," Lance said dryly.

Dan laughed. He decided he liked the young lady. Very much. "She is a mystery. My main interest is, why did she rescue the scholar, then release him to your pal there?"

"Did Fat Joe tell you how he got him?"

Dan shook his head. "I'm just following your assumption. Fat Joe's message was those few lines, nothing more." He paused to light his cigarette. "If our scholar is injured, what do you intend to do with Miss O'Connor?"

Lance grimly stared ahead. "I'll talk to her tonight."

"Command will probably want her brought in," Dan cautioned. "They might cancel her."

Lance cursed. "How much does Command know about her?"

"Just that she'd been seen around the events, nothing more, but you can't protect her for much longer, Lance."

"Tell Command I'll handle her. They owe me that much after all these years."

"I'll pass along your message," Dan said, "but they'll still want her brought in."

Lance's hand fisted by his side.

Dan sat through the stony silence. As he reached their destination, he casually commented, "She's got to you, hasn't she?"

There was a pause, then Lance sighed and admitted, "Yeah, she's got to me and if I don't have her soon, I'll probably cancel her myself."

"Interesting phenomena." Dan grinned at the younger man, as he got out of his car.

"What is?"

"The downfall of a tracker. Miss O'Connor has my utmost respect."

Lance snorted in mild disgust.

***

"Do you think she was successful?" Ed quietly asked as he drove Sandy home. The Charity Invitational had been an exciting mix of politics and celebrity, with insiders mingling with the movers and shakers. He found it interesting so many would attend for the good of those in need, and yet wouldn't leave without first making sure their own private interests were taken care of too, but that was how life was in the Beltway.

"I don't know," Sandra answered. "She disappeared soon after the Chinese delegation arrived, but I'll bet she'd planned everything down to a 'T'. I know she studied blueprints and floor plans of the place yesterday. I'm confident she got what she wanted."

"Too dangerous." Ed's mouth was a thin line. "She flirts with danger like a child's trip to the candy store."

"What does that mean?"

"Our Grace has a sweet tooth," he wryly explained, "so every trip to the candy store is like an adventure to her. What's she going to buy next? Which sweet should she try this time?"

Sandra laughed. "Cute," she said.

"That's the problem." Ed was enchanted with her laughter. He wanted to hear her laugh like that more often. "She doesn't take things seriously enough. It isn't an adventure, Sandy."

"There's where I think you're wrong." She rested her hand lightly on his arm. "Grace is serious about what she wants. It's her demeanor that throws everybody off. Don't assume just because she acts nonchalant she isn't deadly serious. And obstinate too," she added, as an afterthought.

Ed supposed if anybody could understand Grace, it would be Sandy. They both thrived on the chase and the impulse of the moment. He liked being methodical. Things got done faster and more accurately when details had been carefully planned beforehand. He was successful because he never missed any details and always stayed prepared for the next step. Glancing at Sandy's profile, it suddenly struck him maybe he'd allowed too much rigidity in his life, that his need to oversee every angle made him inflexible. By focusing only on the big picture, hadn't he once missed the most significant detail in his life, and thus, was unprepared for its loss?

"Maybe you're right," he softly said.

Sandra glanced at him sharply. When had he ever taken the side of impulse over planning? Hadn't he condemned and refused to listen to her explanations precisely because she'd acted on emotions and not thought? She hadn't blamed his anger. She had absorbed and remembered it, and when she had chosen to be alone three years ago, she'd told herself thought, and not emotion, would be her guide. Now, he left her speechless by even considering one didn't need every detail lined up and considered before venturing forth. That wasn't Ed at all, and certainly not the Maddux philosophy after which she'd dedicated her new life.

"What did you find out tonight?" He wanted to add she looked beautiful this evening, but kept his opinion to himself. She had done her hair in a different chignon, one less severe in style, twisted alluringly low on her nape. His fingers ached with the temptation to pull it loose. He had wanted to kiss her again when he picked her up earlier; she looked sophisticated in her soft while backless culotte, her eyes smiling back at him. The retro style suited her with a cool charm. Instead of pulling her into his arms, he'd given her some homegrown roses, and watched the tint of pleasure bloom in her face.

"I have several links who passed on some interesting information," Sandra told him. "COS Command has a double agent playing havoc inside. I think Lance Mercy was brought in to clean up the situation. Perhaps that's why he needed Grace to ghost for him. He can't trust many within this particular mission."

"So there's a rat inside COS," Ed said thoughtfully.

"It makes sense the double agent is after the missing scholar for more than what our senator seeks."

"Everyone is after the Chinese man. He's certainly gotten my curiosity now. I hope Grace will find out for me exactly what this man knows."

"She'll get good commission from this one." Sandra nodded in approval, pleased her gamble earlier with providing Grace with more access was paying off. "Sounds like more than two groups are after the information."

"If she's ghosting for Mercy, wouldn't he get to know her information first?" Ed knew that he was treading water here. He had no wish to summon any memory of Sandy's ghosting experiences.

She shook her head. "Grace knows the rules. She is first and foremost bound to the institute. There is a strong sense of loyalty in her, and I know she will abide by them. There is a reason why they call us ghosts, you know, Ed." She paused, her head tilted toward him, as if to gauge his mood. "Ghosts in the literary sense just reveal enough clues to point the way to solve a mystery, letting the hero be the hero."

"I think I understand. Ghosts are like Level Three work. Grace will reveal only what she chooses to reveal."

"Or sell," Sandra reminded him. "GNE is a giant ghost."

She did see the big picture, Ed realized. And she did understand the need for detail, only that she chose not to reveal everything. He could learn to accept that. "If I were Lance Mercy," he said, "I'd better be very nice to Grace when I see her."

Sandra smiled as they reached her house. He hadn't pushed, nor had he questioned. It was difficult, she knew, to stop being a field operative, to stay out of the action, especially for a man like Ed. "Would you like to come in for coffee?" she asked, stepping out of the car. She, too, could stop controlling for a while.

Ed paused before closing the door for her. There were many ways to coax a rose bush to bloom, but when an obstinate plant, unaided, surprised one with an unexpected bud, the pleasure was doubled. Such a flower was a lot more precious to him, like a gift freely given. He wanted to savor this particular bud opening to him.

"I would like that," he replied simply.

CHAPTER SEVENTEEN

In a way, Grace was thankful about the arrival of the storm. That ought to drive away the animals, those wild beasts growling outside her apartment. She shook her head indignantly. That was all she needed, helping Mary Tucker earn her next paycheck.

Rubbing at the beginning of a headache, she wandered into the kitchen, making a face when she reached the refrigerator. How could she have thought those magnetic strips a brilliant idea? Trust him to notice them. She muttered something rude about men in general and opened it to get something to drink. Reaching for her ever-present supply of orange juice, she paused, changed her mind, and pulled out one of the bottles of champagne instead. She might as well celebrate her hard night's work by herself. He certainly wasn't going to drink any of this tonight.

She decided she liked champagne. She enjoyed the way the bubbles tickled her nose and how it went down smooth and tangy, like Lance's kisses. Several glasses later, she sighed contentedly. Maybe she should learn how to drink, after all, she grinned, as she savored the slow heat in her tummy. What headache, right?

Picking up her beaded bag, she pulled out the blood-splattered tissue paper and carefully unfolded it. She wasn't sure yet what to do with what the Chinese man gave her, but she was sure they were important. Sipping on another glass of champagne, she held them up in the light, squinting at them, but the alcohol was already making its effect known. Her sight seemed a little lopsided, and she tilted her head first one way, then another. She didn't think she had

191

a chance of finding out anything until tomorrow at the office, anyway. She was tired; it'd been a really full day, even for her. Suppressing a yawn, she carefully rewrapped the objects and hid them away.

Hmm. Why not? One last glass. There was a rumble of thunder, rattling the glass door that led to the back balcony. She stood and watched the rain for a minute. Lifting her glass for a toast, she tossed down the drink with enthusiasm. *Here's to you and good riddance, Mr. Big Cat. Here's to you and goodbye, Tim Halliday. Here's to David Cheng's two false teeth, and good luck in solving the mystery, Grace O'Connor.* The champagne tasted like confidence, sharp and delicious. She would deal with all three problems tomorrow.

***

Rain wasn't a deterrent when Lance Mercy had his target in sight. He was used to storms, the kind that poured down in one big sheet or the kind that lingered for days. They made the hunt more exciting, the sound of thunder and lightning muffled by the canopy of Asian flora. Although there wasn't any jungle right now, the feeling was the same. This was his own mission, without any red tape to untangle, talking heads to climb over, or silly disguises behind doubletalk. Everything was in black and white, as it should be, as he was used to. It was the law of the jungle that ruled him, where political one upmanship was replaced by skill and determination. There was only him and his target.

The lights were still on in the little hellcat's apartment. He wondered whether she was alone. He shrugged in the darkness of her balcony as he lifted the sliding glass door easily out of its tracks. It didn't matter. In the jungle, he would just eliminate anything that got in his way.

He knew his present savage mood wasn't suitable for this moonlit city of D.C., but he was tired of their kind of games. He'd gotten them their scholar, alive, or at least, still breathing, and now he wanted to let loose and be himself. It was his turn to play.

He clicked the sliding door back in place, shut out the rain, and strolled dripping wet into the lit-up living room. Seeing his bottle of champagne lying empty on the table didn't soothe his growing fury. Somehow, he hadn't thought her so callous as to share his drink with her lover boy. She was going to regret that.

The bedroom light was on. Might as well, he sardonically sneered, since he was going to interrupt their love nest anyhow. He hadn't quite decided what he was going to do when he walked in there. Right now, he felt murderous. Somebody had intruded in his territory, and he stalked around the apartment, putting off the inevitable confrontation. Unexpected jealousy blurred his usually cool logic, and he was surprised at the sense of betrayal invading him.

Her responses to him weren't fake. Her attraction to him was real. Yet she dared to ignore the obvious to return to the arms of a young toothless pup like—he couldn't stand it any longer. He could either leave right now and not look back, or go on in there and proceed with her punishment. He chose the latter. Lance Mercy did not relinquish what was his easily. He pushed the door open.

The wave of relief that hit him in the gut almost buckled his knees. She was alone.

And fully dressed.

In fact, she had on exactly what she wore to the function. Sprawled face down on her bed, she hadn't even bothered to even pull down the covers. An arm cradled the right side of her face that was turned toward the door; the other dangled carelessly off the bed. An empty glass lay right beneath her lax fingers. Her maroon outfit was hiked up, like she had tried to stretch in her sleep, revealing black garters holding the top of her sheer stockings. She hadn't even bothered to take her heels off. One was half on still, its heel against the bed sheets with her foot nestled inside the toe end.

Lance slowly walked toward her sleeping figure, feeling his pulse returning to a manageable rate. She was alone. Had been alone. A slow smile formed on his lips—he didn't care to analyze whether it was more out of relief than amusement. The little witch had drunk herself to sleep.

He bent his wet body over her prone one, and bit her earlobe. She still smelled sexy, even though she looked like she'd crawled under some cars tonight, which—his eyes narrowed as he took in dirty smudges and tears on her dress—she probably had. He bit down harder.

"Ouch," she mumbled. "Stupid lion."

"Stupid lion?" he whispered, nonplussed.

"You foul breathed, stupid lion," she said, her lips pouting obstinately, her eyes still shut.

Lance grinned. Dreaming, was she? He pressed his wet body on hers, letting his soggy clothes soak through her ruined ones, then growled gently into her ear. She moved restlessly, trying to get away.

"You don't scare me, you wild beast! You can't have me yet, so quit slobbering on me."

"But I do have you," Lance whispered into her ear.

Grace moaned. Something was doing horribly erotic things to her ear, darting in and out, exploring, swirling, seducing. She tried to twist away from its sexual probing, but found she couldn't move. Hands moved over her body, lips seared her skin. He was good, she thought, fighting off sleep, so clever with that tongue, so strong and tender and—she let out a scream—horribly wet. Cold water dripped down her back and legs. She forced her eyes open, still half asleep, expecting to confront some nightmarish creature frothing at the mouth, dripping all over her.

She was close. It was Lance Mercy in her bed, on her, holding her down. And he was wet from head to toe. His eyes were blazing like those of a wild beast on the attack.

Grace closed her eyes and opened them again, willing her nightmare to go away. It wasn't one. He was still there in person. She shrieked again, trying to sit up. "How did you get in here?" Her panicked voice was hushed, husky from alcohol and sleep.

Lance sat astride her, studying her wakening horror with renewed amusement. He did like getting back at her for making him feel jealous. "Some doors can't be dead-bolted, sweetheart," he drawled.

She frowned, then remembered her sliding door. She called him an extremely unflattering name.

"Tsk, tsk, such language from that pretty mouth," he chided.

"You're wet!" She squirmed. "Get off, you...oaf!"

"I'm sorry. Here, let me get out of these wet clothes."

Grace's eyes widened, as she slowly comprehended his meaning. Her mouth tasted like cotton as she watched him pull his wet shirt off and toss it carelessly over his shoulder. His chest muscles were taut, revealing his mood, the movement of his bare arms tense and deliberate. She started to tremble when his hands reached for the buttons of his pants. She tried to speak but her tongue seemed to have disappeared, her eyes wildly following his hands. Finally, she just shook her head at him.

But Lance wasn't in the mood. "You got wet from my clothes, sweetheart. Let me help you take them off." He held on to the front of her maroon outfit and with one savage tug, tore it down almost to her waist.

Grace came alive, rearing up and catching him by surprise, pushed him off. Rolling off the bed, she scrambled out of the room, almost killing herself with only one high heel on. He hopped off and followed closely.

"Don't think you're going to come in here and find me soft and pliant after the way you acted out there!" Grace fumed, hobbling backwards from him.

"You didn't expect me to be in the best of moods after the act you pulled at the function, did you?" He stalked her as she used the sofa as a buffer between them. "Did you?"

"Did I do anything you told me not to?" she challenged.

"Yes!" he hissed, walking around the sofa. She half-ran, half-stumbled to the nearby chaise lounge. "I told you not to interfere."

"You told me to stay out of the way," she corrected, "which I did. I kept my bloody word, so stop glaring at me! What, do you have any complaints? Didn't you accomplish your mission?"

Using one arm, Lance vaulted over the sofa. Grace hastily retreated away from the chaise, trying to think of a way to calm a savage beast. Half-naked, his hair darkened by the rain, eyes blazing, he didn't look anything like the suave deputy advisor to the Council of Asian Trade. Her heart thumped against her throat at the dangerous look in his eyes.

"You're right, I did accomplish my mission," he informed her, his eyes level, "and now I've come to accomplish my other one."

She swallowed. "What's that?" She stared at him as he kept advancing.

"I told you we would celebrate tonight." He indicated the empty bottle on the coffee table. "Seems like you started without me."

Grace's back bumped into the sliding door that led to the balcony. "I wanted to be alone," she told him, still defiant.

"And I told you I would be back later." He was close enough to grab her. "Did you have any doubts I would?"

"Yes! I don't want you here!"

She turned, slid open the glass door, and ran out into the rain. Too late, she realized her blunder. She was dead meat. Lance followed her, cornering her against the banister. Rain half-blinded her as he twined his fingers in her wet hair, pulling her face up to meet his.

"You have a hearing problem, love. I also told you," he said over the drumming of the rain around them, "game time is over, Grace. I meant it."

He was sleek and slippery, all male under her pushing hands. His dark pants clung to him, unbuttoned and clinging open low on his hips, revealing his flat hard stomach and the tantalizing triangle in the V-shaped gap beneath. Unyielding and powerful, he loomed over her own soggy, tattered body, pulling her toward him even as she tried to pull away. His eyes held hers prisoner and she knew, no matter how much she tried to evade him, he was going to kiss her. And then she'd be lost because she wanted it too. Slowly, his head came down, and his lips captured hers.

She tasted of rain and champagne, a heady combination that shot to his brain. He didn't want her pliant, hadn't expected pliancy, but he wasn't prepared for this need in him. He took her mouth urgently, telling himself he would get her out of his system once he had her. But she was like an addictive drug. The more he kissed her, the more he wanted.

Grace clung to him, drowning in her own passion. She couldn't think when he was this close to her, when he plundered her mouth like he owned it. Surrendering to her own desire, her tongue mated with his, her hands slid feverishly over his chest, down his belly, into his open pants.

Lance lifted his head, feeling strangely elated at her response. She fed his dark urgency to possess her. He wrenched the rest of her soaked dress off her shoulders to her waist, exposing her body to the elements. Raindrops formed rivulets down the soft curves of her breasts, pebbling on the rosy nipples to dance to the storm within and without, and then falling off like sacrificial maidens from the peaks. With his hands around her waist, he lifted her off her feet, suckling on the offerings when they were level to his face.

Grace could only pull helplessly at his hair. It was good that he was holding her. She didn't think she could stand at all. Lifting her face to the falling rain, she felt his hot mouth, his tongue, his teeth on her breasts, and it felt like she was thundering inside as well.

He positioned her until her legs wrapped around his waist, thus freeing his hands to tear off the rest of her clothes. She barely heard the ripping, moaning as his teeth grazed her sensitive nipples and held on delicately to the nubbin until she shook from the pleasure.

She scarcely felt him walking back into the apartment, his teeth still holding her nipple prisoner. He went down on his knees, lowering her onto the carpet, his tongue laving even as he increased the pressure of his bite.

Grace closed her eyes, her head moving restlessly as her need climbed higher and faster. She was aware he'd ripped the last of her wet clothes off. Only her garters and torn hose remained and she wrapped her legs tighter around him. His hands turned from being rough to gentle. His fingers traveled down her belly, touched her inner thigh, and sought pressure points with the knowing experience of a tracker.

Lance wanted her to know this wasn't the young pup. Or any man she'd been with before. His hand slid lower. She jerked up in response and a little gasp escaped her lips. He wasn't done yet. He put his mastery of Eastern acupressure to good use, exerting pressure on a certain nerve. And another.

Grace floated between spasms of light and darkness. She was wet and hot under his fingers and moaned as his mouth burned a fiery path on her rain-cooled skin. Her whimpers became incoherent gasps even as he stopped his assault on her breasts, and started exploring lower. Desperately, she tried to fight the maelstrom of emotions cascading through her. She needed him to pause long enough so she could take a step back. But there was no pause. Only his tongue and fingers and his clever little pressure points. He pressed, and she responded. Here, by her inner thigh. There, below her ear. And there, on her pubic bone. Grace went obediently, peak after peak, until it was a continuous siege of pleasure.

He whispered sex words into her ears, pressing his masculine weight against her subdued body. She felt him flaming hot and hard and her eyes flew open when the pause finally did come, but her reprieve was short and insignificant. There was pressure, and fullness beyond what she had ever felt, and then, the inexorable weight of male on female. Her body welcomed him with heated eagerness, opening up as he pushed in, sheathing around his iron hardness. She emitted another soft gasp as he angled and pushed deeper, pressing her against the floor.

"You're going to break up with him," Lance told—no, ordered—her as he savored the feel of her. Tight. Wet. His. "You're not going back to him. I don't share."

The possessiveness in his voice shocked him, but it was already out and he stared challengingly down at the woman beneath him. She surfaced from her sexual stupor, her eyes large and passion-filled as they stared back reproachfully at him. She writhed in protest at this interruption of her delightful journey, but he shook his head at her. He wanted her answer first, needed her capitulation.

"You never loved him," he told her.

"Never," she whispered in agreement.

"You never wanted him as much as you want me now."

"Never," she said, licking her lips.

He stroked. Little shocks of pleasure rifled through him as she clenched around him. He could feel them both trembling from the effort to not just go wildly at each other.

"You're never sleeping with him again." His voice came out like a growl. God, he wanted to sink deep inside her.

"Never," Grace said, giving him what she knew he wanted.

She didn't mind, didn't particularly care, for she spoke the truth. She'd never felt this way about Tim, and now admitted freely, despite all her fighting, she was falling for Lance Mercy. It felt as if she'd known him for a long, long time. It was a wondrous feeling of belonging, and it made her smile. There was something else her Big Cat ought to know. Her fingers tiptoed down between their bodies, lower, until she cupped him. She stroked him knowingly with her index finger, at the same time tightening her insides around him. His eyes dilated until there were only twin circles of blue around the black orbs. His lips twisted sensuously as his lower body jerked in response.

"Move, babe," she ordered gently, and delicately pressed a certain spot. Her darling tracker wasn't the only one who knew about pressure points.

He hissed and went crazy. She was ready for him, moving easily to his rhythm as his own hunger took over. He slammed into her, and she moaned. He slid out, and she tightened, holding his soul within even as he sought to bring hers higher.

"Grace," he chanted, smothering her cries with his own mindless kisses, and when she moved her index finger again, he shuddered and gave a final deep thrust, holding her tightly as they both exploded in unison, mentally fused in their intimate dance of passion.

Afterwards, they lay there in muted shock, each filled with wonder at the searing pleasure they just gave one another.

Lance understood the nature of pleasure, in its giving and its taking, but he'd never felt this sense of rightness, of the need to take someone for his own. Technique? Finesse? Out the window. This time was something beyond mere sex. Even now, sated from loving her, he wanted her again, wanted to hold her close.

Grace tried to slow her breathing. How did he do this—make her lose sense of time and place? She had cultivated her easygoing personality on purpose, had made it a career to slip in and out of situations with the smoothness of silk, but nothing was easy with this man. His passion overwhelmed her, and how he made her feel wasn't going to make her escape easy. He'd caught hold of something inside her and set it on fire with his touch, and now it roared bright and hungry within. She wanted more from him, wanted to taste and savor him.

He was kissing her with slow attentiveness now, his tongue lazy and teasing, and as she ardently responded, she felt him growing hard inside her.

"Take your pick. Shower or bed?" He explored the hollow of her neck even as he sat up with her legs still around him.

She gasped when he cupped her bottom and pulled her hard against him until his pubic bone rubbed her sensitive clitoris. "You...want to take a shower?" she asked, trying hard to focus. She held on to his shoulders for balance as he easily supported her weight.

"Mmmhmm," he murmured somewhere against her throat, making her arch back helplessly, "but it can wait."

You're going to give me rug burns," she whispered, closing her eyes when the dark pleasure started building again.

He caught her by surprise by grabbing the back of the chaise and standing up in one swift motion. She hung on, impaled, with her arms around his neck. Seating her on the back rest of the chaise, he leaned her back enough until she felt helpless, giving her the choice of either clinging to him or falling backwards.

"Better?" he asked, moving his hips. Not expecting an answer, he bent her even further, using the back of the chaise as leverage. He thrust in all the way, and this way, went in deeper than before. He pushed in again, hearing his name on her lips. She was like a liquid fist, a molten forge. He would willingly melt in her this way forever.

It was an exercise in dominance, but Grace didn't mind. She was too busy feeling good. It was all instinct now, this giving, this taking, this mutual sharing. He touched every hidden corner of her mind, lingered over every sensitive nerve end, until the universe seemed to stand still. There was a tense anticipation, an extra slow thrust, and a moan of release.

It still wasn't enough for him. "Again," he murmured, angling her even further against the chaise.

She grasped the soft material even though he held her securely by her waist, feeling helpless and excited at the same time. Every thrust was slow excruciating pleasure, timing her rapidly ascending orgasm. His experience was devastating, taking her wherever he wanted, up and over the precipice, until she could no longer see or hear, only feel him moving inside her. When he couldn't hold on to his control any longer, he tumbled on top of her, kissing her deeply as they lay upside down.

A little later, she told him, "Now I feel better. The gymnastic lesson could be improved, though."

His chuckle was dark and sexy. "There's no way to stop that mouth of yours, is there?"

"Well, there is a way," she drawled, tongue in cheek. "I'll show you in the shower."

"You're on."

CHAPTER EIGHTEEN

The advantage of being a Level Three, Grace thought, as she lazily stretched, was she could set her own working hours. That was good, since she would probably be mixing up all her languages today if she were still translating. She suspected most of her brain cells had melted the night before.

The arm flung across her middle reacted by pulling her closer. She found herself trapped under one hundred ninety-odd pounds of man. A very aroused man, from what she could feel against the small of her back. She smiled sleepily. The man was an insatiable beast. Her insatiable beast.

"'Morning," she greeted, husky from lack of sleep.

"Awake already?" he murmured. "We didn't exactly nod off till quite late."

"About two hours ago," she informed him, looking at the clock on the bedside table. "Aren't you sleepy?"

"Nope."

"You don't sleep much, do you?"

"Sometimes." He began exploring every inch of her front with a leisurely hand. "Call in sick today. You need to sleep."

Grace grinned. "You mean you're going to let me sleep?"

She turned over and he obligingly let her lie on top of his toasty body. God, he looked awfully sexy, all rumpled and sleepy-eyed. She liked him like this, all naked and all hers.

As she ran her fingers through his hair, she realized that she was beginning to recognize that look on his face. It was what she called his medieval warrior look, when he was thinking he was lord and master over all he surveyed. Not so easy, buster. She needed time to think things through, to understand why she felt this way about him. Darn it! Her eyes narrowed. The last thing she wanted was to fall in love with a tracker.

"I don't like that look on your face," Lance remarked. It amazed him that he wanted her still. She was in his blood, in every cell of his being. He couldn't seem to get enough of the taste of her. This was getting bad.

"Oh? What kind of look?" She idly traced his lips with her fingers.

"You're planning to run away again."

When did he get to know her so well? "I was just thinking I need time alone," she said, a little defensively. "I need to talk to Tim, straighten things out with him."

She also had to solve the mystery of two false teeth.

Lance played with her wavy brown tresses as he studied her face. "I'm eight—nine—years older than you, darling Grace, and absolutely refuse to compete with your young Adonis." He grasped her face between his hands. "And I'm not giving you back to him either."

"Don't I have a choice in this matter?" she wryly asked. "I mean, if I've a choice between a young Adonis and an old man like you—"

"Old?" he growled and smothered her laughter with a kiss.

"Okay, seasoned," she cracked.

He tickled her.

"Weather-beaten," she squealed, trying to escape.

He swung her onto her back, his weight punishing.

"Experienced!" she gasped out. "Experienced and well-preserved!" She shrieked as he tickled her mercilessly. "Uncle! Uncle!" she finally pleaded.

Lance dotted her jaw line with kisses, ending at the stubborn cleft on her chin. "I'm not letting you go," he said softly, cupping her breasts possessively.

She sighed, eyes closing. Things were a lot more complicated when one was in love. A tracker and a ghost. Nonetheless, she couldn't trust him with her secret; it wasn't just her life in jeopardy. It was better to evade the matter for now.

"When are you taking me in?" she quietly asked.

His caress stopped. "How did you know?"

"Sooner or later they'll want to question me. Are you going to let them hurt me?" Maybe kill her too?

Damn her. Why must she bring it up in the middle of lovemaking, when he didn't want to think of the future? "No," he told her, his gaze serious. "I won't let them hurt you."

"But you're still taking me in," she said, gently this time. She wasn't angry. She'd expected it.

"Yes."

"Do you trust me, Lance?" Silence. Trust was a sacred word among operatives, and very carefully given. She arched a brow. "I see." She nodded, feeling a little hurt, but she pushed it determinedly away.

"You don't see at all, little hellcat," he muttered, his blue eyes glinting with irritation. "You're too young to understand about trust in this line of business."

Grace cocked her head. The man was sexy but dumb, or thick in the head, as Dad usually said about her guys, where she was concerned.

"Are you so sure about that?" she challenged. "Too young when it doesn't suit you, right? Great sex but that's how far it's going to go?"

"Damn it, that's not what I meant!" He was starting to lose his temper, not liking the way she purposely twisted his words.

"What did you mean then?" she baited him, wanting him to tell her the truth. "What am I to you, Mercy? Somebody to toy with for a while?"

"Damn it, Grace!"

"I have to know," she whispered. She splayed her hands on his broad back and massaged the corded flesh, lightly scratching him with her nails. There was a strange pain growing inside her, but she banked it down forcefully. She'd been warned about trackers and she wasn't going to regret anything.

"You mean a lot," Lance finally told her. She didn't know how much that was, coming from him.

"Even this young woman can understand that," Grace said casually. "That's probably what I'll say to Tim, too."

"No." He lost it then, and almost crushed her with his weight. "You're not going to compare my feelings for you with yours for your men."

He kissed her hard and possessively, and she gasped when he entered her with one decisive thrust. How could she when she had forgotten everyone else with whom she'd ever gone out? How could she, when she could only feel, taste and see him every time she closed her eyes? Even as he pleasured her and mastered her body, even as they both succumbed to this unrelenting tide of passion that kept them captive, she knew deep down, that as long as they didn't trust each other, there was no future. Besides, he was still taking her in.

Afterwards, they agreed to talk later in the day.

Lance didn't want to leave Grace alone, but there were things to wrap up. If the Chinese scholar was still comatose, he had no choice but to take Grace in for questioning. The missing information was vital. He knew Command would soon issue the order, since she was the last known person to handle David Cheng. They would want to know her motives, and to which agency she belonged. In short, they wanted a file on her.

He frowned. She seemed so calm about the possibility of being taken in, as if she had already known what was coming. Of course she knew. If she were an operative, she knew all the rules. How was it then she didn't run? Or show any fear? Didn't she know she might be in danger? She was so cock-sure of herself...damn it, so like him. He had driven away, after telling her he would try to get around an interrogation, but knew from her mocking eyes she'd understood he was toeing the line.

"Is that why there's an unmarked van right by yours?" she'd queried with a crooked smile.

Dammit. Command wanted her cooperation, and they would get it, with or without his approval. Lance had to make sure he would be the one questioning her. Or, at least, be present. Why did she keep insisting she wasn't an operative?

"It's not me," was all he could say. They were making sure she stayed around.

"I'm not what you think," her parting words replayed in his head, after a long goodbye kiss. "Take me in, if you have to. I can handle this."

Christ, she was either nuts or too confident of her training, or both. There was no way she could possibly understand what awaited her in an interrogation. One thing that made him believe her was she hadn't run away once she'd gotten David. Another factor he could argue in her favor was the fact she'd engineered the scholar back into Command's hands. If she were working for another agency, wouldn't it be the logical thing to take the man to her superiors?

Lance raked an impatient hand through his hair. The curious thing that nagged him about Grace was she seemed to be always willing to help him out, even indirectly. She'd given him clues, even down to imparting her own information, such as the Room 103 debacle. How did she get to know all that before even Command?

Now she didn't even blink an eye at the thought of going with him, hadn't even asked who wanted to interrogate her. He sat up in his seat, swearing softly. Knowing her, she probably knew about COS Command and him. After all, Fat Joe had bandied his nickname often that day when they visited and she'd no doubt researched him. Yet, she'd still aided him in her own way.

He rubbed his stubble, pulling into the gated driveway that led to his penthouse complex. The guard waved and opened the electronic gate, and he drove through. There was so much that was a mystery about the woman. He intended to solve this puzzle himself, even if he had to work around Command. He may not fully understand her or her motives, but he was certain of one thing. After last night, Grace O'Connor was his.

His lips twisted in self-mockery. Yup, that was a fucking archaic declaration. Well, she did say he was old.

***

Back in her apartment, Grace let out a sigh after he left. She had a lot to do today and she'd better ignore these daydreams about the night before. She wasn't worried about COS Command. She still had a few aces up her sleeve. Right now, she needed to get to the office and have Tyler, gadget genius, at her disposal. She paused in the middle of getting ready, her mind suddenly on Tim, wondering where he was, whether he was still in D.C., or had driven straight back to Ohio. She sighed again, regretting it had to end this way. Her initial plan had been to break up with Tim gently, by moving away, then encouraging him to meet other people. She hadn't expected him to drive up to see her so often, hadn't expected a complication named Lance Mercy.

Heat suffused her cheeks at the thought of Lance and the previous night. She'd never felt like that about a man before. The incessant desire to be with him, to make love to him, was alien to her. She had no idea how she was going to deal with this new discovery. Love? Really? She shook her head. No, she was crazy to even consider the possibility.

Tim would be sulking right now, thinking of punishing her by not calling, letting her stew in her guilt. That was Tim, she smiled a little sadly, hating to have to hurt him. Thinking of what was ahead, she took the hidden teeth from the hiding place. Tim would have to wait.

It was easy enough to evade the unmarked van. Eh. They thought her to be an operative, anyway. Fine, she'd act like one. An hour later, she strode into her office, heading straight to Tyler. He was, as usual, immersed in his work, humming a ditty under his breath, as he stared at the computer screen.

"I need your help, Tyler." She sat by him after locking the office door.

"Shoot, babe."

Grace gave him a brief outline of her rescue of David Cheng, leaving out some details of her adventures from last night. "Anyway, he gave me these," she ended her story, showing him the wrapped up teeth in the bloodied napkin, "and I think it's important to my mission."

Tyler didn't interrupt throughout her tale, listening with a cocked head, munching down on some sticky honey toasted concoction. "Does this have anything to do with COS and the Big Cat?" he finally asked.

Grace smiled at her friend. He may look scruffy and absentminded, but his mind was as sharp as a new blade. "Yes, and if I don't find out why these things are important, I'm probably history."

Tyler immediately sat up straight. "History, like——?" He slashed his throat with his forefinger, his eyes wide behind his glasses as Grace solemnly nodded. "God, princess, say you're kidding."

"Okay," Grace obliged. Maybe she shouldn't have emphasized her own danger. "Let's just say they would want to talk to me and I need to have bargaining power."

"Let's look at the babies." After donning a pair of latex gloves, he gently weighed the two false molars in his hand. "You said this Chinese dude has certain information all these people wanted."

"Yes, at least two different groups. The senator and his men, and COS," she said. "The Chinese government is also probably after him, but only to prevent him from giving the information to COS."

"So now they've gotten their guy, thanks to you, so why would they want to interrogate you?"

"I suspect David Cheng had been tortured and given some drug or poison when he was with the senator's goons. He looked really out of it, Tyler. Suppose he didn't make it? Then the information died with him."

"And they would think you might have it, since you went through all that trouble to rescue him," Tyler surmised, his eyes narrowing thoughtfully.

"Yeah, and I think I do. He gave me those for a reason. Suppose they're some sort of clues to where he has the information hidden?" Grace stood up and paced the floor.

"Okay, let's think. He smuggled sensitive information into the country without being detected by the Chinese. I know they censor a lot of websites over there so he couldn't just upload them, not easily anyway. Or he needed a way his sources couldn't be traced at all. Hmm. Other possibilities are videos, micro-cassettes, disks, flashdrives…"

"Microchips!" she exclaimed in the middle of the little room.

"Possible. Where would he hide them?"

"He kept mouthing some words that sounded like *'jeeah lee'* before passing out. I assumed that he was saying 'home.' Maybe he was trying to tell me that he kept it in his house or apartment." She frowned. "I hope not. I've no idea how to find out where that is."

"No way. Why would he go to meet the Big Cat at the rally empty-handed?"

Everything fell into place like the last few pieces of a puzzle. "Hidden. Small enough to be hidden!" She rushed back to Tyler, sitting down again. "Small enough to be inside false teeth?" They both looked reverently at the molars in his palm. "How do we break it?"

"Can't smash it. If it's a microchip, it's a goner." Tyler held one under the light, turning it over and over. Taking out a pocketknife, he pricked the underside of one tooth. "Look, it's quite soft." He started to carefully scrape the material out.

Ten minutes went by. "That's the last of the gooey stuff," he finally said. "Let me wipe my glasses. They're fogging up from all your excitement."

Grace laughed delightedly, draping a friendly arm over his shoulder. "I've always wanted to fog up your glasses," she teased.

"Yeah, well, you're succeeding." He grinned back, rubbing his glasses with a wrinkled handkerchief. He then picked up the tooth and turned it upside down. "Okay, here goes." He tapped it lightly with a finger.

Something fell out. Grace leaned closer, holding her breath. There were two tiny things.

"They're really tiny microchips!" she exclaimed.

"They aren't," Tyler disagreed, poking them with his pocketknife.

"What?" She frowned, leaning even closer to the table for a better look. "Why, they…they look like…"

"Rice grains?" Tyler finished helpfully.

She stared. They did look like two grains of rice. "Open up the other tooth," she said.

Ten minutes later, they had one more rice-like grain to add to their collection.

Grace handled each one in her hand, puzzled. They *were* ordinary rice grains.

"What now?" Tyler stretched from his crammed position. "I suppose they aren't some sort of secret snack our scholar was smuggling out of China."

"Don't crack me up," she warned. "I don't want to drop them on the carpet." She started pacing again, staring at the rice grains. "Suppose the Chinese could somehow detect microchips, and David Cheng had to smuggle the information out a different way."

"All he had to do was memorize it," Tyler pointed out.

"Not everyone has a photographic memory, Tyler-boy," she chided. "Besides, if his English was really bad, then he might have a tough time remembering everything." She placed the grains on her own desk, drawing imaginary circles around them as she stared, deep in thought.

*"For you I will paint
all my secret universe*

on a grain of rice."

"Say what?" Tyler asked.

"That's a haiku," Grace explained, "a type of Japanese poem. It's a love poem I read in college."

"Yeah, well, I don't think this is the time, babe," Tyler said, "your life being on the line and all that."

"Pagan. See, the haiku was written by a man who was in love with a married woman, but he couldn't tell the world about his love."

"So he loved her so much—" Tyler continued, understanding dawning in his voice.

"—he wrote all his feelings on a grain of rice," Grace finished.

"Wow." Tyler sat back staring at her across the room. "Wow. Do you think?"

"Got a microscope among your toys?"

"Yeah, somewhere." He walked over to a cabinet, pushing things aside. "Here."

Five minutes later and the two of them gave each other high fives, their faces smiling triumphantly.

"This one's in code or something," she said, peering through the lenses, "but that's okay. Information is information. I'm going to read out what I see and you write it down, alright?"

"Go ahead. I'm ready."

"Okay. Grain #1," she began.

CHAPTER NINETEEN

It didn't take a rocket scientist to realize she had stumbled onto something dangerous. Grace relied on her father's lessons more than ever. When evasion was impossible, he'd told her, it was best to scatter all information. That same afternoon, she formed a plan with the quick precision of one who had been trained to survive on her own, taking barely three hours to finish up in the office. She yawned. She needed some R&R before any confrontation, that was for sure.

Outside in her car, she shook the package Sandra had earlier given her. During her debriefing, the department head and her supervisor hadn't said a word throughout her summary of the events, only exchanging glances at different points of her story. She understood now they wouldn't interfere with a Level Three as long as she was successful in getting useful information for GNE. After assuring them she'd already released the information in her private online folder, Sandy had given her the package.

"I've anticipated their wanting to take you in," she told her. Quietly, she'd watched her examine the envelope, and at the latter's inquiring look, she explained, "Your emergency package. Read the manual inside and follow the instructions. Everything will be fine, Grace."

Grace tore open the package. She'd better read it now and destroy it. People tailing. People wanting to ask questions. And too many distractions in her apartment these days.

***

As he stood outside her apartment, Lance looked down at the key in his hand and his mouth quirked at the memory of Grace tossing it, along with his semi-dry clothes, to him that morning. "Here, try coming in the normal way next time."

She was a sassy witch, like no other woman he'd ever met. Certainly, he'd never gone out on a limb for a woman like he'd done this afternoon, having spent almost half a day making a case for her not to be brought into a COS facility. He knew once she entered one and failed her interrogation, she might not be allowed out. Half his problem was he didn't know enough to help Grace or reassure Command's worries. Because of his tracker background, they'd finally agreed to use one of the Department of Defense's many interview rooms. They'd accepted his arguments for now.

He wondered how she was. Probably worried, perhaps nervous, but still obstinate as ever. He already knew what she'd done to the tail COS had put on her. The news put the ones in charge in an even more uppity mood, but he felt proud as hell. He grimaced, knowing he had to prepare her for an intense interrogation. He didn't think Grace was going to like it.

"Hello, Lance! I see you won the duel!" Mary Tucker smiled at him as she walked by, laundry basket in her arms. "Absolutely romantic! Wait till the next issue of Beaucoup, darling, it's just going to be sizzling!"

"Nice to be of help," Lance said, opening the door to Grace's apartment.

"How about a one-on-one inter..." Lance politely shut the door in Mary's face, and turned to see what the object of his "duel" was up to. If she was apprehensive, he planned to comfort her, answer any questions she might have. If she was sulky, he would have to convince her to be cooperative.

Music blared out from the bedroom. When he reached the doorway, he stared.

Did he expect a sullen, sulky woman? Did he think she would be a little bit frightened? His woman sat among a mountain of pillows on the floor, wearing nothing but a camisole and panties, and a towel wrapped around her head. Her feet were propped up on a few pillow squares. He could see the little wads of cotton between her toes. For heaven's sake, the woman was painting her toenails as she chatted on the phone, waving her nail polish wand in the air as she joked with her caller. A bucket of Haagen Dazs ice cream sat by her side. No, she didn't look very frightened at all.

Her cheerful laughter rang out over the volume of the music, her attention skipping from her toenails to the television, which was also on. Lance looked at the whole messy room in amazement. She was watching the Three Stooges without the sound on, whooping at the gags, and describing the scene to her friend. In short, the lady was having a grand old time.

Grace felt wonderful. A meditation session to reinforce some mental shields. The long soak in the tub afterwards was exactly what she needed. She decided the best thing to do before facing down a squad of testosterone-filled secret agents was to enjoy herself. She was, she decided as she painted her nails vamp-red, going to look fabulous. No use going to be the only one to sweat. She grinned.

"No, no, Charlie, I'm serious! I'm in love with Moe. He's so mean and tough, just the way I love my men." She laughed at Charlie's teasing comment, oblivious of the approaching mean and tough man behind her. "You like that episode too?" She turned to pick up her ice cream, saw the shoes nearby, and followed the miles of leg and torso until her eyes encountered a pair of sexy blue ones. She smiled prettily up at him, quickly interrupting her conversation, "Uh, Charlie? I've got to go. Yes, let's do lunch. 'Bye."

She hung up and leaned back against the pillows. "What are you growling about now?" she demanded. Honestly, the guy did unfair things to a girl's equilibrium.

For the first time in his life, Lance was at a loss for words. Sprawled at his feet, with her legs parted and those ridiculous cotton wads between her toes, her face scrubbed fresh as a child's, and with that silly turban on her head, she ought to look anything but sexy, anything but seductive. But his cock was totally disagreeing, probably because he was enjoying her half-exposed breasts and sultry, inviting position. He got down between her legs, took the nail polish wand from her and put it back into the bottle, screwing it tight as he looked her over.

Grace's eyes widened. "Oh, no," she ordered firmly. "Don't you dare! I just painted those and if you mess them up, I'm going to kick your ass."

Was that what it took to provoke fear and horror in a young woman these days? Threaten to mess up her just-painted nails? His smile turned rakish, mischievous. Sliding his hands down her thighs, he pushed her legs further apart.

"Better not move then," he advised, as his hands slid back up intimately.

"Lance!" Her voice became a strangled protest as he tore her flimsy panties off.

"Just trying not to mess up those pretty nails, babe," he taunted, pushing her further back into the pile of pillows. "I'll buy you a dozen new panties."

"You can't just come in here and—" Grace stopped mid-sentence as her breath caught in her suddenly dry throat.

"And what?" he helpfully prompted her, his fingers tracing a pattern as he explored and teased.

She couldn't think properly. She lay suspended in pleasure. His hands were magic…

"Can't touch you here?" he taunted, and proceeded to do so.

She inhaled, her pelvis pushing up involuntarily.

"Can't do this?" He teased.

One finger moved in, then two.

"Can't make you feel this?"

They went in deeper, searched for, and stroked sensitive nerves she didn't know existed. She started whimpering as his thumb began its own external torture.

He continued to push her further back, ignoring her incoherent protests when he stopped to put more pillows under her, until she lay wantonly exposed to his gaze. She didn't care; she needed him to resume what he was doing. Desperately.

"You're so beautiful," he murmured, looking down at her. "So wet. I want you hot for me, only me." He touched her softly. "You want me, don't you?"

Grace sighed and nodded, her eyes closed. Just keep going. The music she had on came to an end, and the silence that followed was heavy with anticipation.

"Don't you?" he asked again.

"Yes, damn you," she moaned out, mad that he was keeping his touch light and slow.

"So how come the moment my back is turned, I find you flirting with another man?"

He was killing her slowly, moving deliberate torturous fingers over her aching flesh. "I...I didn't call him. He called...me," she said with difficulty, her mind on more important things being done to her.

"I won't share, Grace. I won't share this." He pushed in deeper, located the spot again and slowly stroked it, feeling her clench around his finger. "I think you need a little punishment, just a lesson to show you I'm the only one who can drive you wild this way, babe."

He meant every word. He explored her like no other man ever had, took her to levels of ecstasy that left her breathless and panting for more. His fingers were cruel, so gentle and insistent, pushing her to the point of madness and somehow keeping her there, with every nerve in her body begging for release. The steady pressure he kept, manipulating the rise and fall of her orgasm, was something beyond her experience. She felt suspended in between layers of pleasure.

"Oh, please, please, Lance, please!" she pleaded finally, grown shameless in her need. Her hands tried to reach down, but were firmly pushed away. She arched and strained against his slow torture.

"More?"

"Yessss!" And she screamed because he started to use his tongue, his mouth. Shock reverberated through her as she felt something cold between her legs. Opening her eyes, she dazedly watched him scooping melting ice cream onto her heat.

"Can't waste good ice cream," he told her, his voice thick with desire, his eyes twin lasers.

Then she was lost. Lost, as he licked and savored and tasted, his tongue slurping up all the ice cream, his fingers in her pressing and stroking and pressing that same spot over and over, his tongue tracking in circles to look for her hidden treasure, and finding it, and deliberately probing it, until she was at the limit, like an arrow pulled back and ready. And still he wouldn't allow her to go over, his sure expertise bringing her close and no closer, over and over, until every nerve he touched responded with silent quivering pleas.

It was a delicious kind of drowning. Grace couldn't breathe, her body struggling to keep up with her pleasure center. She agonized for—needed—that release, too deep in her quest to even moan any more.

"Tell me, sweetheart," he whispered against her. "Are your nails dry yet?" When she gave a strangled reply, he added, "I don't think I can wait, so I'll take that as a yes."

And all of a sudden he was on her, and with a quick downward flick of his zipper, he was inside her in one sure thrust.

"Now."

She climaxed, flying off within, incredibly, wonderfully free.

Lance began to thrust into her heat, feeling every spasm of her orgasm. She was everything to him, so unashamed of her sexuality, so fearless of showing her passion. He loved the way she gave herself, holding nothing back. She tasted of every dream he'd ever wanted, every wish he'd ever made. She was liquid fire, and in demand of more, as she convulsed and came, demanding him to give more, to go with her. He'd wanted this time to be slow, but found it impossible. He kept giving, loving her velvet heat, and she came again, squeezing him until he thought he would go insane with the pleasure. He wanted more, feeding her fire one more time, his hand touching expertly between their joined bodies as his strokes quickened.

"Oh God, Lance, I c..can't...I..."

"Give it to me once more, babe, yes, that's it, tight...like that..."

"Faster...no, don't stop like that..."

"Sweet...hang on...almost there..."

A final thrust. A flick of the thumb. A long exhalation. The ferocity of their simultaneous explosions left marks on his back and bruises on her shoulders. Garbled love words. Soft gulps of air. Delirious moans. Sweet, sweet little death.

***

"You drive me crazy, do you know that?" he said against her neck, his breathing slowly getting back to normal. "I wanted to talk to you first, and one look at you in that ridiculous turban and all my good intentions flew out the window."

The "ridiculous turban" had long ago came off, her thick brown hair spilling out, wavy and untamed, over all the cushions under her. She smiled at him with sexy satisfaction as he tangled his long fingers through its silky length.

"You really have to stop wrestling me to the floor," she said. "I don't think my back can handle this kind of abuse."

"You didn't put up too much resistance this time," he pointed out.

"I have to think about my nails," she defended, pouting at him. She squirmed under his weight. "They're probably all smudged up by now."

Lance rolled over, allowing her to move. Grace lifted her legs to inspect her nails. They were perfect, unmarked, with the cotton swabs still in between each toe. She looked down at herself and started to laugh uncontrollably. What a sight they made. She chuckled at the picture of herself sprawled like a hapless upside-down spider, half naked, with those toes and cotton wads waving up in the air, and him with his shirt pulled to his torso and his fly unzipped.

He, too, started to laugh, after looking down at their bodies lying side by side. "Not a very sexy sight," he agreed, "but I don't think I can move for now."

He pulled her close beside him, and they lay there in contented silence for a while, their hands caressing each other like old lovers.

"When?" she finally asked, softly, so as not to spoil the mood.

Lance sighed. "Tomorrow." He captured one of her hands. "How come I get the feeling you're not too worried?"

"Of course I'm worried," she said, but she smiled as she sat up a little higher looking down at him. "Anything can go wrong." She looked with interest at his open zipper.

"I'll be there with you."

"Really? I'm surprised." She couldn't resist it. She bent forward and undid the top button of his pants. He looked so sexy with the front of his pants open like that.

Her eyes were sending heat waves, and he felt his blood stirring again. Lance struggled to ignore the obvious problem at hand. "Why?" he asked.

"Well, I thought they might try to intimidate me," Grace answered, licking her lips suggestively as she continued eyeing him. "You know, like on TV."

"Not if you cooperate," he informed her, staring at her lips. Ignoring the rising need between his legs, he grabbed one of her feet, set it on his chest, and began to pull out the little cotton balls still encased between her toes. "Why don't you just tell me what I want to know?"

"What, and spoil their fun?" Grace asked, obligingly giving him her other foot when he pointed to it. It was strangely intimate, letting a man do such a mundane little thing. With her toes, she wickedly nudged the interesting thing saluting her. "Besides, it would compromise you if you know all the answers. They'll think I coached you to ask me the questions."

She had a point. It was also getting extremely unimportant. "True," Lance said, sitting up. "It'd have been a lot easier if you hadn't stolen the lists from David Cheng."

That got her full attention back. "Wait a minute," she said, her dark eyes flashing. She wagged a finger at him. "I didn't steal anything from David Cheng. If you're going to accuse me of stealing, you might as well quit trying to talk to me, buster."

Lance studied her, wanting her even more despite her glaring eyes and defiant lips. "What am I supposed to do, Grace? Everything about you smacks of double agent."

Grace sighed and looked heavenward. In one quick move, she straddled his lap and pulled at the collar of his shirt.

"No," she told him firmly. "Your whole outfit has a double agent, and since I don't work for you, it's not me. You have a leak, a rat. I've been answering your questions. Hell, I saved your stupid scholar for you and you can't even give me a little trust?" Her expression softened and she undulated against his burgeoning flesh pushing against her belly. When she kissed him tenderly, his hands automatically came up the small of her back to pull her closer. "You can't keep sleeping with me without a teensy bit of trust, babe."

Lance had slept with many women whom he didn't trust, who would have betrayed him with the right incentive, but he realized none of them were like Grace. They were worldly creatures, beautiful and deadly. He'd gotten used to those kinds of companions, could read them like the back of his hand—usually ambitious, always bloodthirsty, ultimately soulless. Then, there was Grace. He couldn't read her—either she was the most ingenuous and candid woman there was, or she was the deadliest spy on the planet, with the face of a freshly cut flower. She hadn't a shred of fake sophistication to her, her humor was clean and honest, and she was simply the liveliest soul he'd met in a long time. It occurred to him it was that very thing about her that attracted him so much.

"Okay," he finally said, kneading the flesh above her bottom. "I'll take the sex and give you a teensy bit of my trust. But I want the whole story."

Grace's smiled back, feeling happy and tender all at once. Somehow, knowing he trusted her, even a little, was important. If she could make him trust her, that meant she could make him love her, and maybe then, he wouldn't mind all her secrets.

"We both have things we cannot talk about," she told him, as she stroked his velvet hardness. "That's the nature of your business. I promise, after tomorrow, to tell you as much as possible, okay?"

If they let you go, he added silently, suddenly determined he would make sure they did. Her hand tightened around him. There was an urgent need to end the conversation. "Why tomorrow?" His voice grew huskier with each upward stroke.

Because by then you'll know what I am. "You'll see," she told him enigmatically. She ran her nails lightly up and down his erection, fascinated with the way his stomach muscles tighten every time she put pressure…right…there.

"You…worry me," Lance said, his hands going under the silk camisole, heading straight for the soft mounds that had been tempting him. "No agent your age should operate alone. You should…be afraid. The fact you aren't only makes…everyone suspicious."

It was time to concentrate on more interesting things. Grace kissed him, her hand rubbing harder. "Not an agent," she said against his lips. "Not…an…agent."

She kissed him again, pushing up on her knees. "Since you're so suspicious," she added, looking seriously into his eyes as she slid down on his erection, "I think it'd be better if you stay with me the rest of the day and night."

Something primitive flared in the deep blue of his eyes. His sensuous lips curved. "I plan to keep you so occupied you won't think of running away," he warned, holding her waist and pushing her down. His nostrils flared.

"Promises, promises," she taunted, amusement laced with passion as she rode him.

Lance hugged her with more emotion than he intended. She had better know what she was doing, he thought, as his mind started to blank out, or he would have to break a few more rules in the future. For now, he would let her handle him.

CHAPTER TWENTY

Thursday a.m.

Lance didn't like the new development. "Why the hell did they send you?" he demanded.

"Because I was in town," the man at the table drawled. The long fingers of his hands clasped loosely together as he leaned back on his seat, his light eyes studying the younger man before him. He canted a brow at the scowl on Lance's face, then glanced briefly at Dan Kershaw, who chose not to enlighten the newcomer about any problems. He guessed he would have to find out for himself. "How are you, Mercy? Been about five years, hasn't it?"

"About." Lance's answer was curt, his mind racing. He hadn't expected this. "Command didn't have to send you. She doesn't need to be broken."

The man's expression never changed. "No?" he asked politely. "From what they told me, she's somewhat of an evasion expert. They think I'll be able to see through any smokescreen she might throw at you." Interesting, he mused. Mercy had feelings for the subject. "I also heard she managed to evade you a few times. Most fascinating, since even I didn't fully escape your tracker skills."

Lance shrugged. "She's good," he said in a careless voice, as if it didn't bother him. "Have you read what we have on her yet?"

The man shook his head. "No. Maybe later. I like to gauge for myself without prior preparation. Easier to break."

Lance's scowl returned. This was bad news. Command had sent a fucking cold one to test Grace. He had to toe the line again. "She's mine," he tersely informed the man. "I don't want her hurt."

There. He'd crossed the line. Dan, taking notes, as was his job, paused and stopped writing.

Lance didn't wait for an answer. Crossing the room, he opened the door to the adjoining room where Grace was, turned and added over his shoulder, "She came with me willingly and has agreed to answer any questions within reason."

"I see," the man at the table said. He didn't argue or protest, his eyes calculating. His voice betrayed a slight amusement as he asked, "And you accepted this offer?"

Lance turned to give his fullest attention. The interrogator had a reputation and myth not for the weak-stomached. He had tracked him before, had gotten into his head to finally succeed in a particularly tricky mission which took him almost a year. The man was deadly, with the efficiency of a machine. Lance never fooled himself that he really actually found him in the end. He always had the feeling his opponent had allowed himself to be reined back in, and that, all along, he'd been following his own agenda.

A knot of fear grew in his belly. There was no way Grace could handle this ruthless man. After a hard stare, he chose not to answer the man's query, turning to enter the other room instead. The other man followed soundlessly.

***

Grace sat in her chair, which wasn't very comfortable. The room was small and brightly lit, and she was the lone occupant against the wall. In the middle was a long table, with a jug of water and several glasses. The door to freedom was on the other side. Straightening her back, she felt like she was facing a firing squad. Good intimidation tactic, duly noted.

The door opened. She brightened up a little. The first one in was her darling Lance. She quickly took in the scowl and tense body language. Well, he didn't look too darling at the moment. Not a good sign. Two other men followed. Her breath was a little unsteady as she stared defiantly at them. She had an idea which one of them was going to be her interrogator.

Ignoring Lance, she looked at the second man, who was studying her. She returned the scrutiny, her brown eyes narrowing slightly. He wasn't as tall as Lance, but he had an intimidating presence. He had a healthy tan, which made the lightness of his eyes even more pronounced. His hair was a deep bronze, with streaks of red from the sun here and there. He wore it a little too long, like a man who had no time for regular haircuts.

She couldn't help but make comparisons of the two men; both loomed larger than life before her. The new man was older and leaner. There was something very hard about him, and she felt his power immediately as he came closer. A man used to striking fear in others, he wore the quiet menace like a second skin, barely aware of it. Grace understood he was a man who made a living making tough choices, who didn't think twice about taking a life. He exuded coldness, especially in his strange light eyes, which glittered like chipped ice out of his tough, rugged face. They were eyes that looked right into her mind, but she obstinately stared right into them. She wasn't going to be afraid.

"So, you're the evasion expert that have gotten COS's top guns flustered," the man said. He had a slow raspy drawl, almost an accent.

"I was taught by the best," she told him calmly.

His eyes glittered back, but his face was like a statue. "Is that right," he stated, in that soft voice.

Lance watched, clenching his jaw. Did she think she could use mere words to duel with this man? She was going to find out she couldn't play that game with him. Yet, there still wasn't any fear in the way she sat. She looked confident and relaxed, even amused. Only her expressive eyes held a bit of defiance. Damn her, he was breaking out in sweat for her and she was cool as cucumber. He willed himself to do the same, leaning against the door. He had a strange feeling he was going to see yet another side of Grace today.

"So why did you choose to come here, seeing you could evade at will?" the man continued. He jerked his head slightly toward Lance's direction. "Can't resist a tracker, can you? Haven't you been warned about them, little girl?"

The 'little girl' rankled. Trying not to betray her irritation, she leaned back and smiled up at him. "I told him I'd answer only the necessary questions. I don't have to answer that one."

He obviously didn't like her reply, walking up even closer to her. Lance watched, ready to stop him if he hurt Grace. He didn't like the direction the questions were taking, recognizing the tactics of emotional intimidation. Grace seemed to be taking it well. No, his Grace was enjoying the whole thing. He wanted to cross the room and shake her hard. The woman didn't know the tightrope she was walking on.

The man stopped directly in front of her, then said to Lance, "Mercy, I thought you said the girl's yours. How come she's resisted your imprinting?"

Grace tilted her head up to look into the cold eyes studying her so intently. Attack, she decided. "Don't be crude," she said, darting a quick glance to meet Lance's grim ones across the room. He hadn't said a word so far. She wondered whether he was ready for a shock. "Imprinting is for amateurs anyway."

"So, now the young miss thinks she can handle sexual bondage too?" He was being deliberately insulting.

She was aware Lance had started walking across the room. "Like I said," she said firmly, "I was taught by the very best."

There was an odd note in her voice. Lance stopped, watchful again. There was something strange going on here. He breathed in sharply as the other man forced Grace out of the chair by her shoulders. He would have stepped in and put a stop to it if he hadn't noticed her calm demeanor, as she allowed herself to be pulled to her feet without resistance.

"What the hell are you up to, Trouble?" the man asked quietly.

A grin broke out on Grace's face. She relaxed, now that he'd made the first move to acknowledge her.

"Hello, Jed, I've missed you." She stepped into his arms, hugging him. "This is a nice surprise. I didn't know you were in town."

"You better have an explanation for this," he warned, turning his head to look at Lance. "For him too. Another one thick in the head."

Grace sighed and followed his gaze. There was astonishment in Lance's eyes and, she recognized, a growing rage. *Now* she was in trouble.

There was a short silence in the room as the three men absorbed their own conclusions. Grace remained quietly in the arms of the man sent to interrogate her, patiently waiting for the questions to start.

Jed let her go, stood back, and looked her up and down. "You're in trouble," he told her.

"Hardly," she retorted.

"What if it were somebody else they sent to get this information?" Jed again looked at the silent Lance. There was definitely mockery in his voice now. "*He* can't stop it."

"Would I allow myself to be here if I couldn't handle it, Jed?" Grace asked lightly, patting him on the arm. She glanced at Lance, saw his blue gaze narrowly watching her hand still on Jed's arm, and gave him a wary smile. "I suppose you're a little surprised, Lance."

"I gather you know each other," Lance said, folding his arms, as he leaned back against the table. He casually crossed one leg over the other. "I can wait till later."

That sounded ominous. Grace bit her lower lip. Damn, things kept getting more complicated. She returned her attention to the man in front of her, and found him thoughtfully studying her. She knew he was trying to read her mind.

"He doesn't know anything," she told him, knowing Jed would understand her hidden message.

His hard face was inscrutable. Gesturing to the chair behind her, he ordered, "Sit. Might as well see this through."

Grace went back to her seat, crossing her legs. "I'm ready." Then she smiled unexpectedly. This was going to be fun, actually.

Lance frowned. He knew that mischievous look by now. What the hell was going on? And what was the hellcat up to now? How did she know Jed McNeil? He was jealous of the easy manner in which he held her, like he'd known her for a long time. Was he another one of her lovers? That didn't sit too well with him at all. First a younger man, now an older one. Lance Mercy looked on with purposeful eyes.

Jed poured himself a glass of water. He slowly drank it down, not offering Grace any.

Grace's smile widened even more. Oh, he wasn't going to let her off lightly. Well, let him test her, she didn't mind.

"What do you know about David Cheng?" he questioned without warning.

"Chinese citizen here on the pretext of furthering education. He brought with him certain information for COS Command." Grace noticed Lance's lifted brow. It was the first time that she'd ever admitted any knowledge of his agency.

"Why did you help him escape from the Chinese government?"

"I was helping Lance," Grace said, then amended, "I mean, Agent Mercy. He hired me to keep an eye out for the unusual, since COS has a leak within."

"Why didn't you just tell him what you knew?" Jed continued. "By the way, that little adventure with Room 103 and license plate 103 was very you. I should've known."

Grace beamed. "No proof, only suspicions," she told him. "I took a wild guess. I did save COS's guy, and they owe me."

Jed rubbed the bridge of his nose with a long index finger. "I think," he said, his voice that strange quiet tone, "you aren't in any position to bargain."

"Of course I am," she, in turn, informed him in the same kind of voice, her eyes suddenly cool and flat. She held out her hand and studied her painted nails for an interested moment, then answered, "COS can't touch me. I'm a ghost."

An axe could chop through the tense silence that followed. Grace solemnly looked around her, twirling a nonchalant finger in her hair.

Lance finally broke the silence. "You're bullshitting," he said.

Grace smile was smug. "Am I? Here's a recording from my immediate supervisor. She instructed me to give this to the head honcho when there is obvious danger in my situation. Under U.N. section COV63 Paragraph27, you're required to play it through immediately in my presence so I record it for my superiors."

Jed took the small disk from her and handed it to Dan. There was genuine amusement in his expression now, and Lance, watching him, wondered for the umpteenth time what he was to Grace. She had a lot of explaining to do.

Sandra's recorded voice came on. "Gentlemen, my code is Rose. You may call the institute and ask for Sandra Smythe. Grace O'Connor is our field operative and covered by our charter. I trust you'll adhere to it. You may question her, but all information can only be accessed through us, and of course, you know the procedure. We expect you to let her go. Good day."

"Have that sent to Command, Kershaw," Jed said.

"Will do," the man, who had sat quietly all this time, spoke up.

"I don't trust a D.o.D. room," Jed announced, then walked to the door. "Grace, let's walk to your car. I want all the facts."

"I came with La...Agent Mercy." She shot Lance an apprehensive glance, feeling more and more uneasy as his silence grew. "It's his assignment, after all, Jed."

Jed gave Lance a hard look. "You're quiet," he said to the younger man. "No questions?"

"Not for you," Lance replied softly, his eyes unreadable.

"I'm walking her to your car, then." The message was silent, but definite.

"I'll meet the two of you there. I've several things to wrap up with Dan. Five minutes." Message received and warning given.

Grace shook her head. Men and property. She had to write a thesis on that when she returned to school. The thought of college struck her as strange. That world seemed so far away at that very moment. She walked out of the sparsely furnished room with the unexpected newcomer.

Dan Kershaw studied Lance as the younger man watched Grace and Jed walking off together. His old student didn't look especially happy about the girl being so chummy with the Ice Man.

"She's something else," he commented, as he slipped the disk into his pocket. "No one smiles at the Ice Man like that unless she knows him well."

Lance's hand fisted. "They know each other, all right," he said. It was killing him, wondering how well that might be.

"It explains her abilities, though," Dan said.

"What do you mean?"

"Mercy, Jed McNeil is a virus," Dan reminded him.

"I know who he is. He and I crossed paths before, don't you remember? What has an assassin got to do with Grace's talents?"

"Silent assassin," Dan corrected. "Viruses kill without an army. They're programmed to wipe out the target through information assimilation and core attack."

"Information assimilation," Lance murmured, understanding gleaming in his eyes, "like you."

"Only deadlier," Dan said, nodding. "Viruses, you should know, are masters of environment manipulation—"

"And evasion experts," Lance finished, blue eyes blazing. He slipped his sunglasses on. "She's *his* then." There was a painful rage growing in him.

"I didn't say that. Actually, it looks like you've gotten yourself quite a ghost, Mercy."

"She isn't my ghost," Lance answered as he headed out of the building, "yet."

He heard Dan's quiet laughter behind him.

***

"Start," Jed ordered, not even waiting for Grace as he went down the building steps. They both weaved between the groups of people milling inside and outside, ignoring curious glances in their direction. He looked sideways at her, and added with slight humor in his voice, "Your tracker didn't give us much time."

Grace was used to simplifying mass information, had been trained to look at things that way. She finished what he needed to know in two minutes flat.

"How much do you trust him, Grace?" Jed asked, as he led the way to the parking area.

"I trust him, but I haven't told him," Grace replied, matching his speed without complaining, "if that's what you're worried about."

He slowed down enough for her to walk alongside him. "I didn't train you so I would worry about you."

She smiled and slipped a hand in the crook of his muscular arm. "I know, Dad," she said. It was good to see him again.

"A ghost?" he asked, looking down at her quizzically. "I thought you were in school."

"It's a long story, and we're almost out of minutes."

Jed chuckled unexpectedly, his harsh face softening. "He's got you on a short leash."

Grace snorted. Ignoring his taunt, she said, "I want to see you before you disappear again, Dad."

"If you could shake that tracker of yours, we can have a quick dinner tonight, about eight," he told her. "I want to know how you ended up with him. I thought I'd warned you about trackers." He sighed, adding, "It's bad enough I can't control my daughter's dating life, but she had to specifically choose to have the most dangerous tracker in the business."

Grace fondly grinned at her father. She didn't mind not having a mother in whom to confide girlish matters. Her father answered most of her questions more frankly than any of her teachers or her grandmother ever dared, from the mundane to the more interesting ones about the methods in which some agents specialized. There was no other father like hers, that was for sure.

"He's a pussy cat," she assured him of Lance. "I think you might like him."

In the back of her mind, she wondered how she was going to explain to Lance about Jed, when she couldn't reveal that the latter was her father. The truth wasn't possible, given the nature of her father's dangerous job. She was a liability to him, and in the eyes of the world, she didn't exist. She was Grace O'Connor, orphan, brought up by her grandmother.

"Like always, thick-headed where you're concerned."

"What can I say? I have this effect on my guys."

Jed looked over her shoulder. "Our five minutes are up," he dryly informed her, his low voice filled with humor. "By the way, Trouble, your pussy cat's got his claws out."

Grace turned and followed his gaze, swallowing nervously at the sight of Lance striding toward them. He was wearing sunglasses, the sun glinting off the lenses. His stride was slow but measured, very predatory. With his ruffled blond mane and light stubble, shirt unbuttoned and sleeves rolled up, she thought he looked very much like the angry and hungry lion in her dreams. Oh, dear.

A few minutes later, with her head out of the Porsche's window, she gave her father her address. "I've got your Christmas present," she called out, as the vehicle moved. Jed gave her a wave of acknowledgement as they drove off.

Great, she buys the notorious Ice Man Christmas presents. Lance shifted, racing the engine hard. The BMW gave a loud purr as he stepped on the gas. She hugged him. She gave him gifts. She talked like him, even fucking walked like him, which he'd noticed when he was following them across the parking area. They were close, even a blind man could tell from the easy way they chatted with each other, and Lance found he needed release from this strange jealousy that took over every time he saw Grace with another man.

Grace gave him a sidelong glance as he drove with a speed that was going to lure a traffic cop onto their tail, if he weren't more careful. They weren't going back to her apartment. His profile was beautiful, she thought, admiring the strong forehead, the way the sunglasses sat on the straight line of his nose, the sexy curve of his lips, all the way down to his strong, masculine unshaven jaw. If he weren't in such a foul mood, she would kiss him. She was getting mighty curious about where they were heading.

"What time are you having dinner with him?" Lance finally asked, stressing the last word.

They were almost out of the city now, Grace noticed with a start. "Eightish," she told him, too busy trying to figure out where they were to notice him studying her. "Mind telling me where we're going?"

"To a state park."

"A state park," she repeated to herself, very puzzled by now. Would the man ever say something that didn't need explanation?

"Mmmhmm. You didn't exercise yesterday, sweetheart. Since it's partly my fault, I thought I'd make it up to you."

She met his eyes for a moment before turning her full attention to the road. That ought to keep her quiet for the rest of the journey. He could hear the little mind clicking along, trying to figure it all out. He understood how to manipulate her that way by now, just bombard her with information and she would come back for more, until she solved the problem. She didn't know a trap had been set, just for her. With enough breadcrumbs, he would lead her to his lair, and she would find out too late her only solution was to surrender. What did the Ice Man say? Sexual bondage? Maybe she would learn to get him Christmas presents, he glibly added in silence, as they drove on.

Grace looked around in curiosity when he turned down a road that seemed to stretch forever. It didn't look like any highway, deserted and fenced on either side. She noticed the mounted cameras on the poles as Lance slowed down. That didn't seem like standard state park equipment. At the end of the road was a gate with a security booth. Two uniformed men were waiting.

Grace sat up, alert and full of questions. When the BMW stopped, they saluted Lance, who saluted back. A mechanical arm, attached to the security housing, came alive, moving toward the car, then coming to a stop as it reached Lance's window. She could hear the soft whirring of the machine as it slowly disengaged and extended another smaller arm, inserting itself into the car. Her companion didn't look surprised at all; instead, he took off his sunglasses, flipped down a binocular-like device and placed his forehead against it, like one would at the optometrist. There was a clicking sound, and Grace blinked when she heard a computer voice said, "Identity confirmed. Access permitted."

"Wow, they do eye scans for state parks now?" Her question was ignored.

They drove through security. She had visions of strange new worlds in her mind. Aladdin's Cave. Dante's Underworld. King Tut's tomb. This must be how the first man entering those places felt. She had a feeling she was going somewhere very few people were allowed. They drove on for another mile or so, then a circular building came into view. Without a word, she followed Lance when he left the parked car. Taking off his sunglasses again, he repeated the same procedure at the electronic gate, then entered the building when the door slid open.

It wasn't at all what she expected inside—not that she had any idea exactly what she thought she was expecting. She had imagined some sort of cold military-like place behind those doors, certainly not this country club atmosphere with lush carpeting and chandeliers. The man at the shiny counter acted like a hotel manager, except that he, too, was in uniform.

After signing a folder the man at the counter handed him, Lance turned to Grace, taking in her bemused expression. "What size shoes and clothes?" he asked, his voice mild.

Grace cocked her head. *Very strange question.* Oh well, she would play along. "Seven for shoes, six to eight for clothes," she told him, then politely asked, "Want my bra size?"

The corners of his sensual lips quirked, but he ignored her, turning back to the waiting "hotel manager." He repeated her sizes, adding, "Size 12 shoes for me, and large."

The man disappeared for a few minutes, returning with two backpacks, which Lance took from him. "Which courses are free today?" Lance questioned, his eyes looking up at the electronic board on the wall behind the counter.

After consulting his computer, he answered, "Course B, E, and F, sir."

"Which is the smallest of the three?"

"F, sir."

"We'll take that one," Lance told him.

"Real or simulation, sir?"

"Simulation, 2 sets."

The man typed into his computer, then pressed something. A package shot out from a chute to the left of the counter. Grace watched, fascinated with the whole thing, as Lance picked up the mysterious box and said to her, "Come on. That's the changing room. Get dressed and meet me back here."

She watched him disappear down the corridor. Well, he certainly knew his way around. She was tempted to go look around, but thought better. What was this place? In the dressing room, she opened the bag and emptied its contents. She gasped when she saw the army fatigues and boots. She was dying of curiosity. Shrugging, she put them on, then stuffed her own clothes into the empty bag. There were lockers on one side of the room. Well, at least, she knew what those were for.

When she met him outside, he was also in fatigues, looking both tough and sexy. The only thing wrong, she thought, as she critically checked him up and down, was he hadn't shaved. If she were a drill sergeant, he would be peeling a few hundred potatoes for punishment. He was also studying her and was obviously amused by the picture she made. She made a face at him.

"What's so funny?" she demanded.

"Cute," was all he said, as he buttoned her uniform all the way.

"Are you going to tell me what we're doing?"

"You'll find out soon," he said. "Ready?"

Was she ever. "Like I have a choice," she grumbled. Other men took their women out to dinner, to the movies, maybe even a ballet. She got to play soldier in a "state park."

"Come on. We've only eight hours before your big date."

Eight hours. She gulped. "Uh, what about lunch, Lance?" she asked, hopefully.

He smirked back at her as they got back into his car. "You can work up a nice big appetite for tonight, babe."

Ominous, very ominous indeed, she thought, as she studied her surroundings. There was nothing but miles and miles of wood. Very park-like.

He stopped the car, then turned to her. "Listen carefully," he said in a soft voice. "Course F is small, only thirty-five acres."

He opened the package that came out of the chute. Grace's eyes widened at the sight of the two weapons in the case. *Uh-oh.*

"Relax," he told her, pulling one out of its place. "Flexy plastic. Bulky, but lightweight." He unloaded the cartridge and showed it to her. What she saw inside was nothing like what she knew a weapon should look like. He went on explaining, "You have six shots and a seventh in the chamber. Do you see the target on that tree?"

Grace nodded. "Yes," she said.

Lance got out of the car, and pointed the weapon at the target. Grace stiffened, holding her breath. He fired. There was a noisy *Pffft*, like a tennis ball shooting out of one those machines, then a dull thud. Looking at the target, she saw a bright yellow stain right over the bull's eye.

She got out of the car, still staring at the target. Then she turned to Lance, who was grinning at her. "Simulated," he explained.

"Instead of 'real'," she said, remembering the earlier conversation with the man behind the counter.

"Here, you try it." He gave her the other weapon.

It was really quite light. She played with it for a minute, then aimed at the target. She pulled the trigger. A bright blue splattered over the yellow. Wrapping her arm around her chest, with the gun pointing safely away, she looked up at Lance, her brows arched. Okay, she'd done everything he'd told her. It was time for some explanation.

Lance admired her accuracy for a moment, then turned back to her. As expected, she was an excellent shot. It was time for him to find out what she was made of. She could play with words all she wanted, but this time, he would know for sure whether she was for real. He'd come to the conclusion he should just ignore her age and treat her like he would one out in the field. *Let's see the rest of your arsenal, hellcat.* He pulled out a map from the same package.

"I'm only telling this once, so pay attention," he told her. His voice, she noted, had changed into that of someone giving orders, the instructions coming out crisp and staccato. He flattened the sheet on the hood and she looked down at it, following his moving finger. "Follow that path. To the east, there's an incline. Your target is this lodge. You might find lunch there, who knows? But watch out for this stretch before the target. There are six-foot deep holes all over. See? They're hidden. The perimeter is all water and fenced up. Don't try to climb over the fence. I wouldn't recommend it. The other side of the fence is Course D and the soldier told me they're using real bullets there today. Your real goal is here. There are several different ways that lead to it. Pick one. My car is parked there and if you get into it without a shot to your head or heart, you survive."

She digested the flow of information, concentrating on the map. When she was satisfied she'd memorized it, she slowly nodded. "What would you be doing?" She'd gathered from his instructions she was expected to be on her own.

Lance's smile was positively wicked. "I'm coming after you, babe. You have a head start while I hand over the car, then I'll track you and cancel you."

Grace was too stunned to speak for a moment. "This is my exercise?" she asked, incredulous.

He nodded, serious. "You did mention you were taught by the best this morning," he reminded her, the tone of his voice silky soft, with an edge of challenge to it. "Was that all just an idle boast?"

So, now she knew what all this was about. Grace could never resist a challenge. She snapped on the belt that came with the package, putting the weapon in the holster, and accepted the safety glasses dangling from his hands.

"Give me my satchel," she said, her eyes cool, her voice just as dangerous as his.

Lance leaned into the car and pulled out her bag. She slung it over her shoulder, and started to trek down the path leading into the woods.

"Hey, Grace," he called from behind. She turned around and caught what he threw her. "Your compass."

Grace smiled at her opponent. Going to track and cancel her, was he? "Blue is going to look so good on you, darling," she drawled and blew him a kiss, as he got into his car and drove off.

She paused long enough to see his mock salute when he passed by. She snapped back one smartly. Then stuck out a tongue after the back of his car. He could track her as hard as he wanted, but she wasn't the daughter of a Virus for nothing. She would evade him, no problem.

CHAPTER TWENTY ONE

The sun beat down where the trees thinned into a clearing. Grace wiped the sweat dripping off her chin with her sleeve. Squinting, she looked into the cloudless sky that was so blue it hurt her eyes. The color reminded her of another relentless blue that shone out of the face of a certain someone stalking her right now. She sniffed. There was something vaguely familiar about this scenario, but now was not the time to think. She needed to catch her breath, then continue. The incline was a lot steeper than the map had let on; she had fallen and grazed her knee at one point. When she made it to the top, she checked the compass. She could see the rooftop of the lodge to the left. She hoped there was something to drink there. Got to hurry. He wouldn't be too far behind.

Right behind her, Lance pulled at the blade of grass. The first part was easy. She would be heading east, toward the lodge. If he could catch her at the incline, he would have a clear shot at her while she was climbing uphill. However, she was further than he'd anticipated. By the time he reached the incline, all he saw was disturbed foliage, and a patch of sand where she'd slid off. He followed in pursuit.

Grace cursed under her breath. She'd almost fallen into one of those damned holes about which he'd warned. She looked around her warily, her heart still in her tummy where it landed when her foot went through the pile of dry leaves covering the hole. Everything looked normal, but she knew now there was no way she could make it in a hurry. The holes were like landmines, and if she weren't too careful, she would be waiting for Lance in one of them. But if she took her time, he would be able to see her on this level patch of land, and, no doubt, would take her out like easy roadkill. Checking around thoroughly, she caught sight of the tree standing alone twenty-five feet away, with a thick rope of vine dangling down like an invitation. Hmmm. She gauged the jump she needed to make to reach the safe ground on the other side. She might just be able to do it. There were two fallen logs lying on each side of her. Obviously, they were on solid ground. But which one was safe for her weight?

Minutes later, Lance bent down and studied the boot print. One of her feet found a hole here and she had braced her weight on her other foot as she went down. *Good for her.* He grinned at the disturbed area nearby. Here was where she landed on her cute little ass. He looked around, but saw no more clues. His eyes narrowed. There was no way she could run across and not topple into a hole. He caught sight of the scraped wet bark on one of the logs. The little hellcat. So that was how she avoided the holes. Following the log, he jumped close to a lone tree that looked suspicious, set apart from the others as it was. Walking around the huge trunk, he started to laugh softly when he saw the vine. Grace had played Tarzan here and with the help of the vine and her incredible upper body strength, swung out to the pile of rocks there. The ropelike vine resisted his tugs to get it back to him, and he saw, with some consternation, that it was wound several times around another tree trunk on the other side. A reluctant smile of admiration appeared on his lips at her delay tactic. He tested the strength of the vine, wondering whether he should chance walking across the minefield of holes, or be stuck there.

Grace was glad to see the lodge ahead. After almost an hour and a half of hard physical activity, the thirst was getting unbearable. Swinging over with the vine had been tricky, and she was quite proud of her feat. It comforted her parched throat somewhat to know her darling tracker probably cursed up a storm, and thus wasted precious body fluids, when he found out he couldn't use the same trick, seeing she'd made sure that the rope couldn't be retrieved.

Smug, but still thirsty, she hurried toward the little cabin.

A good distance away, Lance dangled upside down by his hands and feet over the clearing. It was good he brought along a pair of gloves. Using the vine like a clothesline, he slowly slid across, using his boots to make sure he didn't slip and fall off. It was slower than swinging over, but better than poking around holes. Sweat dripped into his eyes, then down his chin and under his collar. Ten more feet. Then, he would get her soon.

There was no time to be neat about it. Grace threw open the pantry, grabbing the first bottle of water she saw. Taking big gulps from it, she walked around the tiny shack, looking for things that might aid her. She couldn't haul along any of the gallon bottles of water. Too heavy. She'd better drink as much as she could. From here, she had two choices, either the path to the left of the lodge, or the one to the right. She remembered from the map that both circled back eventually to another main path ahead, but taking either would still put her at the disadvantage of being chased. Perhaps she could hit him first, play tracker instead of prey. She grinned at the idea. Looking around, she noticed a coiled length of rope hanging on the wall. Unwinding it, she found it long enough for her purpose. From her satchel, she took out her Swiss knife.

Lance was thirsty. So was she, he mused, looking at the opened bottle of water. She'd torn through everything, throwing cans and supplies off the shelves. What was she looking for? Pouring a whole bottle of water over his head to cool off, he went to the window and looked at the two paths, trying to guess which one she took. The one on the left had an empty gallon bottle lying in the middle. His eyes narrowed.

Grace lay on her back, holding her breath. She could hear him moving around in the lodge. Then silence. She bit her lower lip. He was probably looking out the window. Well, he couldn't possibly miss the big gallon jug she'd put down on the left path. When he took off up that trail, she would just turn over and aim for that arrogant head of his, turning him into a big Smurf. Then she would stand up on the roof and yell, "Game over!"

Lance stared at the bottle. No way she would bring along a gallon of water out there, drink it, then lay it directly in the middle of the path. Did she think him so easily tricked? He walked out the door, and turned to take the other path.

Damn, damn, damn, he was going the other way! There wasn't enough time for her to make it to the other side of the roof and take a shot at him without him hearing her move. The roof creaked at the slightest shift in her weight as it was. She would have to climb down and take the other path. Oh well, he still couldn't sneak up on her this way. After counting to twenty, Grace started to climb down from the roof.

Nothing along the trail had been disturbed. Lance knew something wasn't quite right. There should be more signs of her after five minutes. He stopped, scowling. She went the other way, that tricky little witch; he couldn't believe he'd fallen for such a simple trick. Pivoting, he doubled back.

Grace checked the compass, knowing she should see another clearing coming up. Then there should be a wall there for her to climb over, and beyond that, Lance's car. She grinned. *Lancelot Mercy, your goose is so cooked.*

Lance grunted in disgust as he pulled at the rope dangling on the side of the shack. He couldn't believe it—she'd been up there all along while he was in the lodge, probably waiting for him to take the path with the bottle so she could shoot him. Dammit, he hadn't thought about her turning the tables on him. Checking his watch, he saw she had ten minutes on him. He broke off in a dead run down the other path, determined to catch her before she reached the wall.

The wall was eight feet high, not tough for a tall man to handle, but a challenge for Grace's smaller build. She wished she had the rope with her still, but she hadn't dared take the time to untie it from the PVC pipe. She knew Lance would know he'd made a mistake within minutes and she wanted to be gone by the time he ran back. Too bad she didn't have a ladder in her helpful satchel, she joked, as she searched for foot holes and cracks along the wall so she could hoist herself up. She pursed her lips at the sound of a broken fingernail. Lance Mercy was going to pay for destroying her nice new manicure.

Halfway up the wall, she heard the cracking of twigs and dry leaves behind her. She looked over her shoulder and gasped. He was running at top speed, zipping among the trees, mowing right through the bushes. She saw him pull the weapon out of his holster as he ran. Starting to panic, she turned back to fully concentrate on her task, desperately pulling herself to the top of the wall as sweat seemed to squeeze out of every pore in her face.

Lance aimed and fired twice while still running. She disappeared over the wall just as he was about to shoot a third time. Two yellow splashes hit the spot where she had been moments ago. Dammit, he almost had her. He was across the clearing in six leaping strides.

Grace jumped off and landed hard, falling to her knees. She could hear him from the other side of the wall, the crunching sounds of pebbles and rocks as he too climbed. She got up in such a hurry, she almost tripped over a rock.

Lance peered over, saw her turning around and aiming. He ducked, an arm holding on to the wall as he almost fell over. Taking out the weapon again, and with his head still shielded, he fired blindly in her direction, hoping he'd get lucky. There was certain smug satisfaction when he heard her squeal.

Grace clutched at her sleeve, now smeared with yellow. The hit didn't hurt but had just enough of a sting to it to make one's adrenaline pump out. The rule was head or heart as target. Oh man, that was close. She fired a shot at him as he pulled himself over the wall and grunted with triumph to see the blue spreading on his shoulder. Knowing he would reach her before she could try another shot, Grace turned and ran for the nearest tree.

Lance jumped off, then rolled quickly, just in case she decided to shoot him again. On his stomach, he trained his weapon at her and got off a shot, just as she went behind a tree. A big splat of blue was on his shoulder. Damn, she was really quite proficient with a weapon.

Grace saw the car at the end of the downhill trek. Ignoring the danger of losing her footing and rolling downhill, she went at full speed, charging toward her target.

He chased after her as she went around a bush, then drove through another, making it difficult for him to get a good shot at her. Finally, the path was clear. His longer strides were gaining ground on her.

Grace was gasping as she sped toward her safety. She could see the futility of reaching it. He would just shoot her in the back of her head and score a 'cancel.' Determined to make sure that wouldn't happen, she turned, went down on one knee, and pulled the trigger again. Lance also fired the weapon at the same time. She got him in the leg; his shot missed, since he was aiming for her head when she knelt down. With her shooting back, he was forced to dive on his stomach to avoid a direct hit. She missed him by inches. She dove forward too, hitting hard on the ground before rolling under the car, using the momentum to move to the other side of the vehicle.

Lance jumped up, weapon ready. Grace was on her feet the same instant, using the car as a shield. They fired, both determined to be the last one standing, triumphantly yelling out.

That was their very last shot.

They were both cancelled, blue paint all over his face, yellow right over her chest. They stood there staring at each other, gasping for breath.

"Are you two lovers?" demanded Lance, in between pants.

Grace leaned her weight against the car, pushing her wet hair out of her face. If she weren't so out of breath, she would have laughed.

"No," she gasped out.

He strode around the car and took her into his arms. Grace laid her head on his chest, still breathing hard.

"Did he make you his ghost?" he demanded again. When she shook her head, he tilted up her face by the chin and gave her a long hard kiss that took the life out of her legs. "Want to be mine?" he murmured against her lips.

For answer, she punched him in the stomach and grimly enjoyed his grunt of surprise. "I'm going to kill you," she told him. He'd been trying to see whether she was good enough for him, damn his dark beastly soul.

"I think we just killed each other," he retorted, rubbing his face and looking wryly down at the blue in his hand.

"I got you first!"

"Did not!"

"Did too! You broke my nail! You're so dead!"

Lance lifted her off her feet and swung her around, making her hang on to him.

"Okay, then I'll be your ghost," he said, grinning, as he hugged her hard. Now that he was sure about her skills, he wasn't willing to let her go so easily. Virus-trained evasion expert or not, he would just track after her till she surrendered.

CHAPTER TWENTY TWO

"She's been released. She was seen walking out of the building and got in the car with Mercy," Ed told Sandra over the car phone. "I'll come by and pick you up for a late dinner."

"Sounds wonderful," she said. "Give me some time to freshen up."

It was just beginning to get dark when Sandra reached her house. The streetlights came on, illuminating the cobbled sidewalk that led to her driveway. She was used to coming home late and looked forward to spending time alone away from the office. The moment she closed the door, however, the hair at the nape of her neck stood up. All her past training rushed back, and without hesitation, she turned around quickly and scanned the dim hallway in her house. Not turning on the lights, she stepped out of her heels and sidled to the wall closest to her.

Her body was rusty, but her faculties were still alert enough to tell her someone had been here, might still be here. She slipped her hand into the inside pocket of her jacket, treading softly into her darkened living room. She wished she'd pulled open the shades that morning, so at least the last of the fading daylight might tell her whether the room was empty.

Without a sound, a shadow stood up from her sofa. She nearly didn't see it, but training had taken over and she was acting solely on instincts. Attacking reflexively, Sandra flicked the tiny weapon in her hand in the direction of the intruder. She heard it whipping through the air, and saw the shadow jump sideways, then disappear. He didn't make a sound, so she couldn't tell whether or not she hit her target.

Must be losing my skill. She seldom missed. Something moved to the right of the window and she flicked her wrist again, dispensing another missile, aiming for the heart. This time the whirring sound ended with a thud against the wall, not the unmistakable sound of metal cutting through flesh.

Sandra frowned. She'd missed a second time.

Her other option was to catch her intruder by surprise, so she flipped the main switch on, flooding the room with bright light. He was standing less than ten feet in front of her, and she knew she wouldn't miss this third time, except she was frozen in shock.

"You're out of practice. You missed me by two feet." His voice was gravelly soft, but he could have been shouting at her, the way her senses were hurting. "Hello, Sandra."

She felt as if a big cork plugging a hole in her gut had popped off. The torrent of feelings buried for so long gushed out in avenging release, all the good mixed with the bad, the joy with the pain, the tender with cruel, everything swirling and washing away her carefully hewn iron control. For the first time in years, she felt emotionally naked. She snapped her half-open mouth closed.

"Sit down," he said. "You're in shock."

She obeyed, her eyes devouring him. He was exactly as she remembered, hard and masculine, deceptively lean. His face hadn't changed; it was like time hadn't affected him at all. He looked the same as when she last saw him, standing there in front of her, unsmiling, his chiseled features harshly defined by the shadows and planes of his high cheekbones and square jaw. His eyes were just as fierce as then, just as secretive. She found her voice.

"What...are you doing here? How did you find me?" It sounded strange to her ears.

"Ghosts don't disappear," he replied, still not moving, studying her, noting the myriad of emotions that raced across her face. She was thinner. Her face was dearly familiar, but the softness he remembered was gone. There was a certain stern quality haunting those full lips, and the usual twinkle in her eyes was now dimmed into shadows. "I've always known you retired from the field."

Answer my question!" Sandra demanded, gathering together the remnants of what remained of her self-control.

"Not yet," he said, his voice gentle, and he walked a few steps closer to where she was sitting. "How are you, Sandra?"

"I'm well," she answered, a little too quickly. "And you?"

"Alive."

"You look good." It was all so awkward, not like the way she'd imagined.

He didn't say anything, just stood there watching her with the same intensity that had always been his trademark. She used the time to gather her wits, to become herself again.

"I've missed you," he finally said. "I've missed us."

"Have you come to tell me this?" she asked, her voice sounding like her own again. She couldn't believe this was real, that he was here in flesh and blood. Clasping her trembling hands together in her lap, she forced them to relax.

"No." He sat down in the chair across from her. A few feet away. A vast chasm separated them. "But I want to know why you look so unhappy."

"Unhappy?" Sandra echoed, tilting her head in defiant denial. "Scarcely. I'm doing very well."

"You made a choice." His admonishment was steely soft, but like always, he managed to say a lot with a few words.

Her eyes flashed with anger. "So I did."

"Was it the right decision?"

The silence in her home wasn't the comfortable solitary one to which she looked forward every day. This was a suffocating gloom, full of choking memories. She looked straight into his eyes, and firmly answered, "Yes."

"Then, live like it is, Sandra," he told her. At her shocked expression, he continued, "You made a choice. I accepted it and let you go. Don't make me regret it."

That swiftly brought back anger, good righteous fury. "It's always been about you, hasn't it?" she asked bitterly. "Somehow, you always managed to make it sound like it's my fault."

"That was never my intention," he denied without any retaliating heat. It still unnerved her, the way he could control his emotions like that. But she faintly noted that she'd touched him somehow, for his eyes were colder, chilling even the beautiful velvet of his dark voice. "It's always been about you."

"I'm tired." She abruptly stood up. She couldn't bear being near him like this, making the same old arguments. "Tell me why you're here."

"I'm here for the same reason why you left me," he told her.

Sandra frowned. He was talking in circles. "What are you talking about? Do you mean you want to hear me repeat I no longer trust you?"

Those were her last words to him and they both remembered that moment in silence. It hung over them like a waiting guillotine.

"You thought I was with another woman while not on a mission," he said.

Why did he have to bring it up? She couldn't control her anger any longer. "A fact you didn't deny." Her voice raised a notch, cold contempt seeping in. "There was a woman and that's why I left." She laughed, a hoarse raspy sound. "Are you saying you're here because of this woman? Has she left you? Did you show up here to—"

"Don't say something you'll regret," he interrupted, a certain sharp edge in that quiet, unemotional voice, just enough to halt her tirade. "Never assume anything, Sandra. Nothing of which you accused me had any basis except for certain assumptions on your part, starting with those phone calls. I didn't deny talking with another woman now and then because I wanted you to know the truth, but you never heard beyond your own accusations. She's still with me. She's never left me."

"Why are you telling me this?" Sandra cried, anger and pain muddling with confusion. "She has nothing to do with me, nothing to do with now!" Didn't he know how much it hurt her when she confronted him and he didn't deny there was someone else?

"You're wrong," he said, so softly she almost couldn't hear him over the furious pounding of her blood. "You didn't trust me and chose to end our relationship. I accepted it, but she has everything to do with you and now. That woman you hate so much is my daughter, Grace O'Connor."

Sandra dropped back down onto the sofa, her surroundings blurred by the sudden dizziness that came. "Your...daughter," she whispered stupidly. Her job dealt with all kinds of information, some so bizarre in nature no ordinary citizen would believe such stories to be true. With all her years in the field, she didn't think she could be shocked any more, yet twice this evening, she'd been left speechless.

She never believed if and when she saw him again, it would be because he sought her out. She'd imagined accidental meetings in public, where she would be in control, where she could smile politely, and move on without more than a few minutes of careful conversation. Even when she sometimes fantasized about a private meeting, she'd practiced the calm and collected repartees she would give to his demanding questions. She'd envisioned herself gently telling him she'd left him for good, and that his being part of her life wasn't going to happen. It was all fantasy, deep dark thoughts played out during the early years of loneliness.

Yet, here he was. He'd sought her out, but not to fill the role her mind had written for him. He was here, playing the part of the ghost of Christmas past, present and future, to reveal *she* had been mean in spirit, that she'd failed the ultimate test of love. She, Sandra Smythe, had lost something valuable to her life because she hadn't trusted enough. She'd walked away without knowing her own mistake and had been paying the price ever since. She closed her eyes at the futile future of such a hateful person as herself.

"You're too young to have Grace for…" she began to form a denial, to reject such a horrible, terrible mistake, but there was no denying it, not when he sat so implacable and cold in front of her, wielding his own brand of justice. Of course he wasn't too young. He would have been barely eighteen when Grace was born. "Not possible," she tried denying again. "Her last name…"

"…one of her grandmothers'. And a play on my middle name."

Jed Conor McNeil. Everything was horribly beginning to make sense. No wonder she'd liked the girl, been drawn to her spirit and intelligence. She didn't know she was responding to something familiar; she was reacting to the similar nature of her father. And her training…yes, she now understood the skills the younger girl had displayed. After all, her father was a silent assassin, trained to evade and destroy. Grace had shown every aspect of her background.

"Jed." Her voice trembled over his name. It had been so long since she'd allowed herself to speak it aloud. "Jed, why did you never mention her when we were…together?"

He cocked his head, lifting a brow. She immediately recalled Grace doing the same unconscious act when she thought the answer should be obvious to everyone. How could she have missed all the signs? "I'm a Virus," Jed reminded her. "Everything I do endangers my family. That's why they don't exist—I can't afford much time with them—and their identities can't ever be revealed."

"So you were married all that time," she accused.

His lips thinned to a grim line. "No, I was a widower," he said, his strange light eyes staring into hers. "You're doing it again, jumping to conclusions. I never cheated on you. All those phone calls were either to Grace or her grandmother. There was an emergency."

She had thought...no, she hadn't thought, Sandra admitted now in forlorn realization. She'd judged and demanded, then without waiting for an explanation, she'd accused and condemned. She hadn't trusted him and that, in his eyes, was what ended their agent-ghost relationship, and killed what they shared. Not that Jed shared much with anyone, but what they had was special and she knew it could have become so much more.

"Why are you telling me this now?" She took several breaths, telling herself she could take any blows from him. She deserved them, after all.

Jed watched her struggle with her internal demons, and understood he could demand his due, an apology at least, and she would give it to him, but he was intrinsically a man used to difficult choices. Whatever one chose, that was the way taken, and the road would lead somewhere. After Sandra's decision, he'd compartmentalized that part away and hadn't looked back, not too much. Much as he had cared about her, he'd had to admit there was a reason he hadn't shared the most private part of him—he hadn't cared enough.

"Because you've given her a way out," he told her, gentling his voice in order to convey the past wasn't what interested him. "She's a ghost now, as you know. I found that out this morning, when I also discovered her supervisor's identity when I heard your voice on the tape. For once in her life, she's protected."

"It must have been awkward to find out the person you were sent to interrogate was your daughter."

Jed gave a hint of a smile, his hard features relaxing. "She wouldn't have broken easily, even if I'd decided to give her a hard time."

"She has one of the best teachers," she acknowledged.

"So she told me during the meeting." Jed sighed, startling her. He very seldom showed any such emotion, except when he...she immediately cut off such dangerous memories. "I don't see her much or I would have told her to stay out of COS's dealings. She's in danger."

"She knows that."

"Yes." He stated it matter-of-factly.

Sandra wondered at this strange father/daughter relationship. He talked of his daughter more like an equal than someone about whom he should be overly protective. But then, how could an assassin, government agent or not, have any normal relationship with his child?

"I needed you to know so you can keep an eye on her. Guide her. That's all I ask, Sandra."

She understood the underlying message. Jed didn't care for an apology, nor did he want recompense. He was asking her to do this one favor, and in his eyes, they would then be even. He didn't want anything more of her, from her, and she now accepted it. What could she say? After all, she was the one who'd walked away, and she knew him well enough to know he wasn't one who retraced his steps.

"She'll go far with us, but she hasn't decided to stay," she told him, her voice calm again. "I've thrown a few incentives in her direction, hoping to win her over. GNE is definitely aggressively going after her services. She's already doing Level Three work, you know."

"She has the training to go beyond your Level Three," he informed her. "I had her with me in the wild for a whole year."

She remembered the period when he'd disappeared and every agency was asking for information on the Ice Man. He hadn't surfaced until about a year later, back at COS. "You trained her for all that time in the woods?" she asked, intrigued.

Jed inclined his head slightly. "Every day. No electricity. No conveniences. Only minimal contact with the outside world." He remembered that one happy year alone with his daughter. It was the most peace he'd had in a long time. "She could survive almost anything, Sandra." Shrugging, he added, "However, it's her choice. I hope she'll stay with your agency."

She understood both father and daughter now. They both made their own decisions; they didn't need to consult each other or anyone. No wonder Grace seemed to just charge along in any situation, unfazed by anything that cropped up. She was her father's daughter, all right.

"She's ghosting for Lance Mercy," she said, a slow flush rising in spite of her trying to sound normal. There was a certain parallel of Grace and Lance's relationship with their past.

He held her gaze, then, blinked slowly. Her breath caught. She'd forgotten how long his eyelashes were, how she'd constantly wondered how a killer with such cold ruthless eyes could have such long, silky eyelashes. She used to just watch him sleep, just stare at those unbelievably long lashes fanning his eyelids.

"She trusts him," Jed stated. He carefully kept his voice toneless because someone else hadn't trusted enough in a similar situation, a lifetime ago. He felt a degree of regret but he was used to separating pain from reality. He absorbed the emotion, registered it, and with practiced ease, slipped it under other layers of subconscious thought, like sweeping and hiding dirt under the carpet. "I hope they make good choices."

So much lost, nothing gained. Sandra didn't want to mourn any more. What was there to mourn about, when her own past misery was over an illusion? No, her eyes were finally open now and she would make the right choice. "I'll do all I can to guide her," she promised him.

"Thank you." Jed stood up, already mentally walking away.

She went with him to the front door. "Contact me if you need help. My old password is still active."

He nodded his head at her offer, looking over her face, the elegant arch of her brow, the clear solemn eyes, the soft curve of her upper lip, the very delicate bone structure. A lost yearning resurfaced in his strictly controlled mind. He wanted to kiss her one last time. That would be a good closure. Before walking off, he gently gathered her in his arms and tenderly molded her lips to his, and it was as if he stepped back into the past, drinking the familiar passion of this woman in his arms. It was enough. He wanted a taste of his memories to see if there were anything different. The kiss confirmed what he already knew deep down. There was nothing in his heart. He stepped away.

"Good bye," Jed told her. It was he who made the choice this time, walking away. He turned and took the few steps down her porch, meeting eye to eye the hard gaze of Ed Maddux standing in the middle of the walkway. The two men stood assessing each other for a long moment as Sandra remained at the door.

"You're the one," Ed said. He felt close to being violent after witnessing that kiss. He wasn't letting her go this time. Not this time.

"I *was* the one," Jed quietly corrected. He knew more about the other man's history than was fair. This was the time to evade, not attack. "Take care of her."

He stepped around Ed's motionless figure, and without a sound, disappeared into the darkness.

Touching her lips, Sandra watched her past walking off, leaving her future standing unclouded before her. Jed had played his part, showing her what her past had been and what her future could be, if she could turn her present around. He'd shown her what was missing all these years, a generous gesture from someone she'd treated abominably. It was time to put some trust in the future. Slowly, she took the steps toward the waiting figure, stopping a few feet away. Ed's eyes were uncertain, his expression bleak. *Please*, she prayed, *don't let me be too late. Please let him trust me.*

She held out her hand. "Ed," she whispered.

Ed looked down at her extended hand. He didn't think he could take another beating. It would be easier to walk away now, with his pride intact, but when he looked back into her eyes, he caught a new light in them that had not been there for a long time. He saw fear and uncertainty, but he thought he also saw hope. He sighed. He'd never been able to say no to her. He wouldn't leave her until she told him to. Slowly, he took her hand in his.

The smile she gave him was brilliant, as if a thousand light bulbs lit up from inside. It made him catch his breath. He recognized her old self, that warm look that always reminded him of a fully bloomed red rose.

"Sandy?" He needed to know what that look meant. All he had left was hope.

"Will you let us try again?" she asked in a low voice, her eyes steady.

"Are you sure?" He needed that reassurance. He dared not hope too much. The smile remained. She was so beautiful, his blooming English rose.

"I'm sure. Can we skip dinner? Come in and talk instead?"

"Yes." *Yes, definitely.*

CHAPTER TWENTY THREE

Lance considered it a generous gesture on his part to watch his personal ghost get ready for a date with another man. She'd answered enough questions for the day and he didn't want to push for more right now. Secrecy was the substance that cobwebbed their kind of life and he understood its two-pronged nature: if one asked for a revelation, one was likely to betray one's secret. This kind of sharing was nothing new. Operatives within an organization had this complex relationship of knowing and not knowing.

Balance. He needed to learn how to hold his own tray full of secrets, his repertoire of truths and façades, while dancing with a new partner named Grace. He figured he would just have to blame it on his own excellent taste that the woman was nimble on her feet. Correction, she could dance up a simoom.

Closing her closet, Grace was secretly amused by Lance. The poor man had all the signs of a male reluctantly trying to live in the twenty-first century. He hadn't asked any more questions, didn't even raise an objection, and she found it particularly adorable he followed her around the bedroom as she laid out her clothes for her "date." She crossed her arms and stood in the middle of the room when he, without a word, picked up her choice of a blouse, stuffed it back into her closet, then replaced it with another more conservative one, with a high collar.

She opened her mouth to make a sarcastic remark, then closed it with the resignation of a woman with the dawning wisdom to tolerate masculine intelligence, or the lack thereof, where territorial rights were concerned. She ruefully shook her head. That thesis on man and property was beginning to sound better and better. After all, she had plenty of material. For revenge, she deliberately picked out a demi-bra and satin panties that were mere triangle wisps of material, feeling ridiculously pleased at the scowl that formed when he caught sight of them.

When he made a move as if to replace them, she snatched them up and walked off to the bathroom. "I don't think so," she told him over her shoulder.

Since it was dinner with her father, she allowed him the male whim of choice of clothes, but she drew the line at underwear. Quickly donning them, she stood at the bathroom counter, putting on some make-up, as he leaned against the doorjamb, watching her.

"The lipstick's too red," critiqued the expert, his blue eyes glaring at her in the mirror.

Too, too adorable. Grace sweetly smiling back at his image as she ignored his advice. "It was just the right shade to get you to kiss it off the other night," she pointed out, trying not to bite her lower lip and smudge her application.

To her mounting amusement, he took the bait. She was just tempting trouble, riling him like this.

"So, are you trying to tempt someone to kiss you tonight?"

She squirted perfume on her body, then breezed past him to where her clothes were laid out. "Maybe," she airily said.

He stopped her when she got to the bed, turning her to face him. With possessive hands, he skimmed her body, caressing her back down to her buttocks, then moving up the front of her body. "Make sure," he said, eyes glinting, "you tempt the right person."

Grace gave him a saucy moue, then intimately touched the front of his pants before turning back to put on the clothes he'd chosen, giving him a wink as she left a few buttons loose down the front.

"What's that?" He pointed to the shopping bag she had earlier pulled out from the closet.

Grace dumped its contents onto the bed. "Jed's Christmas present," she explained.

"Socks?" Lance asked, puzzled, as he counted what looked like a dozen pairs. "You're giving all these socks to Jed McNeil?" It seemed a ridiculous choice of present for an assassin. Ridiculous and, he decided, too fucking familiar.

"Not just socks," she said, holding a pair up. "Thorlo, the best sock maker in the world. See, reinforced toe, double layered here. So soft and comfortable." She spoke like one in love, then laughed at Lance's expression. All right, she didn't see any harm in explaining this one. "Jed was an Airborne Ranger always out on long recon missions and so he was very seldom back on base. By the time he returned, all the socks supplied by the army were usually already picked off. Socks were treasured commodity out in the jungle."

He was beginning to see. "The socks mean something."

Grace nodded as she arranged them in a colorful box. "Many of the army grunts suffered from jungle rot, especially on their feet. After Jed told me about his condition, I decided I would buy him the best socks for every Christmas." She looked up. "It's tough to go shopping for Jed, as you can imagine. This one idea is perfect and he seems to like it."

It was a hell of a story, except that Lance couldn't see someone like the Ice Man actually telling Grace the horrors of jungle warfare. He vowed he would get to the bottom of this mystery. He wouldn't ask her any questions, but that needn't stop him from digging behind her back. Picking up his own shirt, he shrugged into it.

"I'm out of here," he announced. Pride, if nothing else, stopped him from staying around while she entertained another male friend.

Grace followed him to the door. She told herself she wasn't his keeper and didn't have the right to ask where he would be or whether he was returning later. She couldn't resist, however, a jealous dig from slipping out. "Got a date?"

Lance tilted her chin and kissed her on the brow. She smelled delicious. Instead of going out with another man, she should be—he cut off the erotic images threatening to wake up old Tomcat yet again. He hadn't any control over his sexual urges anymore, it seemed, whenever he got close to her. He'd made love to her twice after he brought her back to the apartment, and still couldn't seem to get enough. What was it about her? He gathered her closer, enjoying the womanly warmth of her small body.

"Don't push me, woman," he muttered into her hair, "or I'll show up at your dinner with a date of my own."

251

Grace didn't think she would enjoy the experience. "As long as she's over eighty years old," she said, laying her head against his heart, "then maybe I won't have to scratch her eyes out."

"Eighty?" He was amused. "Not even seventy?"

"Anyone under eighty will still be tempted to bed you," she solemnly told him. "I wouldn't trust you with my grandmother."

Lance laughed, opening the door. Patting her bottom, he teased, "Little old ladies just want to feed me and call me sonny. I'm sure I'll be safe with your grandmother."

"You haven't met my grandmother," was her cryptic reply, but her cat eyes twinkled back at him.

***

Grace decided Fat Joe's Wok Inn was the perfect place for a hungry woman. Ravenous woman, she corrected, smiling. Lance Mercy certainly knew how to work up a female's appetite. She counted herself fortunate she was in tip-top shape, grinning at the memory of how they had matched each other so well that afternoon, both in skills and lovemaking. She grew warm from the memory of the latter part of the day. Changing the direction of her thoughts, she asked her father about the fenced-up area as they walked into the restaurant.

Jed's strange light eyes considered her briefly. "It's a COS training complex," he finally answered, and didn't say anymore.

Sitting down in a booth in the corner, he let Grace order the courses, the corner of his lips quirking slightly at the number of dishes. She'd always had a great appetite; watching her eat her way from a tiny baby into the sleek five foot three woman before him had been one of the few pleasures he'd allowed himself. He never saw much of his little girl, but whenever he did, she would always be munching something, her brown eyes lit up with excitement over daddy's return home. Her little girl voice would tell him every detail of the last few months she deemed important, that was for his ears only.

She was always daddy's little girl, fiercely loyal and so trusting. Her faith in him had always astounded him. No matter how long the duration between his home visits, she'd always welcomed him with unconditional love, and with absolute confidence that he would return. Even as she grew older and understood the nature of his work, she had never questioned or condemned him. His daughter, he realized, was a unique woman, and needed a unique man for a mate. Even if they both hadn't realized yet they'd met years ago. Sort of.

"I see the muscle-bound young man's out of the picture," he cut into Grace's animated reporting of her college experiences.

She was used to her father's silences and sudden questions, knowing very well he heard every word she said before. "Tim," she said. "You never call him by his name."

"He was attached to you, even nine months ago."

Grace grimaced slightly. "You scared the bejeebers out of him when you jumped on him in the dark, Jed."

"It's usually the case when a father comes home to find some stranger in his daughter's apartment." He never did like the boy, anyhow. His first impression was a whiny inexperienced kid, a little spoilt by his rich parents, but he had to remind himself they were all like that in college. "So when did you eventually break off with him?"

"I didn't. Well, not actually, but I've been working up to it, until a couple of nights ago." She gave a helpless gesture. It was too long a story. She frowned. "How did you know I would?"

"He's not your type."

Grace looked at her father with amusement. "Jed, you're my father. Nobody's my type in your eyes." She blew on her hot tea and sipped it. "Tim came up from Ohio and saw me with Lance. It was a rather bad ending. I still haven't really talked it out with him after he stormed off. Well, actually, *I* stormed off." She paused, then sighed ruefully. "It's gotten so complicated, and yes, I'm confused."

His little girl was entering the world of adult relationships. Jed studied her in silence, suddenly feeling old. When had she grown up on him? He'd never had a chance to be a real father to her. "Make up your mind soon," he advised her, "and don't look back."

Grace nodded. Her father was a man who had to live without regrets, and she understood why. He mustn't look back, or he would go crazy second guessing everything he'd ever done as an operative. "I can take care of myself," she quietly told him.

"This GNE world is something new. You already know its asking price; you have only to look at me. Once you're in, the water's deep and murky, and I can't shield you from the dangers any more."

Grace looked at her father steadily. "I've found out everything has a price, but I appreciate the advice. And the warning." The food arrived and she grinned across at him, "Tim was manhandled by Lance too. I don't think they liked each other very much."

Jed picked up his fork. That would have been some scene. Lance Mercy was probably the last person with whom he'd expected his daughter to end up. Sure he was easy on the eye, and a lady-killer, from what he knew of his exploits, but he was also one tough customer, practically unstoppable in any mission, and in a way, ruthless like him. He'd been known to track his object with a relentless tunnel vision; he should know that, having been on the receiving end of a younger Mercy search mission some time ago.

That suave millionaire façade had fooled governments and rival agencies alike, but he knew from experience that behind the model boy face was a hunter of exceptional skill. No one had ever been able to find the Ice Man unless he'd wanted to be found, no one, that is, until young Mercy came along and came so close to discovering his daughter with him, Jed had decided to end the whole game before Grace was ID'ed. That man was a bad ass, and probably the only one who could match and handle his spirited daughter. Jed ate on, silent and thoughtful.

"What about you. Anything new?" Grace laughed at the look her father gave. "I'm not asking about national secrets. Just what you've been doing for fun."

Jed's eyes lit up with humor. "Fun? Are we having small talk?"

"Yeah, fun. You're human, even though many don't subscribe to this." She sniffed. "It'd be nice to know what my own father has been up to the last eight months. Other than his job, I mean."

His expression turned unreadable. She fancied she saw something in his eyes.

"There's someone I'd like you to meet. If it goes the way I want."

Grace stopped eating. Her father had never talked about his women since her childhood, when he introduced Nikki Taylor to her. A very, very rare event. Nikki was special and Grace loved her. Her father never brought any women home since they parted ways.

"Goes the way you want?" she repeated.

"It's complicated." A ghost of a smile softened his face. "And no, I'm not confused."

"And here I thought you were asking my advice for once," she quipped, then leaned forward. "She must be special if you're even thinking about an introduction."

"That she is," her father replied enigmatically.

"At least, a name? Have I met her before? A hint? Pretty please?"

There was a pause. She patiently waited, finding Jed's unusual hesitance very telling. He actually looked as if he couldn't decide!

"It starts with an H. Now eat. Fun news over."

"Yes, sir." She grinned and resumed eating. Wow. Her father finding a woman special enough to meet his daughter. The lady must have gotten to him. Questions, questions, so many questions she knew Jed wouldn't answer.

"Grace, ah, my favorite customer!" Fat Joe's lumpy figure appeared.

Grace wondered with amusement if he only had two fashion statements, as the Pillsbury Doughboy and the fast running Nun. He was jovial as ever, gallantly taking her hand in his, as he nodded at Jed.

"Fatt Choy!"

"Is everything OK with you?"

"Yes," she assured him, knowing he was concerned about her part in rescuing David Cheng. "How about you? Did you have any problems?"

Fat Joe chuckled. "Aiyah*, I suffered all night with you-know-who's incessant questions. Enquiring minds want to know!" he declared, with a wink. "But, how's the food today? Anything I can bring the prettiest customer in my restaurant?"

Grace laughed. "Your dishes are superb, Fatt Choy, the very best." She turned to her father. "Jed, this is my friend, Fatt Choy, the owner."

"Oh, call me Fat Joe," the Chinese man said, as he easily shook Jed's hand. "Everyone calls me that, except Grace here." Jed nodded back. Quiet character, Fat Joe thought, as he excused himself from the table. Something dangerous about him. No

---

* Chinese idiomatic expression, like a "Wow," or "Why," or "Hah!"

wonder Big Cat wanted him to keep an eye on his woman. Hah, the Big Cat was afraid of competition! That was hilarious. Fat Joe had never seen Lance acting so possessive over a woman before, and the thought of his friend finally being noosed brought a congenial grin to his round face, which got even bigger as he walked into the kitchen. Perhaps he could exact some good old-fashioned revenge by telling some tall tales to drive the Big Cat crazy with jealousy when he called later. He should play matchmaker here—those two were perfect for each other.

As the evening came to an end, after catching up with news on family and the few friends they had, Grace and her father gave their usual parting lines. They had always been honest with each other, knowing, with his job, this could be the last time.

"Keep in touch, if possible," she told him, handing him his Christmas gift. "I don't want to wait eight months in between visits."

Jed took the box, smiling fully for the first time that evening. The effect on his harsh face was startling, as a warm look entered his usually expressionless eyes, crinkling attractively at the corners, his masculine lips curled upwards, deepening the dimple in his chin. She liked it when her father smiled. She hoped, whoever that new woman was, she was making him smile like that more often.

"I'll be in town for a little while longer. Stay out of trouble, Grace Audrey."

She made a mischievous face at him. They couldn't even afford a peck on the cheek, not here, in D.C., so for a quick moment, father and daughter held hands.

***

Not everyone was tying up loose ends that evening.

Senator James Richards hated working late in his office. He would prefer to be in his jacuzzi at this time of night, watching some video in his private collection, and maybe have Melanie join him in the tub. He hated having to work past four o'clock, except when Congress had a bill to vote on. Then he would wheel and deal to get his meat in the package deal. Most of all, Senator Richards hated surprises.

Damn it, it hadn't been that complicated a plan. First, get this Chinese scholar who supposedly had a list of other political players who were, like him, currying favors from the Chinese government. How difficult was that? Once the list was in his hands, his whole future would fall marvelously according to destiny, a big bright future for the son of a drunken mechanic. With that knowledge in his possession, he could twist arms to vote with him, to give him more committee power.

But problems started to crop up, least of all was the discovery the scholar didn't even have this list. Someone else named—what the hell was it, the Shark?—yes, something ridiculous like that, had it, and the kidnapping was all for nothing. Then, when he thought he could at least benefit by returning a wanted dissident to the Chinese, Homeland Security had somehow gotten involved and caused a big scene. How the hell did they know about the missing man? Did they know about the list too? Cold sweat broke out at the thought of his name being among those on the take. If anyone of consequence got it...he didn't want to think about what would happen to his nicely planned future.

A simple thing, and it led to mayhem. They blew up the damn car. Richards still couldn't believe it. If the truth ever got out, the political fallout would cost him his election. He'd been juggling lies the last few days after the car was traced back to his office and the questions started coming. He still hadn't come up with a good answer to explain the reason a state-registered vehicle was driven by Chinese representatives.

He didn't think it could get any worse until his own men informed him the car had been switched. One of the chauffeurs had cleaned another car yesterday, and discovered one of the license plates had been attached on with magnets over the real one. He shook his head. What kind of harebrained scheme was that? And of course, with the disappearance of the Chinese man, he now had a new worry. Who had him, and did he know who was behind his kidnapping?

Thank God one of them was bright enough to shut the chauffeur up and do away with the car. If Homeland checked too closely, Richards knew he was going to have a shitload of trouble on his lap. He was already sitting on dynamite, as it was, trying to keep his story straight. He needed the Chinese man found. Picking up his phone, he impatiently punched in the number. When someone picked up the line, he didn't bother to greet him, going straight to the point.

"The only saving grace to this fucked up situation is the Chinese representatives don't know the car they blew up was switched. So they think their man is dead."

"They'll find out the truth if someone decides to question them about the explosion." The man on the other end tried not to sound bored. Actually, he couldn't care less whether they found out or not. He kind of enjoyed watching the senator burn at the stake.

"I will take care of them," Richards barked sharply. "My worry is the scholar. Who took him?"

"It's obviously the Shark."

"Well, what the hell do I pay you for?" he yelled, as he poured himself a drink, spilling some on his expensive desk. Inept bastards. He was surrounded by them. "You told me getting the list would be a piece of cake. Then you got the wrong man. You even managed to bungle something as simple as returning the goods to the Chinese. This is fucking unprofessional, if you ask me. When I requested men to do this job, I'd expected them to send me the best."

The senator was getting annoying, the listening man observed with growing impatience, as he let him rage on about paying covert groups for failed jobs. This flustered windbag didn't even know he was being used, that he was nothing but a cog. There was no group. The one in charge was standing right here, and he, along with an anxious few, wanted to get the list as soon as possible. The other list, the one that mattered.

"We'll get him." He forced himself to sound calm, subservient. The senator still had some future use.

"You'd better," Richards came back darkly. "Clean up this mess before it gets traced back here."

"Of course." The man made a few more reassuring comments before hanging up, then disdainfully flicked cigarette ash into the ashtray by his bed. He had little respect for those who didn't deserve the glory. He would get the Shark, and the lists of names.

The phone rang again. Grounding out his cigarette impatiently, he tried not to lose his temper. If it were the senator calling to chew him out again, he would fucking drive over there and cancel him. "Yeah?" he asked rudely.

"It's Baker. I've an update."

The man relaxed. "What is it?"

"We were scanning for the D.o.D. report on the car bomb and we came across a log schedule."

"And?"

"It had a security code similar to Command. The only entry in the log refers to an interrogation of a possible operative," Baker told him.

"I wonder why I haven't been told." This was definitely bad news. "Did you find out who that was?"

"It looks like Command was in the process of opening a file for this individual. There were photos of her and some profile notes, but nothing about the interrogation today."

"It's probably not been filed yet." A thought struck. "You said that it's a female they brought in?"

"Yeah."

"Could you fax me a copy of the photo on file, Baker?"

"No problem. I'll send it out tonight."

Lighting another cigarette, the man inhaled with a deep satisfaction. Something told him his luck was going to change.

CHAPTER TWENTY FOUR

It was so tempting.

He should do it. It would be easy, and she wouldn't even know it was happening until it was too late.

Lance lay against the propped up pillow, watching Grace with hooded eyes. He'd meant to stay away that night, but the call from Fat Joe triggered his flight back to her apartment. He wouldn't stand for it. Holding hands with another man when she knew very well she belonged with him. Having intimate dinners. Whispering. Fat Joe didn't miss a single detail. He'd driven over with the intention of staying at her place, bringing clothes and paperwork along.

It was time he used his tracker skills. The girl's wings were going to be clipped. With that decided, he'd arrived unannounced, deliberately stating in silence his right to be there. She'd been watching TV, almost asleep, but didn't seem surprised to see him. Without a word, he'd taken her to bed, and afterwards, she'd curled on her side and fallen asleep like a contented cat.

So unsuspecting.

She'd gotten used to him now, used to the way he didn't sleep much, used to the curve of his body against hers. He still put away her gun under the bed on his side and she didn't mind that either, actually taking an amused delight in teasing him about it.

"I really won't shoot you if you fail to satisfy me, honestly, babe," she'd drawled.

It was so temptingly easy. In fact, he'd already started doing it without her being aware of it. He would wake her up in the middle of the night and make love to her; he'd roused her in the early dawn hours with his hands and mouth; he'd taken her while she was still in that half-awake state in the morning. Her response was automatic, eager, unknowingly letting him bind her to him. He knew, from experience, her body had already gotten accustomed to his, and even in her sleep, it sought his warmth for company.

He'd thought about it, analyzed it. He'd never needed to imprint someone with her training before, with that kind of evasive expertise he knew went more than skin deep. Anyone trained by the Ice Man had to be quite formidable, but Lance had stared at her at night, and known he could do it once her body trusted his without question. It was her mind he needed to conquer and the best way to imprint a Virus, he figured, was to override it, putting the quick-thinking training to rest. So he'd made love to Grace until she was sated and exhausted, readying her for the moment when that brain of hers was no longer on.

Then he would attack, imprint her. Clip her wings. Put his brand on her. The secret was not to let her know he was doing it, when her body would just obey his command, and she wasn't awake enough to make love back to him. He needed her very pliant, very obedient, and very exhausted. And every time he changed his mind about continuing, he'd hear the Ice Man's challenge during the interrogation and he was tempted all over again.

She lay there beside him, breathing deeply, relaxed and trusting. Lance felt a tender surge rise inside. He'd taken a weird fascination with watching her sleep. He liked it best, like the last time he'd loved her, when he had woken her up with kisses on her face until she responded with that wild passion of hers, until she shook in his arms. Then, he loved watching her slowly come back down, and like a baby, crawl into his arms and fall asleep again. It was the most satisfying sensation, to feel her utterly give herself to him like that. It was new, to want a woman to wholly surrender herself, to want someone for himself. He wanted more from her than from any woman he'd ever known.

He should do it now. A part of him continued to insist it wasn't fair, to conquer a woman like Grace without warning, but he wanted to possess her so badly. She would never consciously give in to a tracker, so this was the only way. He decided to just do a little test.

Tracing her sleeping mouth, his finger slipped between those shapely lips into its wetness, testing to see how relaxed she was. She was totally asleep, her jaw a little slack as he opened her mouth with his finger. Moving close, he kissed her softly, making sure not to wake her up. He wanted the body to respond, not the mind. Moving lower, he gently sucked her pink nipples until they puckered in anticipation. A low moan escaped her lips, but she didn't wake up, turning slightly toward his body in her sleep.

He lightly caressed her thighs, tracing the soft skin where her legs met with the juncture in between. Skimming, touching, teasing, he felt her respond, heard her sigh as he probed gently into her with his finger, and watched her body grow restless as he circled wetly around her aroused flesh. He was carefully slow and gentle, stopping every time she moaned, and waiting till she fell back into sleep before starting again, tormenting her willing flesh until she was slick and wet. His fingers probed and pressed, and she was so ready that he knew she could climax even in her sleep. And still he stopped. And waited. And continued paying special attention to a certain pressure point over which he knew she particularly went weak.

His own arousal was painful, demanding release, but Lance ignored it. This was a test, and he intended to see it through. He was a cruel bastard, but at the moment, he no longer cared. Her feminine scent enveloped his senses, her softness pulled something wild out of him; he wanted her so badly, he was practically panting with the exertion of self-control.

He waited. Sleep, babe.

It was time to use his tongue. Very, very delicately, he tasted, kissed, laved. She was like wild honey and he took his time, moving from point to point, savoring and tasting. Every part of her body was aroused; he left nothing untouched by his possession, stopping only when he felt her pulse rate going up. He soothed her back to sleep, relaxing her tense muscles. Then, he woke her sleeping body again until it quivered with need. Asleep, her lips parted and her breathing uneven, her nipples pebbled hard and her body sweetly welcoming, she'd never looked more beautiful to him.

Bending to her ear, Lance whispered, "Grace…"

"Grace," he repeated with husky tenderness. Just a soft command. Her eyelids fluttered slightly as she moved against him. He waited until she slumbered again.

"Grace."

His finger stroked slowly over her aroused clitoris, circling and teasing until his hand was wet with her desire. This time she tilted her face up when he called her name quietly, as if expecting a kiss. Lance immediately stopped, patiently bringing her back down with knowing fingers. It was a fine line between relaxation and tension; it all depended on which point of the same nerve one chose to apply pressure.

When her breathing was even again, Lance whispered once again, "Grace, open your legs, baby." There was a moment's tensed anticipation; then, without waking up, his little hellcat slowly parted her legs.

The ensuing triumph was fierce and possessive in nature. He could do it. For an instant, he'd thought his theory failed, but there she was, ready and willing at his command. All he had to do was to take her several times like this, until her body obeyed him. After that he would start with that stubborn little mind when she was awake. By then it would be too late for her. She would be his, unconscious or not.

Grace's eyelids began to flicker and Lance watched her dream. She had the most sensuous expression when she dreamed like this; several times, he'd wondered at what the dream might be as he watched her writhe sexily while she slept. Tonight, she was even wilder, definitely in some erotic throes, caused by his manipulation.

He didn't mind, as long as it was he who was responsible for her little purring noise that never failed to intrigue him. She was getting warmer as she strained against his still fingers. When he moved them playfully, she surged up in her sleep, that deep throaty sound sexy as hell. He continued to ignore his need, feeding hers instead, steadily building her to a peak until the flush of arousal made her body rosy with lust. He stroked her steadily and tenderly, touching her little nub until it swelled in protest, wanting more. All along, she never changed her position, waiting for his next command, her thighs open for him.

He smiled wickedly as he climbed over her. She had passed the test excellently.

***

Friday morning.

"What do you dream about at night?" Lance asked, his hand moving with familiar ease over the silky skin of her back, slowly waking her up.

Grace yawned into her pillow. Didn't the man ever sleep? "I don't dream. I sleep," she muttered grouchily, closing her eyes tighter.

"There's where you're wrong. You have erotic dreams at night," Lance told her.

Grace turned over, and opened bleary eyes to glare at him. "Like you could read what kind of dreams I have," she crossly said.

"No, but you make the sexiest little sounds in your throat." Now that he had her awake, he gathered her under his muscled body. "It's exactly the same whimper you make when I kiss you. So logically, it must be something erotic you're dreaming."

"I don't whimper!" Grace protested, her senses wakened by the intriguing combination of masculine scent and soap. It was a potent wakeup call. "You're making it all up."

Lance kissed her, taking his time as he tasted her, reveling in her sensuous response. As he sucked on her tongue, he pushed her thighs apart slowly while he went deeper into her sweet mouth. Grace started whimpering.

"Like that," he told her, his laughter soft and husky. "That sexy little purring sound. You would do that and start to claw at the sheets, and sometimes, you would even make growling noises, rubbing your butt against my thigh."

"I do not!" Grace laughed at the notion. "You're making me sound like a cat in heat!"

He had to be joking. The image of her purring and rubbing against him was unsettling, and strangely arousing.

"Hmm. A cat in heat. I like that." With expert ease, he got off her, flipped her onto her front, and then climbed back on top of her before she even knew what was happening.

"What are you up to now?" she demanded and gave a sharp gasp when he planted his teeth on the sensitive nerve in her neck, effectively rendering her weak as a baby. She gave a pitifully weak struggle, then stopped as his teeth applied more pressure. There

264

wasn't time to think as his hands roamed all over her body. God, he could turn her on just like that. When his muscular legs dug in between hers and spread out, she felt him hard and ready against her vulnerable flesh and she moaned as he nudged her. She groped blindly at the sheets, trying to push against his arousal, but he wasn't ready just yet.

It's hard to please a cat in heat," he murmured into her already sensitive ear. "She's dangerous, all claws and teeth."

Grace closed her eyes as his tongue invaded her ear, while he teased her lower body by pushing tantalizingly into her softness. Her thoughts scattered like sand in the wind. She couldn't believe how he could make her feel so weak, incapable even of making complete sentences. "You...have... to...stop," she managed to gasp out.

"Why?"

Because she didn't like losing her mind like that. Because she liked to be in control. Because she was still wary about his possessiveness. "You have to," she insisted, barely suppressing another moan as he inched in a little more.

"Let go, Grace," he commanded, rocking against her. "Give in to me. You're the kitty cat in heat and I've got you where I want you."

The image of being caught helpless by a determined male was an erotic charge in the center of her being. His dark seductive voice teased her, made love to her, and made her want him exactly like the cat he was describing. She groaned with the need to have him, all of him, as he pushed in a little more and rocked her from side to side. The tension was unbearable. "Lance," she sputtered, trying to push up. "Hurry."

"Uh-uh." He rocked left and right again. Grace's eyes closed as every feminine nerve ending cried for completion. "I want to hear the cat in heat purr again." He slipped a hand beneath her perspiring body and the bed sheets, and with knowing mastery, used two long fingers to trap the little nub hiding down there, motioning them like a pair of scissors as he undulated. The fleshy part of his palm cupped her pubic bone, effectively squeezing her sex with hand, fingers and hip as he thrust with the same shallow move that was slowly driving her crazy. "That's right, baby. Let me hear you purr."

The tormenting effect of his hand pushing up and his hips pushing down sent Grace into a frenzy of shivers. "Faster. Oh, God."

She started whimpering the way Lance heard her all night, that throaty sexy sound that so fascinated and aroused him. It was what he wanted, her little love call for him alone and he gave her all of him, flexing inward hard and fast. She was sleek and fluid, already trembling inside as she held him greedily. He thrust long and slow, moving with a languid grace of a man sinking into mindless passion. He wanted all of her, wanted her to dream of him, to need this as much as he needed her. All his focus was on the heat building higher as he thrust even deeper, pulling out until he couldn't stand it, then plunging in again, harder. Each time harder, until every sinking thrust shot orgasmic pleasure that was somewhere between agony and ecstasy.

Was that her calling out his name? Grace wasn't sure any more as she felt each of his thrusts deep inside her. Never, ever, had a man taken her like that, deep and possessively, marking her inside, as surely as he marked her with his teeth and fingers. Before, she'd enjoyed the act of sex, in the experience of giving and taking pleasure. Now, she could only react to every sensation crashing down on her like tidal waves. This was beyond enjoyment, beyond sharing bodies. This was, she realized, what making love meant, when each took hold of the other's mind, when each soul held the other's hand, and both surfed and soared on waves of pure pleasure and release. Even as her thoughts shattered and she gave in to his demands, she felt him giving her what she needed. He froze for an instant, then sharply pushed in once before giving a groan as he shuddered and flexed, imbedded deep inside her. Her cries mingled with his, as her sensitive flesh quivered around him, sending seemingly endless spasms of ecstasy.

Their limbs were intertwined, their bodies sticking to each other. Grace didn't mind his weight. She was barely able to move anyway, after being thoroughly made love to like that. It seemed the most natural place in the world to be, even though a part of her secretly worried over their future. She shoved it to the back of her mind, telling herself to enjoy what they had now. A man like Lance Mercy didn't have long-term relationships.

Lance exhaled, slowly surfacing from his sexual stupor. She had the most unbelievable effect on him. He should feel sated and contented; he should be pleased and satisfied, but he couldn't seem to get enough of her. Every time he touched her, the urgent need to have her overpowered every other thought at hand. She made him want to stay inside her all the time, and that knowledge scared the hell out of him. She was becoming way too important.

They lay there, spoon fashion, deep in thought, until the alarm clock sounded. Grace moved first, turning it off. Lance watched the soft play of her back muscles as she sat up in bed, her back to him, her arms stretching skyward. She was young and strong, both in body and spirit, and he worried about her. Youth and strength weren't adequate protection in their kind of life. She lacked the hardened willingness to destroy and distance herself, and although he liked her for that, those missing qualities would eventually put her in danger. Like this time. Her interference went against the grain of her training as a Virus and her recorder status, yet she'd somehow pulled through. Luck couldn't last forever, though. Somehow he had to convince her to stop jumping in head first.

This wasn't the first time Lance found himself feeling protective over Grace's well being. He'd kept telling himself it was just her youth, her naivete, but lately, there was a nagging suspicion it was more than that. For one, he'd never felt possessive where a woman was concerned and the way his blood pressure got going at the sight of her with another man baffled him. He frowned as he watched her back. He got rid of that young wuss, but what was the Ice Man to Grace, besides being her mentor? Why did he pick her to train? What kind of interest did he have in her? The thought of the older man grooming her to be his ghost brought on a scowl.

Grace happened to glance back as she made her way to the closet. Oh-oh. Now what? Honestly, the man went through the strangest moods, morphing from taunting male chauvinist into a sensual beast into a bad tempered grouch without warning. "What's the matter now?" she asked, pulling out a towel.

"I was thinking."

She grinned. "Did it hurt?" When he threateningly sat up on the bed, she slammed the bathroom door shut.

"Coward!" he yelled through the door. "Let me in."

"It's occupied!" she yelled back.

"So? I've seen you naked before." She heard him laugh out loud. "Come on, babe, let me in. I need to use it as badly as you do."

Grace stuck her head out. "My apartment, I get to go first." She let him in, then walked out. "I also like some privacy."

Lance grinned. There wouldn't be much privacy in a hot and dense jungle. The girl had just better get used to being in close quarters with him. "Are you coming back in here or not?" he called out. "I'm getting into the shower." She joined him, sighing contentedly as he soaped her back.

"I like it when you get shy on me," he continued teasing her.

Grace shrugged. It was quite unsettling to see him traipse around her, quite unconcerned about his nudity, doing things only long time lovers do. Like they were a married couple. She didn't want that kind of familiarity with him. It would only make the breakup worse if she got too close to him. He'd already hinted about it just being casual sex and she'd better learn to ignore the panic that reared its head every time she thought of him leaving D.C. or her going back to college in the fall.

"What are your plans today?" she asked instead, as she explored the beautiful broad chest, pouring more liquid soap on it than necessary.

"Check to see whether my people had gotten the information from yours. It's all their little game now. We now have the scholar," his eyebrows rose mockingly, "with a little help."

"How is he?"

"Still out. We don't know exactly what was used on him, so the doctors are hesitant about trying different antidotes for fear of worsening his condition."

"What happens once you get the information?" Grace wanted to know.

Lance shrugged, his hands massaging the underside of her breasts. "There are things to do." He smiled down at her wickedly.

Secretive things, she thought. "Will you be gone long?" she continued asking, her eyes carefully on his body, as she continued drawing soap patterns all over him.

He placed a finger under her chin and forced her to meet his eyes. "One mission at a time, hmm?" he said, his blue eyes suddenly serious. "I have to stay as an advisor for the council to flush out the leak. He's a danger to Command, even more dangerous than what's on the list."

The names of illegal arms traders were a huge danger to the security of the world, but a rat could cost lives and more than mere weapons. He had to take this one out before he found out they had both the scholar and the information. It was still a secret at this point, but how deeply had this double agent penetrated COS's security? He had to work fast. Maybe even talk to the Ice Man today. A plan formed almost immediately.

"I've got to work today too," Grace told him. "My superiors will be wondering where I am since I didn't get back with them yesterday."

Lance grinned down at her. "You lost."

"Ha!" she snorted. "I think the blue on your face pretty much proved you're a lying chauvinist."

"Chauvinist?"

"Yeah, unwilling to admit you lost to a woman." She let him kiss her after he turned the water off. "And kissing me won't make me change my mind either!"

They kept bantering as they dried each other off, and Lance wrapped her in a huge fluffy towel before carrying her back into the bedroom. "I'll make you breakfast if you admit you lost," he bargained, his eyes laughing at her indignant brown ones.

Grace laughed and pulled his earlobe as he set her down. "Make me some of those pancakes you're so good at, and I'll say we were even," she countered.

"Got coffee?" he asked. "No deal without coffee."

"I bought the kind you like," she told him.

"Done," he declared. "You were almost as fast as I was." She chased him into the kitchen.

CHAPTER TWENTY FIVE

He'd done something to her, Grace was quite sure of it, although she couldn't figure out exactly what. All she knew was that every time he whispered her name in her ear, she went hot and cold. There was so much she didn't know about him, so much about herself she couldn't share, and she didn't know where to even start to let him know how much she was beginning to care. If this was being in love, she really didn't want it. She liked the feeling, very much so, but she didn't know what to do about it. Where did she stand with him? Was she just somebody between those glamorous socialites he escorted around the world?

She rubbed her nose in self-disgust. That was another thing—he had, horror of horrors, made her into a Mary Tucker fan. Last night she'd gone online and looked through Beaucoup's archives for past gossip on Lance. Ugh. That had to prove she was in love. When had she ever done such an idiotic thing like that, checking out a guy's past women? It didn't make her feel any better to put faces on those anonymous women either. Too many of them had bodies sculptured like goddesses. Disgusting. Absolutely disgustingly gorgeous.

Grace had never been jealous in her whole life and didn't have a good time last night nursing the green monster. Until he walked into her apartment like he lived there, like a husband returning home. She should have been indignant, but she wasn't. Instead, she'd felt pleased, especially when he set down his bag of clothes and briefcase and took her in his arms. He didn't say a word, but she knew he was staying.

She called in at work to make an appointment for debriefing, after giving Sandra a quick summary of her "interrogation," leaving out the part about her father, of course. Some information was irrelevant. Then she called Tyler to see whether he'd managed to figure out the code on the grains. He was still working on it, so she told him she would meet him at the office.

Because she felt so restless about her feelings toward Lance and partly to get her mind to focus on her job, she took time for another deep meditation session. Dissociation from present reality, her father had called it. The idea was to take a memory and work it into a long form narrative and, within the meditation process, learn to compartmentalize each present memory into segments of the narrative. It sounded complicated when he first explained it to her, but it was easier than she'd expected, since she started doing it as a kid.

Her favorite scene of those lions became her narrative. And through the years, she'd added layers of narrative, having fun and ultimately using it to control her emotions. If the session went well, she could park her growing feelings for Lance here for a while.

She mostly succeeded. Mostly. Because there was a strange combination of Lance walking around naked in her narrative and her lion mate prowling in her apartment. She shook her head and that interrupted her meditation.

Rubbing her hands across her face and through her hair, she stood up and stretched. Bah. Now he was invading her secret domain. She sighed. Let's just focus back on those lists. She methodically went through all the facts.

There was something else about those grains nagging at her. The list of names was easy, most likely abbreviations of people on the take. Senator Richards was surely among them. He'd probably kidnapped David Cheng to make sure COS didn't get the list. No, he couldn't have known about COS. Very few people did, so he must have wanted the list to further his own career. That made more sense.

However, the second grain had foreign sounding names and numbers. That must be the second list Lance mentioned, the one COS was after. If that was true, then the third grain couldn't be an extension of the second grain. That was the one she and Tyler were working to decipher. The numbers looked like coordinates, with digits and dashes. She wanted to crack the code. Information would be more valuable if it made sense.

Besides, she needed to be sure it was a third list before she could make a decision whether to tell Lance. She would have to tell him or her father, in case the information was important. She frowned. How was she supposed to help out without breaking the "no interference" rule? She sighed again. This ghosting business was an exercise in hint-dropping. She wondered how Sandra would handle the problem.

The doorbell rang as she got ready to leave. "Charlie!" She greeted her visitor in surprise.

"Hi there!" Charlie smiled at her, looking pleased. "I'd hoped to catch you here. I called your office and one of your co-workers told me you might still be home."

Must be Tyler. "Come on in. I can't talk for long, though."

"Oh, this won't take long." He looked around. "Nice place. I was wondering whether you would have dinner with me tonight. There's a Three Stooges festival on M Street."

"Really? Oh, I'd love to, but I don't know whether I have anything going on," Grace said. She headed toward her kitchen. "Want a drink? Just pour yourself one from the fridge while I check my schedule."

"Sure. What would you like?"

"Orange juice, please. There's soda and milk in there. Take whichever you like."

"Okay."

Grace knew she didn't have any plans for the evening and she wanted to spend it with Lance. Besides, her father was in town. She'd better leave her options open, much as she loved the Three Stooges. "I don't think tonight would be good, Charlie," she told him, turning around to accept the glass of juice from him, before returning back to the calendar on the wall. She perused the dates as she sipped on her drink. "How about I call you tonight to let you know? The festival's on for the week, I hope?"

"No problem. We can go anytime you want," Charlie assured her. "Actually, I wasn't even sure you would come with me, since you're dating Lance Mercy and all."

Grace frowned. "That doesn't mean I can't go out with friends. He's not my keeper, you know. Besides, he and I are just good friends too." Why let others think she was tied down? She certainly wasn't going to let people she might work with in the future know too much about her, and if she did decide to work in D.C., she would probably be interpreting for the same people repeatedly. Finishing her drink, she smiled at Charlie. "We'll go sometime soon, all right?"

"That would be nice."

"Great! Come on, I'll walk you to your car, since I really have to go."

"Okay. I'm sorry I'm making you late."

"Oh, I'm not really that late," Grace said, sitting down to put her shoes on. She picked one up, then stared at it foolishly. Her shoe was looking terribly out of focus.

"What's the matter?" Charlie's voice was gentle and concerned.

Grace stared down at her feet. They seemed so far away. "I...ah..."

Charlie's shoes came into view, as she continued staring down. "How are you feeling, Grace?"

His shoes. She had seen those shoes before, in the convention parking lot. She looked up, confused, and met his gaze. "Something is wrong." Even her voice sounded muffled.

"Of course." The volume of his voice also appeared to have dropped a couple of notches. He sounded like he was speaking through a bottle. "You're just feeling a slight effect of the drug, Grace. You'll be all right."

"The j...ui...ce," she muttered, her head swimming. Her sight was blurred, like some oily substance was smeared over her eyeballs.

"Relax. I didn't use too much since I need you to walk with me to my car." Charlie went down on his knees to put her shoes on for her. His hands lingered over the tender skin of her arches as he pushed her feet into her shoes. "Come on, up."

Grace licked her dry lips. She was in serious trouble here. Perhaps she could stall. "Charlie," she began, but her speech had been thickened by the drug invading her system, and her tongue had difficulty with speech, making his name sound like...*Ja lee*. Everything suddenly clicked into place. *Jia-li. Chia Lee. Charlie.* Oh God, her good old male nun wasn't speaking Chinese; he was telling her who tortured him! She pushed away Charlie's hand and stumbled back into the sofa.

"Let's try this the easy way. Tell me what's on those lists and then I won't have to take you with me," Charlie said, his hand caressing her jaw.

She stood up again, this time managing to move around the chair while keeping her eye on the blurry figure in front of her. He was faceless, but she heard the menace in his voice. Strange how much harsher he sounded when she couldn't see his face. She stared blankly at the blurry face.

"I thought not," he continued as he advanced toward her. "You'll have to hurry up before you pass out, Grace. Or should I call you Shia Yi, the shark?"

Shia Yi? Shark? Grace wasn't sure she heard him correctly over the beating of her heart. What did he mean when he called her that? She tried to move, but her limbs felt like she was treading water.

"Come on." His voice was insistent now, his grip a little harder. "Since you won't give them to me willingly, you'll have to be persuaded in private. Please come obediently, so I don't have to hurt you. I'm not going to take the chance of any of your friends showing up right now."

"I don't know what you're talking about," she managed to say as she stumbled along. It was getting increasingly difficult to stay conscious. Gripping hard on the stair banister, she made a last effort to resist being herded off but his fingers pried hers loose, and she almost fell down the short flight of steps as he pulled her along at a steady pace.

"Of course you do, my dear. I also want you to tell me about the Big Cat. You were at the rally, as you told me yourself, and even Cheng confirmed that. I want to know everything."

They were standing in the parking lot, by what she assumed was his car. Although the sun felt warm, she shivered hard, reacting to the drug overwhelming her senses. She had to stay conscious. Hearing footsteps coming from behind, she turned to cry for help, but found strong fingers pressing down on her vocal chord, cutting off her voice, and then she felt Charlie's lips kissing her. Out of air, she struggled ineffectively, then sagged against his body as he continued to kiss her.

Mary Tucker was getting mighty curious about her young neighbor. She seemed to have a long line of men forever kissing or manhandling her in the parking lot. Here she was again, in broad daylight, being passionately kissed by yet another young man. Personally, she would prefer Lance Mercy to this one, she added, as she critiqued the new man. This one didn't have what Mary called the 'hungry man' look, like the immensely sexy Mr. Mercy.

She was actually quite surprised at Grace. She hadn't expected her to play around like this. When they had first met, the young woman seemed ordinary enough, with a boyfriend who dropped by once in a while. She had lived a solitary lifestyle. Of that, Mary Tucker was very certain. She prided herself in knowing about these things. Then, in the space of a month, Grace had turned into a very loose young lady indeed.

An idea brought a slight smile to Mary's lips. Wouldn't it be lovely to catch Lance Mercy's face on film if he found out about his current flame's extracurricular activities? Why, the story would be huge! Headline: The Insider's Insider Is Left Outside.

She almost clapped her hands in delight. Getting into her car, she drove off and parked a little ways from the apartment complex. When Grace and her new man's car came out into the traffic, she too pulled out, following them from a safe distance. Let's see where they were going. Maybe she could catch them in the act. No, on second thought, she should arrange for a dramatic confrontation. Excellent, my girl. Picking up her phone, she got hold of her magazine's photographer while watching where the car in front of her turned in. She frowned.

Strange. She hadn't expected a cheap little motel to be their love nest, but this was definitely more than she asked for. The more sordid, the better. Kinky details of the rich and famous were the thing that got her voracious readers eager for the next copy.

Mary didn't wait to see the couple getting out of the car. There should be plenty to see once she got hold of Lance Mercy and enticed him here. ASAP. Mary Tucker smelled a great article for the next issue of Beaucoup.

***

Lance glanced up from his desk at the commotion. His secretary was trying to block someone from entering his office. "This is highly improper—" he heard her exclaiming.

"If you don't move, miss, we're going to arrest you," Dan Kershaw said, flashing a badge and walking in, followed by Jed and several agents.

"Mr. Mercy—" the flustered woman began explaining.

"It's all right, Mrs. Jackson," Lance interrupted. "Go on out. Cancel all my appointments and take a message for any calls for me."

"Yes, sir," she said, and after a last curious glance over her shoulder, closed the door behind her.

"Remind me to nominate you for the Best Supporting Actor," Lance said, lazily leaning back against his leather armchair.

Dan grinned. "I would rather have your kind of pay raises," he countered, sitting down as he looked around the posh office. "Must be fun shaping trade policies."

Lance glanced at his watch. "Fun is relative," he retorted. He studied Jed who stood looking at photographs of him on the wall. "I didn't know you were still around, McNeil." He'd hoped he would be gone by now, actually, and wouldn't be back to see Grace for another nine months.

Jed didn't turn around to face him. "I have time," he said.

"Another five minutes ought to do it," Dan said, looking at his watch too. "By the way, Homeland sends you their thanks for the list, although they would've preferred to do so in person."

"I bet," Lance observed dryly, knowing every agency had a secret agenda to find out the Big Cat's identity. "They've got their list; we've got ours. Once we get our rat, we can kiss the mission goodbye."

Dan nodded. "You still have to continue your role as chair advisor, though."

"For a short period of time," agreed Lance, "but knowing our politicians' penchant to prolong their policymaking, I've no intention to remain for the duration. You can tell Command to get the Commerce Secretary to call in a new man, preferably someone who likes talking round and round a subject."

Dan glanced at Jed, his gaze amused, "I guess that leaves you out, McNeil."

Jed didn't respond, but instead turned and faced Lance, his light eyes intense. "What do you think this double agent is after?"

"The senator hired him to get the list of bribe takers," Lance answered.

"That's what he was hired to do," Jed quietly acknowledged, "but why did he accept the job? The payoff isn't worth what would happen to him if Command found him out."

From behind his mahogany desk, Lance considered the observation thoughtfully. "Only a selected few knew about the second list. Everyone else assumes Command is after the list of corrupted politicians."

"And Command assumes everyone else was after the first list too. What if the rat was after the second list?"

"That doesn't explain why he would need this charade," Dan chipped in. "He could just do an inside job and get the list from Command Center. Why the need to kidnap Cheng from us?"

"Unless he didn't want us to know that Cheng has other information," Jed offered his theory.

Lance sucked in his breath. "There's another list," he asserted, suddenly very sure. Jed just cocked his head and coolly looked at him. There was something very familiar about that pose. He shrugged it off. He needed to solve this new problem first. Three lists. No wonder the dots didn't connect for him. Turning to Dan, he asked, "What did Command ask that genie of yours? Surely they would know whether there are three lists, or not."

Dan shook his head. "You don't understand. The service doesn't give you what you never specifically ask for. We only asked for the list with the names of politicians and arms dealers."

So one only received what one wanted and no more. "Damn it, what's on the third list that's so important?" Lance pondered. Did Grace know about this extra list? If so, why didn't she mention it or at least give him a clue?

As if reading his mind, Jed said, "Grace didn't give any indication there were more than two lists. She mentioned names and coordinate-like codes."

Lance scowled, not liking the fact the Ice Man had Grace's confidence. "What codes?"

Jed shrugged. "She didn't say." There was slight amusement in his voice now. "We weren't talking about her job much."

Lance's gaze hardened, but he didn't take the bait. "What information did Command get, Dan?" he asked instead.

"Just names, no codes," Dan replied, frowning. "We got all we wanted."

"Codes," repeated Lance softly. "We'll have to get hold of this last list to find out the rest of the story." Looking at his wristwatch again, he said, "Let's get this thing over with. Ready?"

The men nodded and Lance led the way out of his office, with curious eyes following his companions as they headed to Senator Richards' office, which was on another floor. The senator's personal secretary was one of their own, and she let them through without warning the politician, just giving Dan an imperceptible nod. She gave Lance a polite greeting for the benefit of the other staffers and waved him and the others through, saying aloud that the senator was expecting them.

"What the—" James Richards looked up from his book in surprise. "Lance. Why—" He stopped in mid-question at the sight of the men behind the deputy trade advisor.

Lance walked straight to the desk, speaking in measured tones. "Senator, I'm going to make this short and sweet. These gentlemen here claim to be from Homeland Security and they're giving me a tough time about certain things to do with our Chinese representatives." He placed his hands on the polished desk and leaned closer to the startled politician. "Seems that there was a car explosion that night we were having our function, and they're telling me the car was used by the Chinese representatives. Is this true?"

Richards remained calm. "Why, yes. I did authorize the car to be used by them, as I already told the officers. You can read that in the report."

Lance's smile was cold. "No need. I want you to get these men off my back. They have very politely informed me they have in their possession a list from a certain Chinese gentleman, Richards, and—" He paused, watching the senator's face turn pale. "—your name is on it. They want to investigate the Council for Asian Trade and all its dealings with the Chinese government. Needless to say, I don't appreciate having my whole life and my work turned upside down because your fucking name turned up on a list."

"Wh..what are you talking about?" Richards was suddenly very nervous.

"Don't even attempt to lie," Lance impatiently warned. "I'm trying to keep the lid down, for your sake." Gesturing toward the waiting men behind him, he continued, "They're waiting."

"Waiting for what?" Senator Richards swallowed hard, looking uncertain. His hands trembled as he closed the book he was reading. Cold perspiration popped up on his forehead as he looked at the official-looking men before him.

"We want to know exactly what you did to the Chinese man, Senator," Dan stepped in, his voice stern. "He'd been drugged and was barely alive. He's very important to us and we want to know what drug you've given him."

"May I add, if you don't cooperate, Richards, I'll personally go to the Commerce Secretary with a report about this?" Lance added, straightening from the desk.

"But I didn't do it!" Richards was in a panic. "I didn't touch the man." He ran a nervous hand across the back of his neck.

"We know you hired somebody else. We want the identity of this person, Senator," Dan ordered.

Richards pursed his lips. "I want your assurance I won't be charged for this."

Lance wasn't going to play that game. He had his victim sighted and cornered; it was time to pull the trigger. "You're in no position to make any bargains. Either way, I'm going to make that report. You'd better cooperate, so you might come off a little better than the traitor you are." He smiled coldly down at the fidgeting man, and added, "I won't have the authorities breathing down my neck because of you. I won't have your little corrupted games interfere with my overseas business. Are we clear?"

Richards' eyes darted from man to man, trying to figure a way out of this dilemma. Perhaps he could seek some sort of immunity by giving them information. His mouth tightened some more. He knew he was in a deeper hole at every passing moment. "I'm entitled to see a lawyer first," he told them.

Jed, who was standing by the entrance, spoke for the first time, his soft voice snaking across the office in deadly polite tones. "If the Chinese man dies, you'll be charged with murder, Senator. Give us what we want."

Richards stared at Jed, feeling horribly certain that he couldn't deal with this one, with his cold expressionless eyes. There was something very final about the comment, like he had no more time to negotiate. His shoulders slumped in defeat. "Charlie. Charlie Bines," he whispered hoarsely.

***

Later, as they left the office, Dan said, "I'll inform Command we can neutralize the situation by today."

"Wait. We need to find out what the third list is," Lance said. He nodded with casual charm at the passing aides and office staff at their desks.

"We could just ask him," Dan pointed out, "when we get hold of him." He motioned to the other operatives to move on without them.

Lance shook his head as they entered the elevator. "I would rather have the advantage of knowing whom we're up against. He's the one who canceled Agnes Lin at her apartment—I've been thinking about it—how very clean and neat the murder scene was. Charlie has a very methodical, organized mind and his search for the list has been done in that way."

"He gets to the source," Jed inserted. "First, Agnes Lin. She didn't have this list. Then, David Cheng. From the senator, we know somehow he didn't or couldn't get it from him, despite the chemical manipulation."

Dan rubbed his chin, looking up at the numbers above the elevator door. "He's been accessing internal files to see who our targets were and when we would meet them. Agnes must have found out about him and…"

Lance slammed on the closed elevator door, startling Dan. Jed studied him with cool expectation.

"He goes for the source. Dan, who's next in our internal files?"

Dan frowned. "I don't—"

"Grace," Jed answered in chilling monotone.

"But I haven't submitted any valid file on Grace that shows she's any major connection," objected Dan, looking from Jed, then to Lance. The other two ignored him, eyeing each other intently.

Lance felt his heart drop like a dead weight to his gut. Grace. The elevator reached their destination but the two men still stayed where they were. Dan kept his finger on the 'open' button and waited. As the information assimilator, he understood the current of exchange between the other two. The tracker was hunting for facts; the Virus was probing through it. With the latter also an expert in information assimilation, they were using each other to get what they wanted.

"Someone is monitoring COS, possibly the group Charlie is part of," Lance said through clenched teeth. He hadn't considered more than one rat. An internal war among operatives was not unheard of, but would certainly be a first for a COS unit. At the thought of Grace in danger, the idea of wiping out a nest of rats held sudden appeal. "Who?"

"People who know the sources. Mercy and Kershaw; Command; Group Charlie," Jed murmured, his mind sifting through the facts. "Group Charlie has access to both Mercy and Kershaw, as well as Command. Grace had contact one time or another with Mercy and Kershaw; none with Command, but once with COS-sent interrogator. Me." He glanced up, his eyes glacial. "Me. Group Charlie accessed the interrogation at the D.o.D. facility."

He sounded like Grace dissecting information, Lance vaguely registered. God, if he were correct in his assimilation—"Grace is in trouble," he asserted, walking out of the enclosed space, and heading toward his office, this time not even acknowledging his secretary as he passed her desk, leaving her staring after the trio. Without pausing, he activated his cell phone and speed-dialed Grace's number.

No answer.

"She's probably at work," Dan suggested hopefully. Lance dialed her office number.

"Group Charlie has D.o.D. cohorts," Jed finished his analysis in his soft monotone, as he watched Lance on the phone, asking for his daughter.

"Which means that elements in the CIA are involved," Dan said, frowning. "What are they trying to get?"

"Rather, what are they trying to hide?" Jed quietly countered. As a Virus, he usually considered the motive for resistance rather than for attack.

"When was she expected in?" Lance impatiently interrupted the other person on the line. He didn't have time for red tape right now. Grace was nowhere to be found. He wanted—needed—the assurance of hearing her voice. "Can you please put me through to Miss Sandra Smythe? I believe that's her supervisor." There was a pause as he listened. "Tell her it's Lance Mercy from Senator Richard's office. She'll talk to me."

***

Sandra hung up the phone and buzzed Ed on the intercom. "Lance Mercy's looking for Grace," she told him, "and she isn't here."

"She's a little late. Maybe she got caught in traffic."

"That's what I said, but she isn't answering her cell. It sounded serious. He wanted me to know there's a third group interested in Grace."

"COS, the senator's men, and?" prompted Ed from his office.

"Ed, you know they never tell anything. He just insisted I get Grace to contact him when she comes in."

"I don't like the feeling I'm getting. She's rarely late, especially for debriefing."

"We'll have to stay prepared, then." Sandra swiveled her chair to face her computer, punching in her code. "I'm going to access Grace's file. She might have finished her report on the lists."

"I'll join you in a few," Ed said.

"All right."

CHAPTER TWENTY SIX

Trouble. Grace's father had called her that ever since she was a toddler. It was an affectionate reprimand for a little girl too bold and independent for her own good, who took advantage of her grandmother's doting, whose father indulged her whenever he was home from his missions.

"Why did you allow her to stay out with that boy so late?" Jed had asked her grandmother one time, absolutely furious to find out his daughter was dating already. "She's not old enough."

"Grace happens." Her grandmother had shrugged.

"What does that mean?" demanded her father, his voice that deadly calm that usually warned Grace. He eyed his obstinate daughter seated nearby.

"Trouble follows your daughter. Trouble tempts her," said the old lady, in her sing-song Chinese accent. "Trouble is Grace. Grace happens." Again she shrugged, then added, "but she's a good girl, Jed."

Grace had grinned back at her father's menacing stare. With her grandmother at her side, she felt undefeatable. Her father had shook his head and said softly, "Think you're such a hotshot, don't you, young lady? We'll see about that."

Six months later, Grace had found herself ensconced alone with her father in the middle of some woods in Florida. There she had stayed for almost a year, under his nose, living a life none of her friends could even imagine. And she'd loved it. She hadn't protested, welcoming the chance to be with her idol, her father.

She would show him, she'd decided, she was more than trouble, that even though she might not be known as his daughter, there wouldn't be any doubt his warrior blood ran in her veins.

Trouble. Grace knew she was up to her neck in it right at that moment. Her vision was clearing, but her reflexes still weren't worth a damn, and she couldn't tell where she was being imprisoned. The room smelled like a cheap motel, enclosed and stale recycled air mingling with lemon air freshener.

"This is perfect for us, don't you think?" her captor asked, as he half-dragged, half-hauled her to the bed. "Sit down, make yourself comfortable. You'll be here for a while, unless," he paused to emphasize his point, "you want to let me have the information immediately?"

Grace felt the cool linen under her thighs. *Use your brain, girl.* Her life depended on it right now. "You mean, if I tell you whatever it is you want to know, you'll let me go?" she asked, keeping her voice bland.

"Of course," Charlie said. "I just need your help."

Liar. "How could I be sure you'll keep your word?" Blinking, she realized the drug was wearing off a little.

Charlie's laugh was short and humorless. "I like you, Grace, I really do, and it really hurts to have to do this to you." Grabbing her hair, he forced her to lie down on the bed. She winced in pain and tried to use her free hands to claw at his eyes, but her strength was still not a hundred percent, and he easily dodged her attack. "You know, they have some very interesting information about you in that file," he continued, as he exerted more pressure on her scalp. "It says you're an expert in evasive tactics, is that true? I know you must be good because they let you go."

Grace eyed the syringe he held in his other hand. Oh-oh.

"Yes," he continued, his smile nastier by the second, "that drug I gave you is wearing off, isn't it? I need all your faculties working at full speed, so I can't knock you out, but I can give you this." He let go of her hair and pressed an elbow on her chest as she tried to escape the needle, easily injecting the fluid. "The first way to disarm an evasive expert is incapacitation. You can't run when you can't move. Don't worry, a dose of Norcuron won't hurt your ability to think and feel what I'm going to do to you. You'll cooperate, won't you?"

It was a losing battle and she knew it. As long as she was drugged, she couldn't physically fight her enemy. It was time to change her strategy. She desperately tried to recall her drug knowledge, ignoring the rising panic of knowing a foreign agent was in her bloodstream.

Norcuron. A neuromuscular blocking agent, used to prevent patients from injuring themselves. Shit. She's going to be totally numb in ten minutes.

"So much I want to do to you, so little time," Charlie softly murmured, holding her fists and pressing them into the bed. "I'll give you a choice. Would you prefer pleasure to persuade you to talk, or pain?"

Grace swallowed down the wave of panic. She didn't need any graphic description to know what he was intending to do. If he were trying to frighten her, he was succeeding, but she didn't need to show it. She must remain calm. Where was Lance when she needed him?

***

Where was Grace when he needed her? Lance broke his pencil in half. Grace, call me, he silently commanded. "He's not in the building," he said aloud. "He's not at his address. Either he's not answering his pages or he's ignoring our calls. I don't like this one bit. He's usually on this floor hovering around Richards. In fact, he very rarely takes lunch anywhere but at the cafeteria."

From the beginning, he'd conceded that Charlie Bines' act as the doormat aide a good way to be inconspicuous in a conspicuous fashion. They had needed eyes and ears around Richards. In fact, he was probably the last person to be a double-agent. He seemed so eager to climb up Command's rungs and his knack at getting information was excellent. Look at Agnes Lin, who, before her death, was persuaded to help procure visas and to act as a go-between for Command and David Cheng's organization. Look at him homing in on Grace. From an agent's viewpoint, she was a good replacement for Agnes Lin, since she was not only an interpreter, privy to private conversations as well as political papers, but she had also recently started dating the trade deputy advisor. Lance's hackles began to rise at the thought of Grace in

Charlie's hands. She'd liked him enough to joke with him over the phone. Dammit, he must find her to warn her.

"I'll go and make sure there's not another list," Dan interrupted his reverie.

Lance nodded. "I'll keep trying to get hold of Grace." He turned to Jed, who had been silent all this time. "Are you in charge of neutralizing the arms dealers?"

Jed shrugged. "Command hasn't decided whether to use them as diversions."

Lance nodded again. It was never the easy obvious route in the game of covert subversion. There were always advantages to consider, as well as worth and value of an enemy, dead or alive. He leafed through the stack of messages on his desk, not really interested, when one grabbed his attention. Jamming a finger on the intercom, he barked, "Mrs. Jackson."

"Yes, sir?" His secretary inquired from outside.

"When exactly did this message from Miss O'Connor come in?" he demanded, furious.

"Just before you returned, sir."

"These are her exact words?"

"That's what she told me to write down. Is something wrong?"

"No. No, thank you." Lance frowned down at the note, perplexed.

"What is it?" Jed asked.

"Grace apparently called me here and asked to meet her in town," Lance told him. There was no mistaking the underlying note in the message. *I have a surprise for you at the Sunset Motel*, it said, with the address. She'd probably called it in as a joke, but it wasn't particularly funny, or did she really want him to meet her at this place? Lance pondered for a moment, then passed the message to Jed, his eyes shuttered. "You know her better than I do. Does she pull this kind of thing often with you?" He hated to have to admit that, but his tracker instincts were giving unusual warning signals.

Jed studied the note, then looked up at Lance. He could tell the younger man didn't like the idea he should know more than he did about Grace's habits, especially when the message was filled with sexual connotation. He considered straightening out the situation, then changed his mind. The tracker hadn't shown how interested he really was in his daughter, besides the obvious fact the two of them were having an affair.

"Grace would never...pull this kind of thing on me," he answered truthfully. "I thought you said she had an appointment with her supervisor."

Lance couldn't contain the relief at Jed's reply. He didn't want to think about Grace and her mentor in a hotel room. "Something is wrong with this. I feel it. Her note. Charlie's disappearance."

Jed felt it too and privately feared for his daughter's safety. "I'll go to the Sunset Motel with you, in case it's a trap," he offered.

"It's a trap, all right," Lance grimly said, already heading out the door. "The address gives it away."

"How?" Jed followed him out.

"If it were really Grace, she would go for a five-star hotel," asserted Lance.

Smart boy. "Who called in the message, then?"

Lance asked the secretary and since it was a female caller, she'd assumed it was Grace. "If it wasn't Charlie, who was it?" he wondered aloud, as they walked out of the building. "Charlie wouldn't want me there."

"Unless Grace knows who you are and Charlie found out she knows," Jed suggested, a steely quietness entering his voice. He was afraid for his daughter. He had trained her well, but she was untested.

"Christ." Lance paled at the same conclusion, feeling sick. He couldn't bear to think what she might be going through, if his suspicion was right. Grinding his teeth, and not waiting to see what the other man's plan was, he took off. Jed matched his steps to the car.

***

Back in the motel room, Grace exerted iron control over her panic as her limbs became a dead weight. She tried to stay calm by being analytical about what she remembered in her father's texts about drugs.

Norcuron, Vecuronium bromide. Muscle relaxant, lasting approximately half an hour to an hour. She could stay optimistic and hope the former would be true for her condition, rather than the latter. Half an hour. She could talk for half an hour, couldn't she?

With effort, she looked up into Charlie's eyes, sweeping his boyish face with contempt. She must be the dumbo of the century—how did she see him as mild-mannered and funny? There was only one way to overcome fear; she would retaliate while she could. "That was quite unnecessary," she said, even as her arm became a helpless piece of meat. "How could a small woman like me escape a saprophyte like you?"

"Saprophyte?" Charlie frowned at the word.

"A plant that lives off organic matter," she sweetly explained. "In other words, a shiteater."

Charlie stared down. Finally, he breathed out, "You're good. No wonder they call you the Shark. You have some teeth."

Grace still wasn't sure why he called her that strange nickname. What better time than now to get him to explain? "How did you find out about the Shark?" she asked.

"Oh, your little Chinese friend told me, of course. He was so like you, obstinate to the end, until I used my special magic potion. It's the newest from our labs, you know, and potent as hell. He talked like an idiot, then, about how he met you at that abortion rally, my little *Shia Yi*. Of course, at that time, I didn't know it was you he was talking about, not until you mentioned about being at the same rally later. Once I realized that, and after I realized you matched his description, I just put two and two together."

And came up with seventeen, Grace noted with disgust. David Cheng had obviously been trained to fight off chemical interrogation. The standard operating evasive tactic was to tell the truth under the influence of any chemical substance, but to control it by controlling the questions. Focus on the irrelevant, her father had taught her, and let the enemy believe it to be the truth. Since David hadn't met the Big Cat at all, he had used his memory of a stranger—her—who'd bumped into him to avoid access to the real truths.

"I didn't think you would assume I would have any connection with the Chinese man," she truthfully conceded. *And no one ever will, as long as I live.* She couldn't let her father down this way. *Keep him talking, Grace.*

"No one else figured it out, except me," boasted Charlie. "It was easy with your friend mumbling your little nickname over and over. You two must have been good friends. Tell me, are you two lovers?" He stroked Grace's jaw suggestively, his eyes roving over her body.

Ah, now she understood. She heard *Jia lee*. He heard *Shia yi*. David Cheng had meant *Char-lie*. He was using Charlie to deflect his own pain and they'd both assumed he was speaking in Chinese. She nearly groaned aloud in dismay. Hadn't her father warned her about quick assumptions? Watching him, she realized he was staring at her body with a strange light in his eyes.

"Lovers?" she repeated carefully.

"You're so beautiful," Charlie said, slowly fanning out her thick brown tresses on the pillows. His hands felt cold against her face as he traced her features with his thumbs. "I wondered about how you are in bed, you know. Oh, you must be a hell of a lay, what with the long line of men at your beck and call. Even got Mr. Model Boy eating out of your hand, according to gossip magazines."

Mr. Model Boy. He must mean Lance. She caught her breath as he started to unbutton her blouse. "I gather you want to join this long line of men at my beck and call?" she asked with heavy sarcasm.

In desperation, she tried to move her hands and feet; she could see them but she couldn't feel anything! Dammit, she wasn't going to go down like this.

"I'm just helping you to be more cooperative," he told her, finishing with the last button.

She'd never felt as violent as she did at the moment. For the first time in her life, she knew she could kill, if she had too. And she would. If he touched her, he wouldn't live, she swore.

"This isn't going to make me more cooperative, Charlie," she warned.

It evidently amused him to hear that. And why not? She was lying there helplessly under his power, after all. His laughter grated on her nerves.

"Oh, you will," he promised, as he drew her blouse apart, revealing her body. Grace sucked in her breath—and felt a slight movement of her toes. *Oh please, let me be able to move soon.* His fingers touched the front clasp on her silk bra, then paused. "I know all the ways to distract the evasive expert, you see. A little fear, a little pain, a little reward, isn't that right?"

She understood what he meant. He was, after all, too by-the-book. Everything he had done so far was textbook procedure, so basic she could laugh in his face. First, he'd sought to make her helpless. Second, he would humiliate her, as he was trying to do now. Third, he would instill fear. He hadn't quite frightened her that much yet, she consoled herself. Fourth, after he'd broken her, he would reward her for obeying him, thus binding her to him. At that thought, she nearly spat in his face. *Talk a little more.* She could move her hands now.

"Do you think you can succeed where COS failed?" she mocked him, her eyes raking his face contemptuously.

That stilled his wandering fingers for a fraction. "I hadn't considered that," he said. Then he gave her that nasty leer that seemed to change his whole boyish demeanor. "But they didn't try the drug on you, did they? See, it's experimental still, but I know it works because I tried it on that Chinese boy of yours. I'll make you talk, no matter how many ways you know to shut your brain off, my dear."

She felt her elbows slowly coming back to life. She commanded all her muscles to work again, desperation descending faster now. She didn't know about this drug or potion, but had seen how it affected David Cheng. The poor man was still in a coma. She didn't think her body could handle another kind of drug, even with her abilities.

Charlie Bines unsnapped the front of her bra, bringing back her full attention to her present dilemma. Her breasts escaped their confines and she strained to move her arms as he looked down with male interest, lust creeping into his gaze.

"Never!" she hissed at her captor, seeking to distract him. "You touch me, and I'll block you out, Charlie. You'll never get anything out of me."

Charlie put his hand in his pocket, then took out a small tube. "You can fight me all you want," he mocked, waving it under her nose. "See this? While I'm distracting your body and you're blocking me out, this will be your pain and pleasure."

She clenched her hands with excruciating slowness. Her fingers felt thick as sausage rolls, but at least she could defend herself now.

"What's that?" she asked, preparing for the worst. With her weakened condition, she had only one try, and she must wait for the right moment to strike.

"This is *the* magic potion. I know for a fact you can't fight me and the drug at the same time. While I'm using this delicious body of yours, the drug will distract you enough you'll have to succumb. I'll get your secrets. Like, who do you work for, Grace? Where are the lists? Who is the Big Cat?" He laughed at her expression. "I got you afraid now, don't I? I turned off my phone so no distractions for me. I'm going to have a lot of fun with you today. Of course, you could tell me where the lists are right now and save yourself a lot of pain."

He twisted the cap off the tube, still waving it under her nose. Grace shook her head. She wasn't fooled. He was going to rape her whether or not she told him. He wanted more than just the lists. He wanted to have access to all her secrets. Fisting her hands tighter, she was only sure of one thing. She used to have only one secret she would give her life to protect—that of her father's identity.

Now, she had two—that of her love's.

***

Lance parked down the road from the motel. He'd made sure Dan knew about the new situation but had refused a full backup. There was simply no time to don a hood and play cowboy just to protect his identity. This one would be done his way—clean and simple. It felt good to be rid of these confines; let Command get another man if they wanted someone to abide the rules all the time.

He paused in the middle of checking the cartridges in his weapons when Jed laid his hand on the steering wheel, breaking into his focus on his plans. He'd forgotten about the Ice Man, so intent was he on rescuing Grace.

"Let me go in first," Jed quietly said.

"No." Lance's answer was equally quiet. Charlie Bines was his.

"If it's a trap, they're expecting you. There won't be time to find out where Grace is."

Lance hesitated. This went beyond the grain; he didn't like going in second, but Grace's safety came first. He wanted her back alive. Unharmed. "OK," he finally said, "scout the target, but you don't make a move without me."

Jed nodded, his silver eyes almost opaque, but that was the only hint of any of this affecting him. His face was a chiseled mask, cold and emotionless. "I'll find out the room number and you can go in. I'll case the outside, check for others."

Jed wanted to go save his daughter, but one look at Mercy told him that short of a fight he wouldn't be the one to enter the room first. There wasn't any time for an argument and he knew the tracker would get his girl out. He could see it in the hard set of his face. That smooth millionaire playboy façade was gone, and in his place, something familiar and deadly, the flat cool-eyed look of one at ease in the frontline of a battle. He must detach emotionally and let things play out.

While Jed was inside the motel, Lance stationed himself across the street and studied the area around the small building. He cloaked his fear for Grace with the icy calm of a waiting predator, surveying with a practiced eye before he made his attack. What he saw answered a few questions. Even though he was hidden in the shadows, Jed didn't miss him when he came out, heading straight to where he was. But he casually walked past his spot and merged into a waiting group at a nearby bus stop.

Lance watched with interest as he seemed to disappear from sight. Grace's teacher, he reminded himself. They both cared about her and he knew he could depend on the man to back him up. Less than a minute went by. Then he heard Jed's voice behind him. Impressed as he was, he didn't turn around.

"Room twenty-seven to the right, rear of building. One man occupies the room, according to the manager, but two or three sometimes show up there."

Lance straightened, unbuttoning his suit to access his guns. "I'm going in."

"I'll be right behind you," Jed told him.

"You have to do something first," Lance said, looking across the street. "There's a blue Saab parked close by the entrance. It belongs to a Mary Tucker, editor of Beaucoup. She's probably there with a camera crew, waiting for me. Get rid of them. I want no witnesses." He didn't wait for a reply, crossing the street. He knew the Ice Man would do what he did best—neutralize a situation before an assassination. And this was going to be an assassination, he added, as he allowed the cold fury to seep through now that he was on his own.

Lance ignored the blue Saab and the innocent looking van parked beside it as he continued to make his way to his destination.

Someone who belonged to him was in Room 27, and he intended to make the culprit pay if she were harmed.

Inside that room, on the bed, with Charlie astride her inert form, Grace endured being exposed to his gaze. Rage curled like a fist inside her, but she hid it, knowing extreme emotions would only encourage him further. *They wanted anger, then fear*, her father lectured in the back of her mind. *Think the opposite. Focus on what you don't hate and what you don't fear. Listen to the enemy and control his questions.*

"Did I tell you I have no idea what the correct dosage is?" Charlie pointed out with silky menace, still threatening her with the tube in his hand.

It looked like a travel-sized toothpaste, a strange cheerful orange color that promised certain death. Grace stared at it as he leaned closer to her, his breath fanning her cheek.

"It'd be better you just give in, Grace. Then at least you have a fighting chance to survive. Turn off your thoughts and you might get your brain fried. And," he smiled unpleasantly as he ran one hand down the front of her body, all the way to her flat stomach, "that would be such a pity. That lively mind gone."

She hated his hand on her, but forced herself not to react to the violation. She needed him closer. She couldn't afford a miss. "Better to be brain dead than to be microcephalic like you," she declared.

Charlie cocked his head. "These big words are just impressing me so much. Micro what?"

"Microcephalic," Grace repeated softly, injecting as much mockery in her voice as she could. "What's the matter, Charlie? Can't stand being a stooge?"

He leaned down over her even more. The tube hung precariously close to her nostril as he pulled her hair, arching her head back for easier access. "It's time to shut you up, I think," he growled, "and pour this up your brain."

It was now or never. With his hands occupied, she grabbed hold of his Adam's apple with one hand, and jabbed blindly upward with her other. There was a popping sound and blood splattered all over her. Charlie howled in shock and pain, holding his nose.

"You fucking bitch!" he roared, and ignoring his bleeding nose, he grabbed her hair again and tried to jam the tube up her nose. "I'll teach you such a fucking lesson you'll wish you were dead!"

His blood smeared all over her face as he squeezed down on the tube. Grace felt a burning trickle and desperately slapped the container away. They grappled with it as their bloody fingers slipped and slid. She bit him, then yelped in pain when he slapped her hard.

Outside, Lance heard the muffled shouts and a scream. Grace. With one swift kick, he broke down the door, his weapon already drawn. His blood ran cold.

His woman lying on the bed under Charlie Bines. His woman's face covered in blood.

He forgot all about strategy. With a snarl, he launched himself on Grace's attacker, who had turned around at the sound. His opponent was well-trained and despite being surprised, put up a fierce fight, but Lance wasn't in the mood to fight. Quickly and efficiently, he punched Charlie Bines to an inch of his life, till Jed stopped his blows.

"We need him," the Ice Man cut in between Lance's fury and Charlie's grunts of pain.

When Jed had entered the room, he'd ignored the melee and headed straight to his daughter. He wanted to make sure she was alive before he stayed Lance's hands. If she were dead, he wouldn't have interrupted. Grace had held his hand, giving him a reassuring squeeze, although she still slouched on her side, weak and out of breath. He took her in his arms, watched Lance for a few moments, and then, made a decision to distract Lance's killing frenzy. If nothing else, he'd just seen a man in love with his daughter.

"Lance, Grace needs you!"

His command finally penetrated through Lance's murderous thoughts and when the younger man looked up, he walked over to him, with Grace still in his arms. He deposited his daughter into his care. Then, ignoring the gasping man lying at his feet, he put a call through to Kershaw. They were going to need him to clean up.

Lance, sitting down on the bed, ran an urgent hand across Grace's face and body as she lay in his lap. He was trembling from anger and fear.

"Where did he hurt you?" he demanded, searching for a wound.

Grace reached up and tweaked him on the cheek. "It's not my blood, babe," she croaked, her throat parched from the drugs in her system. "It's his."

Not her blood. Oh God, she wasn't bleeding. He hadn't known how frantic he was at the sight of the red stains on her face and body until her words lifted the pain that had settled in his chest. A black rage roared through him at the realization she was half-naked, her flesh obscenely splattered. He wanted to go back to punching Charlie for touching her. He carefully closed the front of her blouse, then gathered her tightly against his body, not heeding his own clothing.

"Grace," he breathed out, his eyes closed. He didn't want to ever let her go. He loosened his hold, tilting her head up gently. "Are you all right? He didn't—"

"He didn't," Grace grimly assured him. She grimaced slightly. "Help me stand up."

"What?"

"Help me up," she told him, gritting her teeth at the burning sensation between her eyes.

As Lance set her on her feet, she jerkily turned to look at Charlie Bines, who was still on his back, his face a bloody pulp.

Jed, still on the phone, paused mid-sentence, his eyes narrowing at her unsteady gait. There was an expression on his daughter's bloodied face that he hadn't ever seen before.

Grace coldly stared down at the gasping man, his eyes swollen almost shut from Lance's fists. Charlie was conscious enough to recognize her, and even with a broken jaw, managed an evil grin.

"No more of those big words?" His voice was a hoarse whisper, his eyes bloodshot. "Soon you won't be able to think up any more big words, not when it's going to affect your mind. Gonna burn you up."

"You won't be around to see it," she said, taking another step closer.

"Too bad," he agreed, coughing. He let out a groan of pain. "Your secrets would have been worth quite a bit. Somebody will benefit. Him?" He squinted up at Lance warily.

"Who do you think he is, Charlie?" Grace asked softly and without waiting for an answer, kicked him in the balls. There was an odd satisfaction in watching him double up in agony. She felt distanced from it all, yet thoroughly in control, as she continued in the same emotionless voice. "Pain, then fear, remember? Pity there's no pleasure coming."

Lance's arms circled her waist and she leaned back and let him support her weight. She wasn't feeling too great, but she stood there and continued to watch the man rolling at her feet, unmoved by his pain. He didn't interrupt her, only tightening his arm in understanding of her need for revenge.

"He's...he's...the Big C...Cat?" Charlie finally gasped out. He'd just realized the biggest secret in his short career, and knew that he wouldn't be able to gain anything from it.

"Like I said earlier, microcephalic," Grace told him. She looked straight into his swollen eyes. "You're a dead man, Charlie Bines."

"Micro...micro..." Charlie struggled to get the word out

Grace's knees buckled and she was immediately lifted off her feet. She felt Lance carrying her away.

"Wait! Micro...what is..."

Ignoring the question, Lance looked over at Jed. "Did you get rid of Mary Tucker?"

"They didn't fancy any of their equipment destroyed, so they left. The woman wasn't too happy. I broke her cell phone. Kershaw should be here soon to clean up."

"Jed," Grace said weakly.

Both men were alerted by the softness of her voice, as two pairs of eyes, one blue and the other silver, trained on her.

"I don't feel too good."

Jed was at her side in two strides, pulling up her eyelids to check her eyes. "What did he give you?" he asked very calmly.

Lance gripped Grace closer to his chest as panic assailed him again. Something was wrong. She'd turned deathly pale and her pupils were dilated. He should have known she wouldn't have been this weak if she hadn't been drugged, although she seemed able to function mentally, even as she struggled to answer.

"Something in the apartment. Check the empty glass. Then here, Norcuron. In the end, he was trying to put that up my nose." She pointed at the orange tube lying on the bed. "It's the same stuff he gave David Cheng, but I...didn't inh...ale much. Lance came in time."

Charlie cursed from the floor.

Grace lifted her head and forced a laugh. "Microcephalic," she said clearly, "means your cranial capacity is very small, Charlie."

Her head dropped back into Lance's chest. She was exhausted just from that alone. "I won't let it beat me," she whispered to Jed, even though her eyes were glued to Lance's.

Jed picked up the tube, took a whiff of its contents and turned chilly eyes on Charlie. "Take her to Command Center, Lance," he ordered. "She's going to need the clinic very soon."

"No!" Grace protested vehemently, and when Lance ignored her and turned toward the door, she lifted a hand and pulled his hair as hard as she could to get his attention. His eyes were dark with anxiety. "No, Lance. They'll drain me for information. That drug is experimental and I'd be just a guinea pig. I don't want them to touch me."

"Take her now," Jed said.

"No!" Grace struggled to jump out of Lance's arms.

"The clinic will have the antidote. Take her there now," Jed said again. He understood why Grace was fighting him, but he wasn't going to allow it. Secrets be damned.

Lance was torn, but he had no choice. He saw what the drug did to David Cheng and he wasn't going to let her go into a coma. He would have to make sure Command didn't attempt to pump her for information.

Grace gritted her teeth as the burning sensation sharpened and blinded her momentarily. There wasn't much time...and she was determined to do this her way. She wasn't going to let anyone get in her mind. Seeing Lance was obeying her father, she mustered up all the energy she had left. She would do what she had to do.

"Jed!" she called out with final emphasis. "I'm shutting down. I won't have anyone invading and probing my thoughts."

She vaguely heard some curses but she ignored them, closing her eyes before anyone realized her intentions. She was going away. Calling on her pain to block off the voices, she used her training to seal off any conscious thoughts. No one, no one, she was determined, was going to know about her father. Or anything else in her head.

What you don't hate, and what you don't fear, her father's voice echoed in her blanked mind. She saw the blue eyes. Stared into the blue, blue sky.

Grace settled into her dream state.

CHAPTER TWENTY-SEVEN

Her mind was going blank from this pain.

Sandra rubbed her forehead, trying to get rid of the migraine bent on torturing her. The pounding punishment had dulled into a miserable throb since that morning. Had it really been just ten hours? The day had been one long string of phone calls between her and those COS commandos, from Lance Mercy to the last one, a few hours ago, from Jed.

Jed. She whispered his name softly. He must be worried to death about Grace's condition, but during their short conversation, his voice had been as unrevealing as ever. He'd informed her of the situation; she'd confirmed about the third list, reported in Grace's files, but bound by rules, that was all she could supply. The rest COS would have to purchase when they figured out what it was they wanted. She couldn't have helped much even if she had the inclination to break the rules. What Grace typed in was just a series of digits, plus a four numbered code, which didn't seem to pertain to the first two lists at all. How was GNE going to put this on the market if they didn't even know what it was they had? She sighed in frustration. She had to break the code, find the meaning of the list.

Jed hadn't asked for her help, didn't even go beyond business, as if they were now strangers. She'd felt a nudge of hurt, to be so easily dismissed from his emotions. Even though she no longer felt her old pain, she still couldn't remove all those memories. She sighed again. Where did he encase all those feelings? But then, he was not called Ice Man for nothing. Jed's self-control was the thing expounded in men's war stories, the one warrior in any situation upon whom to depend for constancy. Even when it was his daughter's life that was at stake, he would still be the rock that did battle with the raging waves.

Yet, she knew from experience, how powerful Jed McNeil's hidden feelings were, how those tightly leashed emotions wrapped around him like a cloak, emanating as a dangerous aura that swirled like invisible tendrils. She had been attracted to that power and hadn't understood its source. It would, she freely admitted now, take a very different woman than her to ever know how to deal with a person such as Jed.

"How's the headache, Sandy?" Ed's deep voice interrupted. She hadn't turned on her office lights and the room was lit only by the computer screen and the light from outside. His face was in the shadows as he stood looking in from the doorway, his big frame haloed by the background fluorescent, his jacket slung over one broad shoulder. It suddenly dawned on her he'd always stood outside watching her, always knocking at her door.

"Come on in and shut the door," she invited, pushing her armchair away from her desk.

He did so, coming behind her chair in the darkness, and placing strong hands on her shoulders. "Long day."

"Very," she agreed, flexing as he kneaded the tight muscles. "Hmmm."

"Tell me the details."

"As supervisor to head of department?" she murmured, looking at the screen on the desk.

"That, and as one concerned parent to another," he told her softly, his thumbs pressing down at the base of her neck.

Odd how Grace affected every one of them. They were all worried about her, feeling more than the usual concern for a field operative. "Does she make you feel that way too?"

"You know I've felt protective of her since the beginning," Ed replied. "I wanted to keep her out of this."

"And I didn't." Sandra sighed. "I wanted to utilize her talents."

"Don't blame yourself. Grace was just as determined to be out in the field."

Sandra gave a reluctant smile, remembering how devious her young intern had been. "They still won't release her to us. I want to see how she is."

"Do you think Lance Mercy will let COS use her? This experimental drug and its effects are what worry me. Grace's profile suggested a strong will to fight that kind of subjugation. If they tried to make her talk, I've a feeling that she would rather destroy herself."

Sandra lifted a hand and squeezed Ed's warm one on her shoulder. She agreed. Worse, she knew it to be true, because of Grace's background. "I may not know how she is," she said, "but I've made it clear to COS they're bound by the charter not to harm a recorder. And, I also know one thing. Lance Mercy and Jed McNeil will not let anyone harm Grace."

"She's got powerful allies for one so young," Ed observed, rubbing gentle fingers on Sandra's temples. He could tell there were secrets linked between all the players here, but old recorders like him didn't ask direct questions. Information was sacred, and only shared when necessary. He would know, in time. As head of the department, there were very few resources out of his reach. In silence, he kneaded away the tension he felt in Sandra, concentrating on the shoulders, then the neck, then the temples, smiling in the dark at her sounds of pleasure.

Sandra leaned back, loving the way his hands soothed her. There was a quiet strength in Ed, and his touch was loving and gentle, just like the way he tended his roses. She smiled at the comparison, wondering whether she was just some species of rose in his mind. And who else but an excellent gardener like Ed Maddux to know how to avoid all her thorns? she silently mocked.

"Sandy?"

"Hmmm?"

"Come home with me tonight."

She had been so at ease since that night they talked, opening up to him like she used to, so long ago. Ed wanted her, wanted to push her along toward a commitment. He had a feeling if he didn't press her a little more, she would just be as content to drift and let things be comfortable between them. Comfortable was nice, but not what he wanted. He wanted her in his bed. She could be comfortable later. Very slowly, he pulled her hair loose from her self-imposed knot, and ran his fingers through the baby-fine strands of warm gold.

He spoke so softly Sandra had to strain to hear. "I want you in my bed with your hair loose, like this."

Sandra remained still, her eyes closed, feeling a different kind of tension beginning. His fingers kneaded her scalp and combed her hair with soothing strokes. "Ed, I—" she began to refuse.

"Sandy, I need you."

Need. There wasn't a thing a woman could do to fight when she was needed, and Sandra couldn't say 'no' any longer. She could resist everything else but need. She too understood that yearning, had needed to be needed. "Take me home, Ed," she whispered in the dark.

He inhaled sharply, then stepped from behind her seat. Kneeling down in front of her, he searched her eyes, illuminated by the computer screen. They gleamed back mysteriously but she returned his gaze with calm promise. Still he hesitated.

"I want you to be sure," he said.

"Maybe I can convince you," Sandra told him, and brought her head down to his, pressing soft lips against his firm ones. He had waited for so long. This time, she would make the move and end this gentle patience. She didn't want this stoic waiting of a gardener; she wanted him to know that she wasn't some fragile flower.

Ed closed his eyes. She tasted like the hidden nectar that the hummingbirds in his garden sought. Sweet. Precious. She felt soft as the rose petals of his prize bush of roses. She was everything he wanted and needed, and he drank like a man lost in the desert too long, and tasted more than desire. Here was the taste of need and love.

"Let's go home," he said thickly against her willing lips. He'd recovered something he'd thought lost forever.

***

"No."

Lance's refusal was final. Sitting at the mini-bar in his penthouse, he poured himself a drink, at the same time staring across the room at Jed, who sat at his kitchen table, nursing a cup of coffee. He was afraid. He feared he'd lost Grace.

"She's been out almost half a day," Jed pointed out. "It's our only solution." He took in the bleakness in the tracker's eyes, glazed from fatigue and fear, his lips thinned by worry. Again, he considered telling the young man the truth about his daughter.

"No," Lance repeated. He'd taken Grace here to his own place, cleaned her up, and had somehow hoped she would awaken. But was just lying there in his bed, perspiring like she was feverish, even though her body temperature was normal. "I won't have Command probing her, antidote or no antidote."

Jed continued studying the younger man. Mercy looked like hell. And he himself probably looked the same. He'd forgotten about his daughter's obstinate streak that she would actually shut down rather than betray him. To save her now, they were going to need the antidote and a good COS medic, but even that was no guarantee. If Grace were anything like her old man, she would resist a mind probe, and thus subject herself to more danger. She may end up so deep in a coma that—he didn't want to continue that string of thought.

"It's the only way left to get her mind to respond," Jed continued. "Grace has been conditioned by me to block out any kind of antidote without her mind acknowledging it. If we don't probe her mind, she remains shut down."

Anger was powerless. Anger magnified a problem. Lance kept hold of the destructive tide threatening to take over. He needed every tracker instinct to help him think of another way. He remembered Grace's desperate plea before she decided to do it her own way, how she was against having her mind probed by a stranger, especially by a Command-sent medic. He'd accepted the fact she had secrets, ones so important she would rather die than betray them, and Lance knew he would protect her from this invasion. *But are you willing to let her go?*

"I'm not going to let you or any of Command's damned mind piranhas hurt her, McNeil," he ground out, frustration gnawing his insides.

"We're on the same side, Mercy. I'm trying to save her too."

"Do you know what a mind piranha would do to her?" Lance demanded, his face a grim mask. "Everything she'd ever held dear to her would be exposed. I can't let that happen to Grace."

"Why?" Jed had to know. "She's just one of your passing friendships, isn't she?"

"She's mine," Lance's reply was fierce and swift, "and if you think I'm just going to let Command use her like a guinea pig, you've got another thought coming."

Jed steepled his hand on the table, feeling the steam rising from the coffee cup under his tented hands. He needed more out of this man, much more. "Yours?" he cocked his head in mockery. "She's mine first."

That was the truth, although not necessarily in the way the other man was obviously deciphering. He calmly anticipated the answering angry jerk of the man across the room. Yes, definitely a good response.

Lance wanted to pounce on the older man and beat him up like he did Charlie. His hand tightened around the glass he was holding. "She's just your student," he said testily, his eyes flashing warnings.

"Are you sure that's all she is?" Jed pressed on, not the least perturbed by the crackle in the air.

Lance slammed down the glass. He had about enough of this man's closeness to Grace. Lifting his hands in a gesture to stop, Lance bit out, "I don't care. She's in danger of slipping into a brain-damaged coma, and I don't have to sit here defining what she is to you, McNeil. Just know she's no longer playing that role for you. I intend to be around her for a long time."

Jed continued studying him quietly. There was more than physical attraction here. Softly, he said, "It would be tough for her to relinquish her role, seeing she's my daughter."

A bomb could have blown up outside and Lance wouldn't—couldn't—have moved from his spot. How was that possible? The Ice Man's daughter. As his mind made quick calculations, he slowly lifted his drink to his lips, swallowing the alcohol with a deliberation he didn't feel. He could see the resemblance now—the way they cocked their heads; the way they walked; for God's sake, didn't the way she stood under the tree that first time he saw her snag at his memory? It was the exact pose in which he caught the Ice Man when he tracked him down years ago. Like father, like daughter. He took another big swallow from the glass.

"Jesus," he swore, equally soft. "That's the secret she's afraid to expose."

Jed nodded. "Yes. You know the history of the Virus Program since you were sent out to look for me. Because of the threat to assassinate anyone connected to the Viruses, all nine of us took

303

precautions. Unfortunately, they managed to hit four of us, killing two and their families, so I trained Grace to make sure she stood a chance, just in case they canceled me."

"That year you disappeared, when you left a message with Command you wouldn't return until you were found, you were training her." He'd wondered what the hell Jed was up to in Florida. "Was she with you when I caught up?"

Jed nodded again. "You didn't see her because I'd ordered her to stay far away enough to watch but not to interfere with the tracker and me. As fate would have it, if there is such a thing, you were the one assigned the mission to track me. You've met before, you see. And now, here we are."

"Grace knows you—why can't you go in there and deprogram her mind to respond to the antidote? She trusts you," Lance said, puzzled.

Jed's lips twisted. "Unfortunately, we've struck a devil's bargain, my daughter and I. We'd programmed ourselves not to listen to each other's voice in the event we choose to shut down."

"In case you're used by the enemy to trap the other," Lance guessed. He gazed at Jed quizzically. This was the strangest father-daughter relationship he'd ever come across, but then, nothing in his world was easily defined. "But Grace would technically respond to somebody she trusts, right?"

"Yes."

"I could go in with the antidote and try."

"She can't just respond to a voice, Mercy," Jed said dryly. "She's in a self-hypnotized state. Only a mind probe would get to her, hence the reason I told Kershaw to bring—"

"Fuck those mind piranhas," Lance cut in. "They'll devour her, especially if she fights them, and you know she will, with this secret. Jesus, McNeil, you should know what she's going to do. You'd do the same too."

There was resignation in Jed's response. "I know."

Silence as each man wrestled with decisions. Lance's head slowly lifted.

"I think I stand a chance."

Jed cocked his head. "You're not going to tell me you know how to mind probe," he said. His eyes narrowed as he watched a slow flush creep into Mercy's coloring. The younger man was actually looking uncomfortable.

"Not quite," Lance muttered, then reached for the glass and tossed down the rest of the whiskey. He scratched his chin in disgust. There wasn't any delicate way to put this. "I...er...have been trying to imprint Grace."

"I...see." The silver eyes were expressionless, never leaving Lance's face. The temperature in the room took a dip.

"She...has been...responding subliminally," Lance said, with reluctance. *The Ice Man was going to cancel him for sure now. Imprinting his daughter. Jesus.* He got up to pour himself another drink.

"Grace can't be imprinted with any of your tracker tricks," Jed coldly informed him. "She's been trained by me. Unless, she was willing?"

"Not...exactly." Lance felt foolish, but went on anyway, "I figured she had training as a Virus, so I tried another way."

"And what did you do to my daughter?" Jed asked, wondering whether he ought to be amused or angry, to pat the man on the back, or to cancel him. Mercy was a lot more devious than the ordinary tracker, and he supposed, perfectly suited for an equally devious evasion expert. Slowly, he drank from his coffee cup, his eyes still on Lance. He couldn't gauge any fear in the other man. A touch of embarrassment, perhaps, but no backing down. He liked that.

Lance shrugged in response. What did he expect him to say? That because he thought Jed was a lover, he'd decided to bind Grace through sex by using the Eastern method of controlling sexual energy? As if the Ice Man hadn't done that in his missions. But Jesus. This was his daughter, not a lover. He didn't just step in shit, he was sinking in it. In the gravest of situations, he almost laughed aloud.

"McNeil, she responded a little. I think she'll listen to my voice." He looked directly at his lover's father. "I would never hurt Grace. She means a lot to me."

Jed's gaze turned thoughtful. There wasn't really much time to waste on a moral discussion. Here was a way and they would take it. "When Kershaw arrives with the mind piranha, we'll get the antidote and instructions from him. You'll then administer it."

Action. Lance breathed out in relief. Finally, something at which he was good. Grace's life was in his hands now. "You won't let anyone through till I'm finished," he asked rhetorically. He needed all his focus on saving Grace.

Jed's brow lifted. "I don't think I'd want any one to see what you're doing to my daughter."

Lance had the grace to flush.

***

The mind probe was a woman and she wasn't looking pleased. Lance instinctively didn't trust her. Psychological warfare was part of covert subversion training, of course, and he was no stranger to all the different forms of mind control every agency practiced.

Lance and others like him were action-oriented commandos; whether they attacked as trackers or evaded as Viruses, they were in the midst of a real combat. Mind piranhas, on the other hand, feasted after the work had been done. He abhorred parasites and this one definitely wanted a victim today.

Command sent Laetitia Binoche. He knew her by reputation. Thin and fragile looking, her head seemed too big for her small body, her shoulders tiny and rounded under the shock of badly cut blond hair. She was pale as a vampire, even her lips appeared bloodless. Her eyes were dark as night and as impenetrable. However, she was a tall woman, almost as tall as he was, and she moved quickly for one with such long weak-looking limbs. Her voice was the only animated thing about her. "You wasted my time coming here for a potential asset to tell me I'm no longer needed? Has the subject awakened without an antidote?"

"She's still out."

"Then what's the problem?" She drew to her full height, her eyes narrowing. "You look like you've been through a rough night. Either that, or your file photos have been touched up."

Lance returned her mocking study, for the first time considering her as a female instead of a mind piranha. "I'm sure my files have plenty of bad photos," he said. "Why were you looking at them?"

The pale mouth curved. "I always study all my victims."

The lady was definitely in the mood for mind games. Sorry, but time was short. "I'll let you go back to your hobby then," Lance politely told her, giving Dan Kershaw, who was standing behind her, a meaningful look. "All I need is the antidote and the instructions to use it."

Her laughter rang out in short staccato notes. Lance noted her voice was louder than normal. "Do you think live to service every whim of COS commandos, at the beck and call of your unit? I work by contract and you're costing me a bundle right now."

"How much?" Lance asked, crossing his arms, looking bored.

Laetitia's eyebrow lifted in mockery. "The asset must be important. Let me see her. She might be of use."

"You're not to go near her," Lance ordered, very aware of being emotionally tested. "I'll pay you for the antidote."

"My time and my expertise are expensive. My knowledge and the prescriptions I could give you are worth a lot more than your easy cash, my dear Mr. Mercy. If you want it, you'll have to barter for it."

"You're still contracted with COS Command," Jed said quietly from the other side of the room. "I can get someone else here if you'll hand over the antidote."

Laetitia nailed him with her dark stare. Dislike made her voice even harsher. It was obvious she and Jed knew each other. "I'm an independent, and my contract, Agent McNeil, stated a total evaluation of a new asset under the unusual influence of three drugs, one of which is the new one I helped developed. Command is very interested in what I can learn. Do you think I would just squander this opportunity to dissect this asset for mere cash?" She turned and looked at Lance again. "Well? Believe me, you don't have time to wait for one of *his* friends."

"What's your price?" Lance blandly asked, nonchalantly pouring himself a drink.

"You're a fascinating study, Mr. Mercy. I've generated a great interest in certain tracker abilities." She eyed his masculine frame from top to toe. "The price to assuage Command and to give you one dosage of antidote is one session between you and me."

Silence.

"Don't agree to it," Jed instructed, his own demeanor a frozen mask. "Let her do her job on Grace."

Lance slowly shook his head. He couldn't risk Grace's life. "One session," he agreed softly, still not moving from where he was, his eyes holding Laetitia's. "When and how long?"

"Let's keep an element of surprise in this," she said, smiling unpleasantly. "Anticipation brings a certain excitement to life, doesn't it?"

"Your mind games won't work with me, Laetitia."

"This is a new test on which I've been working, and I'm quite sure you'll enjoy it. It involves massaging the eight holes of the sacrum—" She laughed at the first reaction from Lance, as a scowl marred that handsome face. "Ah, I see I finally caught your attention. I'll call you when the time comes, sometime within a year. We'll make a doctor-patient appointment. For my records, you understand. Uncle Sam is so fastidious about recordkeeping, you know. One session, lasting less than a day. That's my price."

Lance walked the short distance between them, stopping when they were almost touching, so close he could see the telltale contact lens rings on her irises. "Agreed," he told her, very quietly, "but with the antidote, I want your diagnoses, advice and instructions for the patient. If the antidote fails, the deal is off."

"Ah, finding loopholes—a man after my own heart," Laetitia mocked back. "Agreed." She looked around at the other two men. "Nice to have witnesses. I'd have taken Jed instead but I don't think he'd have said yes."

Lance gave a short laugh, startling her. "Why would he indeed?" Little did she know. I would like to start work, if you don't mind."

Half an hour later, he sat beside Grace, watching closely as Laetitia hooked her up to monitor her heart rate and prepared an IV for use, her movements deft and precise. Norcuron, she explained, didn't mix well with the first drug she'd ingested, which was a synthetic mix with a serotonin base.

"Her system is on overload," warned Laetitia, as she attached the bag of fluid "She may hallucinate or become cataleptic, depending on which drug was the stronger dosage. I have no way of finding that out, so that part is the blind factor here."

"English, please," Lance interrupted the instructions, rubbing the back of his neck.

"Serotonin is found in drugs like Prozac, but the compound she was given is synthetic based. You do know how serotonin has an unusual effect on clams, right?"

Lance frowned. "Yes. Clams multiply like crazy when fish farmers feed them serotonin."

Laetitia's smile widened, her small shoulders shaking with what Lance could only construe as twisted delight. "In her case, being human, she may, like some Prozac patients, experience spontaneous—how shall we say it—sexual satisfaction. Her state of arousal will depend on how responsive she is to you. Damn it, Big

Cat, won't you let me experiment with her a little? This could be big for new subversive tactics." She caught Lance's penetrating stare, and then shrugged. "Oh well, I suppose I could simulate this on another asset."

"What is cataleptic?" Lance pressed on, wanting the woman out of his sight as soon as possible. She disgusted him. For her, a human life was an asset with which to play.

"That's what Norcuron does to a person—neuromuscular paralysis with functioning faculties. Our Charlie knew what effect he wanted from his girl here. Total paralysis of her body while her mind is left conscious and functioning. Interesting mind game he prepared for her, I must say. Fear is natural when one is unable to move, and she looks pretty young, so add that to the idea of being undressed and touched—like I said, he was looking to break her down bit by bit. I like his style."

He couldn't bear the idea of Grace helpless, being mauled by that scum, Charlie. He wished now he'd done what he wanted, beaten the man till he was dead. Every time he thought of how close Grace was to being raped—feeling Laetitia Binoche's dark tinted eyes gauging his reaction, he forced himself to stay under control. The bitch wanted to pry into his mind and he wasn't going to give her the satisfaction of knowing how Grace's condition affected him. "So, finish telling me what else I have to do."

"Besides emptying her mind, you mean?" She didn't bother to hide her smug amusement at being the one in control of the game.

"Laetitia, if you don't want to see through the bargain we made—" Lance left the sentence hanging, deliberately walking toward the bedroom door, opening it with exaggerated politeness.

She laughed again. "An impatient tracker. I love it." She sauntered over and turned face-to-face with Lance. "No way would I let you slip away, Mercy. If you could get her attention," she jerked her chin back toward the bed where the sleeping Grace lay, "and somehow make her believe you're to be trusted, then release the IV drip valve. You need to let it in slow and easy because of those two drugs still lingering in her system. Remember, she's either going to hallucinate or be cataleptic, or alternately both, and you have to make sure she doesn't panic and retreat even further. Even I won't be able to help her then. Self-induced coma is tantamount to suicide. Clear?"

Lance inclined his head slightly, already dismissing the woman. He looked out of his bedroom and met Jed's silver eyes. Grace's father looked calm, standing like a statue by the sliding door to the balcony. The older man nodded at him, giving silent permission for him to proceed as planned. Laetitia stepped outside and he closed the door, locking it. He turned back toward his bed.

Grace. For the first time in a long, long time, Lance Mercy said a prayer.

***

The sky was even a more brilliant blue than she remembered. She, the lioness, queen of all she surveyed, lay on her back, lulled by the heat into a paralyzed stupor. She couldn't move from the spot. For the first time ever, she wasn't comfortable in her hiding place. Where was he, her lord and master? She hadn't detected his familiar roar and she was tired of waiting. She couldn't stretch, couldn't explore, and it was too bright to sleep. At first, she was confident he would come and everything would stop looking so strange, and she wouldn't feel so lonely. Nothing. It seemed like forever. Why couldn't she move? She was suddenly afraid.

A distant rumble. Then, soft crackling of disturbed tall grass. She strained to lift her head, and to her relief, spied a familiar pair of powerful paws.

He had come.

He was so beautiful as he sat on his haunches, his azure blue eyes settling on her prone position. Cocking his head, he growled at her, waiting for her to come to him, as she always had, but she couldn't get up this time, couldn't tease him. She mewed softly, trying to tell him not to go. She needed him. Tossing his beautiful head, he roared, and the ground beneath her trembled with the echo. He wanted her to come to him, demanded her obedience. She knew his rage well. Didn't she always purposely make him furious like this, so that he would come to her?

It occurred to her she might be dying. She'd starved herself, lying here like this, and maybe her body was giving up. She began to mew to her lion, wanting to be near him. Pawing the ground, her mate roared again and to her amazement, the sound of her name spliced the heated air between them.

Grace.

She lifted her head with difficulty, staring straight at her love. His golden body was poised to leap.

"Don't be silly, lions can't talk," she scolded him.

"What lions, love?"

Grace blinked. There wasn't any tall grass around her and her lion wasn't looking at her with his possessive blue eyes. Instead, they were Lance's, and his were, she realized, just as brilliant.

"Never mind," she said, trying to understand. Her voice sounded distant, weak. "Where am I?"

"In a safe place."

"Go away. No place is safe right now," she muttered, more to herself than to him. "You're just an illusion."

She closed her eyes, willing him to disappear. She wanted her lion-mate.

"Dammit, Grace, don't close your eyes. Look at me!"

The urgency in his voice made her obey. "Why?" she asked curiously.

"Stay awake. I need you conscious, sweetheart." Lance gently stroked her hair away from her face, trying to break through her glazed concentration. He realized she heard him, but she wasn't really *seeing* him.

"I'm hot and I can't move," she complained. His hand felt wonderfully cool. She tried to shift positions but found herself paralyzed.

"I want to help you, sweetheart, but you have to let me."

"Where's Jed?" she demanded, ignoring the offer. Something just wasn't right. "Where am I? Am I a prisoner?"

Lance sought to reassure her, stroking her gently. "You're safe. Remember? I came into the room when you were fighting with Charlie—"

Grace's face cleared as she recalled bits and pieces. *She remembered shutting down.* "No, I'm hallucinating. You're just trying to drain my mind, make me talk." She squeezed her eyes shut tightly.

"Grace! Grace!" Lance urgently shook her, but her mind had already retreated.

Cursing in frustration, he looked down at her. She'd said she couldn't move. Cataleptic, Laetitia had warned, and hallucinating. He had to get through somehow. Determinedly, he threw off the covers, and unbuttoned the shirt he put on her earlier. Carefully, he removed the IV needle, and slid the shirt off her. He climbed into bed with her, pulling her into his arms. She was warm and so vulnerable, and he wanted her feisty self back. If he could make her respond to him, she might stay conscious. He used his hands. Fingers. Tongue. *Wake up, Grace.*

God, but she was so hot! Grace rolled over and over, stretching. It felt so good to be able to move again. Finally, she relaxed, staring skyward.

His great shadow fell across her tawny body, and she remained as she was, belly up, submissively offering herself. When he loomed over her, she playfully smacked at his whiskers with her paw, eliciting a growl from his golden throat. Lifting both her front paws in supplication, she crooned back at him, urging him.

"That's right, sweetheart, lift up your arms and put them around me."

Her dream-mate became a blur. Grace opened one eye and groaned. "Go away!" She petulantly turned away from Lance. "You're interrupting a good thing." The IV bag hanging on the side of the bed caught her attention and she followed the tube to the needle lying on the pillow by her. "What's that? Are you going to poison me?"

She tried to sit up, to escape, but Lance held her down her back with his weight.

"Stop fighting me, Grace. It's me, Lance."

He sounded so far away. "So?" She was too tired to argue, so she closed her eyes again, but his insistent shaking kept her from sinking back into her dream. Irritated, she glared at him. "What do you want?"

"You. I want you alive," he murmured, then dipping his head, he kissed her, trying to make her realize he wasn't a hallucination.

His tongue was gentle and familiar and as always, sent tingles all over her body. Grace couldn't help but kiss him back. Only one person drove her crazy like this.

"Lance?" she murmured against his lips. She gasped softly when his hand reached lower and cupped her.

"Yes," he answered, planting kisses on her lips and face.

"You're turning me on."

"I know." He could feel her nipples hardening against him, sensed the quivering of her body. He knew her body intimately after all. If he could keep her in this state, she wouldn't slide back into that hypnotic unconsciousness. Deliberately, he explored her intimately, arousing her body even more. She sighed with pleasure when his other hand found her erogenous spots, arching against his fingers as he pressed and stroked.

"Lance?" she whispered, her eyes half-closed. "Don't let them make me talk."

"I won't, sweetheart. That's why I'm here to give you the antidote." He continued to kiss her in between sentences. "You can move again. Try it."

In answer, she moaned softly as she moved her hands lower on his body. Well, at least that mind piranha wasn't lying. The synthetic serotonin was certainly making her extremely sensitive to his touch and she was giving back as good as she got too, as he tried to ignore the busy hands exploring his own heated flesh. His eyes nearly crossed when they found their target.

"I won't let them in," he continued, keeping his voice as calm as he could, "but I need you to be conscious when I hook you back up. I need you to know it's really me. Okay?"

God, she wanted him to kiss her again. If he continued to jabber, maybe she ought to just push him over and show him more fun things to do. Not that she felt stronger than a twig at the moment. Despite her weakened condition, she felt wicked and wanton. The boiling heat rising from the lower extremities of her body was getting unbearable. She touched him impatiently.

"You're so big and hard. And hot. You're burning me up." Then, distracted by a rumble in the distance, she peered over his shoulder and asked, "Where is my lion?"

"Grace, babe, concentrate. Please." Lance found himself pleading, finding it difficult to concentrate himself as she continued to rub against him. He had to hold her attention. "Look at me. Who am I?"

She licked her upper lip, panting. Her eyes were dark and alluring. "L…ance…lot." She giggled. "Lancelot Mercy, my knight in shining armor."

He had to smile at that. He'd wondered how long it'd take before she found out and started teasing him.

"Okay, I'm going to put this into your vein. See? Ea…sy." Shifting sideways, Lance deftly fastened the tape to secure the needle, then held her hand down on the bed with his own to make sure she didn't move it. Her other hand was out of the way, since it was between his legs. Perspiration beaded above his lip as he sought to focus on his goal, rather than on what that hand was doing. "It's just you and me, okay, babe? For God's sake, don't shut down." Putting his weight on his knees, he leaned over and with a trembling hand, opened the valve connected to the tube.

The liquid began to flow down. He turned back to her, kissing her softly. "Are you still with me?"

"Yes." Her voice sounded thick to her. She felt weightless and she held on fast to him, and squeezed. She heard him groan and wondered what was wrong. Did he say he was giving her some drug? Immediately, her defense system woke up at the idea of another invasive agent in her bloodstream.

"No! No, please don't close your eyes." Lance desperately caressed her, moving down her aroused body, trying to distract her. With fierce determination, he shifted his weight, closing his eyes for a second as her hand continued to hold on to him, her thumb pressing down on a tender nerve.

Lord, she was actually using her own form of countermoves to retaliate. His own control struggled, amazed that Grace's Virus training was attempting to defend herself by attacking him. She may be half-conscious but her fingers were sure and knowledgeable as she sought to delay and evade. Lance realized he must make her obey him. Before he started to obey his own selfish instincts.

Grace purred. How she loved it when her lion climbed over her like this, his bushy mane flowing over her as he lapped her face and playfully nipped her ear. He was both fierce and tender, possessive and sharing.

"Grace, open your legs."

She stared at her beloved cat. "Lions don't do it this way," she scolded, then frowned. Why was she speaking?

Her lion solemnly stared back. "I'll do it anyway you want, as long as you keep looking at me."

She gazed into those sexy eyes of his. "Like this?"

"Yes."

"Did you know I wanted your baby when I first saw you?"

"Did you?" He sounded amused.

Grace frowned again. Of course she wanted his babies. She was his lioness, wasn't she?

"I want to have cute little kitty cubs," she told him, then arched up into his lithe muscular body. It seemed so strange, yet natural, to wrap her legs around his lean waist. She shook her head as she kept seeing two different images merging—both blond, both handsome, both with blue, blue eyes. She felt confused, disoriented. "Lance?"

"Yes, my love, it's me. You *do* know it's me, don't you?" Lance wasn't sure whether she was truly aware of her surroundings, since she kept looking over his shoulder and talking about lion cubs. "Grace, who am I?"

"This isn't the time to play question and answer, Lancelot Mercy, which is the funniest name, by the way," she dreamily admonished, as her thighs tightened around him. He was holding one of her arms down, so she could only grab at his hair with her free hand, to pull him closer. Satisfied she had his attention, she demanded, "Faster."

It was good to see some of the feistiness back. Lance smiled down at her, still holding on to her arm in which the needle was inserted.

"Please," she moaned under him. He was all she could feel and see and she wanted more as the minutes went by.

Everything was getting mixed up. Colors, memories, words. It was blue and hot. It was blue and yellow paint.

"Submit," Grace mumbled, and started to give into all the sensations.

"What?" Lance whispered back, trying to concentrate. The serotonin in her blood stream must be trying to counteract with the new agent being introduced. She was incredibly aroused; he could feel the sexual charge coming from her. "Keep your eyes open, babe. Who am I?"

"Lance, the Big Cat," she replied. Rain and ice cream poured on her and she wanted him to lick every drop off.

Then she saw Charlie Bines. She stiffened.

"Retaliate," she said through clenched teeth, and tried to break free.

Lance immediately felt the difference. Confused, he held her down firmly, easily overpowering her. He saw her dilated eyes, filled with panic and anger, and his own fear spread. He couldn't lose her, not when they were so close, but her mind was struggling between reality and hallucinations, and he was totally helpless. He had to do something to keep her mind focused on him. He wouldn't let her go. *Not now. Not ever.*

"Grace," he pleaded, a slight tremor in his voice, "Please don't fight me. It's Lance, darling. You're all right. You're with me, in a safe place."

Safe place. There was only one safe place.

She purred in contentment as her lion-mate licked her all over. He was still possessive, nipping her here and there to remind her who was the master, but she didn't mind as she lazily arched towards him. She would exact revenge later. Right now, she was interested in other things. And his deep blue eyes told her he had them in mind too.

Lance kissed Grace's forehead, her eyes, lips. She appeared to calm down a little as he nipped her, biting down hard enough to draw a reaction so he could see for himself she was conscious. Her eyes still held that strange dreamy look, but the important thing was she was responding to his little nips.

Every bite was a delicious jolt to her system. She turned her head and bit down on the arm holding her hand so securely. "Lance, shouldn't we be in bed?"

"We *are* in bed."

She looked over his shoulder. "If you say so, but don't look up. The sky will be quite a shock." Personally, she didn't care. She would stay in his arms like this anywhere he wanted. "I'm hungry and thirsty."

Lance shook with silent relieved laughter. "Just a few…minutes more, sweetheart. You'll be okay, you'll see. Just keep looking at me. Keep talking."

"I can't."

"Why?"

"I'm feeling too good." She sighed with pleasure. "When did you grow a mane? I mean, a beard," she corrected, fingering his stubble. Why did she keep seeing a lion?

"When you scared me to death shutting down like that. Don't—" he kissed her hard, possessively, "ever—do—that—again." He branded her lips with each word.

"Why?" she asked breathlessly, loving his touches.

"Because you're mine. Because I need you."

Hope blossomed like a flower inside her at his words. Grace just lost herself in those blue eyes, so full of promises, obediently letting him lead her. *He needed her.* The smile she gave him was bright as the sunlit world about which she secretly dreamed. Well, as long as he needed her, she would keep her eyes open.

"Don't go away," her lion-mate ordered.

"I won't," she assured him. I love you, she added silently.

CHAPTER TWENTY EIGHT

"Help!" Grace moaned into the phone. "I'm being held prisoner here! Can you please get me out of this place?" She glanced around wildly, and added, "Look, I don't know the address, but it's definitely an expensive condo somewhere. You've got to help me! The man is torturing me! He—oh, he's at the door, I'll call back later." She hung up, dramatically flopping back into the pillows and flinging an arm over her forehead in pretended relaxation.

Lance lazily straightened from the doorway. "Is that a hint you're bored?" he asked, as he sat down by her, pulling a table on rollers close to the bed, as he'd done every evening when he returned to the penthouse.

"Argggh, the instruments of torture!" Grace struck a look of horror and shuddered at the thermometer that Lance was wielding with mocked menace. "Please, please stop. I'll be good, I really will!"

"You're the worst patient in the world and you know it," he said, and promptly stuck the instrument of torture into her mouth when she opened it to protest such an unfair accusation. Firmly, he cupped her mouth. "You complain, you whine, you leave a mess, and then you start all over again. It's only been three days, Grace."

"*Twzeezayooowong*," she told him.

"Uh-huh, for me too," he agreed. Dutifully, he checked her pulse, placed a hand on her forehead, then without warning, slipped his hand down her borrowed shirt and tweaked her nipple, grinning when she smacked his arm. "If you're good, we'll take you out today."

"We?" she asked, when he took the thermometer out of her mouth. Then sat up excitedly. "Out? As in walking among real people? Oooh, you're letting me out, master? Now? Today? Oboy, oboy, oboy." Grace hugged her legs to her chest. "I've been fine for days now and I want to go back to my own place. When?"

She pouted like a child. Being a virtual prisoner the last few days hadn't pleased her, and her own father hadn't been of much help either, actually advising Lance not to get her any of her own clothes.

"Especially her shoes," he'd said, as Grace, who was still weak in bed at that time, stared at him in utter amazement.

"Since when did you change sides?" she'd demanded, but he merely shrugged.

"Right now, I suspect he's the boss," he replied instead, and watched with quiet amusement as his daughter spluttered in shock.

"What?" Grace glared at Jed, then at Lance, who was sitting negligently by the bed, having his own private fun watching them. She couldn't believe the two of them were ganging up on her. Shaking her head, she muttered, "I think I'm still hallucinating."

Jed's smile had disappeared. "That was close," he reminded her, stepping closer.

"Yes, I know." Grace had tried to sound reassuring and confident, even though she still couldn't shake off moments of fear sometimes. Squirming under the sheets, she continued, "So you're just going to leave me here to suffer under the hands of this tyrant."

She'd hoped to make him see it her way, but her father shook his head. "I've already talked to your supervisor. Everything is set. You're taking a few days off."

And that was that.

Grace discovered that things could happen very fast in a city like D.C., or, like now, it could drag along like a ball and chain attached to her ankle. The first day was tolerable, since she got to actually see the manor of his lordship, as she sarcastically called it, wandering around looking at the expensive furnishings, the silverware in the kitchen, the stuff in his medicine cabinet, even peeking into his underwear drawer. She wondered who did his laundry and touched those cute little briefs. A matronly housekeeper, she hoped. A happily married, matronly housekeeper. Somehow, she couldn't quite see him doing any housework, although she knew he was trained to take care of himself, no matter where he was. She supposed even a tough guy would know how to fold his own clothes.

For the first time since she met him, it occurred to Grace how different their two lives really were. She was, after all, trying to figure out where she was going whereas Lance Mercy knew exactly what he wanted and how he was going to get it. She doubted whether he'd ever not known, the way he steamrollered over everything that stood in his way.

He'd stormed into her life and she didn't know if she could ever handle the calm again. He was the first man around whom she didn't mind rearranging her life, and it had ceased to surprise her how much he dominated her thoughts, and with him now privy to her most intimate secrets, she felt more vulnerable than ever. Worse, she was very aware the end to their relationship could be very soon. After all, what kind of life did he want with her when he could travel all over the world to meet with dozens of women? She grimaced. She certainly wasn't going to sit around and wait for his return, not knowing whether he was alive or not. Been there, done that, with her father before she understood his lifestyle. It wasn't the kind of relationship in which she was interested.

"Babe, did you hear a word I said the last few minutes?"

"Hmm?" She looked blankly at him. Lately, her mind did tend to wander off.

Lance sighed. "Never mind. Here, I've got some clothes from your apartment. Jed wanted to have lunch with you before he goes off."

"Oh. Where are we going?"

"I thought we could eat at Fat Joe's. He wants to see you too. He's been worried about you." Without asking, he casually unbuttoned the shirt she was wearing, and grinned when she rolled her eyes, then pulled her arms out of the sleeves as he helped her.

"Having fun with your Barbie doll?" she asked adroitly. "You've been dressing and undressing, playing doctor, and combing my hair everyday."

"Nice Barbie doll," he murmured, as he pulled her naked form into his arms. "Makes me wonder why I played with G. I. Joe for so long, when I could have been doing this." He splayed his fingers on her bare skin, enjoying its smooth silkiness as he traced her body with the intimacy of a lover.

Grace closed her eyes, feeling the familiar simmer of heat starting. "*I* want to play with G. I. Joe," she said, using her hands now.

"You're going to make us late."

"G. I. Joe never leaves his missions unfinished," she pointed out.

"We're going to be really late." Lance bent his head and lazily licked one rosy nipple.

Jed was already seated at a table when they arrived at Joe's Wok Inn. Grace noticed how the two men appeared more at ease with each other since her ordeal. She'd known, of course, that Lance had been jealous when he didn't know who Jed really was and she was happy they were now friends. Her father didn't make friends quickly.

She checked out Lance, with his dark blond head and piercing stare, wearing casual khakis and a silk shirt that only emphasized his male strength, then her father, with his tanned ruggedness, in faded Levis. Even though they looked different, they shared similar characteristics. For one thing, she wryly observed, they sure made her feel small. They both exuded power and something akin to animal magnetism. She almost laughed; she'd never thought her own father sexy before, but she had proof of it right here, where the women around were devouring her two companions with lusting eyes. Must be her lucky day, she smirked, chewing the inside of her cheek, sitting with two hunks like these.

It may have only been a few days, but Grace actually felt strange to be among people again. It was overwhelming, the way the noise from the traffic and the conversation around her in the restaurant bothered her heightened senses. She knew, from talking to the GNE doctor Sandra had sent over, she would still be affected by the drugs for a while. The bouts of hallucination were mostly gone, although, she smiled mischievously, she did miss the unexpected side effect on her sexual appetite caused by the drug. Oh, she'd enjoyed those indeed. She didn't mind those 'hallucinations' with Lance at all.

"If you don't stop looking like you're thinking about sex, I'll have to cut dinner short and go to dessert," Lance muttered for her ears alone as he served her some five-spiced pork.

In answer, Grace gave him a naughty grin and proceeded to slowly crunch down on the pork. She gave him a wink. She would never get enough of this man.

Jed McNeil sat across from the couple, watching the little flirtation going on, noticing, not for the first time, how the air seemed to crackle between them. He wondered whether his daughter understood the choices she would be making if she continued down this path. Knowing how flighty she could be when it came to relationships, he privately wagered she probably hadn't realized she wouldn't escape this one as easily. Never one to resist testing Grace, he wiped his mouth with a napkin and took a sip of his Chinese beer. After all, he might not see her for a while after today. Better to get some answers now.

"Do you think you have recovered enough to return to work?" he casually asked, knowing that drugs were tough to get rid of, especially for someone unused to them.

Grace nodded, chewing on her food. "Just a little tired, but I'm fine."

A little tired. Lance smiled at the small lie. She'd been sleeping on and off since he rescued her. Her body had obviously decided it needed a vacation after the battle it'd waged against the foreign substances forced into her, and had taken every opportunity to rest up. It still jolted him to know how weak she was, and how close he'd come to losing her.

"Any problems?" Jed continued probing. "Pains? Physical coordination? Concentration?"

Grace took her time chewing, eyeing her father. "None that won't go away," she evaded easily.

"So, you'll be back on the job tomorrow?" Jed sat back, his eyes hooded. "What are your future plans?"

Grace continued chewing. As usual, he attacked without warning. She tried evasion again. "My plans for tomorrow? Hopefully, a nice, quiet day at the office."

"You still have to work on the third list," Jed said. "When are you going back to school?"

Lance gave the father-daughter sparring his full attention. He realized there was nothing unusual going on here, that this was how Jed McNeil got his daughter to talk. Maybe there was something to learn here. The father probably knew a number of ways to sidestep all the evasive training. Her answer interested him the most. He'd forgotten she was still in college.

Grace studied her father, sipping her drink. What was he up to? "Solving the problem won't interrupt my studies, I'm sure," she replied.

"So you're planning to go back to Ohio, then, and not be in D.C.?"

Lance frowned. There *was* something going on here. Jed was trying to get information for *him*! He'd always assumed Grace was—well, what had he thought? That he was going to take her with him—where—to the jungles? For God's sake, he must have been blinded by lust. What was she going to do overseas without an education? For the first time, he realized she might not be with him, after all. Not unless he made a few changes.

"Why are you doing this, Jed?" Grace countered, brown eyes questioning. "I'll be okay, wherever you are. I don't ask you where you're going."

"That's the problem, I think. I've been going in and out of your life so much you've forgotten I have an interest in your future." Jed encompassed the couple with his silver eyes. "I want you to be aware of your options."

"I'm aware of...my options," Grace told her father. Attack when you couldn't evade, wasn't that one of his many rules? "You're trying to cause problems."

Jed smiled. If nothing else, her mental faculties were normal. "Only trying to help, Grace."

Grace's eyes narrowed. Her father never smiled unless he was satisfied with something. She switched to Chinese. "What are you up to?" She didn't care how rude that was to Lance. Her father did the unexpected. He laughed. Grace stared at him, confused and amazed. She couldn't remember the last time she'd heard his laughter. "What's so funny?"

"It is good," he told her in English, his light eyes still glinting with humor, "to know you've met your match."

"My match," Grace repeated, uncomprehending. She turned questioningly to Lance. "Do you know what he's talking about?"

Honestly, her mental faculties must still be affected by the drugs. She used to be quicker than this.

"I think," Lance carefully phrased, his own eyes filled with laughter, "he wants you to know I speak Chinese."

She should have known. The two of them were buddies now, bonded because of her. A light prickle of apprehension stirred inside her. Oh no, not more of this Men and Property attitude. "I see," she said through stiff lips. Turning back to Jed, she accused, "His ability to speak my languages has nothing to do with what you're up to, Jed."

"I want you to think about the future."

"Oh, but you've been doing it for me so well," she pointed out. Jed ignored her sarcasm. "You're already his ghost."

"I'm not."

"I beg to differ," Lance interrupted.

Grace threw her hands in the air. "I'm being manipulated."

"You helped him at every opportunity, girl, and of course, since you've denied being imprinted, it's safe to say you did it out of your free will, right?" Without waiting for an answer, Jed went on, "You dropped Tim for him."

"I didn't!" she denied indignantly.

"Actually, I dropped Tim for her," Lance said helpfully.

"Good move," approved Jed. Grace made a choking sound. "Lastly, when you were half conscious, you told us in all the languages you know that this man was yours. And asked me whether Grace Mercy sounded ridiculous."

Grace nearly spewed out the sip of tea in her mouth.

Lance threw his head back and laughed.

Jed didn't remember ever having seen his daughter so flustered. Good. She needed to evaluate her own reaction to Lance Mercy. Leaning forward, he solemnly continued, "In all fairness, I have to ask, as your father, what your intentions toward this young man are."

This time Grace was truly speechless. She tried to speak in one language, then another, but she was so angry nothing came out. Some father, she wanted to yell, painting her into a corner. She didn't actually say Lance was hers when she was down, did she? She had an awful feeling she said quite a lot more than that.

Lance was having a good time watching her squirm. But he did think it his duty to come to her rescue. "You have an excellent ear for languages," he said, giving her that rakish smile that always made her stomach do somersaults. "Tell me, how did you learn to pronounce so beautifully without taking lessons?"

"Shortwave radio," Grace answered, recognizing an escape route being offered. "I studied learning all the numbers on this station. Then I discovered all the other foreign stations. Jed gave me one for my birthday when I was really young, telling me I would find a secret," she paused, her eyes suddenly staring inward, "...universe." She suddenly pushed her chair back, and smiled charmingly, "Excuse me, I need to go to the restroom."

She darted off, her mind already planning her next move.

Lance watched as she walked in the direction of the ladies' room. He wondered what she would have said to her father, had he not been there. After a few minutes' silence, he said, "She's not happy with your, ah, nosiness."

Jed gave a slight shrug, thoughtfully looking in the same direction his daughter had disappeared. Something had happened just now. "She's always been too wild."

Lance took a swig from his beer. "I'm sure she takes after one of her parents."

Jed returned his gaze to the younger man. "She's still jittery from Charlie's handling," he said instead.

Evasive as the daughter too. "She still gets nightmares now and then," he informed Jed. "She won't admit it, though. Obstinate." He was privately worried about it, having seen her tossing and turning when she slept.

Jed nodded. "She wants to work it out herself, knowing her. Grace doesn't like to show fear or weakness."

"And Charlie made her feel both," Lance finished the thought for the both of them. He frowned, wishing he could help her forget. "Kershaw told me you're going after the arms dealers on the list."

Jed looked up briefly before returning his attention to spooning gravy onto his rice. Not acknowledging, he said, "Homeland passed the first list to the General Accounting Office. Expect Senator Richards to sweat when they start to question him."

Lance stretched out his long legs. He just had to accept the other man wasn't the communicative sort. "He deserves it," he said. "The G.A.O. will have a busy year with that list. Command should have gotten the accolades instead of those cowboys."

"With all the grand juries and investigations bound to happen, I expect you'll be required to stick around with the Council for Asian Trade a while longer." Jed commented, watching Lance's grimace and actually feeling sympathy. D.C. was a tough place to hang out for people like Lance and himself. Nevertheless, he needed to deal out the cards for this man, as he had for his daughter.

Lance decided to try being evasive. "If I'm needed," he conceded, "although my replacement could easily take care of all the needs of the different representatives. Once everything is taken care of, I'll make my exit."

"Meaning, after you find out what Charlie and company were after."

"Yes."

"And where does Grace fit in after that?"

Lance returned Jed's direct gaze without flinching. "I don't need you to show me my options," he told him, softly.

"No?" Jed's dark brow lifted. "So far, I've only seen you thinking about one option while you're around her. She is mine, you know, even though I let her run free, and I take care of what is mine."

There was the father's warning. Lance accepted the challenge. After all, he had flaunted his sexual appetite for Grace in front of him. It wasn't entirely his fault since he hadn't known Jed was Grace's father, or he wouldn't have acted so possessive of her.

"I, too, take care of what is mine," he said. "Anything else?" When Jed just continued looking at him with those light eyes of his, he added, "Since she isn't fully recovered, I want her to stay with me for a while."

There, he'd conceded the point by asking permission.

"I'm sorry to have to tell you that won't be possible," Jed said, finishing off the last of the food on his plate, "seeing that Grace is already on the way to her apartment."

"What?" Lance darted a glance in the direction of the restroom.

"She's gone," Jed told him, calmly chewing. "Made her escape."

"And you didn't stop her?" Lance scooted his chair back.

"Stay. Grace never goes anywhere without leaving me a message," Jed said.

"In other words, if I were here alone with her, she wouldn't have left me any," observed Lance with heavy sarcasm. "Why did she run away? She could have just asked to leave."

"Maybe she just thought of something important she had to do." Actually, Jed thought, she'd looked like some idea had occurred when she uttered that last sentence. What was it? "She probably didn't want you to be with her when she's doing it."

"Nice to know that," Lance muttered. Now he was getting angry. Grace's father had an odd ability at manipulating situations. A Virus' talent, he supposed. He'd known all along Grace was doing one of her disappearing acts and had chosen to aid her. The man was one calculating son of a bitch. He finished his beer.

"Uh, Lance," Fat Joe approached them, smiling apologetically, "I have a message from Grace."

"When was this?"

"About ten minutes ago." Fat Joe's smile became a huge grin. He really was beginning to enjoy seeing his friend being frustrated by that little girl. It was funny, seeing the Big Cat defeated.

"And you couldn't come here a few minutes sooner?" Lance's brow lifted in mockery.

"Umm...she bribed me."

"She didn't have money," Lance said, suspicion filling his eyes.

"She gave a nice kiss," Fat Joe said, grinning again. "A nice, long kiss. And you owe me fifty bucks. She borrowed that too."

Lance shook his head in defeat. "Give me the message." He snatched the paper from the Chinese man's chubby hand, and read it aloud, "Lance, Jed, sorry I have to leave. Something cropped up. I have this urge to get a shortwave radio and listen to some foreign languages. It comes in best around eight at night, so I will be late going back to my place. Love, Grace." Lance looked at Jed. "What the hell does she mean, she's going to listen to shortwave?"

Jed remained silent, apparently not sharing his thoughts. Lance sighed and stood up. One evasive expert drove him quite crazy as it was; two of them were really testing the limit of his patience.

"Okay, Fat Joe, this should cover the meal. And the fifty bucks." He ignored his friend's chuckle.

"Are you going to go get her?" Fat Joe asked.

"No, I think I'd better listen to her and get a shortwave radio." Lance glanced at his watch. "I bet she's going to GNE first. She's trying to tell me something."

Jed stood up, pulling on his jeans jacket. He'd decided he approved of this tracker after all. If he could read Grace as well as he was doing now, she was in good hands. "Lance," he called after him, waiting for him to turn around. "She left you a message this time."

Brilliant blue eyes met hard silver ones.

"She did, didn't she," Lance murmured. Nodding toward his car as they walked out, he asked, "Need a ride?"

"No, I have a few things to do, but I want to see what Grace is up to before I leave town. Say about seven tonight?"

Lance nodded. "Fine. I have a good shortwave radio." He called over his shoulder, "See you later."

He had a few hours to kill and he intended to use them to do something important. Like rearranging his future. First, he had to find out how much longer before Grace finished her college education. Then he would have to arrange a meeting with Command. No way was he going to let that girl slip away that easily. The restroom. Ha! If he had his way, he would never allow her to rest ever again.

The Ice Man was manipulative as hell, he admitted, wise enough to know his daughter would try to escape rather than be close to anyone, even someone who knew so much about her. Lance couldn't blame her. He understood how ingrained training was, that everything was done on reflex and instinct, and Grace O'Connor had, all her life, taught herself to be aloof, on account of her father. He had to make her understand it was different now, that she didn't need to be alone. She had him to lean on.

He would like that very much, to be needed by Grace.

CHAPTER TWENTY NINE

"That Japanese poem was worth a million words," Grace murmured to herself, as her fingers flew over the keyboard while she kept her eyes on the computer screen. It was during lunch, while explaining how Jed had taught her how the shortwave radio could be the gateway to a 'secret universe', when the memory of the poem that had helped her solve the riddle of the rice grains—what seemed like eons ago—flashed another solution in her mind.

Her phone buzzed. When she answered, it was Tyler reminding her, "Time for the meeting, Grace."

"Thanks," she said. "I'm almost ready. Do you have the slides and everything else?"

"Yup."

"See you in the conference room." She rang off, finished typing the last paragraphs. There, the report was in the system for Sandra and Ed, and whoever else was above them, to review after the meeting. Gathering all the material strewn on the table, she stepped out of the office and went downstairs for the informal meeting she had requested.

She looked tired, Sandra observed, as she studied her intern. On the phone, she'd been very business-like, telling of a possible breakthrough about the last list. She admired the young woman for her determination to finish her case. After what she'd been through, most other trainees would still be recuperating, at least, if not quit out of fear. Not Grace. There was strength in her that went beyond her youth, the kind that helped survive personal endangerment like the one she experienced. Their institute needed her, she thought, for the umpteenth time.

"How are you, Grace?" Ed asked, the tone of his voice gentle. "We've been worried."

"I'm not one hundred percent, but I'll be fine," she assured him.

"You should have taken a few more days to rest," he said.

Grace shook her head. "I'd rather be working than lying on my back thinking about Charlie Bines all day long." She wanted to change the subject, unwilling to explain how she was having flashbacks of her abductor's hands all over her whenever she was alone. She impatiently waved such thoughts away. "Anyway, I have an interesting theory."

"Let's hear it," Sandra said, and sat down when Ed pulled out a chair for her.

Turning to Tyler, Grace nodded. He fiddled with the keyboard, then nodded back. She switched off the light. "These are the three grains of rice."

Tyler tapped on a key and a picture of the rice grains appeared on the overhead screen.

"The three grains are actually three lists, smuggled out of China," Grace began. "I first met the Chinese scholar, David Cheng, at the rally. Of course, he was disguised as a nun, and I had no idea at the time he carried with him three important lists. In fact, I think I've figured out nobody knew he had three. Everyone who was involved in this adventure, including us, thought there were only two lists. Mr. Cheng was there to meet Lance Mercy, whom we know works for COS Command. However, the meeting was interrupted by the bomb scare, not to mention the arrival of two different groups of people."

She signaled to Tyler.

"This is Grain number one, magnified. It's the list of important political players who are, or have been, accepting bribes from the Chinese government. The people who kidnapped the scholar at the rally were after this list. They worked for Senator Richards. I know because I recognized the car they used when I visited the senator's residence with Mr. Mercy. Senator Richards was probably after this information so he could use it for himself, and I suspect he truly believed there was only one list.

"This is Grain number two. There were three Chinese men at that rally who were also after our scholar. I think they were sent by the Chinese government to get the scholar before he met up with Mr. Mercy, who was there for exactly this grain of information. COS wants this list because it contains the list of arms dealers who were doing business with the Chinese. Because there was a double agent within their ranks, COS was using the list on Grain number one, which deals with an internal rather than international problem, to divert attention from their real target."

Grace stopped to take a sip of water, then continued, "Grain number three, however, became the catalyst that tangled all of the groups involved. It is the strangest and the most important. Look at this close-up. Instead of names, this list has numbers in code-like sequence. We now know Charlie Bines was the double agent in the COS unit. He was working for certain rogue C.I.A. elements. He used Senator Richards to get to David Cheng before his immediate superiors could, in hopes of getting this information. Somehow, he found out I had these lists, especially this third one, and," she took a breath, pushing away the unpleasant memories, "that's why he came after me.

"I think I know what the codes mean." She waited a beat, then said, barely holding down her growing excitement, "This list contains codes that give special instructions of some sort to certain operatives. Whoever listens to the sequence will understand what is required of him or her. See, these are numbers, in a certain pattern, that always end with the four numbered codes, which are codes the operatives will recognize as theirs."

"How come you're so sure?" Sandra cut into Grace's detailed speech.

"You'll have to accept for a fact I know certain operatives are given codes like these for communication purposes," Grace solemnly told her supervisor, "but number codes have always been used in communications, all the way from World War II. During the Cold War, Russian agents coded all their targets that way. Hey, even our ever-popular James Bond has a 007."

Sandra shook her head, wondering at how Grace always managed to inject humor in any situation, and said, "All right, I can accept the codes within the ranks, but you'll have to explain to us how you made the conclusion these numeral sequences are instructions. Where did you make the jump?"

"It's a long story," Grace said, "but I can easily prove the point. You can hear similar patterned numbers read back to you tonight."

"What?" Ed sat up, intrigued.

"On shortwave, but it must have global frequency," Grace said, leaning against the wall, standing next to the screen. She grinned at the sudden rapt attention she was getting, even from Tyler. "I used to listen to shortwave radio as a kid, and today, I remembered how I would always tune in to this station that carried nothing but a woman's voice in monotone, at certain times of the night, repeating numbers in several different languages. I used to practice saying my one-two-threes with her. See here, at the top of the grain, is actually the date these sequences will be read. The Chinese use the lunar calendar. That's what threw us off."

"If that's correct, we only have three days," Ed said.

Grace nodded, and said, "That's why I was in such a hurry to get this done; I needed the information out tonight because there isn't much time left."

Ed tapped his pen. This is big. Real big. "We can get it out, but since, as you pointed out, nobody knows about this list, who's going to ask for it? And how would they know what to look for?"

"I, uh, hopefully, have arranged that," Grace replied, thankful no one could see the guilt on her face. "I didn't say anything about the third list, since I don't really know what these codes are, but I've generated some interest in, ah, well..."

"Shortwave radios?" Sandra chimed in helpfully. Tyler snickered.

Grace nodded. "Yes. It's for them to figure out what's going on, since they're the ones who communicate with each other that way," she reasoned. "My job was to let them know there is a possibility some of those agents listening are rats like Charlie Bines, and are somehow tied to the arms dealers and political bribery stuff."

"How did you come to *that* conclusion?" Ed asked, looking at all the numbers on the screen.

Grace loved this part. Information assimilation was like making a block of coherent shots out of a bunch of loose photographs. "The main thread here," she began, her voice slow as she tied together all the relevant points, "is Chinese influence buying. Grain one, buying from policymakers to get trade favors; Grain two, buying from arms dealers to get offensive power; Grain three, buying operatives—and this is speculation—to compromise their agencies so their own rats won't get caught.

"I think COSCO knew about the arms dealers, but couldn't figure out their identities or sources, and David Cheng was their first chance in getting to the bottom of this. However, our scholar brought along something even bigger—the third list, which revealed corruption in even higher levels than expected. His intermediary, Agnes Lin, worked at the Chinese Embassy, and she was the one who arranged his student visa and meeting with COS. She told Charlie Bines about this third list, but of course, he never passed the information back to the COS Commandos. I think he murdered her too, to keep that list a secret."

Tyler gave a soft whistle. "Yowsah," he said, softly.

"Good work," praised Ed.

Grace turned the lights back on. "Everything is in the main directory. I've printed out a preliminary report. I don't know exactly how they're going to phrase the question, but I've written it in the simplest way possible..."

"Don't worry," interrupted Sandy, as she leafed through the papers, "BB will sort all this out. This is going to bring in quite a bit, I suspect." She looked up, smiling, and added, "It'll be a good payoff."

Grace thought of that offshore account GNE had set up for her. She made a mental note to check and see exactly how much she was being paid for this kind of work. "I also need to talk to you in private about my future," she told them.

"How about tomorrow, after we've gotten this taken care of?" Sandra asked.

"That's fine," Grace said. She helped Tyler rearrange all the scattered files and machines. "I'll see you in your office tomorrow."

The two of them walked out with the boxes and materials. Tyler's *sotto-voce* exclamation floated clearly back into the conference room where the two older adults sat.

"You make money out of this? Babe, you got to let me in on this deal!"

Ed and Sandra exchanged glances, remembering. It used to be fun, just like that.

"Well, that was quite a performance," Ed mused. "It's going to be interesting to see the Committee's reaction when they read her report,"

Sandra agreed, smiling. "They're going to insist on getting her to stay aboard. I would give her an A for her intern work, don't you think?"

Ed got up from the table. "I wonder what her decision is," he said as he followed Sandra on the way out of the room, distracted by her walk and then privately thanking the inventor of the high heel. Genius, whoever he was. He wished they could leave the office early, but with Grace's case, it would be closer to ten tonight before he would get to feel the smooth skin underneath that white silk skirt.

At the door, Sandra caught Ed's heated perusal and a slow, warm smile bloomed on her lips. "Incentives can be very persuasive in certain jobs," she told him, her voice low.

He smiled back intimately. He no longer feared the possibility of rejection, knowing he was welcomed to share, to joke, to confide. "And what would be Grace's incentives?" he teased, stepping closer to her.

Sandra turned around fully, leaning her weight against the door, closing it. "Lance Mercy?" she suggested.

"Ah, a man." He stepped even closer.

"A man can be a wonderful incentive," she said, her voice husky. She lifted one hand, unbuttoned the first three buttons of his shirt, and slid it in, right over his heart. "A good man is hard to find."

His need for her, as always, came sharp and fast. Ed crowded her against the door, leaning his weight on her, as he breathed into her ear, "And a hard man..."

"...is very good," Sandra agreed.

***

Lance started tuning around a quarter to eight, playing with the dials and different shortwave frequencies. Dan sat at the kitchen table, a book on global shortwave frequencies opened in front of him. At the far end of the living room, Jed stood studying an Escher litho print of a pair of hands drawing each other with a pencil. Foreign voices came in and out as Lance moved up and down the dial.

"Try this one. One-ten." Dan pushed the book toward Lance.

333

Lance looked at the page, then returned his attention to the radio. The voices faded in and out as he turned one way, then changed his mind, and turned the other.

"Slower," Jed instructed, as he backed away from another Escher lithograph, this one called 'Another World.' He liked this one, he decided, as he listened to the radio. Something caught his ear. "Slower," he repeated. He remembered that Grace liked this station, how she used to show off her imitation of a British accent. "Stop."

A woman's voice floated out, in the middle of reading. It was a smooth, quiet voice, and in English, she read out nothing but numbers. There was silence in the penthouse as the three men listened to the soft voice. Then it switched to German, repeating the sequences. Then Russian. Then Chinese. The process was repeated and the woman signed off.

"Grace said she learned how to say numbers from this particular frequency," Lance said, his eyes deep in thought. "So, what is she saying?"

"She wanted us to listen to the numbers," Jed said, as he walked to examine yet another Escher print.

"Hell, we know what these channels are used for. Every cowboy wants an assignment like that—get a code, hear your instructions, do it." Lance shrugged. "Not quite our style."

"More C.I.A.'s," Jed agreed.

"And we know Bines doublecrossed us with those particular cowboys," Dan pointed out. "He confessed just as much. Nothing new here."

"How many names did Bines give?" Lance asked, his eyes hooded. He ran impatient fingers through his hair, wondering what Grace was trying to tell him. She would never give him such a big clue if it hadn't something to do with Charlie Bines and the Chinese scholar.

"He only knew a few. Obviously lower echelon," Jed told him. "Nobody that would be of consequence for a third list."

"A third list of..." Lance's gaze turned intense. "It's got to be names. The other two lists were names."

"But we just heard numbers," Dan interrupted, not looking up from his writing.

"Yes, but we know how they work. Remember when I had to track that operative who was on the lam? He told me what his job was, navigating other operatives with coded radio instructions. I thought he meant hand radio, but this works that way too."

"What's the connection?" Dan looked up. "Overseas operatives getting instructions and Bines' group, I mean."

"They're on the list," Jed supplied the information, his back still to them.

"Jesus," Dan Kershaw voiced out softly.

"He's not on the list," Jed dryly came back, finally turning around, his silver eyes glittering in the darkened room.

"Grace's got a fucking whole list of them!" Lance started to pace the floor. "A whole fucking list of scums listening for instructions."

"But what do they have to do with David Cheng's lists of corrupted politicians and arms dealers?" Dan asked.

"Think, man, what were the Chinese getting from the arms dealers?"

"Cheap rockets. Cheap plutonium. Weapons they can reverse-engineer." Dan watched Lance walk back and forth.

"Who would ensure delivery wouldn't be intercepted by their governments?" Lance demanded. "What could be a more convenient way to distribute than at the very same locations where these agents are, with them as the middle men? Nobody would be able to find out how the Chinese received their weapons. Untraceable. Loyalty among thieves, remember?"

"So, Bines wanted the list to protect a lucrative part time job," Dan said.

"And to rise within the ranks," Jed added. "Don't forget. Information is power."

"Command will want this list ASAP," Lance muttered, opening the refrigerator. God, he needed a drink.

"It should be ready for sale at GNE right about now," predicted Jed, turning around again, now that his daughter's little riddle had been solved.

While Dan got on the phone, Lance walked over to the sofa and sat down. He twisted the cap off a beer bottle, as he watched Jed examine his art collection. "Want one?" he offered.

"Thanks." Jed accepted the beer and sat down in one of the armchairs. The two men studied each other as they drank quietly. "I'll be taking care of the arms dealers. My men and I have been working on certain missing weapons. The connections will work to our mission's advantage. "

"Command will want me to track down the bastards in this last list," Lance said, drinking down his beer slowly.

"Looking forward to escaping D.C.?"

"Yeah. But only for a while." Lance easily read the hidden question. "I'll have a talk with Grace when I get back. With the names and sequences, it shouldn't take me long to neutralize them."

Jed turned the bottle on top of his thigh, studying Lance like he was one of those lithographs on the wall. "Ever read the book *Godel, Escher, Bach?*" he asked.

"Yeah," Lance replied, curious. Godel was a famous philosophical mathematician, Escher was the artist who used clever optical illusions to show paradoxes, and Bach was the master musician whose fugue and canon arrangements showed his mathematical genius. The book fused the three different subjects together to study different perceptions of ordinary problems. It wasn't an easy book to read but Lance had enjoyed it.

"Our world moves in and out of the same paradoxes, like those Escher prints on your wall," Jed said quietly. "We're the hands drawing ourselves; we're the reflection on the dewdrop. We're used to moving from shadow to light and back."

"And not Grace?" Lance ventured a guess.

"Oh, Grace understands more about it than you think," Jed said, drinking from the bottle again. "She likes Escher too, you know. But she's young. She'll turn twenty-three in November."

"I think I already told you I don't need any of your options laid out for me."

Jed went on, ignoring Lance's warning, "Both of you have to survive within all your illusions. Set one rule for yourselves. That is, if you're interested?" He arched a quizzical eyebrow.

Intently staring at the hard face of the older man, Lance said, "Go ahead."

"Answer each other's questions truthfully."

"Such as?"

Jed's lip curled back derisively. "When she asks you who Laetitia Binoche is, tell her."

"My problem," Lance said. Grace need never know.

"She may not know, but there are worse things than not knowing," Jed told him, as if he had spoken aloud. "Believe me, because of how we live, she'll only create more illusions instead of the truths."

"You speak from experience," Lance said, suddenly sure.

Jed's answer was enigmatic. "Don't we all?" He stood up abruptly. "Tell her when she asks, Mercy. You know she'll find out about her."

Lance sighed, exasperated. "There's nothing to tell her, except what Laetitia wants from me. Why would I want to make Grace feel responsible?" How could he explain to her he would have done anything to get the antidote? How could he tell her if he had failed to save her, a part of him would have died? How could he, when he himself didn't even understand this bond he felt toward her? All he knew was he couldn't lose her.

"Have you forgotten Grace is an evasion expert?"

Jed ended the conversation, letting that last question hang between them. If this tracker couldn't figure out Grace could help him, maybe he deserved to have her accuse him, just like Sandy did, out of jealousy and suspicion. He hoped his daughter wasn't like that, but love did strange things to perception, and he knew his daughter was in love with Lance Mercy. It was in her eyes, in the way she said his name. He walked back to look at the lithographs, ignoring a brooding Lance. Let them make their own choices, then. He loved his daughter, all of her independent, obstinate spirit, and had always respected all her choices. He wasn't sure, though, if he could accept she wasn't his little girl anymore.

CHAPTER THIRTY

Grace didn't like her apartment any more. Every little sound rattled her nerves. It was too quiet. It was too noisy. For the first time in her life, she wasn't comfortable alone. She wondered why she didn't feel elated about how things turned out. After all, she had everything solved, hadn't she? She did her job and was paid well for it. She'd gotten promoted and was offered a position for which she would have given her eye teeth a year ago. She should be on top of the world.

Yet, there was a hollow feeling inside her. Maybe she was still being influenced by those damned drugs. Determinedly, she stopped prowling around her apartment, and for a few minutes she stood in the living room, trying to feel safe.

She jumped when her phone rang, and knew who it was. With relief, she answered the call.

"Grace?"

She clutched the phone tightly at the familiar sound of his male timbre, wishing she were with him at his penthouse at that moment. She'd chosen to return here instead, to be alone, to overcome her new fears. She hadn't told anyone about them, that she was afraid of being alone and that sometimes, she had nightmares.

"Yes, Lance," she forced herself to sound calm. "Been doing anything interesting tonight?" She wanted to ask him to come to her, to hold her while she slept.

"Lots," he replied. "It's going to be busy for a while."

Grace had heard that line before, from her father. She closed her eyes. "I see," she said slowly. "Well, I'm glad I've been of help." Her throat felt constricted, and she swallowed down the lump that had formed there.

"I have to go off for a couple weeks, but when I get back, we'll talk, okay?"

He sounded so impatient, as if he couldn't wait to leave. Why didn't he just come right out and say it? Forcing herself to sound as offhanded as he, she said, "Sure."

"I'll be out of the country, so don't bother to call the office. I'll call you If I can."

If that didn't sound like the classic "don't call me, I'll call you" brush off, she didn't know what was. A cold heavy feeling settled in that hollow place inside Grace.

"I understand." Her voice sounded polite and far away. Of course she understood. She had always known that this moment would come.

Lance frowned at the coolness in her voice. Something was wrong, but he didn't have time to press her for an explanation. He wanted to yell at her for not returning to him for the night, so he could hold her for the few hours before he left, but he didn't want to quarrel with her before a mission. She was, after all, still recuperating. She hadn't admitted it, but Lance knew she hadn't truly recovered from that incident with Bines. *Go gentle.* "Will you be all right by yourself? I don't want you feeling lonely."

She hated his saccharine concern. He needn't feel obligated about her. She would be strong about this, about everything. "I can take care of myself," she said smoothly, ignoring the screaming inside her head. "Good luck, Lance."

There was a slight pause, and he said, "Okay. In a couple of weeks then."

"Right," Grace said, and pressed her thumb down to end the call. She couldn't bear to say goodbye outright.

In the dark, she sat down in her favorite chaise lounge, her eyes open but seeing nothing. She felt numb, helpless, like she didn't know what to do next. Giving a weak smile, she muttered out loud, just to break the silence, "Well, I really need some practice with this breaking up bu...business."

The last word got caught somewhere in her throat, and Grace curled into the soft pillows of the chaise and bawled her eyes out.

She never, ever cried, and she hated Lance Mercy for making her do something she'd sworn never to do.

***

When the first major snowstorm hit in November, Grace decided to walk to class instead of taking the car. It was very bright and clear outside, and if not for the crisp arctic air, it looked like a regular summery day. The sky was so blue, everyone was wearing sunglasses, along with the usual assortment of parkas and heavy jackets. Everyone was trying to hurry, to escape from the decidedly cold fingers of the November wind.

Grace didn't mind. She had been cold since September, when she had to return to school. GNE had accepted her decision, once she'd told them she would finish her three remaining quarters in two, graduating after the winter quarter. If they were still interested, she'd said, then she would join the institute in spring, but she wanted a degree under her belt. Ed had backed her, and Sandy, in her usual efficient way, had told her everything would be taken care of. One of them called her once a week to touch base and to make sure she was all right. She was touched by their concern, since she hadn't ever thought of them as anything other than her bosses, but looking back now, she realized the two of them had given her a lot of advice and direction.

She told herself she was happy to be away from D.C. Memories of Lance haunted her apartment and she'd gladly found someone to take the remaining time of her lease, moving her belongings into storage in Ed's garage for now.

She didn't want to think about *him*. She hunched into her jacket, walking against the icy wind. Two weeks. Sure. That had stretched into two months now, and she had yet to hear from him. Not that she'd expected it, but she'd hoped... She pursed her lips in disgust. Why did he always creep into her thoughts when she didn't want him to? Pride stopped her from asking her friends in D.C. about him and her conversations with Ed and Sandy were always carefully general in nature.

She learned from the news about a bribery scandal brewing on Capitol Hill. Heads were going to roll. She recognized all the names mentioned but, of course, that was her little secret. She knew where her father was, courtesy of her new connections at GNE, and for that she was grateful for her new job because it was another way to keep tabs on him. However, despite her privileges, she'd avoided the subject of Lance Mercy and the third list like a contagious disease, choosing not to access any information about traitorous spies being caught. She'd thought that by banishing him from her everyday life, he would cease to exist in her mind.

How very wrong she'd been. He was with her everyday. She couldn't escape at all. She couldn't stop herself from thinking about his face, how his eyes crinkled when he mocked her, how his body tensed under her seeking fingers. Most of all, she missed his heat. She'd been so cold since that night he broke up with her.

Ha, classic words—*Don't call me at the office; I'll call you...You'll be all right by yourself, won't you?* Scarcely two weeks was up and women were calling for him at *her* place. She still fumed at that memory, balling her gloved hands into fists inside her coat pockets, her anger and indignation making her stomp faster down the brick sidewalk. It was one woman but she sounded like she knew Lance very well, asking for him because she couldn't get him at his penthouse. How did she get her number? Grace had asked her politely. Lance and she were very close, purred that hateful voice, and he'd talked a lot about her. When she saw Lance, would she kindly pass the message she had the date with him all planned out?

Grace remembered how furious she had been, how she'd gone down to the weight room and worked out until she could barely walk back to her apartment. Then she'd started packing.

It was better now, that pain. She had it under control, turned down like a volume gauge. It was a muffled kind of pain and she had learned to exist with it—by going to school, keeping busy, by taking long walks with her grandmother, by simply, not thinking. Until, that is, she saw a blue sky. Or a tall athlete. Or worse, bumped into Tim in classes. She had a long talk with her ex when she saw him the first day back on campus but his male ego had been hurt, so he'd been ignoring her ever since, walking past her with his newest girlfriends. He probably thought her depression had been caused by envy and regret, and she managed to grin at *that* idea. She had been right about one thing all along, though— there was no comparison when it came between Tim Halliday and Lance Mercy.

Today was her birthday. It was cold and she was miserable. Fuck class. She made up her mind to walk into town and go to

O'Hooley's, order Irish coffee and people-watch for a while. It was her favorite hangout, a cozy Irish café-bar, just across the main campus. She'd been doing that lately—people watching. Funny how many different kinds of couples there were when one set about studying them.

Sipping a hot cup of Irish coffee, she lazily let her eyes wander, looking at fellow students trudging back and forth from their classes, smothered in heavy scarves and hats; gloves and boots; thick jackets, woolen coats, furry capes.

Then she saw him.

Lance Mercy standing all by himself at the campus gate right across from the café. How could she miss him? The man was standing there without a coat, only in a denim jacket, and jeans. There was no hat covering that familiar mane of hair, glinting gold in the bright sunlight. Tanned and fit, his face leaner and unshaven, he looked positively dangerous among the colorless wintry backdrop. He had a leg raised on a brick planter, and was leaning on an elbow anchored on his knee, a casual stance that didn't deceive her. She knew better. He wasn't missing a single detail of everyone passing by.

He was looking for her. Grace's heart did a slow somersault. It would be so easy to just take the back exit and run away. She didn't particularly want to get burned again. Why was he doing this, coming here, after all these months? And why did he have to look so infuriatingly good? On the verge of turning away, she caught sight of a particularly pretty student walking by and blatantly sizing him up. Grace's eyes narrowed as she witnessed the girl mouthing something to him and was rewarded by that easy devastating smile of his. The effect was not unexpected: the girl stumbled. Grace wanted her to fall on her face.

The nasty thoughts changed her mind about getting away. Nothing was ever going to get better if he was still capable of making her jealous while standing across a street. She was tired of evading Mr. Smooth, anyhow. It was time to teach that bothersome tracker a few things about pain. She went to pay her bill.

Lance was used to waiting, knew the endless preparation it needed to finally get one's target. Waiting was part of the hunt and he was very good at it. But his style had always been to lie in the shadows and make his move at the precise moment, not like this, out in the open, where his opponent had as equal a chance to see him first. He reminded himself he wasn't there to track an enemy. Acting on a hunch, he'd chosen to be where he was, hoping to catch Grace going to classes. God, he was a goner; he was actually hanging out in front of a college gate among a bunch of fresh-faced kids, looking for her.

Two months. The last man on the list was a lot wilier than the others, and had led him on a chase through several countries. His downfall came when he made the wrong decision to hide in the jungles. Apparently, the man didn't know the Big Cat's domain, and Lance located him with deadly ease after that.

When he returned to the States, Grace had already moved on, seemingly having forgotten about him without trouble. She hadn't left a message at his office, hadn't even asked for messages from him there, even after the two weeks went by and he hadn't returned. She obviously didn't care enough to even wonder whether he was alive or dead and it had rankled. Had she really forgotten him already? His ego dismissed that notion but he suspected she was capable of burying him as her past, and again, that thought had driven him to instant action.

He cursed silently at his predicament. He had almost nine years on her; among these kids, she must remember him as some exotic summer adventure. Not knowing about her future plans, he came here determined to let her know she was going to have a fight on her hands, if she thought she could evade him.

Besides, it was her birthday today. He wanted to see her. It'd been too long.

She suddenly appeared out of nowhere, standing across the street. Lance blinked, not sure whether she was real, and then, she wasn't there any more. Grimly, he straightened up, looking at the spot again. He was sure it was her. It was the way she stood, the way her head tilted to one side, which told him she saw him too. He was about to cross the street when he saw her again to his left, leaning against the low brick wall that surrounded the college green.

He couldn't see much of her with all those winter clothes she was wearing, but her face looking back at him had the same questioning and mocking stare she'd given him that first time he'd seen her at the rally. She just stood where she was, her right hand scraping the snow on top of the low wall, not moving when he began to walk toward her.

He looked at her hungrily. It'd been too damn long. Startled, he realized she was thinner in the face, the slight hollow underneath her cheekbones giving her dark eyes an even more catlike slant. Her lips were soft and inviting, and he walked a little faster to reach her. He badly wanted to kiss her but he just stopped a foot or so in front of her, forcing her to look up at him.

They stared at each other like duelists. She wanted to touch him, but didn't. He wanted to pull her into his arms, but didn't.

"Well, do I at least get a welcome back gesture?" Lance drawled, slightly annoyed at the way she just stood there looking at him. He had expected more emotion. Dammit, he had missed her; hadn't she missed him too?

Grace's two-month-old icy calm cracked at his words. The man had played with her emotions, then dropped her, so what did he expect after all this time? Had he shown up thinking to find her soft and eager?

"You want a welcome back gesture?" she yelled at him, ignoring the startled looks from passersby. "Here's your welcome back gesture!"

She started pelting him with globs of wet snow, hitting his face with several on-target aims. Caught by surprise and half-blinded by snow, Lance took several steps backwards, using his arm to shield his face.

"Damn it, you hellcat, stop that!"

When it became obvious she wasn't going to, shooting missile after missile at him with her usual accuracy, he decided that retaliation was the only way. He scraped snow off the wall and went after her.

Grace was angry enough not to feel the first cold blast that hit her face. Nor the second. She vented her frustration at this man, who dared to invade all her secrets, dared to seduce her, and made her feel something for him.

"Here's your welcome, Lance Mercy," she shouted, hurling words and snow. "Here's another gesture! Here's your damned gesture!"

"Grace, quit it!" He circled her tightly with his arms, astonished at the fury she was exhibiting. Not understanding, he gathered her close, and let her rant and rave into his chest, her words muffled. He didn't miss the curses and her threats to several of his body parts. Nor did several amused spectators. God, the woman certainly knew how to stage a fight. "Grace, baby, calm down!" He hadn't expected this much anger. "I know I told you two weeks, but the business lasted longer than I thought."

She went still. "You actually meant it?"

"Meant what?"

She lifted her face, snow on her brows and lashes, her brown eyes still fierce with some emotion he couldn't fathom. "Meant to call me when you got back."

It was important to her, Lance realized. She'd thought he wasn't going to call her again. That explained the coolness of that last conversation. He gave her a measured look. "Did you think I wouldn't?"

"It sounded like a line," Grace said, but she didn't sound sure any more.

"I'm not some college kid with a collection of lines," he told her, his blue eyes glittering with temper and astonishment. "You know how these things go, with my work."

"You could have called when you were delayed," she accused.

"I was chasing bad people, for God's sake. I've been a bit busy trying not to get killed." This time, it was his turn to yell.

He had a point, she conceded. But she remained obstinately angry. "There are other ways to communicate. Email. A postcard would do nicely."

"Jesus, Grace, where I was, the postman doesn't call. Besides, if you'd moved that pretty ass of yours to my office, you might have seen the messages I told Kershaw to leave for you." That was mostly what pissed him off, to return to D.C. and be told she hadn't once called or been there to get his messages. He had never done that for anyone, and hadn't expected his concession to go unnoticed. "And if you recall, we never emailed each other. I don't have your email address. I didn't think about it, that's all."

Grace frowned. "You left me some messages?" Had she really misread him so badly? A little flare of hope returned.

"Yeah." He stared down at her. "I don't know why you're so mad, you should be used to this. Your father doesn't show up for nine months, and you accept that."

That rekindled her anger. She smacked his chest with her palm, yelling, "You're not my father! If you think I'm going to sit around waiting and wondering like I do when my father doesn't show up when he's supposed to, you're in for a rude awakening, Lance

Mercy! I want more than that, a lot more. You want a pliant waiting female, you go back and date that woman waiting for you in D.C. *She*'s waiting eagerly for that date and I'm sure she's just the type for you." She struggled to get out of his hold. "Let go of me! Nine months! You aren't my father!"

"You tell him, girl!" a passing student loudly approved as she walked by, glaring at Lance for hurting a fellow sister. Her companions yelled similar encouragement.

Lance was taken aback by her tirade. He'd never before thought her capable of losing her temper like this. The Grace he knew was sarcastic and witty, and when angry, usually evaded a confrontation. No, this Grace was truly upset with him. He gently held her till she ceased struggling, then bent his head and placed a kiss on her lips.

"I don't want to behave fatherly," he said huskily. He nibbled her lower lip and reluctantly released her. "Let's get out of this cold and go somewhere we can talk. Somewhere public." At the question in her eyes, he told her, "I won't be talking if we're alone. Unless you want to see how absolutely unfatherly I feel about you?"

Grace eyed him warily. Talk. There was nothing to talk about that he hadn't shown through his actions these past few months, unless…unless…he really did try to send her a message? Did that mean he cared? Maybe they should talk. They hadn't spent much time doing that anyway. She took him back to O'Hooley's across the street.

Lance examined her critically as she draped her heavy coat over the back of her chair before sitting down. "You're thinner," he observed.

Grace raised an eyebrow. She wrinkled her nose. He looked like a disgustingly tanned and well-fed wealthy man. "I didn't know you could see through this bulky sweater," she said, then turned and ordered another cup of Irish Cream from the waitress.

Lance asked for the same, and continued, "Aren't you eating well? Are you still having nightmares?"

She'd forgotten how he could always deflect her evasions. "Is that why you're here, to update my health report?" she quipped defensively, fiddling with the utensils on the table.

He captured her restless hands and pulled them toward him, forcing her to lean across the table, closer to his face. "Is it so difficult to answer my questions?" he asked softly.

"That's what you always do—question, question, question— since the very beginning," she accused, her eyes darkening as she tried to ignore the way his thumb was rubbing the inside of her wrist.

"What am I supposed to do when all you do is run, evade, mislead?" he countered, but unlike her, his tone was gentle. "I never said life with me was going to be easy, Grace."

She was suddenly short of breath. "I didn't think there was a life with you," she murmured, staring into his eyes. "You made it sound like you were saying goodbye the last time we talked."

The intensity in his eyes grew and the hold on her hands tightened a fraction. "You were looking for a way out, so don't blame me if you chose to read my words that way." He was angry again but he pulled back, trying to explain. "We should talk more, this is very enlightening. I didn't know you had such a low opinion of me, that I would just end it like that."

Grace bit her lip. "I don't know how millionaire playboys— façade or not—" she stopped his interruption, "break up with their women. I didn't want to be a toy, Lance, some fling before you go back overseas."

He caught the past tense. "Didn't?" He cocked his head.

Grace decided she liked this new role of being on the attack. Maybe she had the makings of being a tracker herself. She knew when a fish had taken the bait. Now all she had to do was to let him chomp on it a little bit, before reeling him in. She gave Lance her most serious look and nodded. "I've changed my mind."

"Changed your mind," he repeated, puzzled.

"Yes. I would like to be with you while you're stationed in D.C.," she said, "and continue where we left off. I understand this kind of social etiquette a lot better now, having talked with Mary Tucker." She was really enjoying the look on his face. "She told me a lot about your social life, how you...enjoy yourself so much. I thought I would do the same."

"What the hell are you talking about?"

Grace smiled. He was coming in without a fight. "You know, the kind of relationship you like. I don't see why I can't enjoy you and other men as well."

"What?" In his surprise, Lance let go of her hands. All at once, fury and exasperation took over. He sat back, glaring at her. In deliberate measured tones, he asked, "What you are saying is that when I'm away, the mouse will play?"

She studied the back of her hands, seemingly unaware of his murderous look. "Well, I wouldn't put it that way. However, I think it's only fair. You've all these dates with other women, so why can't I?" She hid her smirk behind her coffee cup.

"Let's make this clear. When I'm in the vicinity, you'll be exclusively mine, but once I'm out of sight, you'll be busy entertaining somebody else?" The thought of her dating another man was enough to make him want to forget all his earlier intentions of being gentle with her and letting her finish her studies. If he had to, he would put her in isolation in a jungle. See whether she could go on a date with another man there, he thought, with a satisfying viciousness.

"Perfect!" Grace looked up, smiling. "Makes things simple, doesn't it? Besides, you won't be that long in D.C. anyhow, seeing you've wrapped up this mission." She studiously counted his accomplishments off her hand, as she continued, "Got your rat, got your weapon dealers, got your greedy politicians. There's only the Council for Asian Trade left, and you can easily get out of that."

Lance's eyes narrowed. "I'm sorry to inform you, babe, there's been a change of plans," he silkily told her. "You see, I arranged certain things before I left and will be sticking around until after you graduate, maybe a little longer. I was going to tell you before I left."

Now it was her turn to be surprised. "What?"

The enormity of his decision was very clear. She forgot about baiting him. If she wasn't mistaken, Lance Mercy just committed himself.

"So you won't really need to date anyone for a while, seeing that you agreed to an exclusivity clause," he said, then paused to drink his coffee down, a smug expression on his face. "And since Miss Smythe had already told me you're returning to GNE, I can always make certain to track you, wherever you choose to disappear to." He came forward and said in a low voice, "You can't ever escape me, Grace."

She made a face at him. "So we're at an impasse." It dawned on her they were both playing fishermen, reeling each other in.

"We can try something different," he suggested.

"As long as it's your way, of course," she pointed out, used to it by now.

"You'll like it," he told her. He took her hand between his again. His voice became lower, huskier. "Suppose we just stick with each other, exclusively, and I promise it'll just be you?" He brought her hand to his lips, looking at her seriously. "Well?"

Grace exhaled slowly. "Well." That was all she could think of saying. There it was. Bait. The long awaited cheese for the mouse.

"And my mother wants to meet you."

She stared at him. Then grinned. "I get to ask her why she named you Lancelot Mercy?"

"Will that make my offer more attractive?"

"Let me think about it."

He bit her fingers. "Is it so hard for you to forsake all others too? To be mine, exclusively?"

"Actually," Grace said, still grinning, "I thought I've been doing just that. Haven't I given up Tim for you?" Her expression changed. "I would like to know, though, about this other woman." When Lance just looked quietly at her, not answering, she persisted, "Laetitia something or other. She was looking for you, calling at my place."

It would be simpler just to lie. Why cause more trouble? But Lance remembered the Ice Man's advice about telling the truth regarding Laetitia Binoche. "Are you sure you want to know? It's not what you think. Sometimes it's better not to know, Grace."

She shook her head. "That's a lame evasion. Remind me to teach you how to do it right," she told him, a touch scornfully. "Come on, you were the one who wanted to talk. Tell me about her." If she had competition, she wanted to know about it now.

Lance kept his gaze steadily on hers as he told her about Laetitia Binoche, keeping the details to a minimum. Her eyes had rounded in shock then became almost black as she silently listened. Carefully, she laced her fingers with his, and the short silence that followed was filled with angry tension.

A sense of wonder thawed away what was left of the icy ache inside Grace. Dare she assume, for the very first time, dare she hope he was here because he wanted her long term? Wasn't that what everything meant? That he would agree to a session with a mind probe to save her; that he would stay out of his beloved jungles for a while, *for her*.

"Lance, you didn't have to make the bargain or change your plans. Why?" She looked at him hopefully.

Her face was such an open book. She'd never been good at hiding her emotions from him. "Do you want me to admit how important you are to me?" he asked, exasperated. "These last few months without you have been hell, sweetheart. I've not been a joy to work with, as Kershaw will tell you."

"I'm glad you've been miserable," Grace said, smiling. "I wasn't a happy camper myself."

Later, she would help him deal with this Laetitia Binoche. She hadn't any intention of letting this woman touch her man, neither his body nor his mind. Right now, though, they needed to make up for lost time.

"Did you miss me?" His voice was low, intimate. "Or have you been busy replacing me?"

She touched the side of his face, her nails scraping his stubble. She was about to answer when a couple sat down at the table by them, one of the chairs bumping into another on one side of their table. Looking up, she caught sight of the culprit and her smile widened. Following her gaze, Lance found himself being scowled at by Tim Halliday. He wasn't alone; a pretty girl sat next to him. But the kid's whole attention was on Lance and Grace.

Lance turned back to Grace and demanded, "Did he have a part in making you so thin?" He didn't like the way she was smiling at the punk.

Grace looked away from Tim. "He thought I was pining for him," she said, her eyes were shining. "I think he's finally getting the message."

"Were you pining?" Lance asked, smiling back at the humor in her voice. He felt relaxed and carefree. The way she was looking at him told him volumes.

"Questions, questions," she said, softly. "Why don't you let me show you?"

"Deal." Lance slapped down some cash on the table and helped her into her jacket. Not even noticing Tim's baleful glare, he guided her back out into the cold. "Did you drive?" When she shook her head, he pointed down the road. "My car's parked down there."

"Wait!" She held on to his sleeve, pulling him back. "Kiss me. Now."

She didn't have to ask again. While the temperature dropped, Grace's reached a fever pitch. He relit the fire in her, his lips moving intimately against hers. It was a possessive kiss, giving no quarter, telling her how much she was wanted, and she returned it with passionate abundance, needing him so badly it hurt.

"You could have just told me when I saw you at the gate," she said, when they broke apart to breathe, "instead of telling me to treat you like my father."

"It didn't strike me when I was trying to duck a bombardment of snow," he dryly reminded her. "I bought you a birthday present."

"You're lucky," she said, her eyes lit up with laughter. "I was going to drop snow down your neck if you forgot to bring me one."

Lance gave an exaggerated sigh, bent over, placed an arm under her knees, the other around her shoulders, and swept her off her feet. He walked with his usual surefootedness down the road, nodding at passersby as if nothing unusual was happening.

"You always did enjoy manhandling me," she sighed into his chest, slipping her hands inside his jeans jacket, caressing the corded muscles under his shirt. She didn't mind being carried off at all. It was kind of romantic.

"It was either that or kill you," Lance muttered, as he felt himself growing hard from her bold little hands. "I still might, if you don't stop trying to shove your hand down my pants."

She ignored him, delighting in the furnace of his heat as it enveloped her. God, she'd been cold for so long. "Can I put in a request?" She pulled at his shirt impatiently. "No strangling. Too painful. No knife. Too messy. No drowning. Too uncomfortable. No…"

"Are you going to list every method?" he cut in, then muttered a soft curse when her hands found flesh. "Woman, I'm going to kill you slowly," he promised.

"Hmm, one more thing." She raked him with her nails gently, too engrossed to notice that he had set her down on the hood of his beloved BMW.

"What?" God, she was like a drug, the way she affected him.

"Where are you going to put my body?" She tilted her head, still smiling.

He gave her that golden smile, the one she loved. He bent down and kissed her deeply, his tongue mating with hers. When he looked at her, his eyes were a searing blue, hot and full of promise.

"Where it belongs. In my bed." He didn't need to question her any longer. "I love you, Grace."

She didn't need to evade or run away any more. "I love you too," she murmured. Their adventures together had just begun. "But you've got to learn to text and email more."

"Hate that stuff. I'd rather show you what I—" Lance paused just before his lips caught hers again. He lifted his head slightly, as he listened. A soft, deep rumble filled the air. "What's that growling?"

"Thunder," Grace replied, pulling his head back down to meet her embrace.

That was no growl, that was a purr, but she was too busy to correct him.

THE END

AUTHOR'S NOTE

Dear Reader,

When Jed and Grace McNeil first appeared in **Big Bad Wolf**, they generated a lot of emails asking for their stories. I felt I had to give some time for both characters to grow, especially Grace, since she was only sixteen.

Grace's story was definitely a fun write for me because of her youth and enthusiasm. Not only that, it was great to see how that time out in the wilds with her father five years ago had shaped her into the woman she is now. I loved being in her point of view because she is young and still have much to learn, definitely a departure from my usual worldly/cynical/damaged heroines. And yeah, I was surprised Lance's very, very brief appearance in **Big Bad Wolf** was actually the seed to the crazy couple in **Tempting Trouble**.

As for Jed, I discovered so many layers to "His Jedness," as his fans like to call him, as he showed up more and more in subsequent books. He is a tough character to "know" and is a challenge to write as a romance hero because of his uncompromising attitude.

You can read Jed's story in the Super Soldier Spy series (**Virtually His** and **Virtually Hers**, so far). I don't regard them as *romantic* romance, by the way. The series is my techno spy-fy romance, with emphasis on mind games and some fiddling with current cutting-edge research on virtual reality and robotics. And yes, the heroine's name starts with an *H*.

These books have a more erotic edge. Because, you know. This is Jed. And so, you've been warned.

Good to see y'all in the Glow World!

Thank you and best to you,
Gennita

P/S For those who enjoyed the Super Soldier Spy series and love the computer, COMCEN, he has a blog where he chitchats much about his observations on COS commandos and their (love) lives (. Check it out at http://fyeo-gennita-low.blogspot.com/

ABOUT THE AUTHOR

Gennita Low writes sexy military and techno spy-fi romance. She also co-owns a roof construction business and knows 600 ways to kill with roofing tools as well as yell at her workers in five languages. A three-time Golden Heart finalist, her first book, Into Danger, about a SEAL out-of-water, won the Romantic Times Reviewers Choice Award for Best Romantic Intrigue. Besides her love for SEALs, she works with an Airborne Ranger who taught her all about mental toughness and physical endurance. Gennita lives in Florida with her mutant poms and one chubby squirrel.

To learn more about Gennita, visit www.Gennita-Low.com, www.rooferauthor.blogspot.com and www.facebook.com/gennita

OTHER BOOKS BY GENNITA LOW

BIG BAD WOLF

~ ~ Crossfire Series ~ ~
PROTECTOR
HUNTER
SLEEPER
HER SECRET PIRATE (short story in SEAL of my Dreams) &
also available separately

~ ~ Secret Assassins (S.A.S.S.) ~ ~
INTO DANGER
FACING FEAR
TEMPTING TROUBLE

~.~.Super Soldier Spy ~ ~
VIRTUALLY HIS
VIRTUALLY HERS

~ ~ Children's books as "Gennita" ~ ~

A SQUIRREL CAME TO STAY